I0542535

ASININE ASSASSINS

Edited by Weldon Burge

Praise for
UNCOMMON ASSASSINS

"It's rare that every story in an anthology will knock my socks off and this one is no exception, but the vast majority of the stories are highly enjoyable. ... UNCOMMON ASSASSINS is a nicely put together anthology and there's something to love for crime and mystery fans alike."

— *Crime Fiction Lover*

"While I'm not normally a big fan of anthologies, this one was a blast to read! Viking assassins to an 'all in the family' group of assassins and more! It was a fun read, all the way through."

— Khinasi

Praise for
INSIDIOUS ASSASSINS

"Excellent anthology with stories by modern masters of the macabre. Lansdale and Ketchum are worth the read, but so are Mosiman and Dorr and Mannetti. These are my kind of stories!"

— Paul Dale Anderson

"Another entertaining anthology from Weldon Burge that is certain to get your adrenaline flowing and to cost you hours of sleep. What a wonderful collection of stories. What are you waiting for?"

— *Fair Reviews*

ASININE
ASSASSINS

Edited by Weldon Burge

Smart Rhino Publications
www.smartrhino.com

This book is a work of fiction. Names, characters, places, and incidents are used fictitiously. Any resemblance to actual persons (living or dead), events, or locales is entirely coincidental.

Asinine Assassins Copyright © 2021 by Smart Rhino Publications LLC. All rights reserved, including the right of reproduction in whole or in part in any form.

"Payback: With Interest" by Matt Hilton was first published online on his blog and later published in the *True Brit Grit* anthology (2012).

"Shooting Fish" by James Dorr previously appeared in *Forgotten Worlds* (Autumn 2006).

Original cover artwork © Georg Schultschik; cover design by Ju Kim.

ISBN-13: 978-0-9985196-6-1

CONTENTS

ACKNOWLEDGMENTS

Thanks go to Georg Schultschik for his amazing cover illustration, to Ju Kim for designing the cover, and to Terri Gillespie for her excellent proofreading skills.

And, of course, to my wife, Cindy, who came up with the anthology's title and was the first reader!

RIP HO, JASPERS!

BY RICKY SPRAGUE

The whole thing was the fault of those prossies. Taking that money I gave them for a right jolly rogering and not using it for, say, social disease treatment. If they didn't have one before our biblical encounter, you can bet twelve teacups full of diamonds and gold they had one now. Bit irresponsible if you ask me. I assumed it was implied, especially when I gave them a full fifty quid per hole, that they would remain in their social stratum and not blemish mine.

Certainly, I never expected them to pool their money and treat themselves to a fine dinner at Nourriture Prétentieux, which just happened to be my Aunt Dot's favorite West End restaurant. And of course as the fates would have it, my Aunt Dot just happened to be dining there one evening with none other than the Dowager Amplebotham and Lady Dryheaves from the Ladies Chastity and Temperance League when the old slaggy-vags were seated just one table over and began chattering and chomping about how they happened by their recent windfalls.

Such was the impetus that drove her unannounced sojourn to my flat in the Wodehouse Towers, where she broke with protocol in a real humdinger of a way, clobbering in and trilling, "Barnie Brewster, you are a vacuous, venal, frivolous little bounder."

"I must say, Aunt Dot, you usually couch your descriptions a bit more euphemistically."

Despite my cheery demeanor, her face took on a rather magnificent shade of magenta as she laid out the scene alluded to in this story's corker of an opening.

"It seems to me, poor old Aunt Dot—"

"I *hate* when you call me that when I'm furious with you!"

"Indeed, you do," I conceded in a merry tone, to keep it light, as it were. "But the point is, it seems to me your beef, or perhaps I should say *ton bœuf*, is with the management of said fine French dining establishment, for even entertaining such filles de nuit—"

"They were giggling about *you*!"

"Sur moi?" I asked, still in the French mode.

"They said they acquired the funds to encroach on our territory from a client of theirs—a wealthy, idle, glassy-eyed, tousled-haired goofball who cries out 'Sweet Pumpkins' when he *achieves sexual climax*!"

I had to admit that old Aunt Dot had me there. Aside from the "goofball" bit, it described me to a T. And there was probably no profit in denying it, as Aunt Dot knew firsthand my favored sexual climax expression. Such being the case, I decided a bit of rhetorical jiggery-pokery was in order. Sadly, I am not a person with much du cerveau, as it were. Still, I gave it the old Eton try.

"And what kind of management do they employ at that Nourriture Prétentieux place, anyway?" I asked in high dudgeon. "Letting just any old coterie of smutty Janes in for plates of escargots and ratatouille and tarts—wait! I've just had a pip of a pun come to mind! Now, what was it? I've just lost the train. Something about prostitutes eating tarts … Oh well, perhaps that train will get back on the track and come zooming into the station of my brain. Regardless—what's the management doing at that restaurant, letting a bunch of tarts in to eat tarts? Those tarts are for the easy moneyed! Wait—I think I've just thought of another pun—"

"Barnie!" she howled in pain and anger.

"Aunt Dot—*Dorothy*—it's true I've had occasion to get a bit rambunctious with the old pego—"

She gasped.

"Sorry, Aunt Dorothy. I just had to satisfy certain urges in a venue where our family name and rep would remain free of the old lascivious smut. Hence, it seemed strictly boss to make the two-backed beast with a prossie now and then."

Now Aunt Dorothy's face took on the color of strawberry pudding, with a dash of sherry. "While I appreciate your attempt at discretion," she intoned imperiously, "something needs to be done about these women."

"I shall give them a stern talking-to."

"As long as they remain breathing, they are a danger to the 'rep' you claim to want to protect."

"I shall endeavor to ask them to hold their breath."

Her nostrils flared like she was about to use them to insult me twice at the same time. Instead, she said in a rather disconcertingly dulcet tone, "Eliminate them."

"But—you seem to suggest they be, well, *murdered*."

She held up her hand. "Do not use that common word in my presence. This is a necessary elimination for protecting our family's name, our family's fortune, and your allowance."

That brought me up short. "The old life of idle luxury's in peril, is it? Well, this *is* a bit of a pickle, framed in that manner."

"Not only that, but I also think it's just entirely possible that you need to restrain yourself to the conjugal bed of a single woman."

"No!"

"I've had my eye on Celeste Waterloo-Penguins as a possible suitable match."

"Ugh," I groaned without thinking. If ever there was a woman less suited to satisfying the carnal needs of a red-blooded son of the realm, it was old flat-bottomed, sunk-chinned, pear-shaped, pasty-skinned Celeste the Pest.

"There were five of them there. And they made an impression. See that they are silenced." Aunt Dot turned on her heel and began to storm out of the room, then suddenly turned back on her heel and added, in a highly serious tone, "*Forever.*"

When she'd left, I looked to Jaspers and said, "Well, I suppose that's final, then."

"Indeed, sir," my valet replied with his usual calm-cool collection.

"And why didn't you help me just now? You know you're the brains in the outfit, and you're the one who procured the services of those ladies."

"It didn't seem my place to talk back to your Aunt Dorothy."

"Can't say I blame you there. All in all, if I had my way, I'd prefer not to talk back to her, either. Nevertheless, I asked you to find me some ladies of the night, and apparently you went out and retained some ladies of ill repute who couldn't be trusted to keep their mouths shut, when they weren't full, so to speak."

"I offer my sincerest apologies. Next time I shall find you someone who is more discreet."

"Indeed. In the meantime, if we don't silence those whores, it's off to the wedding chapel for me. And, as you know, I prefer good old Whitechapel to the wedding chapel. Hey—that's a ripe pip of a pun, isn't it?"

"Indeed it is, sir."

"Wish I'd thought of it while old Aunt Dot was here. But she befuddles my bean and, let's be honest, the old noggin isn't the most cloud-free skull in all of Christendom to begin with."

"No comment, sir."

"Really, it's all *their* faults, you know. They broke through to the upper crust before their particular bread was baked, in a manner of speaking."

"I'm not sure I understand, sir."

"Neither do I. The point is, I tried to help those unfortunates. Fifty quid a hole is so much over their asking price it qualifies as charity. And what happens when you give underclass people charity?"

"Are you asking me, sir?"

"No, it was a rhetorical question. We all know the answer. Giving charity to the lower classes softens them. The hand that takes the handout grows no calluses, as the saying goes."

"I'm not familiar with that particular expression, sir."

"No? I think I just made it up. Looks like the old bean's recovered from Aunt Dot's withering presence, as it were. Anyway, I won't be able to help any more unfortunates if I lose out on the old allowance."

"You're all heart, sir."

"Quite." I gave him a strong pat on the back. "How will you do it, old man?"

"Do what, sir?"

"I expect you'll perhaps invite them all to a Paphian convention or something, then fill the room with burning sulfur pitch. Quick as a fiddle, no more mouthy whores."

"I'm not sure that's quite—"

"Hm, yes. I see what you mean. A bit complex, logistically speaking."

"No, sir. What I mean is, murdering prostitutes is outside my general duties and, honestly, is not necessarily in keeping with my character."

"Surely you don't expect me to lose my allowance? Or marry Celeste the Pest?"

"We do seem to be on the horns of a dilemma."

"The *whores* of a dilemma, so to speak. Now, there's a ripping pun for you! That ought to be worth one whore killing in itself."

"I rather expect that, should I endeavor to take on this particular responsibility, I'd be paid in more than just terrible puns."

"No such thing as a terrible pun," I tut-tutted at him. "And I do not appreciate your judgmental tone."

"Apologies, sir. But I am afraid I'm going to have to draw the line at killing prostitutes for you."

"I have to say I find this very offensive, Jaspers. You are, after all, the servant in this relationship."

"Now I'm afraid it's my turn to be offended, sir, as I am a *valet*, not a *servant*."

"Well, let's try not to let this impede our relationship."

"Indeed, sir."

"So you'll get started topping the trollops?"

"I'm going to decline the opportunity."

"Not even for, say, fifty quid apiece? It's what I gave them. Well, per hole, I mean. To be fair, I'll give you one hundred-fifty quid apiece."

"A tempting offer, sir. But I'll decline."

"Hm. Well, I suppose it's going to have to be up to old Barnie Brewster to defend the honor of the manor. Any advice before I get started?"

"I'd suggest wearing a hat with a brim, that might shade the eyes."

"Ripping suggestion. Let me write this down. Something along the lines of a deerstalker, perhaps?"

He nodded, which made me feel I was on the right track. "Also, perhaps a cloak," he said.

"And how about gloves? When I get up to them and strangle them, I'd like to—"

"You're planning on *strangling* them, sir?"

"I gather from your tone that you don't approve?"

"I'm not entirely certain you have the constitution for that. Have you ever strangled anyone before?"

"No. Have you, Jaspers?"

He nodded, and his face took on a gloomy expression. "Unfortunately, during my time in India, I had occasion to do and see things of which I am not so proud."

I gasped. "But surely a few more neck-twisters won't overtax you too much. Especially at, say, two hundred quid per?"

He shook his head. "I'm not interested in this assignment. But I will say that strangling a person is much more difficult than it looks. It takes a lot of hand strength just to crush the windpipe. Moreover, generally speaking, people do not just sit placidly while you're strangling them. It is physically and mentally taxing to kill someone in such a manner."

"You make an excellent point. A firearm then?"

"Too loud, sir. Might I suggest you draw a blade across their throats?"

"That's the best way, huh?"

"Be sure and go in deep at the start. Plunge and slash, severing the artery. It's a bit messy, so you'll want to stand either behind or to the side."

"You get a lot of blood spray, do you?"

"Indeed, sir."

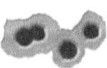

I'm afraid I made a bit of a botch about the job, this being my first intentional murder and all. Stick one was the fact that I couldn't remember exactly who all of them were, and even when

Jaspers provided me with a list of their professional names, I still had to do a bit of asking around, subtle as I was.

Then I tried going to the locations where I'd met them. However, Jaspers had been driving, and I don't know if you've ever been down in Whitechapel at night, but between the darkness and the fog and the soot-covered buildings and the tatty-looking natives, all of it blurred together into one rather sticky bit of soup.

It was sheer and blind luck that led to my finding the first one. She spotted me as I just lifted the old deerstalker to wipe some sweat from my brow right as I stepped beneath the light of the gas lamp. At that moment, a voice cackled, "Sweet Pumpkins!" and then roared with laughter.

I approached her. She was covered in sores and smelled vaguely of sea life and sheep skin. Her eyes were ringed with provocative dark circles, her teeth pointed in seven different directions at once.

"Well, aren't you a lovely vision," I said, relieved.

"And you—what a charmer!" she declared.

I looked round. There was some foot traffic despite the late hour, although not too much. Still, it seemed a capital idea to retire to an alley. "Have you got a few spare moments for a bit of hide-the-Johnny?"

She laughed. "I've already earned me nut for the night, but one more, especially the likes o' you lot, won't hurt me none!"

She threaded her arm through mine and led the way to an alley. She took a coin, and then turned to face the wall, hiking up her skirts to display her scabby, smut-covered backside.

"Get it in there good an' tight, lovey!" she said in a husky tone.

I'm afraid my courage deserted me at the last, and not even the prospect of losing my allowance was enough to keep my eyes open. This was exactly the sort of thing Jaspers was employed to do—protect me from having to do any dirty chores, i.e., the elimination of dirty whores. Yet, here I was, one hand over my eyes while the other, holding the blade, flailed about wildly.

"What'cher doin'?" she asked confusedly.

Then suddenly she made a horrible hacking and heaving. I gathered the gumption to remove my hand from my eyes and saw her standing off to the side, leaned against the wall, laughing at me.

"I'm sorry, is this amusing?"

"I suppose I'm up for a bit o' role-playin'!"

Now tell me if this has ever happened to you. You're all set to ribbon-slash a mouthy harlot, and she thinks you're playing a knock-knock based Punch and Judy show. I decided in a flash of inspiration it would be much easier to dispatch the slag if she were to play along with me, so I replied, "There's ten more quid in it for you if you'll be my 'victim.'" I made sure to carefully place a cracking set of matching rhetorical quote marks around that last word.

Alas, even with her "assistance," I had a rather rummy time of it. Jaspers wasn't just having a laugh about a struggling victim being an uncooperative inconvenience. Once she realized the bodkin wasn't so odd and I intended to use it, she started punching and kicking with a zest that was shocking, given how little she had to live for. I ended up with several knocks and scrapes and a right jolly bash on the skull that literally rattled the old lemon.

Her body was rather a mess, I'm afraid. So much so that in the confusion of the set-to, I ended with a piece of her innards in one of my cloak pockets.

"It appears to be part of a kidney, sir, if I may be so bold as to guess," Jaspers said, examining the gooey bit on the dresser. "Shall I dispose of it?"

"It may sound daft, but I actually feel rather sentimental about the oozy thing. I'd like to keep it."

"Perhaps I can preserve it, sir. Otherwise, the smell might become alarming."

"Yes! Capital idea! Pickled kidney. I do rather feel I accomplished something. It's a bit pleasant. I imagine it's not unlike the pride you must feel when you've made me a satisfactory breakfast."

"Speaking of which, sir, I thought perhaps some coffee and a savory—"

"Oof. Can't even bring myself to think about food. The old Yorick is still ringing like Big Ben at New Year's and the stomach's turvy-topsy."

"Hm. Your expression is a bit more glassy-eyed than usual, sir. I'd venture to guess you suffered traumatic encephalopathy."

"That a social disease?"

"Not in most cases, sir."

"Good. Because little Barnie hasn't had his helmet lubed in several days. Anyway, I expect that after a few days' rest I'll be back in the pink and well and truly pipped that the sequel to last night's adventures will go much greasier."

"I don't see how it could go any worse."

"That sounded a bit insubordinate. Don't forget which one is the valet in this relationship."

"Indeed, sir."

"Now off. I've some strenuous resting to do."

It was all rather humorous, in a dry sort of way, when the story first started hitting the broadsheets. Apparently, a few jackanapeses claimed to see some old bird conversing with Miss Kidney just before the deed, but there was little consensus as to said bird's size, shape, and sound of voice.

Then the local rabble became convinced that the culprit must have been an immigrant or a member of some religious sect. It was all rather rummy to follow, but it did call to mind something that hadn't before penetrated the concrete of the bean. Some other someone might be arrested for the dispatching of these women, if such activities could be viewed as against the law in the first place.

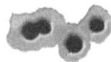

From an action standpoint, the next one was a touch more conked. I went straight for the throat just as quick as you please, and she was on the ground, spurting and gurgling like a champ. I lingered a little until her body stopped entirely.

It was all rather a bit too easy, the lemon kept telling me, but I heeded the message about gift horses, and so on, and managed to make my way back to the flat in Wodehouse Towers well before three tolls.

But my God, the things they claimed I did! Reading the broadsheets was ghastly, and I expressed my disgust to Jaspers in no uncertain terms.

"I rather thought the authors of these first drafts of history would have been impressed with my improved efficiency at dispatch," I said gloomily. "The first event was all rather a sloppy ruffle, I grant you. But this second one was a real ripe pip by comparison. One slash right across the old gullet and she was out like a light. But the things they've written about it here! Say—do you think they got my thing confused with another whore killing?"

"Not likely, sir. Might I suggest the authors are inventing sordid details to goose the sales of their publications, so to speak."

"I'm all for a bit of goosing now and then. One hardly expects one's news outlets to convey the simple unvarnished truth, what with so much competition from books and plays and so forth. But these things—they've made me out to be a right undignified desecrator of the human form!"

"Indeed, sir."

"If I'd done even half of these things, I'd make myself sick!"

"They are rather rude, sir."

"Even to read about them makes one yearn for a nice long soak in the tub. Say—I have an idea. Perhaps I should start writing letters to the papers and the police, sort of clearing things up about the situation, as it were?"

"I'd advise against that, sir."

"Not smart?"

"It's possible you might—inadvertently—write something or use some piece of paper or ink that could be traced back to you."

I was just about to deliver a rather corker of a rejoinder to that one when I suddenly heard the front door slam open. In all my years, I'd only known one person who could so convincingly slam a door open.

"Tell Aunt Dot I'm sleeping."

From the front Aunt Dot intoned, "Barnie Brewster, you are summoned! Come out here this instant!"

"If you'll forgive my saying so, sir, I doubt your aunt would believe that anyone could have slept through that particular beck and call."

"Hue and cry are more like, what ho?" I said morosely, leaving the warmth and comfort of the old down mattress.

"I'm rather more disturbed by the fact that I believe I heard the sounds of *two* sets of feet walking into the apartment," Jaspers said.

"You don't think she's brought Celeste the Pest along with her? She's not going to force me into some kind of marital conundrum?"

"I'm afraid that such an outcome might be more desirable than what is currently in the offing."

"Indeed?"

"Indeed. The second set of footsteps had a much more constabulary sound to them."

"Your ears really take the cake!"

"Thank you, sir."

Indeed, when we stepped out into the sitting room, I perked up with some alarm at the sight of the civil servant-looking chappie who'd accompanied Aunt Dot, and whose clonking shufflers had so impressed Jaspers's magnificent auricles.

"This is Constable Bottledeck," Aunt Dot said. Her expression was rather like that of someone who's just swallowed a lemon filled with castor oil. "He works in the Whitechapel area."

"Oh. A picturesque area, so I've heard," I said, by way of being coy.

Aunt Dot produced from her coat pocket—as if by some form of transcendental conjuring—a copy of the very broadsheet over which I'd been scowling just a few minutes prior. "Just what have you been up to, Barnie Brewster?"

"Well, certainly not *that*," I said in a bit of a dander. "What I mean is, the press often gooses things in order to goose up the sales, as it were—"

She pointed a bony yet menacing finger at me and said, "You. Silence." She then turned said finger, which was still bony but now somehow slightly less of a menace, in the constable's direction and said, "You. Explain."

He started in all hecks-and-goshes. "Ah. Yes. Well. Then. You see, Mr. Brewster, most of the police in the area are well aware of your Whitechapel activities."

"What? Whitechapel? That name sounds familiar." I pretended ignorance with genuine authenticity, I felt.

"Stop it, Barnie," Aunt Dot said, unimpressed.

"We know about you killing whores down there," the constable proceeded apace. "At least twenty-eight witnesses have come forward describing a glassy-eyed doofus in a deerstalker and dark cloak, talking piddly-poddly type West End, idle-rich argot, looking for, quote," (here he removed from his jacket pocket a small notebook and skimmed the leaves) "'these whores I made the nasty-in-out with,' unquote."

"Could be anyone," I said cheerily.

"Three witnesses heard you say, while committing the first crime, and I quote," (again his beady little soul-windows went to the notebook) "'If it weren't for dotty old Aunt Dot, you can bet your bottom quid that old Barnie Brewster would be back at the Club Strawberries Club with Pippy Hyde-Chatsworth-Haynes and Philsy 'Bobo' Baldwin-Wylden and the rest of my gang of sweet old birds engaged in some good-natured jiggery-pokery, instead of killing off the whores I made the nasty-in-out with, to protect the name of the Brewsters and my allowance and keep from having to marry old Celeste the Pest.'"

"That does sound a bit of a floater, that," I admitted. "You see, I was rather frustrated with the lack of a willingness on the part of said prossie to expire in a timely manner, and I'd also suffered a rather cracking corker on the old lemon—"

"Barnie!" Aunt Dot intoned.

When I shut the old pie-hole, the constable continued. "The point is, sir, that the police have had to cover for you on these two murders. We've had to convince witnesses they were wrong about what they clearly saw and heard. We've had to plant rumors about the possible involvement of members of certain immigrant and religious minority communities. We've even accentuated your work a bit to confound evidence-gathering and help stoke fears about the crimes."

"Good show, old man!" I clasped his hand warmly and clapped his back like an equal. "Thanks for pulling me out of the soup, even though I wasn't aware I was in the soup and, come to think of it, it's rather part of the constabulary's job anyway to clear things up for us."

"Well, you're welcome, sir."

In a rare philosophical mood, I went on. "I suppose I did rather get above myself in the old murder racket. I expected something more penny dreadful-ish. As it was, it was just dreadful. But now I know you're on the case, I suppose I'll just give you the list of the three other women I need taken care of and I'll let you handle things. Which, I admit now, I should have done from the start-go."

The sheepish look on the constable's pan, and the blazing hot angry look on Aunt Dot's, seemed to indicate that I'd put my foot in something, rhetorically speaking.

"About that," the constable said. "You see, there are some investigators who are of the impression that you—or the person responsible for these crimes, at least—should be arrested."

"What? Me? Arrested? For something other than a good-natured night of carousing and singing 'round Piccadilly Circus in the evening's thatch? Absurd!"

"It's bad enough," the constable went on, "covering for you. But to take anyone out on your behalf would be too much, even for those of us who are sympathetic to the plight of someone of your social standing."

"I think what the constable is trying to say is," Jaspers finally deigned to speak after I'd done so much of the conversational heavy-lifting, "*you* will need to continue your activities. Those in law enforcement who are willing to help cover for you will do so, but they can't actively participate, as such a proactive stance might disrupt the equilibrium within the halls of justice."

"Exactly," the constable said.

I looked at them gloomily. "It's a lot of fancy jargon, but when you add it all up you get old Barnie Brewster having to slash up three more slatterns. Do you know how many pairs of pants and shirts I've ruined with gore?"

"Two, sir?"

"Well, yes. So far."

"Might I suggest, sir, that under your cloak you wear clothes you don't mind soiling?"

"Why on earth would anyone keep clothes they didn't mind soiling? If you've got something you care so little for, dispose of it."

"That is a good point, sir," Jaspers conceded.

"Enough!" Aunt Dot shrilled. "Jaspers, unless you intend trying to find other employment elsewhere, you will help Barnie in his task."

"If you don't mind my speaking frankly, that's rather outside my job description."

"When I say 'elsewhere,' I mean in the spirit world, because I have friends in prominent places who can make certain you commit suicide in a painful and grisly manner."

"Jaspers!" I cried. "What's all this suicide pish? You're not depressed are you?"

"If I may speak with candor, I think your aunt is threatening me," Jaspers said in what sounded like a bit of a funk. "Very well. I shall help Mr. Brewster."

With an air of satisfaction that fairly oozed, Aunt Dot turned to the constable and said, "And you and your friends will continue to help with clean-up. I'll see that you're all rewarded."

"Thank you, madam," the constable said unctuously.

It was rather a lark heading out for the next one with Jaspers in tow. I made a valiant attempt to offer some practical advice, but he pointed out that I'd been fairly rummy at it so far and perhaps I should let him assume first chair. Although I was a bit relieved, I still made a point of pointing out that he was the valet in the relationship.

Through all the pea soup of the fog and the mélange of the smut-smog and the dark of the moonless night, it was heavy going for a bit. As it turned out, my previous activities, plus the addenda provided by the police and the journalists, had caused a bit of a mass hysteria and the meretrices were doubling up for protection. Getting one alone was going to be a bit of chore, I could tell.

Then, after nearly three hours of shuffling, old Tyche herself smiled on us. Two walking together on the cobblestones—and both were floozies who'd had a taste of little Barnie!

"We can have a bit of a double event!" I gasped at Jaspers.

"This *is* a bit of luck," Jaspers said. For the first time that night, he seemed, if not pleased, at least not entirely in a snort.

"I'll sidle up and get the ball rolling," I said, being the old hand, as it were. I was so quick in approaching them I barely heard Jaspers's scorning objections.

"Hello there, chippies," I said cheerily. "My friend and I would like to—"

"It's Sweet Pumpkins!" one of them cried out from her filthy mouth.

"He's the one what's been knockin' us off! Halp! HAAAALLLPPP!"

They turned and ran in the opposite direction. I stood dumbfounded because I don't care if you intend on slicing them up or not, it's a real dash to the ego when a smut-and-scab-covered harlot runs screaming at the sight of you.

"Come on!" Jaspers said as he dashed past me in chase.

Jaspers grabbed the slower one by her scarf and jerked her backward and to the side, toward the ground, while continuing to scamper after the other, fleeter one. I assumed Jaspers intended on me taking the one he'd knocked down, so I pounced on her, tabby-like.

I was nice and quick about it, but not so quick that there weren't a pair of constables standing watching me by the time I was finished. I turned toward them, wiped a little blood away from my cheek, and said, "I hope you're two of the jolly, helpful ones."

"We are," one of them said. "But you'd better get going so we can start fixing the scene up."

"Right ho. Did you happen to see which way my valet went?"

"Left at the next street."

As it turned out, it wasn't too difficult to find Jaspers, as he'd attracted a bit of a crowd himself. Thankfully, they were of the constabulary, so no actual harm done. They watched him with such glassy-eyed wonder that it was, for me, a bit like wandering into a hall of mirrors. When I finally got past them and could espy his handiwork, I could uptake their shock.

Jaspers, you see, had been a boodle boy in India, and, as he'd previously mentioned, he had seen and done some rather knock-down things. Apparently, they all came roaring back into his noodle, and suddenly he was back there in India. He let her have it right proper, including long after she'd already been well and truly eliminated.

"My God, man," I said when he finally rose, panting, from the piece of meat that had once been a scabby source of pleasure. "You've taken some of the best of her inside bits and strewn them around her outside."

"Indeed, sir. I seem to have lost my head for a moment." He sounded as dazed as me after a night at Club Strawberries.

Despite Jaspers's alarming vim in attacking his subject, I couldn't help but to think that things were going to be oojah-cum-spiff again soon. I woke with rather a light and breezy affectation, thinking all was right with the world, what with only one harlot left to hack. I lay in bed and waited for Jaspers to bring me my eggs and b.

And I waited.

I'm afraid I waited rather a long time. Finally, I made my way out of bed and into the quarters occupied by Jaspers. The old bird had a look of gloomy confusion. I said, "Everything hunky-dunky?"

"I'm afraid not, sir," he replied in an alarmingly emaciated voice. "Last night's events resurrected in me some impulses and instincts I'd hoped had been buried."

"Sorry, old bird. Glass half full, though—only one more to go. You plan on making breakfast any time soon?"

"I'll get right on it, sir," he said.

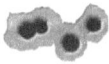

Jaspers's gloom was a bit of a knockabout, and to keep from being gruntled by his negative influence, I decided to take on a side project.

I was a bit miffed over the fact that the shenanigans that Jaspers and I had worked on were getting so much play in the broadsheets. They'd taken to calling us "Saucy Jack, the Whitechapel Ripper," which seemed presumptuous if you ask me. Still and all, they were selling so many copies I felt it only sporting I get a commish. Obviously, that wasn't in the offing. Also, a bunch of rounders had sent in missives, ostensibly from Saucy Jack's bespattered quill, all of which sounded daft to me.

So, I fired off a rather amusing little bit of bally. Keeping in mind Jaspers's admonition that I might accidentally give myself away, I wrote it with my left hand, which was not the one I was most accustomed to using. And, moreover, to ensure that they recognized my blather as the true bucks, I enclosed the bit of pickled kidney I'd fortuitously purloined.

That turned out to be a bit of floater, as it produced yet another impromptu visit from old Aunt Dot. This time, with a journalist friend in tow.

"What did you do *this* time, Barnie?" she demanded.

"Can you add a bit more detail to the query?"

In answer, the journalist produced the note I'd fired off.

"You're the lucky man who found my—I mean, who happened to come upon an authentic Spicy John original."

"Arthur Feelingood-Herewell knows who you are, Barnie," Aunt Dot said with a world-weariness that almost broke one's blood-pumper.

"Well, why'd you tell him?" I asked Aunt Dot, momentarily forgetting my general unease over her regard for me.

"*You* told him!" she shouted.

By way of explanation, the journalist stated, "You signed the letter, quote," (he regarded the letter) "'Sincerely, the real culprit behind the slayings of the Whitechapel floozies, Barnie Brewster, but please don't publish my real name if you print this, call me Spicy John if you don't mind. Thx,' unquote."

"Rather explicit instructions, I should think, and easily carried out, even by the dullest of dullards."

"If I may be so bold as to offer a bit of advice," Jaspers said in a harshed-down voice.

I turned to look at him and was rather flabberflopped by what I saw. He had a frenzied expression, not unlike that on the face of my Uncle Oswald when they were carting him off to the funny farm after twenty-two years of life with Aunt Dot. His entire bod was saggy and disconsolate. Perhaps worst of all, his shirt was buttoned in a rather lopsided manner.

"What's that, old chap?"

"Please do nothing further and allow me to finish things. Tonight."

The journalist's eyes widened. "You're gonna do a final one, eh? You don't mind if I get an exclusive? You know, as a consideration for not exposing old glassy-eyes here."

"How are you sure you'll be able to find the last one?" I asked. "She's been a bit incognito, as it were."

"Our friend Constable Bottledeck reached out to me last night. He's found the place she's been holing up. I will once and for all—and rather spectacularly—put an end to this whole sordid business. Maybe then I can rest again."

"You sound a bit serious," I said.

"I am." His voice was harsh and empty at the same time. I was rather glad he asked me not to venture out with him that last night.

When he returned the following morning, he was exhausted and sopping with the red gooey bits. He retired to his quarters, leaving me to manage the upkeep of the flat and to cook my own meals when I didn't want to dine at the Club Strawberries.

It wasn't until the next day that I got some inkling of what Jaspers had got up to the night before. I have to say, it was rather appalling. He'd apparently done up something of a berserker surprise party, as it were, with her innards as the decorations. It was two days later before I finally worked up the gumption to ask him, "Jaspers, old man, how much of what I read in the broadsheet was your handiwork and how much was the fancy of the journalist and the help of the constabulary?"

He smiled. "If you'll forgive my suggesting this, sir, perhaps it's best you not know the full story."

"Agreed. Mine's a delicate constitution. Rugged as we Brewsters are, we are afflicted with sensitive souls. It's what led me to engage in such heavy-tipping with those floozies in the first place."

"Indeed, sir."

"You could say it was my sensitive disposition that caused the whole mess, in a way."

"You could say that, sir."

"I just did. And now I might also add that my sensitive disposition is guiding me toward a yearning for the company of a member of the fairer sex. What say you run out and procure me someone?"

"If you'll forgive my presumption, sir, perhaps you'd be better off finding someone who is less local."

"A trip to the country?"

"I was thinking, perhaps, that we might travel abroad for a few months."

"Jaspers, it's just that kind of advice that makes your counsel so valuable."

"I am a person of many talents, if I say so myself, sir."

Ricky Sprague is a writer and cartoonist whose work has appeared in *Mystery Weekly*, *Ellery Queen Mystery Magazine*, *Mysterical-E*, *MAD*, and *Cracked*, and various short story book collections. He is the author of the crime graphic novel *Gut-Shot*, inspired by Ed Gorman's story "Stalker," from *Short, Scary Tales*, and a Kolchak novel from Moonstone, and the colorist for Chris Wisnia's *Doris Danger* from Fantagraphics.

DUMBASS

BY F.J. TALLEY

My boyfriend is a dumbass. That's not a criticism, just a fact. Mind you, he's a good-looking dumbass, but a dumbass nonetheless. Let me go back and fill in the blanks.

My boyfriend used to work as a low-level enforcer for Jackie Ray, the biggest drug kingpin in our little city by the bay. But he wasn't satisfied with being the biggest. Jackie Ray wanted to grow even more.

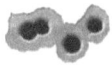

"Sammy, what about that bitch who's been taking more and more of the southwest side—Angelina Cortez? What can we do about her?" Jackie Ray asked.

Sammy Collins was a wiry, rat-faced man who never expended more energy than he had to. He raised his eyes. "She's bringing in the people, boss. I heard people aren't complaining, she treats her dealers good, and—"

"I don't care about that, Sammy!" Sammy sat up straight at the noise, but before he could say a word, Ray had risen and begun pacing the room. "She's growing an empire in the southwest, and I don't like it."

Collins frowned. "I don't understand, boss. You always said the people in the southwest weren't worth your time, and—"

"That was before Angelina moved in and started making money! I want that money, Sammy. It's supposed to be mine." Ray sat, caught his breath, and looked up again at Collins. Taking one more deep breath, he asked, "How are we going to do that?"

"Do what?"

"Take back what's mine."

Collins pursed his lips and thought, finally saying, "We could move into the southwest, and—"

Ray held up his hand. "You already told me Angelina has a loyal following. And the last thing we want to do is to get tough with customers, since they can buy from anybody they want to."

"So?"

Ray rubbed his temples. "Think, Sammy," he said. "We need to take that broad out, hurt her organization, then move in and take what's ours."

"Oh."

"Right. Now, who do we have who can take her out?"

"Really take her out, like, kill her?"

"You got a better way of taking somebody out than by killing them?"

Collins winced, his eyes darting about the room. "No, it's just that killing somebody is a little much, don't you think?"

Ray shook his head. "You know, the big drug dealers in the movies don't have these problems. When they ask for somebody to be killed, they just snap their fingers."

Collins shrank in his chair and muttered, "Sorry."

Ray waved his hand. "So, who do we got?"

"Muscle who could do this?"

"Yeah," Ray said. "What about Pooky, he's pretty tough?"

"Don't you remember, boss, he's in jail."

"Oh. Yeah. Well, we still got Lorenzo, right? He's a mean son of a bitch."

"He was until that last shootout with the cops. Lorenzo started going to that Jehovah's Witness Church when he got out of the hospital and is thinking of moving."

Ray stared, wide-eyed. "Jehovah's Witness?" Collins nodded. "Dang! That's a tough outfit." He sighed. "Um, how about Billy Don, and—" He paused as Collins shook his head.

"We sent him out of town after that last arrest. We can't risk him coming back so soon."

"I don't believe this. Who do we have left?"

Collins searched his brain. "Well, we do—"

"Yeah?"

"Kody is available."

Ray laughed out loud. "You've got to be kidd—"

But he saw Collins shrug.

"Times have been tough," Collins said.

"I didn't think they were *that* tough." Ray sighed again. "I guess you got to bring him in." Ray thought for a moment, then his face brightened. "And since he's not in the inner circle, the cops won't know him. This could be good." Ray smiled to himself, not seeing Collins shake his head in disbelief.

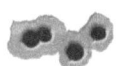

If you wonder why they were so concerned, it was the fact that Kody—Kody Parker, that is—isn't going to set the world on fire. He's a nice guy who will do what you tell him, and not screw it up too badly. However, Kody was pretty green. The most he's ever had to do is threaten thirteen-year-old users to pay up. Taking out a rival was way out of his league. But when the rest of your muscle is unavailable, you take what you can get. Ray found that out when Kody walked in.

Parker ambled into Ray's house, more befuddled than usual. Parker was a well-built man, over six feet tall, handsome and well-proportioned, and carried himself with an innocence that charmed many a woman, though he had little success with them. Being summoned to the big man's house for a special assignment scared the bejesus out of Kody. He scaled the steps, and Ray stared back in amusement. Turning to Collins, he asked, "This is Parker?" Collins nodded. "What's that he's wearing?"

"It looks like a fedora."

Ray sighed. "Parker?"

Parker stood at attention. "Yes, sir. I'm ready, sir."

"Ready for what?"

Parker's face fell. "Oh, uh, whatever you need, sir."

Ray pointed to a chair. "Sit." Parker sat, perched on the edge of the chair, eyes expectant. "Parker, do you know Angelina Cortez?"

"Is she that actress, from that one movie?"

After a quick glance at Collins, Ray sighed and said, "No. She's a major drug dealer in the southwest, Parker. Ring any bells now?"

Parker shook his head. "I only know you, sir."

Ray frowned. "Were you in the army or something?"

"No, sir," Parker said. "But my mother always taught me to be respectful." He smiled.

Ray suppressed the urge to scream. "Well, she's growing her business in the southwest at my expense, and I want to take over the southwest from her, do you understand?"

Parker frowned. "Uh—"

Ray rolled his eyes. "Look, Parker, I want her gone, kaput, washed, you understand?"

Parker looked confused. "Which of those did you want, sir?"

"You know what dead means, right?"

"Yes, sir."

"Good. Then that's what I want."

Parker looked at his hands. "I wouldn't know how to do that, sir. I mean, I've never shot nobody before."

Collins raised his hand. "We don't want you to do it that way."

"No," Ray said, his annoyance increasing. "It should look like an accident."

"What kind of acci—"

"Use your judgment," Ray said, ignoring the wide stare from Collins. "Look, go over to her place and learn her habits, like when she leaves the place and stuff. Then, when you have the chance, hit her with a car, or maybe use a pipe bomb in the car—something like that." He pointed to Collins. "Sammy can help you with the details. But the first thing you gotta do is learn her habits to make it look like it just happened. You feel me?"

Parker stood at attention again. "Yes, sir!"

Ray turned to Collins. "Now, once you leave, if you need anything from us, we're always hanging here from 4 to 6 p.m. That's when we count the day's money, okay?"

"Yes, sir."

"Good." Ray turned to Collins. "Can you get the address and anything else Parker here needs, Sammy?"

Collins stood, looking like he was heading to a firing squad. "Sure, boss. Let's go, Kody." As Parker and Collins left the room, Ray sat back and wondered how big a mistake he was making.

It's one thing to give someone an address and basic instructions, and quite another to make them smart enough to get a tough job done. Parker didn't have nearly enough tools, but he had *some*. The following day, he found himself in Angelina Cortez's neighborhood, checking out her modest home with a pair of binoculars and plenty of drinks in case he got thirsty.

I'm one of Angelina's neighbors, and I was just parking my car when I noticed him. At first, I looked around, thinking he might be a strange bird watcher, but there was far too much concrete in this neighborhood for the birds to hang around. Plus, who wears a fedora and trench coat to watch birds? He was a good-looking guy, if a little strange, so I shrugged and walked to his driver's side door.

"Hey."

The man started as he turned and hit the binoculars on the doorjamb. "Ouch!"

"Sorry about that," I said. "Are you okay?"

Rubbing his forehead, the man said, "Yeah. I'm good. But you know, I'm not here."

"Okay," I said. "But I can still see you, so . . ."

The man looked around, then back to me. "Well, I guess you can see me, but I'm not supposed to be here. I'm, uh, actually I shouldn't tell you, but I'm working."

I shrugged again. "I can see that. But most people who use binoculars are looking at something interesting."

The man looked through his passenger window again. "I'm looking at something important—the lady who lives here?"

I frowned. "In the house there?" He nodded. "You mean the house you're parked right in front of?"

"Yeah."

I leaned on his driver's side door and tried to smile. "You know, Slick, if you're trying to check out Angelina Cortez's house, you shouldn't do it right in front of the house, you know?"

"I didn't want to miss anything."

That's when I first realized that this man—as gorgeous as he was—was not the smartest tool in the toolbox.

I stood straight again. "Look, if there's something you need to know about Angelina Cortez, I can help you."

He smiled. "Really? I mean, that would be great!"

"Sure. I live in the neighborhood, and I know a lot about her. I'm Patty, by the way. Patty Alvarez."

"Kody Parker."

I pointed down the street. "How about we meet at the Roasted Bean coffee shop? It's three blocks down that way and on the right. I'll even buy the first round of coffees."

"I guess."

I shook my hips enough to get his attention. "You don't want to have coffee with me?"

The man's face fell. "Oh no, I don't mean that. It's just that I have to learn her habits, and if I leave the street, I might—"

My upraised hand stopped him. "Slick, uh, Kody, I can tell you anything and everything you need to know about Angelina Cortez. Trust me." I inclined my head toward the end of the street again. "And I could use a latte right now." I returned to my car and started down the street, his car right behind mine.

When we got to the coffee shop, he pulled his six-foot-plus frame out of the car and my jaw dropped. He was a hunk! Chiseled features, strong, and I suspected dumber than a box of rocks—but I could live with that. He opened the door for me, and we ordered coffees, sitting at a corner table.

"So tell me what's so important about Angelina Cortez, besides the fact that she's a major drug dealer in the southwest?"

Kody's mouth dropped. "You know about that?"

"Everybody knows about that, Kody," I said. "And a lot of people want to take her out, because she's good at what she does, and she's a woman." I frowned. "Is that why you want to know more about her?"

Kody hesitated again. "I can't say."

"You don't trust me? The first person who offered to help you?" I sat back in my chair and pouted. "That's not very nice, Kody."

"I didn't mean it like that," Kody began. "It's just that I was trying not to be too obvious, and—"

"By using binoculars right in front of her house?"

"Well, there is that, I guess."

"Exactly," I said. "Now, I can help you, but I need to know a few things first." I leaned forward, closing the distance between us again. "I mean, I'd want to know if the person who's going to move in is a kingpin who's going to hurt people or one who will leave well enough alone, and—"

"Oh, Mr. Ray wouldn't hurt anybody!" Kody cried. "He's a decent guy. He gave me a job when I finished high school and had nothing else to do." Kody shook his head with a vengeance. "No, he's not like that at all."

"Sorry," I said. "I didn't mean to insult him. And if he's going to be okay, then maybe it isn't so bad that Angelina Cortez gets taken down." I smiled. "So, how are you going to do it?"

Kody shrank back, studying the table. "I don't know yet. Mr. Ray wanted me to make it look like an accident."

"And you haven't figured out how to do that?"

"No."

I sat back, thinking. After a minute, I raised my eyes. "Maybe you should ask your boss about a couple of options, like poison or something like that. I mean, once you learn her habits, I mean. Can you do that?"

"Sure," Kody said. "They told me I could see them between four and six most every day. That way I wouldn't have to always call them in case phones were tapped or something."

I nodded. "That's a good plan." I stood. "Tell you what. I'm going to help you out. Maybe Mr. Ray will be better around here than Angelina. Why don't we meet here in a couple of days, like on Thursday at noon? We can compare notes."

Kody smiled. "Sure." I touched his hand, smiled again, and left.

Now, some would say that I was using Kody, but that wouldn't be fair. He had a job to do, and I had a job to do, and I just arranged it so we helped each other, you know? No, Kody Parker and I were two partners, he just didn't know it.

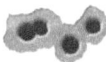

I smiled when Kody walked into the coffee shop. He was still wearing that annoying fedora, but I ignored it. "Did Mr. Ray approve? What did he say?"

"He said he didn't care, so long as I got the job done." Kody smiled. "He seemed thrilled that I had learned anything so far." *That was hardly a surprise.*

"Good!" I said. I waved Kody closer to me at the table. "And I've come up with a great way of doing the job."

"Yeah?"

I nodded. "We can go with carbon monoxide poisoning. It's common in older houses . . ." I stopped because Kody's face was blank. "What's the matter?"

"What's that?"

"What?"

"The carbon thing."

"Carbon monoxide?"

"That's it!"

Oh, boy. "It's a gas that you can't see or smell, but it can kill you. And the cops almost always think it's an accident. That way, nobody will get caught."

Kody frowned again. "Where can I get this carbon stuff?"

I waved my hand. "That's the easy part. It's everywhere, even with something as easy as turning on the gas and not having the pilot on, especially in older houses like Angelina's." I saw the confusion on Kody's face again.

"Something wrong?"

"It seems too easy."

I shrugged. "The best plans always seem too easy."

"Yeah?"

"That's what they say." I leaned forward again and smiled. "Let's get this plan started."

We figured a good time to pull off the job was to schedule it for the same time when Mr. Ray—Kody's boss—had an alibi. If either of us got questioned, we'd say we were out of town taking a drive when Angelina died. That way, we'd both be covered. The next time we met, I gave him the little space heater. It wasn't much bigger than a small suitcase and had a special canister attached to it. When Kody looked at it, I could tell he was confused again.

"Here's the deal," I said. "I found out that Angelina likes to watch soap operas in the afternoon."

"I used to watch those with my Mom!"

"Focus, Kody. Now, Angelina watches these shows, but she's embarrassed about being a big drug trafficker who likes to watch soaps. She sends all her people out of the house for a couple of hours each day, and half the time she falls asleep." Kody nodded.

"So," I continued, "all you need to do is to take this heater into the house, and—"

"Nobody's gonna stop me?" This was an outbreak of smarts that surprised me.

"No. Like I said, Angelina sends everybody out of the house then. I mean, everybody knows why, but they don't say anything. In fact, the house is seldom locked, because who's gonna break into Angelina Cortez's house?"

I pulled out a hand-drawn floor plan of the house and pointed. "This is the bedroom and sitting room she uses to watch her shows. She hardly ever leaves those rooms for two hours. Place the space heater by this door, turn the knob so the pilot goes on, close the door and leave. Maybe an hour later, the job is done." I smiled and handed Kody the floor plan. He studied it for a minute, nodding his head a few times, then stood up.

"I can do this."

"Yes. You can. And when it's all done, meet me at Roasted Bean tomorrow at 6:30 and we'll celebrate!" I kissed his cheek and sent him on his way. I didn't worry about Kody following through. Creative he ain't, but he can follow simple directions with the rest of them. In the meantime, I had more work to do.

I was waiting for Kody the next night until way past 7 o'clock when I realized something had gone wrong. I drove to the neighborhood and saw a single parked police car with its flashers on. Kind of defeats the purpose to have flashers on, don't you think, guy? I drove by the car and parked at the cross street, then walked to Mr. Spinelli's house. He always kept his eyes open. "What's up?" I asked him.

Mr. Spinelli looked at me, and with no emotion in his voice, said, "Angelina. Looks like gas or something." He glanced at the police vehicle. "They'll be calling you sometime soon, so get ready." I turned to go away when he grabbed my arm. "One busybody called in a suspicious car, and they arrested somebody, I heard." His eyes locked on mine, and I nodded.

"Gotcha." He released my arm, and I approached the detective, ready to show the proper amount of shock and grief.

I sidled up to the detective and looked innocent. He finally noticed me. "May I help you, miss? Do you live around here?"

"Yes to both," I said. "I wanted to know what was going on. I just got back from a drive."

"And you are?"

"Patricia Alvarez." I pointed to my house. "I live in 2116."

The detectives flipped to a new page in his notebook. "When did you start this drive?"

I looked up for the answer. "Sometime around 1:30, I'd guess, and just got back. What's going on?"

The detective thought a moment, then shrugged. "There's been a suspicious death, ma'am." He inclined his head toward Angelina's house. "Angelina Cortez has died under suspicious circumstances."

"I don't understand."

The detective hesitated again. "It was with carbon monoxide gas, ma'am, and it was probably an accident, but we have someone in custody who we believe might have been involved."

"Oh?"

"Yes, ma'am. A man wearing a fedora and a trench coat was seen leaving the house and drove away in a car, and a neighbor of yours called it in."

"And this man is already in custody?"

The detective smiled. "Your neighbor got the license number." He pointed down the street to Mrs. Sanderson's. "You should thank her. She's really on the ball." *Oh, I'll be sure to do that.*

The detective turned back to me. "Look, if you weren't around then, I've got work to do. We'll contact you if we need you. You said 2116?"

"Yep."

He closed his notebook. "Got it."

This was a wrinkle I hadn't counted on, and neither had Kody, but as always, I had a backup plan, which Kody discovered the following day.

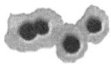

Kody was led into the visiting area and told what to do. He even looked good in that orange prison jumpsuit as he saw me and brightened. He sat and picked up the telephone.

"Hey."

"Hey to you." I looked at the glass partition. "Not what you were hoping for, huh?"

"No," Kody said. "But I should be getting some help."

I shook my head. "Don't count on it, Kody."

"But I—"

"Stop." I raised my hand to quiet him. "They record these calls. Ray and somebody named Collins were killed yesterday. It was in the papers."

Kody looked stricken.

"Then how do I—"

"Do you trust me?"

"What?"

"I asked if you trusted me."

"Sure."

I smiled. "Then let me take care of everything." With that, I hung up the phone.

The following day, a guard walked Kody Parker to an interview room where an older man in a suit was seated. The man pointed to a chair and waited until the door was closed to speak.

"My name is Steven Graham, Mr. Parker, and I'm your defense counsel."

"I can't pay for a lawyer."

Graham waved his hand.

"My fees are being taken care of, Mr. Parker. What I want to tell you—very clearly—is that you are to say nothing to anyone, do you understand?"

"Well, I—"

"No. Nothing to anyone. That your fingerprints were on the space heater that killed Ms. Cortez complicates this case. We can't deny that, nor that you were in the neighborhood when this happened."

"Well, I have an alibi, if you'll just—"

"You do and you don't, Mr. Parker," Graham continued. "If you use that alibi, it wouldn't work, since you were seen at the house. And it would only implicate Ms. Alvarez. And you don't want to do that, do you?"

Kody shook his head. "No."

"I thought not." Graham smiled. "Leave this to me. Remember, say nothing to anybody, that means nothing to any other prisoners, guards, police—anyone. Do you understand?"

"Yes."

Graham rose. "Good. We'll be in court tomorrow. You may have some prison time and a fine to pay, but it won't be too bad. Are you okay with that?"

"How much jail time?"

"Standard is one year."

Kody looked around the room. "That doesn't seem like a long time for a murder."

Graham smiled again, a shark-like smile. "And if this were a murder, a year would be impossible. But . . . just leave this to me, okay?"

"Okay."

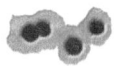

Kody sat stunned throughout the entire court proceeding, confused by all that happened. Since he couldn't be made to testify against himself, the prosecutor didn't bother to call him. And he was surprised when his lawyer rose and gave papers to the judge and the prosecutor.

"You see, Your Honor and Madam Prosecutor, Mr. Parker was simply helping Ms. Cortez with assisted suicide. She was terminally ill and truly had no hope of recovery, which these records show. You will also see receipts in this packet using Ms. Cortez's credit card and her signature on receipts for the space heater and fuel canisters, indicating her intent. Mr. Parker was assisting Ms. Cortez so she could have a Christian burial. It was unfortunate that Mr. Parker did not wipe his fingerprints from the heater." He raised his hands in surrender. "That would have been dishonest, of course, but also would have absolved him of culpability in this case.

"My client is guilty, Your Honor, and is willing to accept the consequences for assisted suicide, but not murder, and we will stipulate to that fact."

The judge was open-mouthed, but turned after a moment to the prosecutor.

"Madame Prosecutor, have you considered and agreed with this?"

"We have, Your Honor."

"The defendant will please rise."

"Mr. Parker, I understand your intent, but to assist another person with ending their life is still a crime in this state, and therefore I am sentencing you to one year in county lockup and a fine of ten thousand dollars. Do you understand that?"

Kody was silent until his lawyer nudged him. "Now you can answer. Just say 'Yes, sir.'"

"Yes, sir."

"And will you be able to pay the fine?"

"He will, Your Honor," Graham said. "We've prepared a cashier's check to cover it."

"Very well," the judge said. "Given the circumstances, and the plea agreement of the prosecutor and the defense, this court is adjourned."

Kody turned to his lawyer. "But how—"

Graham pointed toward the gallery where Kody saw me smiling.

And that's the story. Kody helped take out a rival to his boss. At the same time, he gave me the chance to take out his bosses—between 4 and 6 o'clock in the afternoon. My sister worried about what would happen when she died and hoped I would survive in the cutthroat world of drugs in the city. She didn't think I had the killer instinct. Kody gave me the perfect opportunity to take them out, and he helped my sister die with dignity.

So, he may be a dumbass, but he's my dumbass. And he's going to look damn good on my arm when he gets out.

F. J. Talley writes primarily in the mystery and science fiction genres. His novels, *Twin Worlds* and *Take Hart*, were published in 2017. F. J. is the winner of the 2019 prize for fiction from the Gulf Coast Writers Association for his story "Thirteen." His short story, "By the River," was selected for inclusion in the Maryland Writers' Association's 30th-anniversary anthology. He lives with his family on the Western Shore of the Chesapeake Bay.

THERE'S ONE FOR YOU, NINETEEN FOR ME

BY CARSON BUCKINGHAM

"Metcrumb, get in here!" Mr. Bunson yelled in a voice that could open clams at twenty paces. "Now!"

Bob Metcalf exploded from his cubicle and stood in front of his fearless, if somewhat rumpled, boss within seconds.

"When I say *now*, I mean *now*, Metcrumb,"

"Yes, sir." How he could have arrived any sooner without the benefit of teleportation was anybody's guess. "And it's 'Metcalf,' sir."

"What is?"

"I am. My name is Bob *Metcalf*."

"Don't correct me."

"Right, sir. 'Metcrumb' it is, sir."

"How's the family, Metcrumb?"

"Huh?" The switch from ogre to concerned citizen was a little jarring.

"Your family. How are they?"

"I don't have any family, sir."

"What, none at all? How about a wife or girlfriend ... or boyfriend?"

"No to all three, sir. I'm all by myself and have been for a long while."

Bob Metcalf was the new guy at the Special Collections Division of the Internal Revenue Service. He had been beyond delighted to be tapped for this plum of a job and the huge raise that went along with it. If Bunson wanted him to crawl through rabid tarantulas while playing "The Pina Colada Song" on the accordion, he was more than ready to don the kneepads.

"How may I be of assistance, sir?"

"I have a special assignment for you—a really tough collection. Think you can handle it?"

"Oh, yes, sir. Absolutely, sir."

"Good. You'll be flying on our private plane to Russell Springs, Kentucky, in a few hours. We have our own airstrip there. The deadbeat you'll be seeing is in Jamestown, so you'll need to rent a car or travel by cab—if you can find one. Oh, and here, you'll be needing this."

Bunson handed him a Glock 9 pistol.

Despite the tarantulas and accordion, Metcalf involuntarily shrank back from his boss. "Why do I need *that*?"

Bunson sighed. "What did you think we do in Special Collections, Metcrumb? Send out little cards with flowers in them saying 'Pretty please pay your overdue taxes?' No. By the time the demand gets to this office, there is no longer any hope of payment."

"But then how does killing them help?"

"When things reach this point, the IRS takes out a life insurance policy on the deadbeat that covers the amount owed plus interest. We are only just *so* lenient at the IRS, Metcrumb."

"I didn't realize we were lenient at all, sir."

"Don't talk rot, Metcrumb."

"I have never talked rot, sir."

"Well, for a beginner, you're damned good at it, then. So are you going to do this or not? I need a strong agent for this job, Metcrumb."

"I'm your man, sir," he said, taking the Glock between thumb and forefinger and carefully pocketing it.

Bunson looked on with amusement. "Know how to use a gun, Metcrumb?"

"I should think I just aim and squeeze the trigger, sir. After turning the safety off, of course."

"Close enough. Where'd you learn that?"

"CSI: Miami, sir."

"Fine. Here's the deadbeat's file. Familiarize yourself with it in the plane on your way there."

"Thank you, sir. I won't let you down."

Metcalf returned to his cubicle.

"Schmuck," Bunson muttered, shutting his office door.

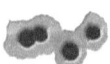

Metcalf dumped the contents of the manila envelope onto his desk, sat down, and began sorting through it.

First, there was a photo of the guy—a Mr. Norbert Bunch—looking like he had just crawled out of a pipe. Metcalf himself was about a hundred pounds overweight, bald, and was certainly no oil painting himself, but *this* guy! He was reed-thin, hadn't shaved since Christ left Chicago, had hair that would please

Medusa, and, from the looks of things, was the proud owner of three, maybe four, teeth.

"How does he not trip on that beard? Norbert Bunch makes Jed Clampett look like Robert Goulet. Oh, this is going to be a cinch!"

He read through the rest of the file and discovered that Mr. Bunch owed the IRS in the neighborhood of fifty thousand dollars—their share of the mega inheritance he received from a wealthy relative, who had probably never met him. Oh, and the interest of twelve-and-a-half thousand dollars yearly, which comes to one-hundred twenty-five thousand of interest alone, and a grand total of one-hundred-seventy-five thousand.

No wonder the IRS wanted him dead.

He tucked the Glock into his briefcase and grabbed his go-bag—a packed overnight bag he always kept under his desk, just in case. Metcalf liked to be prepared.

But how to approach this deadbeat? What would be most effective? This was his big chance to impress the boss, and he didn't want to blow it.

Then it hit him.

Wouldn't it be better to look like a local rather than an IRS agent? Might be easier to get close enough to him that way.

He had just the thing.

"Judy, I'm going to run out for about an hour. Please notify our private plane and get a rental car squared away so I can get on my way to Logan when I get back."

"And who are you again?"

"Oh, sorry ... Bob ... I'm new."

"You sure are. You can make your own damn arrangements when you get back. I'll leave the phone numbers on your desk ... *Bob*."

"Uh, OK, I guess. Thanks."

"Blot on the landscape," she muttered at his retreating back.

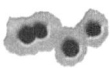

A few minutes later, Metcalf strode through the door of Costello's Costumes. "This is the best idea! That guy won't suspect a thing."

The football-field-sized store was a bit intimidating, and he had little time. He looked around for a clerk.

"Helpya?" trickled a female voice from behind a counter piled high with whoopee cushions and fake plastic vomit.

"Yes. I need to look like I belong in a rural area."

She glanced over the plastic vomit and looked him up and down. "As opposed to the undertaker you look like now?"

"A comedienne. How charming."

"What, you mean like a farmer or something?"

"Kind of like that, but not that specific."

"Just, like, a redneck or a country hick, then?"

"Yes! That's exactly it!"

"No prob." She unfolded herself from her stool, drifted around the counter, and in a scant twenty minutes and seventy-five dollars later, put together the perfect look.

He stuffed the bulging plastic bag into his car and headed back to the office.

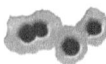

"Judy, I'm back."

"I'm all aflutter."

Metcalf went to his cubicle, scooped up the numbers she'd left, and made his arrangements. He'd have to get going to reach Logan in time. Though he'd be the only passenger on the IRS private plane, they still had a strict schedule. Everything about the IRS was strict. And they also had a private gate to their plane, without a metal detector, so the gun wouldn't be an issue. He grabbed his briefcase and go-bag.

As he passed the front desk, he said, "I'm off. I'll be staying at the Cumberland Motel in Russell Springs in case you need to reach me."

"Mnmm-hmm. If anything comes up that only your sage advice and extensive experience can help us handle, I'll be sure to call you," Judy said, not looking up from her copy of *Elle*.

He dashed to his car without replying.

"Eyesore," she muttered, shaking her head.

Ten minutes later, Metcalf pulled into the short-term lot at Logan Airport. Theoretically, he could have the business with that Kentucky hayseed squared away in one afternoon. But he wanted to get there a day early to see what the area and the people were like—it might help in dealing with Bunch.

The plane would be ready to take off as soon as he boarded, so he grabbed his bag, briefcase, and "country duds," and legged it.

Once airborne, he settled back and relaxed. It was the first time he'd flown on the IRS private plane, though he'd worked for the "Service" in different capacities for the past twenty years. But now ... now he'd arrived. The big time. The Special Collections Division. Top honors, the pinnacle of success. He was so excited about this first assignment that if he were a puppy, he'd be wagging his tail at the speed of light and wetting himself.

What people like Metcalf failed to realize was that Fate had a way of sneaking up on them with a length of lead pipe behind its back.

About an hour into the journey, Metcalf felt a bit peckish. He pressed the intercom button on his chair arm.

"Yeeeeeessssssssss?" came the irritated reply.

"Could I see a menu, please?"

It took a minute or two for the hilarity to die down. "If you're hungry, I have been instructed to serve you a lunch appropriate to your station in the company. I'll bring it right out."

Oh, fantastic, he thought, clicking off. *I'm in the top division of the company.* Visions of chateaubriand and a fine Bordeaux danced in his head.

This Dancing with Meat came to an abrupt halt when the flight attendant (the boss' unemployed and heavily tattooed and pierced niece) unceremoniously chucked a plate of saltines and cheese at him and plunked down a glass of water that looked like it was fresh from Wooley Swamp.

Metcalf drew himself up. "What is the meaning of *this*?"

"New guy, right?" she asked, snapping her Bubblicious.

"Well, yes."

"Be grateful. Last guy got a pickle and a breadstick." She sauntered back whence she came, leaving Metcalf open-mouthed.

So, as long as his mouth was open anyway, he made the best of his stale crackers and processed cheese food slices that were getting hard and curly at the edges.

After lunch, he read Norbert Bunch's file for the rest of the flight.

"Hey, wake up—we're about to land. Stow your tray table, put away all that crap, and for God's sake, sit up!"

Metcalf stared groggily at the flight attendant, whom he was sure graduated at the top of her class in the subject of chewing nails and spitting rust, and hastened to obey.

She cleared his plate and untouched toxic wastewater and ambled back down the aisle. He gazed out his window and saw that they were landing on a grassy strip in a field. No airport, no nothing.

The touchdown was so fraught with peril that he wondered if they'd landed or been shot down. Finally, the plane came to a bone-jarring halt. The pilot, dressed in basketball sneakers, spandex bicycle pants, and a tee-shirt that read, *I Pooped Today!*, opened the exit hatch, threw out a rope ladder, looked at Metcalf, and said, "Oh. You made it," and then descended to the ground.

Metcalf hit the intercom button again. "Can I get some help with my luggage, please?"

"Oh, sure," the flight attendant replied. "Be right there."

In a moment or two, she strode up the aisle. "Where is it?"

"These and that," he said, pointing to the two bags and his briefcase.

"Terrif." She picked them up and heaved them out of the open hatch. "There ya go."

He sighed, making a truly inadvisable mental note to speak to his boss about this dimwit's attitude. He then rose from his seat to attempt the precarious descent. It lasted about two rungs before the ladder decided, "Oh, no you don't" and broke in half.

The pilot, stepping away from the bale of marijuana he was in the middle of purchasing, helped Metcalf up and checked for broken bones. Finding none, he returned to his deal.

Metcalf surveyed the area. He had rented a car from Cardinal Rentals, but there was no building in sight. "Hey, where do I pick up my rental?" he asked the pilot.

"It was already delivered. It's right over there."

"Right over *where*? That's nothing but a ..."

"That's it."

"A *lawnmower*? A riding *lawnmower*?"

"Sure. Why not? There's even a place to strap your bags to the fender, see?" The pilot took his bags and a bungee cord he pulled from his pocket and fixed them in place.

"Does no one have a car who can give me a lift?"

"Sorry. We're flying back in a couple of minutes. It's this or walk."

"Grand."

"So, how far are you going?"

"The Cumberland Motel."

"Hey, Felicia. He's at the Cumberland Motel!" he shouted to the flight attendant.

"Ooooooh, he'll love it there, fer sure."

The pilot turned back to Metcalf. "OK, you'll probably have to stop three or four times for gas, since this baby only holds a gallon, and it's not the most efficient model, if you know what I mean."

"Anything else? Poisonous snakes in the wheel wells, perhaps?"

"Nope, they cleared them out of there yesterday."

"I guess I'll be on my way, then. Can you point me in the right direction?"

"Thataway, until you get to 127, then hang a right and keep going until you get there."

"Fine. Thank you." He started up the lawnmower and, after a backfire or two, he was moving. At two miles an hour, but he was moving.

It was 2 p.m.

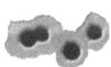

Metcalf pulled into the Cumberland Motel parking lot at three in the morning—after four refuelings and one traffic ticket. How was he supposed to know that he couldn't drive a lawnmower on 127? He escaped any further trouble with the law by mowing the grass at the side of the road all the way down to the motel.

He was hungry, exhausted, and covered with cut grass that the wind had blown back at him.

He looked like Jordy Verrill.

He was not in the best of moods.

He rang the front desk bell.

"Hol' yer horses, I'm comin'," a moth-eaten voice shouted.

The owner of the voice was about three days older than dirt, with the same customer service skills. "Yuh wanna room?"

"I have a reservation. The name is Robert Metcalf."

"Lemme look. Yep, here 'tis. Room 5. Right this way."

"Where's my key?"

"Don't got none."

"What? No room keys?"

"Nope. The dope-fiends jes kep' breakin' down the doors and it got too 'spensive t'keep replacin' 'em."

"So, what? I should just put anything valuable outside my door before I go to sleep?"

"S'what most folks do. Saves time."

"Just show me to my room, please."

The relic wambled to the end of the hallway, opened the door to Room 5, and walked in.

Metcalf followed. "Where's the bed?"

"Oh, we got them there Murphy beds," he said. He pulled a frame down from the wall. Inside was not a mattress, but several bales of hay.

"I'm supposed to sleep on that?"

"Best sleep a'your life, believe me. Just lemme find the sheets. Ah, here they are." He tossed them onto the hay. "Now over here's the bathroom."

Metcalf glanced in. "Can I get some towels?"

"Them's extra."

"I'll splurge." He turned the sink tap on—nothing. "Some water would be good, too."

"No water? I don' unnerstan' it. We just had this room remodeled."

"Oh, then that huge rust stain in the sink is new?" Metcalf stepped over to the shower and pulled back the curtain. "And the mother with her six puppies? Do these go with the room?"

He scratched his chin. "Well, they *could*, if yuh want …"

"I most certainly *don't* want! What I *do* want is a room with a bed that hasn't come out of Bethlehem on Christmas Eve! I want a sink and a shower that have hot and cold running water! I want towels!"

The geezer narrowed his eyes. "Fussy, are yuh?"

"Evidently."

"Well, then, we'll just upgrade you to the Presidential Suite."

If Metcalf hadn't been too tired to remember his Glock, he might have given it a test run.

They trudged down to Room 12, which had the most basic of amenities and cost three times the money. But Metcalf didn't care at that point. Amazingly enough, besides the bed, there was a chair in the room, which he pushed up against the door after the ancient baggage returned to the front desk.

Since there was actual water, Metcalf took a shower to scrape off the grass and road dust from the day. Once clean and dry, he discovered that the television worked too, but only got one channel and that was exclusively devoted to tractor repair. Even after the day from hell that Metcalf had just put in, he wasn't quite that desperate for entertainment. He switched it off, climbed into the bed, with a real, if lumpy, mattress, and spent the next eight hours in the deep and dreamless.

At eleven the next morning, there was a series of taps at his door that sounded like they were being executed with a jackhammer.

He bolted from the bed, removed the chair, and flung open the door.

"G'mornin'," a female prune with legs twittered. "Gotcher comp'mentry breakfast."

He stared down at the cracked red cafeteria tray she held, which, in turn, held burnt toast with jam, an ounce of oatmeal, a slice of fried bologna, and a runny concoction that he couldn't identify, but regarded with deep suspicion. Oh, and cornbread.

He took the tray. "Thanks very much," he said, closing the door on further conversation.

He was starving, but it somehow didn't seem prudent to play what amounted to gastric Russian roulette first thing in the morning. Deciding to live another day, he bunged it all in the wastebasket, knowing they'd never discover it for years.

He dressed, checked out, revved up the lawnmower, and went in search of actual food, which he found two hours later at Linda's Diner in Jamestown.

He parked, stepped inside, and seated himself. Turning to look at the blackboard menu, he perused the bill of fare.

MENU

DEEP-FRIED CHICKEN   **DEEP-FRIED PIGS FEET**

DEEP-FRIED HOT DOGS   **DEEP-FRIED LIVER**

(All come with deep-fried fries and deep-fried green beans)

SIDES   ## DESSERTS

DEEP-FRIED FRIES   **DEEP-FRIED APPLE PIE**

DEEP-FRIED CORNBREAD   **DEEP-FRIED TWINKIE**

DEEP-FRIED COLESLAW   **DEEP-FRIED PUDDING**

DEEP-FRIED PICKLES   **DEEP-FRIED JELL-O**

DEEP-FRIED SALAD

Metcalf sighed and ordered a deep-fried cup of coffee.

The noise of the Fryolators was deafening.

Today was not going to be a stellar day. He could just feel it.

After forcing down the coffee and paying his bill, he took his rural costume into the men's room and got changed, trying hard not to touch anything.

He inventoried his look in the mirror. Straw hat—check. Faded plaid shirt—check. Bib overalls—check. Old, beaten-up barn boots—check. Pitchfork—check. Piece of hay to chew on—check.

Studying his reflection, it suddenly occurred to him that he could have gone to Goodwill and gotten the exact same look for about eight bucks. Well, too late now.

He was ready. He walked outside and, after consulting his map, jumped back on the lawnmower and headed for Sheep Dip Road and the Bunch place.

Fortunately, it wasn't far. He pulled into the driveway and killed the motor—which was just as well because he was about ten seconds away from running out of gas.

As he stepped off, a bullet whizzed by his left ear.

A cheery voice inquired, "Who the hell are you and whaddya want?"

Metcalf felt his side pocket to be sure the Glock was still there. He thought fast. "I'm from Publisher's Clearing House, here to talk to you about a prize you won."

"Oh, well, that's different, then. Come on up."

Metcalf picked up his pitchfork and sallied forth.

He was met at the door by none other than the deadbeat himself, Norbert Bunch … or at least Metcalf guessed it was Bunch. It was hard to tell. This man was well over six feet tall, clean-shaven, wearing Ralph Lauren slacks and a Pierre Cardin dress shirt. His Cole Hann loafers were polished to a high sheen. He had a complete set of teeth and a perfect haircut.

"Norbert Bunch," the man said, thrusting out his hand.

"Bob Metcalf." He offered a firm handshake. "I barely recognized you. You don't look a thing like your picture."

"Oh? And which picture is that?"

"I saw one of you with no teeth, looking kind of rough."

"Aw, that was taken at a Halloween party years ago. Where'd you happen to see it?"

Metcalf realized he'd put a major foot down wrong. "Ummmmmmm … on the internet, I think."

"Well, no matter. Come on in, then. You can leave your pitchfork outside."

The interior of the small brick house was nothing like Metcalf expected. Where he thought he'd see peeling paint, there was tasteful, subtle wallpaper. Where he expected chairs and sofas losing their stuffing with exposed springs, there was a Chesterfield living room suite. Where he was sure there'd be a kitchen with cheap pine cabinets and rusted appliances, he found mahogany cabinets, Tiffany pendant lights, stainless-steel appliances, and granite countertops. There was soft music in the background, which Metcalf recognized as Beethoven's *Fur Elise*.

All he could do was stare.

"I'm about to have me some lunch. Care to join?"

Metcalf's stomach roared at the mention of food.

Bunch laughed. "Here, have a pew. Won't be a moment." He pulled out a Stickley chair at a matching Park Slope Hex table. Metcalf felt a little self-conscious in his overalls.

"You like Reubens? On rye? With a kosher pickle?" Bunch said.

Metcalf had a hard time speaking around the tsunami that his salivary glands had unleashed, but managed a rather moist, "Great!"

Ten minutes later, a mile-high sandwich on a Spode Pure Morris dinner plate, along with the promised kosher pickle, was put before him. Bunch poured Pellegrino water into Waterford crystal tumblers and then sat down behind his own sandwich.

Metcalf was kind of sorry he was going to have to kill this guy.

There followed much chewing and no talking.

After the meal, Bunch served espresso with chocolate mousse cake.

When the last crumb was finally consumed, Bunch gazed across the table at our hero and asked, "OK, why are you here, Bob Metcalf?"

Metcalf sighed. "Guess I didn't blend as well as I thought I would. OK. I'm from the Special Collections Division of the IRS. You have a ten-year delinquent tax bill, and I am here to … take measures." He tried to look tough, but it was hard to do when that idiotic straw hat kept falling over his eyes.

"In other words …"

"I'm here to kill you." He withdrew the Glock and pointed it at his host.

Bunch raised his hands. "All right. I guess I got it comin'— but can I make a last request?"

"You can."

"I want you to kill me with my own gun. It's a shotgun and it'll be faster."

"I guess I could do that, sure." Metcalf was happy that things were going rather smoother than anticipated.

"All right, I'll take you to it. Then we can go outside. I'd hate for there to be a mess in the house." He led Metcalf to his gun case and pointed out a Mossberg break-action shotgun. Metcalf pocketed the Glock and removed the weapon from the rack. "Is it loaded?"

"Gun's not much use if it ain't. C'mon, let's get this over with."

They trudged outside into the middle of the backyard, and Metcalf was just raising the gun when a fellow walked out of the barn and headed their way.

"Hey, Norb. I wanted to ask you about—oh, hello," he said to Metcalf, looking him over. He turned to Bunch. "Circus in town?"

"Nope. This here's Bob Metcalf from the IRS."

"Oh."

"I'm about to get shot for nonpayment."

"Seems a little extreme. Can I have your van Gogh?"

"Sure. Take what you want."

"Who *is* this guy?" Metcalf demanded.

"Him? That's Caleb, my hired hand."

"Can we please get on with this?"

"Fire away."

Metcalf raised the shotgun, got Bunch dead center in the sights, and squeezed the trigger ...

... and the gun exploded in his face, shearing off half his head and depositing it all the way into the yard.

The two men stood over the twitching corpse.

Caleb asked, "So, how many is that now?"

"Twenty. We get two every year."

"Wonder why nobody ever comes lookin' for 'em."

"Don't matter. We got sausages to make, now that we got more of our secret ingredient. He's fat, too. What with smokin' and mixin' in with the other ingredients, he oughta last six months 'til the next one shows up. Gimme a hand. You take grab his legs and I'll get his arms."

"So, what'd you plug the barrel with this time?"

"Old cartridges, packed in real tight.

"You'll be right up shit's creek if they ever send a guy who knows to check that the barrel's clear before shootin' yuh."

"I ain't worried about it."

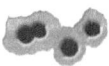

A month later, back at the Special Collections Division, Mr. Bunson slit open an envelope from Kentucky and withdrew a two-thousand-dollar check, which he pocketed. It was his ten-percent share of the quarterly profits from "Norbert's Farm Fresh Sausages," which were wildly popular throughout the south.

He smiled. "I don't care if that guy never pays his taxes." He rubbed his chin. "Now … who else is expendable around here?"

Carson Buckingham knew from childhood that she wanted to be a writer and began, at age six, by writing books of her own, hand-drawing covers, and selling them to any family member who would pay (usually a dime) for what she referred to as "classic literature." When she ran out of relatives, she concluded that there was no real money to be made in self-publishing, so she studied writing and read voraciously for the next eighteen years, while simultaneously collecting enough rejection slips to re-paper her living room … twice.

When her landlord chucked her out for, in his words, "making the apartment into one hell of a downer," she redoubled her efforts, and collected four times the rejection slips in half the time, single-handedly causing the first paper shortage in U.S. history.

But she persevered, improved greatly over the years, and here we are.

Carson has been/is a professional proofreader, editor, newspaper reporter, copywriter, technical writer, novelist, short story writer, book reviewer, editor, blogger, and comedy writer. Besides writing, she loves reading, cooking, and gardening—but not at the same time. Though born and raised in Connecticut, she lives in Kentucky now—and Connecticut is glad to be rid of her!

UPCHUCK CHUCK

BY BRUCE HARRIS

"I want to tell you something," Roland said. We were alone, yet my older brother looked over his shoulder. "I shouldn't be doing this, but what the heck. Retirement is in my near future. I guess it doesn't matter."

"Shouldn't be doing what?" I asked.

"This." He produced a blue yarmulke. It sported a lower case, white-stitched *NY*, the New York Giants logo.

"You're converting to Judaism?" I asked. Roland shook his head. "You're becoming a Giants fan? Go, Big Blue?"

"It's evidence," he said disgustedly.

He held the skullcap at arm's length. I supposed it was because none of the Giants' players on his fantasy football team performed particularly well this season. The now-veteran NYPD beat cop looked like he could still fit into the uniform he wore as a rookie patrolman twenty-five years ago.

He continued. "A clue. I found it the other day at a murder scene."

Roland paused, and I stared at him. Other people usually moved their hand in a circular motion to encourage my terse brother to share details. But I'd always simply stared, knowing that soon enough he'd get frustrated and—

"Murder. My erudite partners call him Upchuck Chuck. The guy puked his guts after he killed. What a mess."

"Where?" I asked.

"1276 Lombard Drive."

"That's not far from here."

"Right." Roland flipped the yarmulke in the air a few inches before catching it. "I didn't show it to anyone else. I was first on the scene. It doesn't belong to the victim. His wife swears she's never seen it before."

"Why are you showing it to me? Shouldn't it be locked up at the police station?" I was no cop, but I'd watched enough TV to know that much. This was the first time Roland had ever shared evidence with me. With thumbs and index fingers, I pinched the corners of my eyes shut. There had to be a reason.

He shrugged. "Like I said, several more weeks on the job, and then I drink beer and watch sports 24/7. We'll catch him with or without this yarmulke."

"How do you know?" I asked.

"It has amateur written all over it. According to the victim's wife, her husband did time for robbery. He talked and received a reduced sentence. His partner, a three-time loser, swore he'd send someone to kill him. He must have picked one hell of an assassin. The guy left his vomit but took about thirty dollars in cash and a cheap watch with a broken crystal. That's it. It's a first-floor apartment. The killer broke the window and gained entry. Messed up the place a bit, but I've seen a lot worse."

"Maybe the puke was the victim's? Or the wife's?" I asked.

"Nope. No DNA match. It's the killer's. Probably not his first job, either."

"How do you know?"

"Two months ago, another murder scene with vomit. Nothing missing except some cash and the victim's tie. Upchuck Chuck must get nervous. Anyway, I'll hang up my uniform soon enough and this killer will be caught." Roland looked over his shoulder again, then whispered, "Since you and I are the only two who know about this," Roland held up the yarmulke, "let's see if we can find this killer, this public puker, this heaving hombre, this retching—"

"I get the point."

A beat cop for two-and-a-half decades, my brother never received a promotion. I'm sure he felt bad about that. I don't recall him ever solving a big crime, or any crime for that matter. Usually first—or one of the first—on a scene, he gathered evidence for others to solve the mystery. Maybe this one time, Roland wanted to be the one to crack the case. His time to finally shine. And he's honored me with sharing in that accomplishment.

"Hmm … could be interesting." I was out on disability following knee surgery. I still had a week before returning to my job as a shipping manager for an auto parts wholesaler. I could move around pretty well. "Sure, why not? I'll probably make a better cop than you."

Roland punched my shoulder. "I can still beat you up, just like when we were kids."

"That'd be police brutality," I said.

"I'll wait until I retire," Roland said, "when it will be nothing more than an older sibling beating up on his annoying younger brother." A smile appeared on his face.

"Where do we begin?" I asked.

"With Arthur Brinkman."

"Who?"

Roland turned the yarmulke over so I could see the three lines of red lettering inside. I read:

BAR MITZVAH

ARTHUR BRINKMAN

SEPTEMBER 2, 2019

I looked up. "Is he our suspect? Our man?"

"Technically, he *is* a man since his bar mitzvah has come and gone. But I'm confident he'll lead us to *our man*," Roland said. "Just because this name is on the yarmulke doesn't tell us much."

"One thing it tells us is Arthur Brinkman likes football."

"If you call what the Giants play football, then yes, I agree," Roland said. "I'd argue the opposite. I'd say, if he likes the Giants, he knows nothing about football."

"You're the cop, older brother. What's next?"

"Let's start with a list of temples in town. We'll find out where this young Giants fan attends Hebrew school."

An initial internet search revealed six synagogues. Further digging informed us there were two each of reform, conservative, and orthodox houses of worship.

The first temple we visited told us they wouldn't permit sports teams or any type of advertising logo on a yarmulke. They suggested we try a reform temple.

Roland and I found what we were looking for at Shalom for All, the second of two reform temples we visited. We showed the receptionist the yarmulke and explained the reason for our visit. She confirmed the Brinkman kid was a student there.

"I think I'd better get the rabbi," Debbie Franklin said from behind glass. She spoke through a small, circular opening.

Moments later, we shook hands with Rabbi Harold Kantor.

"Please, follow me. My office is this way." Rabbi Kantor was tall, thin, with light hair and a close-cropped beard. He had small, twin, blue-diamond earrings that matched his eye color. He wore a suit but no tie. We sat around a polished wooden table in his book-lined office. The image on his computer screen was an exterior shot of Shalom for All.

"Debbie tells me you are from the police?"

"Yes, I'm officer Roland Sanderson and this is Sheldon." He paused. "Sheldon is assisting."

Rabbi Kantor nodded. "And Debbie says you are looking for Arthur Brinkman?"

I watched, listened.

"That's correct, rabbi." Roland produced the yarmulke from his pocket. "We found this in an apartment that was ... um ... burglarized. It didn't belong to the victim. We believe the perpetrator dropped it while committing the crime. We're hoping you can help us ... you know ... generate some leads based on the yarmulke?"

Kantor rubbed his stubble. "Leads? I don't—"

"Who would have received these yarmulkes?" Roland asked.

The rabbi tapped a pencil on his desk. "The ushers handed them out to the men on the morning of Arthur's bar mitzvah. Of course, it's possible some males brought their own yarmulkes. Then again, it's also possible the men didn't wear a yarmulke at all. We don't require it at Shalom for All. Thinking back, there may have been roughly twenty-five men, typical for a Saturday morning bar mitzvah."

Roland spoke. "Just because someone wore their own yarmulke or didn't wear one doesn't mean he, or even she, didn't take one as a keepsake. True?"

"That's correct," Rabbi Kantor readily agreed.

"I'd like to contact the Brinkman family and obtain from them a list of all the guests that attended Arthur's bar mitzvah." Roland was direct, forceful, his police experience on display.

The rabbi's pencil tapping increased. "Debbie can provide you with their address. It'll be up to them if they want to cooperate."

We thanked the rabbi. Debbie handed us Brinkman's information. Roland left his card with her and we departed.

The following morning, Roland and I paid a visit to Karen and Eric Brinkman. Roland was masterful. His uniform persuasive. We had the names in less than ten minutes.

"We'll drop the list off at the station, have them run it to see if anyone has a prior record."

"Good," I said, my first word since meeting the Brinkmans. "Then can we get something to eat? I'm starving."

Roland got caught up with another officer discussing some administrative matters. It was noontime when the two of us sat down at a diner.

Over lunch, Roland's words depressed me. "I'm thinking maybe this was a stupid idea to begin with. I'm serious. I think we should just call this off. We aren't going to find this killer at Shalom for All."

"How do you know?" I asked.

"I just know."

I wasn't enjoying our brotherly bonding experience. I didn't want the investigation to end without a solution. Roland's impending retirement had to be bittersweet, even stressful on some level. This was his last opportunity to prove to himself he could solve a case, a really important case. "Tell you what," I began, "Why don't we do this ... let's wait until after we run the Brinkman family names through your police database. We'll see if any names show up with a criminal record. If there's a hit, we question that person or persons. If not, we throw in the towel. What do you say to that?"

"Deal."

Later that afternoon, ROLAND illuminated on my phone's screen. "What's up?"

"Brian Letterman."

"Who?"

"He attended Arthur Brinkman's bar mitzvah and guess what?" Roland asked.

"What?"

"Three years ago, as a juvenile, he was arrested for breaking and entering. Year after that, convicted of a minor drug charge."

"Whoa! He's our man!"

"Not so fast, Sheldon. Innocent until proven guilty. Ever hear that expression? And it's a long stretch from breaking and entering or marijuana to murder."

An hour after our phone conversation, we discovered Brian Letterman was the eighteen-year-old nephew of Mr. and Mrs. Brinkman, Arthur's first cousin. He lived alone less than thirty miles from 1276 Lombard Drive, the crime site. Letterman's address turned out to be a decent-sized, one-family home. As Roland and I ascended the driveway, I couldn't help but wonder how a teenager could afford such a house. Roland double-checked the address. He confirmed we were at the correct location when I noticed two mailboxes. That explained things. Young Letterman rented a room in the house's rear. One mailbox had an old-fashioned Dymo plastic label. The badly cracked label read:

REAR APT

LETTERMAN

"Would save us a lot of trouble if it said 'Upchuck Chuck' instead," I said. We went around back. There was no screen door. Roland knocked.

"Who is it?"

We lucked out. He was home. "Police. We'd like to speak to you for a minute, Brian."

The young man in front of us wore sweatpants and a T-shirt. He was shoeless. His hair hung down to his shoulders. "What's this about?" he asked.

Roland was still in uniform. This time, it seemed certain, intimidation was his goal. "We want to ask you a few questions. Can we come in?"

Letterman looked us up and down. "Got a warrant?"

"No, but we can get one," I said, channeling my inner Joe Friday.

Letterman stepped back. "C'mon in. I don't have nothing to hide. I'm clean. You won't even find no weed here." His tone indicated nerves rather than confidence. I hope he wasn't nervous enough to upchuck in front of us.

The three-room abode was messy. The bed was unmade, and dirty dishes and glasses were piled in the small kitchen sink. Rumpled clothes were scattered across a carpet that begged for a shampoo. My mind might have been playing tricks on me, but I could have sworn my nose detected a faint vomit scent. Now I hoped I wouldn't get sick. A laptop sat on the floor, plugged into a wall outlet, screen up. The homepage displayed a young bikini-clad woman. It could have been his girlfriend. Roland and I glanced around. I was more convinced than ever the job of an auto parts shipping manager suited me better than police work. Roland produced the yarmulke.

"Ever see this before?" he asked Letterman.

I detected a slight smile on Letterman's face. "It's a yarmulke. From my cousin's bar mitzvah. He's a Giants fan."

"Do you own one?" Roland asked.

"Yes—I mean, I did. I got one at his bar mitzvah. But I'm not sure where it is now. Why?"

"We'll ask the questions. You lost it?" I asked, eyebrows raised.

Letterman shrugged. "I don't know. It might be around here someplace. I haven't seen it since the bar mitzvah. I'm not in the habit of wearing one. Besides, if I did, it wouldn't be a Giants one. They suck. Anyway, it was a while ago."

"September second," Roland said.

"Right. What's this about? Arthur done something bad?"

Roland explained to him about the break-in and burglary at 1276 Lombard Drive. He said nothing about the murder. "We found the yarmulke at the scene."

"How does that involve me?" Letterman asked. His Adam's apple jerked.

"We haven't accused you of anything," I said.

"I didn't do it." Letterman stared into my eyes. "A lot of people were at that bar mitzvah. Why are you picking on me?"

"I think you know the reason, Brian." Roland let the ensuing silence work for him.

Ironic. Roland could never stand it when I stared at him in silence, waiting for a response or confession. Now Roland employed the same trick on our suspect.

"I was a kid." Letterman bowed down his head. "I learned my lesson. I got a job now and I'm on my own. I had nothing to do with whatever happened on Lombard Drive. I swear it."

"And you've looked for the yarmulke but haven't been able to find it? That's what you said, right?" I asked.

"I didn't say that. I haven't been looking for the yarmulke. Why should I? I just said I don't remember seeing it since the bar mitzvah. What's wrong with that? This whole thing is ridiculous."

The kid was right. I shut up and let Roland do the talking.

"Do you own a watch?" Roland asked.

Letterman automatically touched his left wrist. "No. I used to wear one, but since it broke, I just use my phone."

"Do you remember where you were on December seventh, the night of the ... burglary?"

"Hell no ... I mean, no. I have no idea."

"Okay, Mr. Letterman. If you can think of anything regarding that night, you'll let us know?" Roland asked. He didn't wait for an answer. Instead, he handed Letterman his card.

"I really don't think—"

I cut Letterman off. An idea struck me. "Did you wear a suit to the bar mitzvah?"

Letterman's head tilted like a curious puppy. "Yes. Of course."

"Is the bar mitzvah the last time you wore the suit?"

Letterman didn't have to think hard. "Yup. I don't normally wear a—"

"Has the suit been to the dry cleaners since you wore it?" I asked.

He reddened. "Um, no ... but I only wore it the once, so it's not dirty or anything—"

"Where's the suit now? In your closet?" I turned toward a door off his bedroom.

"Yes. Why?"

"I'm thinking maybe the yarmulke is still in a pocket of your suit."

Roland grinned, walked to the closet, and pulled out a hanger with a poorly hung suit precariously clinging to the wood.

"Wait a minute," Letterman said. "You can't do that."

"I just did," Roland said, reaching into the suit jacket pockets. "Nothing." He then placed his hand into the pants pockets. "Noth—wait." He reached deeper and pulled out a NY

Giants logo yarmulke. "Almost missed it. You have a hole in your pocket."

Letterman took the hanger from Roland. He did his best to straighten out the suit, but it still looked like a mess.

Roland placed the yarmulke on a battered dresser. "Sorry to have bothered you, Brian."

"That's it? I'm in the clear?"

"That's it," Roland said. "Oh, one word of advice." He let the words hang in the air.

"Oh?" Brian asked.

"Get the suit cleaned and pressed and have that hole sewn before you wear it again."

On the drive home, Roland sighed. "What's the point?" he asked. "We can't go around questioning innocent people because I found a yarmulke at a murder scene. Whatever. At least we tried."

I'd seen the look. Roland's words belied his true feelings. His mood matched his uniform color. I hated to agree with him, but there didn't seem to be any use in continuing the investigation.

Roland was trying to convince himself. "Well, it was fun anyway."

I tried to lighten the moment. "I'll just stick to packing and shipping rotors and drums."

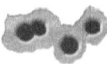

Weeks later, Roland and I were settling down to watch an afternoon of football. The Upchuck Chuck case was still unsolved. Roland's phone rang. He checked the caller id, put the call on speaker.

"This is Roland," he said.

"Officer Sanderson, this is Debbie Franklin from Shalom for All."

Roland studied what must have been my amused and confused look. "How are you, Ms. Franklin? How can I help you?" he asked.

"Could you stop by the temple this afternoon? There is someone who wants to speak to you."

Roland told her to hold and put the phone on mute.

"I'm retired. Remember? Turned in my badge. We'd be impersonating police officers. Besides, I've put it behind me."

"We started something. Might as well finish it."

Roland's eyes widened. He aimed the remote, turned off the television, and unmuted the phone. "See you in an hour," he said.

We again found ourselves at Shalom for All. Rabbi Kantor was away at a conference. After a brief "how have you been" conversation with Debbie, she introduced us to the Temple's former president, Harvey Bristol. His egg-shaped head was shaved bald. Smooth facial skin glistened. There wasn't a hint of hair. The man's dress was Brooks Brothers-conservative. Bristol stood at attention and then extended his hand. He had a vise-like grip. Roland must have noticed my discomfort. He grinned and said, "Let's get down to business."

"Debbie informed me about your investigation. I found something I thought you'd find interesting," Bristol said.

Bristol moved to a computer. He began punching keys and arranging multiple screens on the desk. He looked like an old techie.

"We recently installed new security cameras. Before archiving the old footage, I watched several minutes of video captured by various cameras." He squinted, bent closer to the middle screen. "Here," he continued, pointing. "Watch this."

Roland and I stared. The video showed a man, first looking over his shoulder, then grabbing fistfuls of what appeared to be yarmulkes from a basket and shoving them into his jacket pocket. The location was the synagogue's front lobby.

"That's Malcolm Burnside, one of our congregants. Did you see him grab a handful of yarmulkes?" Roland and I nodded.

"The video is dated only days after Arthur Brinkman's bar mitzvah." Bristol turned back to us. "Follow me."

The two of us walked with him to the front lobby. There, on a table near the front door, was the basket we saw in the video. Despite having walked past it more than once, I hadn't noticed it. The basket was filled with yarmulkes of different colors and sizes.

"We keep these here for anyone who wants to take one," Bristol said. "We buy some, like these inexpensive, thin kippot."

Bristol noticed the dumb looks on my and Roland's faces.

"Kippot. Sorry, that's another name for yarmulkes," he explained. "After bat and bar mitzvahs, the families usually dump the extra yarmulkes into this basket."

"People keep them or return them?" I asked.

"Both. Some return, some pocket them and take them home."

"Wait," I said. "Are you saying after the Brinkman bar mitzvah, this basket was filled with those New York Giants yarmulkes?"

Bristol grinned. "That's right."

I looked at Roland. He wasn't saying anything. I figured he was having a hard time playing a cop in retirement. I, on the other hand, was enjoying my revived role.

"Anyone in the congregation could have taken an Arthur Brinkman yarmulke. Our suspect list just increased … I don't know … how many members do you have?"

"Three hundred."

"Three hundred?" I repeated, sighed.

"Technically true," Bristol confirmed. "But not likely. As you saw in the video, Mr. Burnside pretty much single-handedly reduced the suspect list."

"Where can we find Malcolm Burnside?" I asked.

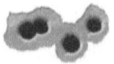

Less than thirty minutes later, Roland and I found ourselves in a small, overheated apartment. Despite the temperature, Malcolm Burnside wore a woolen beanie hat and a sweatshirt. We didn't identify ourselves as police officers, rather as two people who were just at Shalom for All and we wanted to follow up with Burnside on something. I mentioned the yarmulkes and what we witnessed on the security videos. Burnside's age was difficult to determine. He could have been forty years old or on the wrong side of fifty. He squinted almond-shaped eyes. He denied nothing.

"It's not stealing. How can you steal something that is given away for free?" Burnside asked.

I didn't know how to answer. Roland came to the rescue. "How many yarmulkes do you have?"

A grin appeared on Burnside's face. He walked to a dresser that was missing a drawer. He opened the bottom drawer. One knob was loose, and he struggled. "Thirty-two. I have six from Harry Yeager's bar mitzvah, five from Jessica Altman's bat mitzvah, three from—"

"We're just interested in the Arthur Brinkman yarmulkes," Roland said. "Have any of those?"

"Sure do," a proud Burnside said. His collection was strewn in the drawer. After a few seconds, he pulled out the familiar blue Giants yarmulkes. "Ten. Had eleven, but sold one."

"You sold one?" I asked.

"That's why I take them. I sell some at the Community House Apartments."

I was familiar with the federally funded Community House complex. It was a halfway house, catering to recovering alcoholics and drug abusers. They offered addiction and mental health counseling there.

Brinkman continued. "I used to live in that place. Trouble is, I have only one Jewish friend there. He was my best customer. He'd give me two dollars for one. Sometimes three if he really liked it. But he died. So, I don't sell too many now."

"Who did you sell the one Giants yarmulke to?"

"I didn't sell it. I gave it away, to Pete Standish. He isn't Jewish. I felt bad for him. He works sometimes down the street at the deli and he's always complaining about nearly getting hit by cars going into the Temple on Saturdays and holidays and it makes him nervous and late for work. I convinced him wearing the yarmulke would bring him good luck." Burnside laughed.

"What's so funny?" I asked.

"I don't think it brought him any luck. I knew it wouldn't. I just told him that to make him feel better."

"Why do you say it didn't bring him luck?"

"Because he lost it ... day after I gave it to him. Then, guess what?"

"What?"

"He showed me a new watch he said he found. But it wasn't working! He said he had nothing but bad luck since he wore the yarmulke."

"Did you get a look at the watch?" Roland asked.

"Yup. The glass was broken. Not that he'll need a watch now. Or a yarmulke."

"Why is that?" I asked.

"They do random checks. They found drugs in Standish's apartment and called the cops. Poor guy. He puked his guts out when the cops arrived. He's in jail now."

The next evening, Roland and I got together again to watch Monday Night Football. By the time he arrived, it was the fourth quarter. For the first time since his retirement, Roland looked content.

"How are the Giants doing?" he asked.

"Getting killed."

Bruce Harris writes crime and mystery stories. His work has appeared in *Mystery Weekly Magazine*, *Rock and a Hard Place*, and *Shotgun Honey*, among others. He lives in New Jersey, but his heart is in Maine.

DIRTY POOL

BY CHRIS BAUER

They stumbled past the real estate sign at the corner of the property, then climbed into the freight elevator, him and this old barfly, the two of them late from tonight's last call at Thunder Wonderland Bowling Lanes. She mentioned something about handcuffs.

Right. Like that was gonna happen.

The Anthracite Beer Company, 1899-1937. Twenty for Active Seniors on tap. For sales info call …

Her place. A conversion on the second floor of what used to be a brewery. When he was through with her, they'd never sell another unit.

Her name was Sissy. Retired security guard, late fifties was his guess. The name didn't fit. No matter. *Anything between eight and eighty, blind, crippled, or crazy.* A cliché he'd heard as a horny teenager. Randall Burton's motto ever since.

How he liked them at this age—older, even. Unless he could find himself a young one. Except he'd had to stop that shit. That shit made him leave Detroit. Major crackdown on predators. He'd headed east across Pennsylvania, his destination: Justus, ten miles past Scranton. Coal country. Home to a large senior population enjoying their golden years in the Poconos. New talent, some maybe willing, some maybe less than willing, in a small town that received national attention as a statistical aberration.

Takes an aberration to know one, he mused.

The elevator opened onto a second-floor hall. She led him out, him commenting on one label next to the floor buttons. "A pool, too. Nice."

"It's being cleaned," she said.

Blue pool water turning dark crimson, rippling away from a floating, bloodied corpse. Oh my my *my*. The mental visual was incredible.

No. Stop. Too risky moving a body, even at 2 o'clock in the morning. Too careless to act on impulse again. Like this afternoon, at the edge of this sleepy little burg, where he'd taken advantage of an underage gas-pump jockey who'd been in the throes of a distracted, one-handed text-messaging frenzy. The kid got more than a fistful of dollars when Randall had him reach into his lap for the money. It was humorous and thrilling to Randall, and it ended with one knockout punch to the kid's face after the kid caught on. But it was also death-wish stupid on Randall's part.

Sissy tossed the handcuffs onto her bed, her grin sloppy, lopsided. She winked at him. "Maybe we'll change our minds," she said.

Fuck no, cunt.

The fight; the beating; restraining her with his bare hands; the maiming; the submission. It would all be so sexually gratifying, so ... euphoric. He didn't need no stinkin' handcuffs, but seeing them had taken him out of his game for a second. He caught himself too late to keep her from wandering out of the bedroom, her fat ass cheeks wrestling each other for continued cohabitation of her tight lavender pants.

"Be right back, honey," she said.

Damn it.

So be it. His wood was still seasoning, anyway.

"Lowest Crime, Small Metro Areas: #1 Rockingham County NH … #8 State College PA; #9 Kingston NY; #10 Glen Falls NY. FOOTNOTE. The list excludes ineligible small-town venue Justus, PA …"—PARADE Magazine.

Randall Burton parked the Chevy Impala in a lot that served the town's post office, its newspaper, and a bowling alley. Sixteen hours on the road, staying at or below the speed limit all the way from Detroit. Martha Spezak, the car's owner, had vouched for the car's low mileage.

"Nineteen thousand, six-hundred miles is accurate, Stephen," she'd said, addressing his alias, another in a succession of many, all of them chewed and spit out like sticks of Juicy Fruit. As Martha's boarder in her suburban Detroit rancher, he'd stayed long enough to steal her identity and drain her bank accounts. "Driven more than twenty-five years by, yes, a little old lady, yours truly. To the grocery store on Fridays and to church on Sundays," she added, beaming a warm, dentured smile at her new friend just before he crushed her head with the car's tire iron and put her in the trunk. Her body went into a dumpster somewhere along the Ohio Turnpike.

Randall needed a good muscle stretch, some greasy bar food, and lots of whatever beer the bowling alley bar had on tap. And he was frisky for more tail.

The rest of the footnote in the PARADE article had closed the deal: *"Justus receives Honorable Mention for this statistical aberration. No—repeat NO—crimes have been reported within its jurisdiction for the past four years."*

Cable news stations had picked it up, and Randall also saw it on a Nickelodeon TV feed when he exited the women's toilet in a Monroe, Michigan, Chuck E. Cheese restaurant after strangling little Morgan Hobart. He paused to watch the rest of the news stream—*"Retired sheriff never replaced. Town has no police force."*

Wow. Tax-free shopping.

Randall glanced at the magazine article on the seat next to him, opened to a photo. He'd parked near where the picture had been taken, and most likely around the same time of day, twilight, the sun setting behind the bowling alley, a cobalt sky blended with a subtle orange above the alley's marquee of sequentially flashing Vegas-style lighting. He climbed out of the car.

"That's a lot of fucking lights," he murmured mid-stretch. "Podunkers and their bowling. Made for each other."

At street level in hand-arranged black letters below the glittering marquee, a small white message board boasted *"Good Food and Drink–Senior Women's League–Monday & Tuesday."*

Today was Monday. He'd died and gone to heaven.

"No food or drink on the lanes, fellas," the bartender-fry cook-cashier-bowling shoe guy said. A second bar patron, a short thirty-something with a monk haircut, acknowledged the directive with a nod, grabbed his drink, and headed toward a children's play area in the farthest corner, close to a building exit. Randall stared.

Red flag. The play area was only ten feet away from the exit.

Are these people for real?

"Got it," Randall said to the bartender and picked up his food.

He wandered the width of the building, eyed the women bowlers three steps down at lane level, read their team names as he sipped his draft Genny Cream Ale—local merchants, small companies, celebrity fan clubs, friendly coworkers.

He passed lanes seven and eight, Newman's Own vs. Clooney's Concubines, stopped short of setting foot on the polished wood floor at lanes nine and ten, settled into a black, contoured plastic seat in the carpeted second row, the other spectator seats empty. His wide-mouth beer cup sat high in the cup holder, the paper-plated food next to it on a shared table between seats. Chomping on deep-fried fish fillets, manhandling some greasy fries, licking his fingers, and gulping his Genny, Randall wanted to be noticed and was. With a cherry-cheeked complexion, fifty extra inner-tube pounds, and a fleshy, full face, Randall was a large man who at forty-seven could pass for a grandfatherly sixty. The image came in handy, with kids and seniors alike.

He ogled two teams clad in untucked bowling shirts plus one woman in a wheelchair. Their score-sheet was projected overhead, game two of a three-game match. Lethal Women, lane nine. Fighting Cadavers, lane ten. Sure, why not?

After each team bowled a frame, he'd figured out who was who. Lethal Women was Dody, Myra, Penny, and Sissy. The wheelchair-bound Charlotte kept their score. Sissy, the team's anchor, a left-hander with a wicked curve, was striking her way through the tenth frame and most likely bowling her weight, her score nearing two hundred.

The women's conversation—kids and grandkids, aged parents, pets, ex-husbands, boring husbands, dead husbands, dead beat husbands, boyfriends, big colored balls of the bowling and non-bowling variety, and the joys of sex with and without a partner. Randall was feeling the tickle, would need a few minutes before he could stand to get himself another beer.

Halfway through the final match, he'd learned enough. The Fighting Cadavers were four current or former hospital nurses. Lethal Women included one retired security guard, one retired dental hygienist, and two retired lawyers, their elderly scorekeeper a retired surgeon. A Mel Gibson fan club, the Lethal-Weapon-series Mel model, overlooking for the time being the new Abusive Mel model. Made sense to him, considering they had these beautifully hand-stitched bowling shirts with the team's name already on them.

Third game, ninth frame, the match nearly over, he peeled his girth from the plastic seat and headed for a bar stool.

The bartender lined up multiple shots along the rail for both teams. Randall would treat the women real nice, would foster their feeling of safety in numbers, would settle on the loneliest. Or maybe whoever the loneliest was would settle on him. Nearly all of them accepted his generosity, Sissy downing the leftovers. The women asked him to join them at a table.

Including Randall, they were six. He was smooth and witty and charming and humble and cuddly while the entire women's team sized him up, him asking questions that were age-, lifestyle-, and conversationally appropriate for a person sensitive to the local environment and the folks who enjoyed it. He addressed their comments and questions.

"You're not from around here," Sissy said.

Guilty. Will be moving here from a Midwestern city where there's too much urban crime. Looking for good people, clean air, a less worrisome environment, Mayberry RFD, blah-blah-blah-gag. After all, there was this news story about your town— no reported crime for four years running.

"Yeah, we've heard a lot about that lately. You a bowler?"

Yes, many years, two-thirty-seven average, he'd competed professionally while in his twenties. All lies.

"Married?"

Yes, she died. True. He'd killed her.

"Kids? Grandkids?"

Two and five, respectively. Lies. Loves all kids to death. So very true.

Finally, after chatting each of them up, a *Welcome to Justus, Randall* chorus echoed cheerfully around the table. He smiled in return, liking the sound of his name on each of their gussied bright red or hot pink or deep cranberry wrinkled lips, thinking maybe he'd keep this alias, maybe hang around here longer than usual if the feeding stayed abundant. Might as well sully the town's no-crime record real good, seeing as how these gullible old bitches seemed so—

"… friendly. And protective of all our neighbors, mind you, once we get to know a person," Sissy said.

After three more shots, as many beers, some nachos, a few rum-and-Coke refills, and eventually three departures, Sissy made eye contact with Myra, and Myra, too, departed. Last call from the bartender brought two more drinks. Brassy-haired Sissy stirred her glass, her eyes down, demurely observing the melting ice, then asked, "Got a place to stay tonight, honey?"

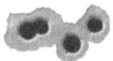

Sissy had been gone less than five minutes. Came back to her bedroom with a six-pack of beer, a devilish grin, and her bottled blonde hair pulled out of the way and arranged in a ponytail, ready to play. Smelled better, too, as she got closer. How sweet was this, her getting all perfumed up just for him?

Time to get down to business. Soon as he had himself another beer. The six-pack was at the pillow end of the mattress, near the brass bedrail. He reached for a bottle.

The handcuff snapped closed around his wrist, the bottle still in his grasp, the second handcuff click as quick and smooth as the first. Randall was now attached to the bedrail.

"How's that, honey?" Sissy said sweetly. "Oh come on now, don't look so upset, lover. We're still going to have fun."

He pulled at the bedrail, tested its strength, was sure he looked as pissed as he felt. He calmed himself into a fake smile, decided it would be best to play along. But once the sex on her terms was over and she let him out of the cuffs—whoa baby— was she going to suffer for this. Soon as he was back in control. "Sure, Susie, whatever you say."

"Sissy. The name's Sissy. But what do you care what my name is, right? Just like I don't much care what your name is either. And neither do my friends."

Three women entered the bedroom, two of them Myra and Dody, the third he recognized from the opposing bowling team they'd faced tonight, the Fighting Cadavers.

"Right now," Sissy offered, "you're thinking us old bitches are going to fuck your brains out or do something else with you, and you'd be right. About the 'something else' part."

Another person entered, the team's scorekeeper Charlotte, her wheelchair pushed by a sheepish kid with a bandaged nose and eye sockets black as a raccoon's.

"You met Charlotte already. Her grandson here, Justin, is fourteen. He's got a broken nose underneath all that tape, from a sucker punch he got this afternoon, so he doesn't much look like himself right now. We woke him and brought him over here just so he could meet you." Sissy turned to the boy. "Justin?"

"That's him, ma'am. The pervert who punched me. Asshole."

"Thank you, Justin. Dody, Justin can go home now."

Randall was quiet, waited for the boy and Dody to leave the bedroom before he tugged at the handcuffs again, the result the same as before. He glared at Sissy, standing nearest him but just out of his reach, sized her up again, then glared at the smaller Myra, guessed her to be in her early to mid-sixties. Charlotte, in the wheelchair and seventy if she was a day, looked shaky as hell. The fourth one, nameless to him, was clad neck to knees in a rumpled white nurse's uniform and, like Sissy, she seemed physically fit and large enough to give him trouble.

"This is false imprisonment," he said. "You could all go to jail for this. Why don't you sweet ladies just let me out of these cuffs? I'll get in my car and leave. We'll call it even."

Sissy raised her eyebrows, tilted her head, and pushed out her lower lip in seeming consideration of his offer. She turned to face her friends. In one swift move, she turned back, the cold steel barrel of a large handgun rudely greeting Randall's eye socket. He heard a click—she'd cocked the gun's hammer.

"That doesn't work for us, Randall. Ladies ..."

Three more clicks found him facing four handguns, shaky Charlotte's included. The pause that followed was the longest five seconds of Randall's life.

"Let's get you comfy," Sissy said. "And secure."

Staring down a gun barrel, Randall was handcuffed spread-eagle to each post on the bed, two pillows under his head.

So this was what it had come to. More than sixty murders over thirty years. Countless rapes, multiple identity thefts. Anonymous cities. Constantly on the move. State police, the Feds, local Andy Taylors—far as he knew, no one had gotten even remotely close to catching him. Until now. Until these women, in this small town. These *old* women. Un-fucking believable. He shook his head, cracked a smile. None of the women smiled back.

"Chances are, ladies," he said, undaunted, his charm returning, "you'll be proud of yourselves once it gets out just how difficult a person I've been over the years." Randall had their attention now, was enjoying the audience. He couldn't help himself. He had to share.

"I've, ah, killed people. Quite a few of them, actually."

Maybe he knew it was coming to this, the end of the line, his last hurrah, right here. So careless, so cavalier were his recent attacks. No planning, taking too many chances, so little attempt at being discreet. His last two murders, both the same day, one in a public restaurant for Christ's sake, the car he was driving stolen from one of them. He hadn't ditched it, instead drove it all the way here, the old lady's body now in a dumpster on an interstate. Quite a trail he'd left. All cries for help, the courtroom shrinks would call it.

"Fitting that I get caught here, huh? In the town with the perfect no-crime record? Only downside for you guys is, the record's fucked." He gave a sarcastic, oh-well shrug. "But look at the upside. The media loves this shit. When they hear about it, you'll have them eating out of your hands."

And the media would hear about it, if he had to mention it himself during the questioning or profiling or whatever the authorities did to build their case. Sure, they'd take him down, but the darlings of evening cable TV and tabloid journalism would chew on his case for months, would make this a media circus. He could feel the excitement even now.

The overnight fame ... wow ... what a rush—

Yes, Mr. District Attorney, I'm ready for my closeup now.

The four women remained stone-faced and silent. His smile dissolved.

They're in shock. This must be traumatic for them. Close to giving them coronaries ...

Charlotte, the oldest, powered her wheelchair over to the side of the bed next to Sissy. Behind them, some foot shuffling ended with the bedroom door closing. Sissy helped Charlotte to her feet. The two stood next to the bed, Sissy with her handgun now tucked into her waistband, the lump visible under her bowling shirt, and Charlotte leaning over him, taller than he'd thought. Charlotte addressed him, her voice cracking.

"Dylan, Lightfoot, or Petty?"

Randall's face pinched. "Huh?"

"I'm not sure what I'm in the mood for. I'm giving you a choice."

"What? Uh ... hell, I don't like any of them. How about Zeppelin?"

"Dylan it is."

A pair of bookcase speakers above the bed came to life, Bob Dylan's twang now delivering the poetic, dissenting lyrics of "The Times They Are A-Changin'."

"My being here," Charlotte said, her smooth-skinned pinkish cheeks dimpling into the barest of smiles, "and my probing you on your music preference presupposes your answer to the next question."

"What the fuck are you talking about?"

"Your secrets about your indiscretions, past and current, are safe with us, Randall. You have but one more simple decision to make."

He grew impatient, figured he'd help her out by cutting to the chase. "You mean like deciding on my plea? I can tell you right now it'll be not guilty. More fun that way for everyone involved, right? The media, the police, the lawyers. Everyone gets a piece of the action. Everyone gets a piece of the murdering degenerate Randall Burton. People will eat it up. And so will I."

He heard the click before he felt the barrel. Sissy's handgun again, this time against his temple. He froze.

"Fact number one," per the hovering Charlotte, "as a reminder. Justus has no police force. No police means no arrest, no plea, no analysis, no trial. Fact number two, about our enviable string of years with no reported crime. See fact number one. We do, unfortunately, suffer from crime here. Like everywhere else, we have too many politicians doing too little about too many misdeeds. So very … frustrating to us older ladies. So crimes get reported elsewhere, off the radar. Like yours was."

The last woman in the room, the one in the rumpled uniform, appeared alongside Charlotte, her nurse-white smock gleaming in the light from the bulbs affixed to the ceiling fan.

Charlotte lifted a tremoring hand waist-high, turned it palm up, narrowed her eyes, and stared the tremors down, willing her hand into perfect stillness. Her faint smile relaxed. Her cheeks drooped to become fleshy parentheses around thin, straight lips.

"Fact three is—"

A sliver of surgical steel appeared in her palm, slapped there by her nurse assistant.

"—we've decided to clean up the gene pool, dearie. I'm thinking you'll choose my approach toward this end rather than, ah—"

Charlotte repositioned the scalpel handle between her thumb and forefinger. The nurse cut away his trousers, stood waiting with a syringe. The overhead lighting glinted off the steel in Charlotte's hand, strobing Randall's horrified face.

"… rather than, you know, Sissy's alternative." Charlotte nodded at the gun against his temple. "But I've been wrong about these things before. So answer me this and we'll respect your decision:

"What would you rather be? A dead rooster, or a live hen?"

Chris Bauer is a brute force novelist. "The thing I write will be the thing I write." His novels include thrillers *Zero Island* and *Hiding Among the Dead* from the Blessid Trauma Crime Scene Cleaning series; *Binge Killer*, which had some of its bones in this short story; and horror-thriller *Scars on the Face of God*, all from Severn River Publishing, plus *Jane's Baby*, a political crime thriller about the landmark Roe v. Wade U.S. Supreme Court decision, from Intrigue Publishing. Find Chris at chrisbauerauthor.com, facebook.com/cgbauer, twitter.com/cgbauer.

MR. BENEDICT'S
WILD RIDE

BY ROBIN HILL-PAGE GLANDEN

Arthur Benedict stood impatiently in front of his Park
Avenue real estate office, waiting for his driver. Roger was never
late, and he should have been there twenty minutes ago.
Something must be wrong. Arthur's cell phone rang. It was
Roger.

"Sorry, Mr. Benedict, but the car died on the Long Island
Expressway. I'm waiting for the tow truck. But don't worry, a
buddy of mine who drives a gypsy cab is coming to pick you up
and get you home. His name is Elvis, and he should be there in
about fifteen minutes."

Arthur rolled his eyes. *A driver named Elvis. Really?* "Damn it,
Roger, didn't you take the Lincoln to the shop just last week?
How the hell could it break down?!" Arthur was furious.
Anything that inconvenienced him or caused his discomfort
made him angry.

"I don't know," Roger replied. "They did a tune-up and said everything looked fine. I'll have it towed to your mechanic and they'll check it out in the morning. Sorry for the inconvenience."

"Okay, well, see that the car gets fixed—pronto. Keep me updated." And with that, Arthur hung up and stuffed the phone back into the pocket of his cashmere overcoat. He pulled his collar up against the chilling wind and shivered. An ice-cold gust ruffled his salt-and-pepper hair. He was tired of these New York City winters and had been thinking of moving somewhere with a milder climate. His *Big Six-Zero* birthday was coming up fast, and at his age and with all his wealth, he didn't need to put up with frigid winter weather anymore. Benedict Blue Ribbon Realty could operate just fine from an office in another location, and he could summon his private plane to get him back to New York whenever necessary. He had often thought of opening an office in another state. There was a lot of money to be made in real estate in California and Florida.

Arthur spotted a black car easing out of the flow of uptown traffic. It stopped in front of him, and the driver lowered the passenger window. "Yo! Are you Arthur Benedict?"

Arthur leaned down and peered in the open car window. He saw the shadowy figure of a man seated behind the wheel. "Yes, I'm Benedict."

"Hey there! Roger sent me to come pick you up."

"It's about time," Arthur grumbled as he glanced at his wristwatch.

The driver bounded out of the car and ran around to open the door to the back seat for Arthur. "Elvis Potter at your service, Mr. Benedict!"

In the bright city lights, Arthur took in the sight that was Elvis Potter. He was a tall, gangly, painfully thin fellow— probably somewhere in his thirties. Roger always dressed in a suit and tie when he drove for Arthur. Elvis was dressed like a bum in baggy, camouflage-print pants with holes in both knees. His tan hoodie had splotches down the front that looked to be yellow mustard stains. He wore scuffed work boots, and his black, curly hair stuck out from the sides of a neon yellow trucker hat emblazoned with what Arthur presumed was supposed to be a witty saying: I'M OUT OF MY MIND. BE BACK IN FIVE MINUTES. Elvis gave him a wide, buck-toothed grin. Arthur placed his briefcase on the back seat, then got in. Elvis slammed the car door shut, ran back around, and hopped into the driver's seat.

Arthur immediately regretted not calling a reputable car service. He found himself seated in an older model sedan that clearly had many years and many miles on it. The back seat was cramped, and the upholstery was torn in several places. There were a couple of empty McDonald's French fry containers under his feet, and a huge wad of pink bubble gum was stuck to the back of the seat in front of him. The interior of the car was filthy and reeked of cigarette smoke. Arthur considered getting out and calling a service, but he was feeling chilled to the bone and dead tired. He had a headache, too, and just wanted to get home. It wasn't all that far, so he decided to go with the ride at hand. Tomorrow he would give Roger a stern reprimand for sending such a horrendous car for him.

Arthur had been in an exceptionally good mood when he left the office. He had just stolen a juicy multimillion-dollar listing out from under a competing real estate agent, and he already had a buyer lined up. He had also just clinched a deal for the purchase of a fabulous building on the Upper West Side. Those were a couple of big wins. Never mind how he had done it—he lived by the rule that you do what you must do to get things done. Arthur Benedict was a winner. He always figured out how to get what he wanted and prided himself on being a master manipulator and negotiator.

He had gone to work in his father's Manhattan real estate office shortly after his twenty-fifth birthday, but Ronald Benedict didn't always approve of the way his son conducted business affairs. After learning the ropes, Arthur left and started his own real estate company. He built a lucrative business with his ruthless formula for success. For the past three years in a row, he proudly held the title of Top-Selling Real Estate Agent in Manhattan. Never mind that some of his tactics were dishonest and immoral, not to mention some that were downright illegal. Arthur was smart and devious. He played by his own rules, and he knew how to work the system. But now, with the transportation issue, the disgusting car, and this geek of a driver, his good mood had dissipated.

Elvis turned around and gave him a thumbs-up gesture. "Okie dokie, we'll be ready for take-off as soon as you fasten that seatbelt, Mr. Benedict!"

The car made a strange clicking noise as it idled, while Arthur secured his seatbelt. "How the hell old *is* this car?" Arthur asked. "Do you think it'll make it to North Hills?"

"No worries, sir. This car is *very* reliable. It gets me everywhere I need to go." The driver was cheerful and reassuring. Elvis steered the car into traffic, then looked at Arthur in his rearview mirror. "So, you're that big-time real estate mogul! Roger told me all about you. I see your picture on ads all over town. Saw your mug bigger than life on the side of an uptown bus yesterday. You're a famous guy. But you know, *I'm* gonna be famous one of these days real soon. My mama was the biggest Elvis Presley fan in the world, and she named me after The King.

"So I have a name already associated with fame and fortune. Don't think that drivin' this car is my calling in life. No sir, it is not. I was in a couple of local theater productions in South Jersey, and everybody told me I got talent, genuine talent. So here I am in the Big Apple, trying to get my acting career going. I'm lookin' for agents and auditions and such. But in the meantime, I'm drivin' folks around and deliverin' pizzas. I also do a little dealing on the side, so if you're ever wanting some weed or whatever, I can hook you up. You gotta hustle in this town just to pay the rent on a crummy little studio apartment in a crap neighborhood. Man, rents are freakin' sky-high in this town. But hey, you know all about that, don't you? Real estate is your thing. I like your slogan on the side of that bus. *Be a winner—play the real estate game with the #1 agent in New York City*! Sounds like you're rockin' the real estate world pretty good."

Arthur sighed. A driver who's a talker *and* an aspiring actor. Dear God, how he hated that. One thing he liked about Roger was that he always just drove the car. He didn't ask questions or engage in senseless small talk. He just drove the car from point A to point B in silence. But because this driver was being so complimentary, Arthur felt compelled to respond. "Yes, I do very well, thank you, and I guess I *have* made a bit of a name for myself."

"Roger says you're quite the expert wheeler/dealer—a real pro. Not to mention that you're part of the elite Manhattan social scene. Roger says you know a lot of celebrities. Hey, maybe you could introduce me to some famous actors and directors to help me get my acting career movin' along. That's how show business works—it's all about who you know. You know? I read an article about you a couple months ago in *New York Magazine*. Sounds like you got some kind of wild life goin' on. There was a picture of you makin' time with that supermodel, Anastasia. Wow, she's hot. You lucky dog!"

Arthur ignored the request for introductions to celebrities, but he enjoyed having his ego stroked. "Let's just say I've mastered the skills of negotiation and not-so-gentle persuasion. And yes, I do have an active social life."

Elvis laughed. "That's cool. Man, I wish I had a knack for making deals and making the big bucks. But I got no business savvy. I guess maybe it's a God-given talent, and I just didn't receive that particular blessing."

"I'm just curious, Elvis. How are you acquainted with Roger?" Arthur asked. He was genuinely perplexed how his quiet, reserved, always well-mannered, and impeccably dressed driver could be connected to this buffoon of a guy.

"Oh, he and my brother, Paul, hang out together sometimes. One night about six months ago, Paul and I met up with Roger and his cute, and *very young*, girlfriend, and we went out for drinks. Boy, Roger sure can pound down the booze."

This morsel of information sent up a major red flag. Roger had been his driver for nearly ten years, and Arthur thought he knew him pretty well. Roger always said that he didn't drink. Often, Arthur had offered his employee an alcoholic drink—a fine wine, aged scotch, the best bourbon—when they were at his home. Roger always politely declined and requested club soda with lime. He finally told Arthur that his father had been a raging alcoholic, and Roger decided early on that he was never going down that road. So this account of Roger drinking heavily in a bar was a revelation. Also, as Arthur seemed to recall, Roger told him when they first met that he was happily married to his high-school sweetheart. Just last week Roger had taken Tuesday night off to celebrate their fourteenth wedding anniversary. *That's strange,* Arthur thought. *Maybe Roger isn't the straight arrow he seemed to be. Maybe I don't know him as well as I thought I did.* Arthur made a mental note to discuss these issues with Roger in the morning. What his employees did on their own time was none of Arthur's concern, but he would not tolerate being lied to.

Elvis continued. "We got to talking and found out that we're both drivers, so we kept in touch. We go out drinking and just shoot the shit occasionally. Roger said one of us might need backup one day, and sure enough, he was right—here I am pinch-hitting for him tonight. He and my brother been buddies for years. Paul is a big shot attorney. I guess he got the brains and smarts from my dad. Our dad was a college professor. I don't know what I got from my dad except a kick in the pants sometimes. Hahaha! But it's funny how some people seem to inherit stuff from their parents. Sounds like you got that business savvy from somebody on your family tree."

Arthur shrugged. "Who knows? My father was a successful businessman, but he was too soft and easygoing. Not me—I go for the throat when I want something. I just go at it full blast when I have to get something done. But maybe I did inherit good basic business sense and smarts from my father—and then I added a touch of evil."

"Evil! Ha! That's a good one! What you got goin' on these days? Any big-time deals? Got any hot babes on the line?" Elvis asked, seemingly fascinated with the man in the back seat of his car.

Arthur never passed up an opportunity to sing his own praises. "Well, as a matter of fact, I just out-foxed another realtor and got a multimillion-dollar listing on the East Side. And I bought a great apartment building on the Upper West Side.

Practically stole it from the old couple who owned it for over forty years. The steal made the deal even sweeter."

Elvis gave a thumbs-up sign. "You get it any way you can, right?"

"Ah, Elvis, it appears you understand my philosophy of life."

"I believe I do, sir. I believe I do. You wanna rule the world, you gotta just reach out and grab what you want, right?"

"Damn right," Arthur replied. "Real estate, money, women, whatever … you just have to take it. I could steal candy from a baby, and I wouldn't feel the least bit guilty. I'm a firm believer in that it matters *not* how you play the game—as long as you *win*."

"And you, Artie, I can see that you are a winner in every sense of the word."

Arthur puffed out his chest with pride as he overlooked being addressed as "Artie." He despised that nickname. His ex-wife had called him that, even though she knew he hated it (or maybe *because* she knew he hated it). *Well,* Arthur thought, *she was a knockout in the looks department, but she was a bitch, a nag, and an all-around hateful woman. Glad to be rid of her.* Thanks to a prenup she signed right before the wedding, she got precious little in the divorce settlement.

"Hey, wait a minute!" Elvis said. "Didn't I see you on the news the other day saying you might run for mayor of New York City?"

"Yes, that's right. I'm not so sure I want to get into politics, but I'm giving it some consideration. The current mayor is an incompetent idiot. I could beat him in an election any day—no problem."

"I'll bet you could!" Elvis exclaimed. "I like your confidence, and I agree—I don't care much for that mayor we got now. If you run, and I think you should, you got my vote!"

Arthur was starting to like this new driver, and his line of cheerful, flattering banter had lifted Arthur's spirits considerably. Maybe he'd fire Roger and hire Elvis as his full-time driver. There would, of course, have to be a drastic wardrobe adjustment for

Elvis and much less chatter. He would also have to abandon his absurd notion of becoming an actor. Arthur thought about the possibility of buying a new car—maybe he'd trade in the Lincoln and get a Mercedes. Or he could splurge and buy a Rolls-Royce. Yeah, now that would be sweet.

Arthur's cell phone rang. He fished it out of his pocket. Probably a call about the closing on that West Side apartment building.

"Arthur? This is Barbie. How you doing?"

Arthur sighed. Here she was—last night's mistake. "Hello, Barbie. How did you get this phone number?"

"Hi, Sweetie! I found one of your business cards in your coat pocket while you were sleeping last night. I thought you might forget to call me today, so I wanted to make sure I could call you. Can I come over again tonight? I love your apartment and we had such a wild time together. What say we do an encore?"

"No, you can't come over, Barbie. I'm not even at my apartment. I'm on the way to my home outside the city. Won't be back until Monday and, even then, you *cannot* come over—ever again."

"Why not?!"

"Look, no offense, and I hate to use a cliché, but you're just not my type."

"Well, I was your type last night."

"That was last night. It was a one-night-only engagement, my dear. I thought you understood that."

"I *didn't* understand that, and I *don't* understand it! We had a great time, Arthur. What's wrong?" Barbie sounded weepy. Time to end the call before he had a sobbing woman to deal with.

"Sorry, honey, but y*ou're* wrong—for *me*. That's all. Now don't call this number again." And with that, Arthur disconnected the call and muted his phone.

Elvis chuckled. "Sounds like you gotta fight off the ladies, huh?"

Arthur nodded. "Yes, sometimes. I've noticed that quite a few women seem to go for famous men with lots of money. Gee, what a surprise, huh?"

"I'll bet you can have pretty much any babe you want, can't you?"

"Well, I don't know about that, but let's just say that finding female companionship is never a problem for me."

Elvis shook his head. "I got no luck with the ladies. I usually find my sugar downtown with one of the gals on the street."

Arthur was tempted to offer some advice to Elvis about how cleaning up, dressing well, and getting a decent car might be a good start on improving his image and sex appeal. But suddenly Arthur felt drowsy. It had been a busy week. He could hardly wait to get back to the comfort of his spacious, elegant house and away from the noise and frantic pace of the city. They should be there soon. Surprisingly, the traffic had been light, and they had been speeding along without delay. The traffic was never light on a Friday evening. Arthur saw road signs up ahead, confirming that they were nearing their destination. Elvis stopped talking and put some soothing classical music on the radio. Arthur dozed off.

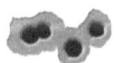

Elvis looked in the rearview mirror at Arthur, fast asleep with his head resting on the back of the seat. He reached over and felt for the revolver inside the Duane Reade bag on the seat beside him. This was going to be an easy hit. They should arrive at the cemetery soon—a quiet place on a cold winter's night with residents who can't testify as eyewitnesses. It was the perfect place to knock off this rich asshole. Elvis started contemplating what he might buy with the paycheck Roger had promised him for doing this job. A big-screen TV and a PlayStation 5 were at the top of his wish list.

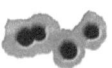

The sound of a cell phone blasting Elvis Presley singing "Burning Love" jolted Arthur awake. Elvis answered, whispering at first, but then his voice grew louder and hysterical. "What are you talking about? Wait, what did you say? Hey, don't hang up!"

Arthur sat up and looked out the car window. There were no street lights, and they were on a dark stretch of road he didn't recognize. He checked for the time, but the face on his smartwatch was blank. The digital display didn't appear. Instead, he got a dead battery signal. Arthur thought they should have arrived at his house by now.

"Elvis! Where are we?" Arthur shouted. "I must have dozed off. I don't know what time it is. My watch battery is dead, but I think we should have arrived at my front door by now. Did you get us lost?"

Elvis laughed, but he sounded nervous. "Don't worry, Mr. Benedict, I'll get you where you need to go."

"I *need* to go to *my house*. Now!"

Suddenly Arthur Benedict broke into a sweat. He had an alarming thought. Maybe he was being kidnapped and held for ransom. As a wealthy man with deep pockets, he was a prime target. He had made quite a few enemies through the years because of his abrasive personality and ruthless business practices. His very life might be in danger! He had always been so cautious, but he let his guard down with this stranger who had been sent by his trusted servant, Roger. Arthur grabbed his cell phone. He would dial 911 and call for help. His cell phone location could be traced. He looked down at his phone. He touched the dark screen, then pressed the ON button. Nothing. His cell phone was dead.

"Who were you talking to on the phone, Elvis? What is this—a kidnapping? Grab a rich guy and hold him for ransom. Is that it? Well, it won't work. Nobody at my office will pay you one thin dime, and I have no family you can squeeze. So you might as well just forget whatever scheme you've cooked up." Arthur's mind was racing. "Oh wait, I know—you mentioned earlier that you heard me say I might run for mayor. I'll bet our incumbent mayor is afraid to run against me in an election because he knows I'd beat him in a landslide. Are you one of his henchmen hired to dispose of me? Take out the competition—is that the plan?"

"Good guesses, Mr. B, but you're wrong on both counts. This is not about money and ransom, and this is not about politics."

Arthur punched the back of the seat in front of him in exasperation. "Look, stop playing games. I just want to get home." Arthur checked his phone again, but it was still dead.

Then Elvis's phone rang again. He grabbed it and pressed it to his ear. "C'mon Roger, tell me what the hell is going on."

Arthur lunged forward. "You have Roger on the phone? Let me talk to him!"

Elvis hit the speakerphone button. "Hello gentlemen," Roger said in his usual calm voice. "I'm sorry for the inconvenience this evening. Don't worry—I programmed the car to arrive at your final destination, and you will soon receive the payment you have earned in this life."

"Wait!" Elvis screeched. "What the hell are you talking about, Roger? This is just a job for me. I deserve a *fat paycheck* when I'm done here, *that's* what I deserve. That was our deal! My final destination tonight is my apartment. And what's that about programming this car? That's impossible!"

Arthur was totally confused. "Damn it, Roger!" he screamed at the phone. "What is it with this driver and this car? We should be at my house by now."

Roger's serene voice emanated from the cell phone. "Hello, Arthur. I'm sorry to spoil your weekend plans, but the universe has other plans for you. At least you won't be going alone. You have my friend Elvis there to keep you company. Now I must sign off. Goodbye and good riddance to the two of you." And with that, the line went dead.

The inside of the car was getting hotter. Arthur tried to open the window, but it was stuck. He loosened his necktie. "Elvis, tell me right this minute where we are, and will you *please* crank up the air-conditioning? It's stifling in here."

"There's no air-conditioning in this car, Mr. Benedict. And I honestly don't know where we are." Elvis sounded terrified.

"Pull over and let me out of this blasted car!" Arthur demanded.

"I wish I could," Elvis replied, as sweat poured down his face. "But I'm not even driving. I'm not in control of this car. See?" He tried frantically to turn the steering wheel, but it was locked in place. He pumped the brakes, but they didn't respond. He pulled the emergency brake, but the car kept speeding along. Elvis lifted both hands off the wheel and turned around to look at Arthur. A flash of bright light illuminated the interior of the car, and Arthur saw genuine fear on the driver's gaunt, pale face. There was another flash of light and suddenly red-hot flames licked the sides of the car, leaping past the windows.

"Elvis, the car is on fire! For God's sake, man, stop the damn car!" Arthur screamed as he struggled to breathe. The interior of the car was filling with smoke, sending Arthur and Elvis into a fit of coughing.

"I … can't …" Elvis cried as he wheezed and choked.

The old sedan picked up speed. Frozen with terror, Arthur and Elvis stared out the windshield. Straight ahead, they saw a blazing wall of crimson and orange flames. Arthur was unbearably hot, and his heart was beating wildly. Elvis pounded on the steering wheel. All the two men could do was hold on tight as the car sped through the wall of fire, then took a sharp turn—straight down. Arthur Benedict and Elvis Potter were on the way to their new home—the *hottest* piece of real estate known to man. And as an experienced agent in the real estate business, Arthur was quite aware of the importance of the mantra that all realtors know so well:

Location, Location, Location.

For twenty years, Robin worked as a professional actor, musician, and writer/editor in Philadelphia, New York, and Los Angeles. She attended the UCLA Writers' Program, edited books for authors, and wrote feature stories for two Los Angeles magazines. Family matters brought Robin back to Delaware, where she works as a freelance writer and editor. Her short stories and poetry have been published in many anthologies and magazines, and her fiction has won Delaware Press Association awards. Robin is a regular contributor to two of the *Guideposts* magazines. She also conducts writing workshops, performs her poetry and music, and produces cabaret variety shows.

PAYBACK: WITH INTEREST

BY MATT HILTON

Having his front door smashed in at 5 a.m. was becoming an occupational hazard for Ronnie Stout. The cops always chose that time to execute a warrant, expecting someone like Ronnie to be deep in slumber after a night of booze and women. They thought they'd catch him with his trousers down—literally. On three previous occasions, they'd done just that. After the second time, he didn't bother replacing the locks, so it was much easier this time for the door to be slammed off its hinges. Less damage to contend with afterward was fitting with Ronnie's ethos. He kind of expected the cops to come, so why bother making things more difficult for the city's finest—or for him, for that matter? Last he wanted was to be kicked loose from the cells and have to come home to the inconvenience of a full evening's carpentry. Fuck the hassle. All Ronnie wanted these days was to be left alone, to get a little peace and quiet. He needed to get his fucking head together.

He heard the crash of the door rebounding from the hall wall, sat up in his bed, and adopted the position. He kicked the sheets free from his legs, sat there in his boxers, and outstretched his arms, palms open so there'd be no mistakes. Feet thundered up the stairs. Christ, the cops were keen this morning. Sounded like they meant real business. Seemed a lot of trouble to find his little stash of weed or the prescription meds he'd boosted from the corner drugstore. Unless this was about that other *thing* ... nah, he thought, how could they have pinned that to him? This had to be about drugs.

The cops usually came in shouting, another tactic to confuse and disarm a suspect roused suddenly from sleep. This time they didn't make a sound, just that of boots on the bare boards of the upper landing. He heard a door thrown open. Something crashed to the ground.

"Hey, for fuck sakes! Are you lot stupid? I'm in here where I'm normally at."

Ronnie shook his head. Probably rookies on their first warrant, he decided. Full of adrenalin and keen to show their sergeant they were up for the job.

The footsteps slowed, came to a halt on the landing outside his door.

"Come in," Ronnie called out, trying to sound jovial. Jovial equaled nonthreatening in his book. "The door's open, officers. I'm unarmed."

He just tacked that last morsel on as an after-thought. It wasn't the same cops who regularly busted him, that was for sure, so he didn't want any stupid mistakes made.

The doorknob twisted and the door swung open.

Ronnie was surprised. When a search warrant was executed, there was usually a squad of cops on hand. Certainly, there was always more than one man. That thought was troubling enough, but nothing like the next thought that spun through Ronnie's head. "The fuck's he wearing a ski mask for?"

The man entered, and it took Ronnie all of about two seconds to realize that he wasn't a cop and only one man would leave this bedroom afterward.

The man didn't say a word. He just sprang forward and grappled Ronnie, throwing him down on his back on the bed. Before Ronnie could squirm away, the man moved in, kneeled on the mattress with one knee shoved between Ronnie's legs. It was an almost intimate gesture, the way the man leaned close. His body was little more than an inch from Ronnie's bare skin, and Ronnie felt heat waft off him. The ski mask held most of the man's breath off Ronnie's throat, but he still felt a whisper of it along his chin as the man leaned close to his left ear.

"Psst," the man said.

At the shocking realization that his early morning caller hadn't come to arrest him, Ronnie's voice had caught somewhere deep in his chest. Now it leaked from him in a breathy exhalation. "Psst? What the hell does that mean?"

"It's the sound of your death, Ronnie. Only you won't hear it. The way Carl Dunn didn't hear his death coming."

The man reared up and showed Ronnie the silenced pistol in his right hand.

"Oh, my Go—"

Ronnie never finished his sentence.

The man caressed the trigger and the bullet in Ronnie's skull ended everything.

The gun hadn't been as silent as promised. It made a noise more like a ball slapping a catcher's mitt. But Ronnie's killer had been correct in one respect. Ronnie didn't hear a thing.

Jason Corrie had no driving license. They had taken it away from him after he'd blown the legal alcohol limit three times, after the cops tugged him after a hit-and-run collision. Why the fuck had the other car been parked there in the street anyway? Inconsiderate bastards should have known better than to leave a motor parked on the same street as his local. The cops had been arseholes. When one fat-faced cop asked him to blow into his little contraption, he hadn't got the joke when Corrie pulled out his dick and said, "Wanna blow into mine?" He'd been arrested for refusing or failing—or summat—to give a sample of his breath and thrown in the cage in the back of a Maria. The same cops had then thrown him in a cell until it was time to be put on the machine by the custody sergeant. Once he'd been tested, he was escorted back to his cell and again thrown inside. There'd been a lot of throwing around that night, so Corrie repaid the gesture by throwing up on the fat-faced cop. In hindsight, it wasn't his best way of avoiding a charge, but that's what he got.

Luckily, nobody was hurt or he could have done time. The judge just slapped him a fine and took away his license for three years. But that meant little to Corrie. Who needed a fucking driving license when you were driving a stolen motor?

He was pissed as well.

In for a penny, in for a pound, he thought. If they caught him, he'd definitely go down this time. In fact, he knew he was on borrowed time as it was. The other day, when he and Ronnie Stout burgled the chemist shop, Corrie had been pissed then, too. But he'd still been the one behind the wheel of their getaway car. Safer for them both with the cold snap setting in. But it wasn't because of the ice he'd elected to drive. Ronnie was as high as fuck on a cocktail of weed, magic mushrooms, and diazepam, seeing funny colors everywhere, and in no state to drive. Fuck, maybe it would've been better if Ronnie had been the one driving, cause maybe he'd have seen the red light Corrie ran. Corrie didn't see the kid on the bike. He only felt the collision, felt the bucking of the wheels as they squashed the kid's ribcage and forced splinters of bone through his lungs. He'd hit the brakes, but it hadn't helped. Actually, the locked wheels only dragged the kid and his bike along the icy road a few hundred feet, and made Corrie hit the lamppost on the next corner. Corrie had to reverse over the kid to get away, and this time his skull had gone under the wheels. Corrie didn't give a fuck for the young lad, he was just one of them scrotes off the housing estate anyway, he'd heard, and no miss to anyone. That time of night, riding a bike without lights, the little fucker was probably out robbing, and Corrie decided he'd done his local community a service. He hadn't expected the noise that people made about the little shite's demise. Why the fuck did any of them care? They were crying about the brutality of the kid's death. The kid didn't suffer. He was deaf as a post and hadn't heard a thing when Corrie had hit him from behind. Didn't feel a thing either, he bet.

He wondered if Ronnie Stout had suffered when he died.

When they'd reversed off the steaming pile of flesh and bones, Ronnie had been giggling hysterically, and Corrie had pulled him over the front seats and nutted him. Only way he could get the drugged-up fucker to shut the hell up. Then Corrie had checked that nobody had witnessed the smash. He was certain that no one was around, but some twat must have seen them and told the scumbags on the estate who'd done their kid in. It was the only thing that'd explain how someone knew to go to Ronnie's place and put a bullet in his melon.

Well, Corrie wasn't going to hang about. Not so no screaming mob could come and tear him a new arsehole. He'd boosted the car—fuck the lack of a license—with a plan to get the hell out of town. As he drove, he supped from a bottle of Bell's whisky he'd shoplifted from a Spar shop, wondering where he should go. Thing was, that boy had connections all over the town. He'd never heard of a family as large as the Dunns were— there were fathers, brothers, and uncles, not to mention cousins and half-cousins, and cousins by marriage—and wherever he went he'd soon be on their radar.

He thought about going to see Johnny Boy Stout.

Johnny Boy was Ronnie's cuz, and he was also the big man around town. Nobody fucked with Johnny, not even a crazed family baying for blood. If they wanted war, Johnny would give it to them, and there'd be only one winner. But Corrie knew what he'd get if he went to Johnny. It was one thing Ronnie asking for protection. Corrie would get his arse handed to him on a plate. In Johnny's eyes, he'd lay the blame for his cousin's death firmly at Corrie's door. He wouldn't get a neat bullet in the skull from Johnny. First, Johnny would set his boys on him. Big Jimmy Hurt and Crazy Bobby Bowlam would soften him up with pickaxe handles before Johnny Boy did him the kindness of cutting his head off with a rusty saw.

No. He had to leave town, as much to avoid Johnny Boy as the tribe of Dunns after his blood.

The blue lights came on behind him.

Fuckfuckfuckfuckfuck …

Corrie dropped the whisky.

No, wait.

He could still get out of this. Play it cool, be nice to the cops, admit to being a little drunk and to driving a stolen vehicle without a license, and ask them to take him in. He'd be safer in a cell tonight than he would be out on the streets like this.

The cop car pulled in behind him as he brought the stolen motor to a halt. Corrie checked the mirrors. Apart from the flashing blue light in the windscreen, he could make nothing out of the make or model of the cop car. It was one of those unmarked cars that the traffic coppers used to sneak up on you. If it was a regular cop, on any other occasion Corrie could have spoken his way out of being lifted. But you didn't fuck with those traffic Nazis. Corrie watched the door come open in silhouette and a big fucker get out and walk slowly toward him. Corrie knew not to get out of the car. He hit the button and the electric window motor whirred. He waited calmly, hands on the steering wheel.

The cop walked directly to the window, his body filling most of the opening.

"Evening officer," Corrie said sweetly. "I've an offense I'd like to admit to."

"Have you been drinking again, Corrie?" the cop asked.

The use of his name didn't surprise Corrie. Most of the cops 'round here knew him well. But the cop's actual words that came next surprised him.

"I'd like to take a sample of your breath. Would you please blow into this?"

As he opened his mouth in an incredulous gasp, the silenced barrel of a handgun was shoved between Corrie's teeth.

The back of his skull was blown out, spattering the passenger door and part of the windscreen with blood and tufts of hair.

Big, red-faced Jimmy Hurt stepped through the open door, stamping his feet and blowing into his cupped palms. His coat was done up to his chin and he had a woolen hat pulled low, but he still looked frozen. "I guarantee you, boys, there'll be more snotty noses than standing cocks tonight."

He came into the kitchen, still blowing warmth at his blue hands. "I'm telling you, boys. You know it's fuckin' cold when your dick shrivels up like a prawn vol-au-vent!"

No one answered him. No one laughed. They'd already heard Jimmy's lurid take on the cold snap on three separate occasions.

"Close the door, will ya?" Bobby Bowlam was hunkered down in front of the oven. The meager blue flame inside was the only source of heat in the old house.

"Thought all the power and stuff was off?" Jimmy moved toward the oven, holding out his palms.

"It is, but the oven's Calor gas. There was a bit left in the bottle." Bobby shoved him away. "Fuckin' hell, Jimmy, I can feel the cold coming off ya! You a fuckin' ghost or summat?"

"Gotta admit, I feel like I'm about three days dead," said the other man.

Jimmy and Bobby looked around at the latest speaker.

Johnny Boy Stout stood up and walked over to Bobby and shoved him sideways. "Stop hoggin' all the fuckin' heat."

"Yeah, move it," Jimmy added.

"Tosser!" Bobby called Jimmy, but he reluctantly gave way to the older man, his face twisting as he was shunted away from the small flame.

Johnny Boy was in his late forties—heavily built, his jowls drooping and his hair turning gray at the sides—his nickname a bit of a misnomer at any stretch. But he was also the hardest of the three, and neither Jimmy nor Bobby would argue too stringently. Johnny Boy put his arse to the oven, lifting the tail of his coat to warm his lower back. He stood there smiling at the other two, but there wasn't the slightest mote of humor in his eyes.

"Is he home yet, Jimmy?"

Jimmy shoved his hands in his pockets and fiddled round like he was adjusting his underpants. "I froze me fuckin' bollocks off, but it was worth it. The grass was right. He lives at the house across the road. He's there, Johnny Boy. Alone."

"Good." Johnny Boy allowed his coat to drop as he transferred his hands to his own pockets. He pulled out an illegal semi-automatic pistol, an imported Sigma. From his other pocket, he pulled out a magazine and slapped it in place. He racked the slide. "You two packin' like I told ya?"

Bobby pulled out a sawed-off shotgun with a chopped and taped stock. Double-barreled. A farmer's gun adapted to fit under his armpit. He clicked it open and fed in a couple of 12-bore cartridges.

Jimmy said, "I've a pick handle. Don't trust meself to pull a trigger, my hands are so cold."

"Keep rubbing your balls like that and the friction'll set 'em on fire," Bobby said.

"I'm not rubbin' me balls," Jimmy said. "I'm still trying to find 'em!"

Bobby laughed this time. "Heard you often have that problem with your dick."

"You wouldn't like it as a wart on the end of your nose," Jimmy said. Another of his sadly overused rejoinders.

"Shut up," Johnny Boy grunted. "Fuckin' idiots I have to work with …"

He led them out of the house and into the biting cold. It was dark outside, no moon, no stars, just a heavy mist that covered everything. The mist dampened the sound so much it felt like they were walking through a void between worlds.

Johnny Boy felt the mist clinging to his face, turning to ice crystals on his eyelashes. He rubbed a palm across his jowls, and they felt like they were as tight as a virgin's arse. He exhaled, and a cloud of frozen breath streamed around him.

Three days dead, he thought. It was as cold as the fuckin' grave, right enough.

But soon, things were going to heat up.

His cousin Ronnie had been shot like a sick dog, fucking executed. So had his pal Corrie. Not that he gave a flying fuck about either drug-addled punk, but he couldn't allow any transgressions against his name. If he allowed one hit on his family, it would only invite others. He had to make an example, and he had to do it now before the fucking Dunns got ideas about completely taking over his parish. And he couldn't think of a bigger example than going after the target he'd chosen. Killing Jack Dunn would make the others shit their pants.

A faint glow poked through the mist. Yellowish—like piss spreading in a swimming pool. They had to move closer before they could make out that it was the light from the living room in the house opposite.

"Can you see him?" Johnny Boy whispered.

Jimmy pointed, using the pick handle he'd lifted from outside their hiding place. "Saw him in there about five minutes ago. Dunno where he's at now."

Johnny Boy nudged Bobby. "You're the smallest. Sneak over there and see if you can see him."

"What if he sees me?"

"You've got a fuckin' shotgun, what're you afraid of?"

Bobby sniffed a dewdrop from the end of his nose. "It's fuckin' Jack Dunn we're talkin' about. Hard bastard, I've heard.

Even with the gun, I don't want to go up against him on me own!"

"He's not fuckin' bulletproof," Johnny Boy snarled, but even he wasn't so sure that he'd be here without Bobby and Jimmy backing him up. "Fuckin' big man! Maybe the cops couldn't prove he was the one who capped my cousin Ronnie, if I told them, but I know it. An' he's gonna pay. Now get over there and see where he's at. Soon as you give us the nod, we'll be on him like stink on shit. Right, Jimmy?"

Jimmy didn't answer and Johnny Boy turned, searching for him in the mist. All that remained of his passing was a faint swirl.

"Where the fuck has he sneaked off to?" Johnny Boy completed a slow pirouette. There was no sign of the big man. Only his pick handle lying on the ground. "I don't believe this. The fucker's bottled it!" He turned toward Bobby. "Well, it's just me an' you, Bobby, but don't worry, we can still do this ..."

Bobby was nowhere to be seen.

"Bobby? Bobby! Where the ..."

Johnny Boy gripped the butt of his Sigma, but now the gun didn't seem the equalizer that he'd originally thought. In fact, it felt woefully inadequate. A bit like he felt, really. Moments earlier, he'd planned on making the Dunns shit themselves. Now it was his guts that were fluttering.

He took a slow step back, turned, and was about to leg it.

A form reared out of the mist in front of him.

Johnny Boy couldn't make out the face of the big man. It had nothing to do with the cloying mist, but everything to do with the sawed-off shotgun barrels jammed against the bridge of his nose.

"Going somewhere, Johnny Boy?" Jack Dunn asked.

"Oh, fuck," Johnny Boy moaned. His eyes darted sideways, hoping that Jimmy or Bobby would rush to his aid.

"You needn't look for those two idiots. They're out of the fight. Same as you're going to be, Johnny."

"Jack. C'mon, man. This is one big misunderstanding."

"Is it? Way I heard it, you were planning on killing me, payback for your cousin Ronnie. Well, Johnny, you got the right man all right. It was me who capped Ronnie and his mate. See, the Dunns wanted payback, too."

"Well, you got it, Jack. Let's leave things at that, eh? Come on. Let's call things quit, yeah?"

Dunn shook his head slowly.

"I want payback with interest," he said.

Johnny Boy didn't even think about lifting his gun. If anyone cared to listen, he'd have told them that his fingers were too cold to pull the trigger anyway. The truth was, he was decidedly warm. At least he was in his trousers when he shit himself.

It was shameful, soiling his pants like that, but he didn't have long to worry about his reputation.

The shotgun was reversed quickly, and the stock slammed against the side of his head. Like deaf Carl Dunn, Johnny Boy didn't hear his death coming either, though his was much slower than either Ronnie's or Corrie's had been.

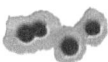

It was three days before they were found. The slaughterhouse had closed on Friday evening, so it wasn't until Monday morning that the staff arrived and found Johnny Boy, Jimmy Hurt, and Bobby Bowlam trussed together in the meat locker. The Scene of Crime Officer was already on scene and a uniformed constable guarded the door, recording movement of personnel in and out of the freezer. The constable had to step aside for the Detective Sergeant who arrived at the scene.

"What have we got?" the DS asked.

"Three of them this time."

"Same gang?"

"Yeah, it's the Stouts," the constable said. "You think the Dunns did them?"

"We've no proof of that, Constable. And personally, I'd rather you didn't mention that name in that tone of voice."

"Uh, sorry, Sarge," said the constable. "It's just that …"

"The Dunns have got a bad name around town?"

"Well, yeah. There is that."

"You should show a little more respect. The Dunns lost one of their children in a vicious hit and run. Not only that but—" he aimed a finger at where Johnny Boy swung on the end of a chain "—I heard that scumbag threatened to desecrate the child's grave if the Dunns didn't give up the man who shot the boy's killers."

"Isn't that a bit like the kettle calling the pot black?"

"When did you last complete your race and diversity training, Constable?"

"Uh … oh, I didn't mean …"

"Forget about it. But watch your mouth in the future, OK. Not all the Dunns are bad guys, Constable." The DS tapped his chest. "Some of us aren't."

"I wasn't suggesting anything like that, Sarge."

"Forget it," said Detective Sergeant Dunn. "I've lived with it all my career."

"Are you related to the boy that was killed by Ronnie Stout and Jason Corrie?" the constable ventured.

"Distantly."

Moving past the constable, the DS stepped inside the meat locker and immediately shivered. "Bloody Baltic in here," he muttered, rubbing his hands together.

"Minus thirty," a SOCO investigator said from the center of the room. "They were still alive when they were tied up in here, poor sods. It looks like they froze to death, Jack."

Yeah, the DS thought, thinking about Jimmy Hurt's words that he'd overheard as they planned to kill him, I know there were more snotty noses than standing cocks that night.

Matt Hilton is the author of thirteen high-octane Joe Hunter thrillers, including his most recent novel *Fourth Option*, and eight books in the Tess Grey and Po Villere thriller series, the latest being *Blood Kin*. His first book, *Dead Men's Dust*, was short-listed for the International Thriller Writers' Debut Book of 2009 Award, and was a *Sunday Times* bestseller, and was recently a Kindle bestseller. He has also published thrillers and horror and supernatural novels, including *Darke*, the first in a crime/supernatural crossover series featuring DI Kerry Darke. Check out his website at www.matthiltonbooks.com.

SHOOTING FISH

BY JAMES DORR

The problem with Supreme Invasion Commander Fakhboom, Brrolz reflected, was that he insisted on taking everything so Peshwar-blessed literally. That and his caution, refusing to let the Blukwark armada leave its hidden holding orbit behind Earth's single moon until Brrolz could prove a silly point.

But still, it was Advance Scout Second Class Brrolz's own fault. Nevertheless, who would have thought . . .

He turned toward Glomo, his beauteous female lieutenant—who, on the side, was also his lover—who he had wheedled the Supreme Invasion Commander to send back down to the planet with him as Assistant and Witness. "Who would have thought," he said out loud, trilling the syllables through his Earth disguise mask's mouth-filters, "that the entirety of Blukwark pride, its invincible war fleet, might yet be sent in shame back to the Home Worlds without a single enemy vessel engaged should our mission fail, and all because of a simple utterance of Earth slang."

"An utterance by you, my blue-tentacled dream-kreeb," Glomo sighed. She waggled a tentacle of her own, seductively thrusting its tip through the right nostril of her own simulated-Earthwoman face-covering. "Had but your preliminary scouting mission not been so successful."

Yes, Brrolz reflected. Or had his speech-orifice not been so commodious—that was the Earth slang, was it not, that one's "mouth" was too "big?" Had he not, solely to impress his dear Glomo, laced his report on what he had found of Earth and its customs with real Earth expressions? His mind went back to the fateful interview, Supreme Invasion Commander Fakhboom squatting on his throne, Glomo and the rest respectfully groveling at the Commander's anterior siphon. "So," Brrolz had concluded, "conquering these Earth beings will be, to use an expression they use themselves, 'as easy as shooting fish in a barrel.'"

In the silence that followed, Brrolz nearly bit off his labial appendage—that is, as the Earth beings would say, his "lip."

Fish in a barrel.

At last, the Supreme Invasion Commander spoke. "This 'fish,' what is it?"

"An Earth creature, Honored Sir," Brrolz replied. "One that, I believe, inhabits 'barrels,' er, large containers of water. That is, they live in liquid."

"I see," the Supreme Invasion Commander said. "And what is this 'shooting?'"

"A sacred ritual of the Earth people. A thing they do much of in their entertainments."

"Then you could do this, too, if it is so easy," Supreme Commander Fakhboom declaimed, puffing his mantle until his crest shone red. "We cannot take chances. All Blukwark depends on us, that we do not fail. Therefore, Scout Brrolz, we must prove your statement: Before I can let our invasion proceed, you will go back to Earth and 'shoot' such a 'fish' and bring it back to me, yourself having come to no harm in this effort. One can, after all, never be too cautious, as is according to our own expression, that 'cautiousness is next to Peshwarkiness'."

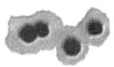

Brrolz remembered also how Glomo had stealthily extended a pseudopod, sliding it gently against his telson until his crest, too, glowed red. Just as it did now beneath his Earth hair toupee, under the hat he wore to disguise even *that*, as he and Glomo, having purchased an Earth surface "ranch house" with funds supplied by the Fleet Quartermaster, filled their new bathtub with real Earth water. They had both decided that it would be safest to do this indoors, away from possible Earth counterspying eyes, that which the Honored Fakhboom had ordered.

And so he now raised his "twenty-two rifle," an Earth artifact that he had purchased at a celebration referred to as a "Gun Show," where, as the Earth people said, "no questions would be asked." He called out to Glomo:

"Release the fish!"

Glomo complied, having purchased a "goldfish," a creature that looked small and harmless enough, at a place called a "Pet Shop" where, also, she was not asked to answer questions, a ritual protection that seemed important in Earth people's dealings. Or so at least Brrolz's research had implied.

She dropped the fish in.

The rifle went *BOOM!* Its recoil, tiny as it was, sent the weapon flying from Brrolz's surprised grip while he, himself, went into a skidding spin on the bathroom's smooth-tiled floor. Glomo, surprised as well, shook water clumsily from her Earth-disguised woman's face and limbs, from the splash from the tub as the gun, too, fell in, then helped Brrolz stop himself. What was the saying the Earth people had for this, "slippery when wet"?

They looked in the tub.

The fish was still swimming, perhaps a bit frightened. Perhaps irreparably harmed psychologically, doomed to die an early fish-death, but most assuredly not a corpse *now*.

And, more to the point, not one that had been shot.

Their mission, thus far, had failed.

It was Glomo who first found words for it: "This 'shooting of fish,'" she said, "perhaps it is not so easy a thing after all. That is, you have shot. But the fish has survived it."

Brrolz, less hasty to jump to conclusions, reluctantly agreed. Something had been done wrong.

"Look," Glomo said, "how your 'rifle' is damaged, too." Her voice sounded frightened. "Has the fish done this? That is, the Pet Shop person assured me that fish are harmless, but look how the tube part appears to be bent. Is it possible, then, that this fish-thing could beat *us*?"

Brrolz, still somewhat dizzy from his spin, inspected the rifle, leaning half in and half out of the water. He pulled it toward him, noticing that the bend disappeared when it was wholly out of the water. He stuck it back in again, just a little, just the tube part's tip, seeing the bend come back, but just on the part he had re-immersed.

"Aha!" he said.

The fish, still swimming about, looked puzzled.

"Aha," he said again. "No, Glomo, don't worry—the fish are indeed harmless, just as your Earth informant has told you. No doubt all fish are so, otherwise Earth people would fear shooting them. And this, this bending of the rifle, is an illusion, caused by the properties of light being reflected differently through water than through air.

"But you are right about one thing, I fear, Glomo. That this fish shooting will *not* be so easy."

Thus it was three days later, days that Glomo had spent inspecting the swimming pool in the ranch house's back yard— an artifact surrounded by a bathroom-floorlike, smooth-tiled patio, it in turn surrounded by a fence, so protecting it, too, from intruding eyes. Thus making it an ideal place to continue their mission. So it was that on this patio Brrolz awkwardly set a genuine handmade, wooden-staved barrel, purchased at what

Earth beings called an "Antique Store." Although, to Brrolz's eyes, it had seemed no older than the shops on either side of it. "So," he explained, "I can shoot directly down, thus avoiding the 'bending illusion' causing me to miss like the last time."

Glomo, meanwhile, had come up with a theory, that the crafty Earth people themselves turned, sometimes, to fish—that it was, perhaps, a liquid-dwelling phase of their life-cycles—and that their saying of "shootings" and "barrels" was itself a kind of ruse, meant to trick innocent spies like her and Brrolz. Nevertheless, she kept that to herself. To plant seeds of doubt *now* would surely destroy the invasion effort. As Supreme Commander Fakhboom had said, one could not be too cautious. Therefore, instead, she had used the three days, those times when she was *not* inspecting the pool, to seek a "Gun Show" and go herself and purchase a shotgun for Brrolz to use, to minimize the negative effect a slightly deviant aim might have.

Also, nothing if not a practical Blukwarkan female, she purchased a somewhat larger fish, one she had found at a place called a "Fish Market," still alive but scarcely moving from being packed in "ice." This, called a "mackerel," she placed in the barrel.

Slowly, the mackerel swam. Around and around.

"Glomo, the 'lawn chair' please," Brrolz commanded.

Glomo placed the outdoor chair that had come with the pool, that had come with the one-story California house, next to the barrel where Brrolz now pointed. Taking the shotgun, Brrolz climbed on the chair.

Looking down, he aimed at the mackerel.

Oblivious to this, the mackerel swam. Around and around.

And around and around.

And around and around.

And around.

And around.

A bit dizzy, recalling his spin on the bathroom floor, Brrolz felt himself falling. He fired both barrels—perhaps too quickly. Water splashed everywhere. Brrolz hit the tiled deck as fish and wooden staves flopped and bounced toward the pool, sliding and slipping. Glomo herself nearly slipped as well as she rushed to the side of her fallen scout-lover.

"Are you unhurt, Brrolz!" she screamed.

Brrolz nodded weakly. "Did I miss again?" he asked.

Glomo inspected the jagged holes in what was left of the barrel's bottom, then glanced at the pool where the mackerel was now swimming in larger circles. "You hit the barrel," she answered. "*That's* something."

"No," Brrolz said sadly. "The barrel doesn't count. It is shooting the *fish* in the barrel—that's what's important."

"Look," Glomo said. "I have an idea. At the place I obtained this latest fish, surely some were already dead. They wouldn't be so hard to hit. We could *simulate* a fish pool shooting."

"No," Brrolz sighed. "As tempting as it is, such a stratagem would not deceive Supreme Commander Fakhboom, I fear. He would have its wounds inspected. He must be absolutely sure, you see. No hint that the fish might have resisted, somehow, us successfully shooting it properly."

"Then can't we give it up, this madness?" Glomo said. "That is, of shooting the fish ourselves? We have passed, so far, in our disguises among the Earth people. We have deceived them, at least. Why can we not hire one of *them* to shoot this fish for us, since they are the experts?"

Brrolz shook his "head"—that which had successfully passed for his Earth person head, that is. "No," he said, "Supreme Invasion Commander Fakhboom would still find out in time. He has his methods."

But then Brrolz's crest brightened—or at least it must have, even if Glomo couldn't see it, disguised as it was underneath his wig and hat. "What you said, Glomo, about 'fish pool' shooting. This 'swimming pool' itself, is it not just a kind of larger barrel? One made of cement perhaps and not of wood, but one that could hold an even larger fish—easier to hit. Indeed, perhaps, several such large fish, so that, even shooting at random, one could scarcely help to hit at least *one*. Possibly even fish that are accustomed to leaping from the water into the air—perhaps when they're hungry. I saw pictures of certain of these on my last mission, before my report—so that I would not even have to look down at them swimming in circles."

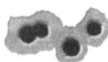

The fish they finally selected was called a "Pacific barracuda," the largest of them nearly five Earth "feet" long, and prone to leaping when they were excited. They had to change the swimming pool's water to Earth ocean saltwater to keep these fish healthy, because Commander Fakhboom would find out if the one they shot was not in its prime—whereas, if it were, Brrolz could surely expect to receive a promotion to Scout First Class—and they had to apply to the Fleet Quartermaster *twice* for more money, confessing that they had hit a "minor snag."

They went back to Gun Shows to improve Brrolz's weaponry, selecting a "Chinese knock-off AK-47" with extra "banana clips" ("Isn't that some kind of food?" Brrolz had wondered, but Glomo shushed him, fearing the phrase might be some kind of spy-thing, to trick and expose them) for the actual shooting.

At last, they were ready.

The fish were delivered in a tank truck that backed into their "driveway," its operator then running a chute-like device through the gate in the fence to their pool. He opened a large valve and fish swam and flopped down the chute to the water, splashing and flailing.

Oh, they *were* excited.

Leaping and gyrating.

Water was *every*where.

"They look mean," Glomo said. "See their eyes? All kind of squinty-like? These are not nice fish."

"Good enough eatin'," the truck driver interrupted, folding

his truck's chute back up into sections. He held out his hand for Brrolz to pay him. "Some say it's high-flavored, but the meat is firm, kind of like swordfish back when you could eat them. Back before them mercury troubles."

But who is eating whom? Glomo thought. A practical female, she knew not to cast doubt—to not disturb the concentration one iota of her hero-lover. Was it not true their triumph, and with it that of Commander Fakhboom and the Blukwarkan invasion armada, was all but assured already? The fish were large, sufficiently large that Brrolz should be able to hit at least one. They had practiced with the "AK-47" and knew how to make it shoot in bursts, almost like the shotgun, but without so great a "kick." The fish splashed, silvery, into the air so Brrolz could fire at them without the need to compensate for the bending of light at the air-water interface.

What could go wrong?

And yet, the teeth of the fish still looked so sharp.

She shrugged off her misgivings as, the delivery Earth being having departed, Brrolz put an "arm" about her "shoulders." Familiar bulges flexed beneath clothing, pseudopod against telson, tentacle tweaking beak, mandibles touching briefly through mask-mouths.

"Do not worry, my passionate kreeb-blemsh," Brrolz murmured into her hearing orifice. "All is as it should be." He gripped his AK-47 and, uropod in uropod, they advanced together to the pool's side.

"Perhaps I should mop the tiles first, though," she said. But Brrolz shushed her with a squeeze.

He raised his weapon.

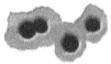

That's when Brrolz slipped once more.

Indiana writer James Dorr's The *Tears of Isis* was a 2013 Bram Stoker Award® finalist for Superior Achievement in a Fiction Collection. His latest book is *Tombs: A Chronicle of Latter-Day Times of Earth*, a novel-in-stories from Elder Signs Press. Dorr has been a technical writer, an editor on a regional magazine, a full-time nonfiction freelancer, and a semiprofessional musician. He harbors a Goth cat named Triana. Follow him on his blog, http://jamesdorrwriter.wordpress.com, and Facebook, https://www.facebook.com/james.dorr.9.

JUG HANDLES

BY ALBERT TUCHER

I had a lead.

Two leads, in fact. The first came through pure luck, which I don't rely on, but I never turn it down either. It seems a guy saw Phil in Atlantic City and tailed him. That earned the guy some points until he lost him again, which put the guy back at zero.

The boss kept detailed accounts.

I liked the sound of Atlantic City. It meant Phil was getting careless. Up to now, he had done everything right—cutting up his credit cards, losing his cell phone, never flying or even taking an Uber. But apparently he couldn't live without the craps table.

The guy who spotted him tailed him to the ends of the earth. Or Sussex County, whichever you prefer. I mean, who lives there?

The whole story led me to think Phil might give in to his other itch, which can be scratched anywhere. By which I mean Phil is a pussy hound. I understand because people might say the same about me. No shame in that, is there? Just don't let it rule your life. But if Phil made that mistake, I would be there to catch him at it.

I did some reconnaissance in Sussex County, and I was sure a town called Driscoll was the place to start. Most of the area is newer bedroom communities sprouting around Driscoll, but the town itself has been there a long time and hasn't been doing well for most of it. The state highway that nicks the edge of Driscoll has grown a strip of motels, fast-food places, and a bar.

Obviously, I started with the bar. I picked a time a little before 3 o'clock in the afternoon, which gave me a half hour before the after-shift crowd started showing up.

The bartender looked like a guy I could talk to. That sounds like a job requirement, but you'd be surprised how many bartenders don't have it. Or maybe you wouldn't.

I ordered a draft.

"I'm staying across the street," I told him.

"Uh-huh."

Okay, he was going to make me work for it a little.

"A town with as many motels as this, I figure there must be people around who know what motels are for. If you know what I mean."

"We have a reputation for sleeping. So I'm told."

And maybe his attitude needed adjustment, but that would have to wait.

He was looking me over, which I can tolerate within reason, but he was going over the line. I was about to explain his error when he nodded.

"Some people would know what you mean," he said. "I don't. But if you were to go back to room ..."

"One-oh-seven."

"One-oh-seven and relax, no telling what might happen."

"I like your style."

"Might want to be sure you have three bills on hand."

"For whatever might happen."

I was curious to meet this woman who was charging Atlantic City rates in the boonies, but she didn't have to be worth it. It was a business expense, even if I ended up paying her.

I downed my beer, tipped him a ten spot, and left the place.

One thing that drives me crazy about New Jersey—the highway was divided, and the traffic was homicidal. I had to drive a half mile and hang a jug handle U-turn, complete with a stoplight, just to get to my room fifty feet away from where I started. Nowhere else in the country have they even heard of jug handles.

Eventually, I got back to number 107 and settled down. Sure enough, less than an hour later, there was a knock on my door. I opened it, and there she stood.

"Hi. I'm Diana. I hear you'd like to meet me."

Now you don't see many of these, but when you do, you know it. She looked like a blonde, tanned lifeguard, which is fine with me. But that was only the beginning. I wouldn't call her exactly beautiful, not like a movie star, but right away I wanted to sweat up the sheets with her all day long, and then I wanted to take her home to meet my mother. And Mom would have said I had done something right for a change.

"Uh, come in."

Best of all, the total package was available by the hour. Three hundred wasn't looking out of line all of a sudden, especially since I could be sure she knew Phil. He would have found her the way I did and had the same reaction.

I had originally planned to get right down to my business, but I decided to get down to her business first. I didn't have an envelope, which was a minor violation of the etiquette of these transactions, but she made the bills disappear into her bag.

And I was right. The sheets got plenty sweaty.

And that led to my usual issue. I started squirming as my skin started crawling. My ex-wife always had Freudian bullshit to spout on any topic, including this one.

"You hate needing me. You crave sex, but you hate women. That's why you have to wash me right off."

Whatever. I just knew I couldn't stop itching. I tried to suppress it, but this Diana had seen it before. I had the feeling she had seen everything before.

"It's okay. Go shower off. You have thirty minutes, and I run an honest business."

I believed her, and when I came back in control again, she was still there in the bed. I didn't join her. I almost hated what I had to do, but I couldn't think of a way to fool her into cooperating.

"I'm looking for a guy, and I think you know him."

"If I do, I can't tell you. I don't talk about clients."

"You'll talk to me. Nothing personal, but you will. I'll show you a picture, and you'll talk."

She sat up cross-legged, which is an interesting thing for a naked woman to do.

"Vince didn't like you."

"The bartender?"

"That's why he told you three hundred. Mostly we charge two around here."

"Okay, he didn't like me."

"I've always told him I don't want him deciding for me, but this time I guess I should have let him."

She shrugged.

"Go get your picture," she said.

I went to the cheap bureau against the wall and opened the drawer. The picture of Phil was there, and my burner phone. But something important was missing. I turned to find her holding my thirty-eight. I'm partial to revolvers because they always work.

And she knew which end of a gun to hold. I couldn't help thinking it looked pretty hot.

"Call this number," she said. "Put it on speaker."

She recited a phone number from memory. I raised my eyebrows, and she caught me at it.

"I never write down anything about business," she said.

I thumbed in the digits, and a familiar voice answered with a guarded, "Hello?"

"Jack, it's Diana. You know I wouldn't normally call you, but there's somebody here I think you need to talk to."

She gave me an expectant look. That and the gun got me talking.

"Hey, Phil. What's up?"

"Shit."

"That's probably going to be my name with the boss. She's something else."

"Diana? Hell, yeah. And now I'm going to have to move on, thanks to you."

"You knew it would happen eventually."

"I guess."

"Take care, Phil."

"You, too."

He disconnected. I pointed at the gun in her hand.

"Don't hang onto that. It's got a few bodies on it."

"I figured. Maybe you should talk to somebody about the itching."

"Maybe I will."

For a moment we just looked at each other.

"Why?" I said finally.

"You messed with my business. Jack was a regular. Or Phil, or whoever."

"Wish I could be a regular."

"A little late for that."

Albert Tucher is the creator of prostitute Diana Andrews, who has appeared in more than 100 short stories in venues including *The Best American Mystery Stories 2010*. Diana's first longer case, the novella *The Same Mistake Twice,* was published in 2013. In 2017, Albert launched a second series set on the Big Island of Hawaii, in which the forthcoming *Blood Like Rain* will be the latest entry. He is also an associate editor of *Rock and a Hard Place* magazine. He lives in New Jersey, and he loves NJ Turnpike jokes.

SHORT-ORDER CROOK

BY J. GREGORY SMITH

Florida, just outside The Hamlets retirement community

She was late.

Willie Coates peered through the tinted windows of his huge, black Raptor pickup. The lift kit and extra-large off-road tires added to his vantage point in the back of the Target parking lot. The open space allowed him to make sure no one would overhear his conversations.

Most of the lazy customers would park as close as possible to the entrance of the store. So, when he saw the pearl-colored Lexus SUV roll past some choice, empty spots and head toward him, he knew it wasn't just a shopper worried about door dings. The boxy Lexus pulled up near the truck and backed into the adjacent space.

Willie waited. Soon, the driver's side window slid down to reveal a woman with magenta-dyed hair cut in a reverse bob. She looked to be in her late fifties. So far, so good. He lowered his own window and leaned out.

"Can I help you?" he asked.

"Are you Willie?"

"Depends on who you are." He realized that didn't quite make sense, but she didn't seem to notice.

"We spoke on the phone. You solve problems? Isn't that what you called it?"

Willie nodded. "Cordelia Sinclair?"

"That's right." She paused. "Uh, now what? I've never done this before."

He almost said he hadn't either, but that might botch the deal from the get-go. "Step out of the vehicle, please." She did, and he saw she looked athletic for her age. Probably a tennis player. "You aren't with the police, are you?" he said. Best to cover that base right away. If she was a cop, she had to identify herself.

"Don't be ridiculous." Cordelia pressed her lips together and looked around. "Are you sure about this?"

Willie reached to the passenger seat and picked up a manila folder. "Of course. Most public places turn out to be the most private. Stand back, please." He opened the heavy truck door and held the steering wheel while his feet found the running board. When he hopped to the ground, his cowboy boots made a double-tap sound as the heels struck the pavement.

He looked up at Cordelia, who had covered her mouth like she was trying to smother a cough.

Willie held the folder in front of him like a shield. "Fine. Let's address the elephant in the room."

"Elephant?"

"Whatever. Do you need help with a problem or not?"

"I'm sorry. You sounded … taller on the phone."

"I get the job done."

"I'm not so sure, Herb—that's my husband—may be older, but he's still tough."

"You didn't say it had to be a cage match." Willie struggled to keep his temper. Screaming at prospective clients wasn't going to make the payment on the Raptor. Neither was his job as a cook at Denny's nor the small scams that came up from time to time. Time to go big.

She seemed to calm down. "Of course not. But I did say it absolutely must look like an accident. I'm not spending my best years in prison."

Willie held out the folder. "My specialty. I never get caught because they never suspect a thing," he said.

Cordelia took it and perused the newspaper clippings. "Hunter suffocated after getting head stuck in a rabbit hole?"

"Keep going." He beamed.

"Chef preparing exotic cobra dinner dies after accidentally scratching hand on fangs of the snake's just-severed head?"

"Had to think fast on that one. The guy probably thought an animal welfare officer had busted him, but he wished all he got was a ticket!"

"And they never even questioned you?" She looked at him with fresh eyes.

"Nope."

Of course not. He'd never even heard of those fools until he'd researched their stories online.

"Now I have a coupla questions for you," he said.

"All right." She handed the papers back to Willie.

"First, why do you want this … accident?"

"Why do you care?" She sounded insulted.

Willie took a deep, patient breath. "*I* don't. But the more I know about the objective, the better my chances to arrange things to your satisfaction."

"Well, if you must know, we've been married twenty years, which is nearly two decades longer than I expected. Herb's just entering his seventies. He was only fifty when we met. He was a widower and had just recuperated from an acute heart attack."

Willie nodded and scribbled in a small notepad. "Heart problems. Good."

"I figured we'd have a few laughs, he'd check out, and then leave me with his roofing business that I'd sell."

"Marriage must have agreed with him." Willie couldn't resist.

"Tell me about it." Cordelia shook her head. "He recovered, and I talked him into giving up the business he loved and retiring, thinking he'd die of boredom. Sinclair Roofing was his life. Next thing I know, we've moved to the Hamlets. And I swear he's getting younger!"

"Not to chase business away, but if you can't stand him, ever consider divorce?" Willie said.

"Wow, why didn't I think of that?" Sarcasm didn't improve her looks. "Herb did well, but he's not a Rockefeller or anything. I can't live right on just half."

"Fair enough. Before we go further, we should discuss the fee," Willie said. "Eight grand and I'll need half up front."

"Six grand, plus Herb's Hummel collection, worth four grand easy," she countered.

"His what?"

"Hummels. Ceramic collectibles. They sell like crazy at the flea markets around here."

"Seven, and keep your china dolls. Cash only."

"Fine, but you'll have to wait. Herb has me on an allowance, and he watches every penny."

The truck's upcoming payment loomed over Willie. "All right. Now, any phobias, triggers, stuff like that?"

"He's a neat freak? Plays too much golf? He hates snakes?"

Willie smiled.

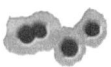

The Hamlets, two days later

Willie sat in the truck a half block away from his target's home. Despite the unseasonable pre-dawn chill, he knew the white uniform was going to be warm once the sun rose in the sky. He should be done with the hard part long before that happened. At least the giant green thumb logo and GT Lawn Service matched the removable magnet stuck to the truck's door.

It was a gated community, and the guard at the gate barely nodded to him when he arrived. Something on the man's phone had been far more interesting. Willie probably had added the gaudy fake sideburns for nothing.

Just as Cordelia had promised, shortly after Willie arrived pretending to study a clipboard with paperwork, he saw the small garage door open, and out came a custom golf cart.

It looked just like a miniature vintage Chevy Bel Air, right down to the Regal Turquoise and white paint scheme. Herb took no notice of Willie in the bland lawn-service vehicle as he went to the garage to retrieve his golf clubs.

Herb looked like an old version of James Dean, with a deep tan and a shock-white pompadour. He wore a T-shirt that proclaimed, "Roofers Like It on Top!"

Herb put the clubs in the cart, donned a windbreaker, and sped off down a path, eager to get to his usual first tee time of the day.

Not long after, Willie heard the familiar sound of a postal truck. He watched while the Sinclairs received their daily dose of junk mail. As soon as the truck putted around the corner, Willie pulled the truck over in front of the house. He had a plastic spray can he'd specially modified. There were air holes drilled near the top, and this one was going to dispense more than fertilizer.

He pretended to hit a few spots on the immaculate green turf until he reached the mailbox. Once there, he pulled open the bottom-hinged door of the mailbox, removed the mailers, and quickly unscrewed the top of his spray can. The cargo was still there. Willie tipped the open container until the surprise slid inside. He winced while he replaced the mail, but needn't have worried.

After closing the mailbox door, he pulled out a fake flyer for GT Lawn Service and tucked it behind the flag on the side of the mailbox. He then added a few more flyers to mailboxes while walking the area in the direction Herb had driven.

Satisfied he'd made a sufficient, half-assed marketing effort, he returned to his truck and moved it, so he'd have a good vantage point without being too conspicuous. The sun shone between a cluster of homes and warmed his truck to the point that he began to sweat in the uniform. The truck's feeble A/C system barely took the edge off the rising temperature. Herb's yard, still in shadow, looked like a cool oasis, but he needed to maintain a discrete distance.

Cordelia said this was Herb's "speed golf" day when he'd only play nine holes and the final score would include a time component. That meant Willie wouldn't be kept waiting.

Sure enough, it wasn't too much longer before Herb and his Bel-Air cart barreled around a tight curve on the cart path. Willie could swear that it looked like the top-heavy cart nearly flipped over, with Herb grinning like a maniac.

Yeah, keep smiling, old man.

Willie pretended to eat from a bag lunch, but he was sneaking peeks through a small pair of binoculars. He watched Herb pull the cart into the driveway and hop out and walk straight toward the mailbox.

That's it.

Willie held his breath.

Herb opened the mailbox, reached inside, and …

… took out the mailers and envelopes. He closed the door, snatched the green flyer from the outside of the box, and marched back toward the house.

Nothing?

Willie had to know why, but then Herb emerged from the house in an old shirt, pushing a gas-powered mower. The sun continued to climb in the sky as Herb worked and worked on his damn yard. Willie contemplated just driving off. No, he had to know what went wrong. Had the thing escaped? Was there a hole or something in the back?

After an eternity, Herb went back inside. Cordelia had told Willie that Herb met some friends for cards in the afternoon, so the guy must be getting a shower. Here was his chance.

Willie pulled up again. When he got out of the truck, he was struck by how much warmer the sidewalk felt. He glanced at the windows of the house and, just in case, took out another flyer and his modified sprayer. He opened the mailbox door carefully. Nothing but darkness.

What the hell?

He rapped the side of the box with the sprayer nozzle. Still nothing.

Willie peered in the front. But with the sun behind the house shining right in his eyes, all he could see was a black space. He took out a penlight and peered closer.

Before he could even shine the light inside, he sensed a flash of movement and then felt searing pain as the ball python sank its teeth into his face and latched on.

Willie staggered backward and clawed at the snake's head while the rest of its body emerged from the mailbox like a magic trick. The snake's full weight pulled from his face at the expense of the flesh on his cheek.

"Hey, buddy!" Herb rushed out of his house in a bathrobe and bare feet. "What part of 'No Solicitation' do you not ...Whoa! What happened to you?"

The python coiled, still facing Willie, who continued to back away, his hand clasped over the shredded skin on his face.

"Aw jeeze, *another* one?" Herb yelled. Willie wasn't sure if he meant him or the snake.

The snake quickly slithered for a small rain-catcher pond across the street.

"Are you okay?" Herb asked. "You need me to call someone?"

Definitely not.

Willie pulled a handkerchief from his pocket and pressed it against his bleeding cheek. The salt from his sweat made the wound sting even more, but he'd live. "I'm good." Willie looked down to keep Herb from seeing his face.

"How the hell did that thing get in there? Damn kids around here think it's cool to have a pet snake. Then, as soon as it grows up, they just turn it loose." Herb slammed the mailbox door shut. "You sure you're all right?"

"Yeah, just a scratch," Willie lied. His face was throbbing.

"I'll have to call animal control before that thing eats the Johnsons' Pomeranian. Can you stick around to make a report? They'll act faster if they know it already got somebody."

"Sorry, can't. But I'm okay. I must've scared it." All Willie wanted now was to get out of there.

Herb shrugged. "Suit yourself. Me, I hate those things. Can't imagine why anybody'd want 'em as pets."

Several days later

Genius. He should have thought of this earlier, but he'd been sure the snake would do the trick. Not his fault the pet shop guy forgot to tell him how sluggish those things were until they warmed up.

No matter. This time for sure. Willie had found the perfect ambush point. Right by the eighth hole on Herb's favorite course. The cart path had a sharp bend and, from the way the guy would come, he'd face a clump of trees and ornamental bushes with thick ground cover to the left. To the right of the path, the grass sloped down at a good angle toward a bone-white sand trap.

Willie found the foliage downright comfy after he'd crept into the cover and shed his white coveralls, revealing a black outfit suitable for a ninja. More important, judging by the idiots who already rolled by, he was completely hidden.

Speaking of traps, Willie checked the twine and felt a resistance that told him his friend was ready and waiting. He'd better be. There wouldn't be much time.

Willie craned his neck from his prone position in his makeshift hideout. He got a glimpse of turquoise before losing sight of it behind a rock. Willie could almost hear screeching rubber as Herb put the cart through its paces.

"Ready for your close-up, Mr. Squirrel?" Willie whispered and tugged on the twine.

The resistance felt more like a fish on the line. He pulled harder and now could see the cart barely slow for the last turn. Herb's grinning face scanned the "road" ahead.

The string gave, and Willie was sure for an instant that it had simply snapped. But then he saw his handmade, fake squirrel leaping over the slope's crest. Well, all except for the tail that had apparently snagged and pulled off, leaving his decoy looking like another kind of rodent altogether.

Way too late for repairs. Willie tugged the rest across the pathway in what he hoped was a realistic animal movement.

"Rat!" Herb shouted.

Willie reeled in the furry thing and heard the cart tires moan as they changed direction.

He couldn't resist a peek at the impending carnage, but he realized that instead of veering away from the decoy, Herb was doing his level best to run it over. He was heading straight toward the bushes and Willie.

"Die, you filthy … oh crap!" Herb's eyes bulged in terror as he swerved to avoid a tree and lost control.

Willie tried to roll away as he heard the cart's tires slide on the grass. The cart finally stopped in a hydrangea bush.

Willie froze, nearly underneath the cart. He waited for Herb to say something. Any thought of an excuse vanished from his brain.

"Screw it," Herb muttered. Willie peeked and saw Herb looking everywhere but the ground around the bushes. Herb put the cart back into drive and sped off, rolling right over Willie's ankle.

Target parking lot, two days later

Late again. Worse, Willie didn't know what she wanted. He sat inside the truck and thought about starting the engine to run the A/C, but decided against it to save gas.

Maybe Cordelia saw all the effort he'd put in and decided to front some of his fee after all. Something needed to break soon, besides his ankle, which felt like it was on fire and trying to burst out of the walking boot he'd be in for at least the next six weeks. Damn golf cart.

He'd pulled an extra shift at Denny's, working the kitchen in a desperate effort to placate his manager, Ron, who had warned him already about missing time. The only good thing about the ankle was that the pain made him forget about his swollen face.

Finally, Cordelia pulled into the parking space next to him. She got out and waited, leaning against her front fender and inspecting her manicure.

Willie opened the door and grasped the knotted rope he'd tied to the passenger's side door handle. Sure, it was embarrassing to rappel out of his truck. But the last time he'd dropped onto the walking boot, he'd almost passed out from the pain.

"Really?" Cordelia watched Willie descend.

"Any idea what those damn carts weigh?" His arms burned with the effort to land extra slowly.

"Sorry about your luck. The good news, for both of us, is that somehow Herb still doesn't suspect a thing."

"Perfect. We're nearly there," he said.

"Actually, we're there now. You're fired."

"Excuse me? It doesn't work like that."

"Says who, shrimp?" Cordelia lit a cigarette. "I'm calling it off before you get us both arrested."

"We had a deal. You want to back out, that's fine. But my fee is the same. Seven grand." Willie used the rope to raise up to his full five-foot-three.

"Yeah, no. You should stick to flipping pancakes, you'll live longer." She ground out her half-smoked cigarette and opened her door. "Or you could always ask Herb for the cash."

She then got into her car and drove away, not even looking back at him.

Willie waited for Cordelia to get out of sight before climbing back into his truck, which took far less effort and pain than getting out of it.

"Careful what you wish for, lady."

The Hamlets, one week later

Willie parked the GT Lawn Service truck in front of the Sinclair driveway and waited. Soon the garage door opened, and the turquoise cart backed out of its space. Herb turned around and noticed Willie for the first time. Willie took satisfaction in the long scratch down one side of the cart from its off-road adventure. He hauled himself out of the truck.

"Hey! Move that tin can!" A light of recognition. "You again?" Herb stared. Today he sported a T-shirt with a cartoon picture of a muscular guy on a roof that said, "Wanna Get Nailed?"

"We need to talk," Willie said.

"You need to stop blocking my driveway. And what did I tell you about solicitation?" Herb looked at the walking boot. "What happened to your leg?"

"Skiing accident."

"In the summer?"

Oh. "Water skiing."

"Whatever. What do you want? I do my own lawn work and probably better than you." Herb crossed his arms.

"I'm sure. See, I'm not really a lawn guy, but I do have a proposition," Willie said.

"I don't have time for games."

"Make time, and it's no game. Your wife wants you dead."

That got his attention.

"What are you talking about?"

"See, she hired me. I'm giving you a chance to buy out her contract. For only—"

Herb's scowl turned to a slight grin. He flashed capped teeth as white as his hair. "Who put you up to this?"

Willie felt the first threads of panic in his chest. "You think that snake was a joke? You're in danger, pal." Willie's voice picked a terrible time to crack.

"And she picked *you*?" Herb laughed so loud Willie could see that he'd had his tonsils removed.

"You're in our way. We're having an affair and she wants you gone." Willie let the lie about the affair just tumble from his mouth.

Herb turned red and struggled to catch his breath. "Stop. I can't breathe. You win. I'll go get some cash. Funniest shit I ever heard."

Willie felt his head spin. Herb vanished inside, and Willie didn't know what to do. The old geezer was *laughing* at him. Laughing, for Christ's sake!

One minute turned into two, then three.

Why'd he really go inside? Was he getting a gun? Or calling the cops?

Willie decided to cut his losses and sped off before he found out the hard way.

He could still hear Herb laughing as he drove off.

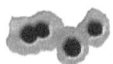

Denny's, one week later

"Coates, you have a visitor," Ron, the manager, called back while Willie and the crew cleaned up after the breakfast rush. "This counts as your break."

Willie was too surprised to argue. Repo men didn't announce themselves, did they?

Just outside Denny's front door stood Cordelia. "You didn't think I'd show up?" she said.

"Lady, I don't know you." Was this some kind of setup? "They're expecting me back inside soon."

"This won't take long." She stepped closer. "I have something for you."

"You have me confused with someone else," he said. He wasn't out of the ankle boot yet, so running was out of the question. Was this Herb's cue to come around the corner with a nine iron?

"First, I owe you an apology." She sounded like those words hurt her throat.

"You think so?" It sounded halfway between a question and a statement.

"For doubting you."

"What's your game, lady?"

Cordelia glanced over her shoulder and nodded. When she spoke again, she whispered. "Okay, I understand."

That made one of them.

She reached into her purse. Willie flinched before seeing it was a thick manila envelope. "It took me a while to get it all from ATM withdrawals." She held the envelope open and let him peek inside. Lots of dead presidents looked back. Far more than he'd negotiated. Way more.

"Why'd you change your mind?" Willie said. "You fired me, remember?"

"I'm glad you didn't listen."

"How can you be so sure?" Willie pictured a hidden tape recorder while he spoke. "I never touched the guy. Just ask him."

Cordelia looked confused and then shook her head. "I get it. You think I went to the cops? I'm an accessory, too, you know."

"Of course." Willie feigned more confidence than he felt. "Accessory to what?"

"Your plan was brilliant. Herb called 911 because he was having heart palpitations. When the EMTs arrived, Herb was laughing so hard his heart gave out right there. When I got home, he was still on the floor, and they were zapping him with a defibrillator. The coroner later ruled cardiac arrest."

Cordelia handed him a newspaper clipping of the obituary. Herb grinned back at him from the grainy black-and-white photo.

A calm washed over Willie's body. He'd flipped his last pancake, sure as old Herb had eaten his final one.

"What did I tell you?" Willie took off his apron, dropped it to the ground, and then reached for the envelope. "They never see me coming."

Greg Smith is the bestselling author of the thrillers *A Noble Cause* and the *Flamekeepers*, and the Paul Chang Mystery series including his breakthrough novel, *Final Price,* and the sequels, *Legacy of the Dragon* and *Send in the Clowns,* all published by Thomas & Mercer. Greg is now working on The Reluctant Hustler series, starting with *Quick Fix*, *Short Cut*, and the upcoming *Easy Street*. He lives in Wilmington, Delaware, with his wife and son.

BLOOD IN THE URINE

BY MARTIN ZEIGLER

Tooby or no Tooby, that was the question.

For over fifteen years, we had it all worked out. I'd decide the *who* and *when*, and I'd leave the *how* and *where* up to Tooby. You know, to give him a chance to stretch his imagination. I never wanted him thinking he was slogging away in a pickle plant, every day the same.

Not that we did this kind of thing every day. Maybe two, three times a year. It would've been great if we didn't need to do this at all, but every so often in the business world, the market needs what's called *correcting*.

For instance, take last year. Early on, I gave Tooby a call. As usual, I kept the assignment simple: Dave Granger, March thirteenth, 5:30 p.m. The who and when.

The next day, March fourteenth, I read about it online. How the body of one Dave Granger was found impaled over the spiked fence outside the Museum of Natural History. I figured Tooby must have remembered what I'd told him once about

Dave. Hell of a nice guy, but when it came to finances, a dinosaur.

Near the end of the year, I sent Tooby out on another mission. Joey Ginsburg. November twenty-eighth. Eight a.m.

Name, date, and time. Clear and straightforward.

And sure enough, come the twenty-ninth of November, the morning news reported it. The head of someone IDed as Joseph Ginsburg was discovered in a dumpster outside Tino's Pizza.

A day later, the rest of Joey was found, but by then I had all the information I needed.

Did Joey Ginsburg deserve the pruning Tooby gave him? Joey made a few mistakes, but he was a bright and witty guy, always quick with the comeback. I would have just shot him. But as I say, I left the method up to Tooby. And maybe what inspired him was hearing me mention what a head Joey had on his shoulders.

That's what I liked about Tooby. He thought outside the box. He took the initiative. Over all these years, he never once shirked his duties, ever. Always finished his assignments on time. Always got the right guy or gal, even when it came to the person in question having a name like John Smith or Jane Doe.

But a few days ago—on February nineteenth, to be exact— something changed. Paul Teleman was seen stepping out of an afternoon matinee. Trouble was, Paul Teleman shouldn't have been seen doing anything because, on the *eighteenth* of February, I called Tooby and said, "Paul Teleman. February nineteenth. Three a.m."

So, on the afternoon of the nineteenth, I had to make another call, one I never had to make before.

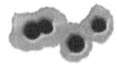

"Tooby," I said. "What's the story with Teleman?"

"Oh, hey, Marcus," he said. "Yeah, I was just about to call you up about that. You see, it's like this. I figured, since I'm earning a good living going to work three days a year, I better make sure I get to those jobs on time. So, I bought a brand-new alarm clock. What I never figured on was the alarm not waking me up the way an alarm should. And that's why I didn't get up in time. The clock's a complete dud."

"What's wrong with the old one?"

"Uh, old what?"

"Alarm clock. It's been working up till now, right?"

"Yeah, but it's … uh … been making a funny sound."

"What do you mean, funny sound?"

"Like gears grinding. Rrrrr-rrr, like that. You know, a funny sound."

"But it still wakes you up, right? It got you up in time to chop Ginsburg's head off out there at Tino's Pizza."

"It wasn't making a funny sound back then."

"That was just a few months ago. You haven't used the clock since then. Now it's making a funny sound?"

"Yeah, you're right. I can't explain it."

"What difference does it make anyway what kind of sound an alarm makes, as long as it's loud enough?"

"Well, Marcus, I figure, something makes a funny sound, it can go haywire any second. That's why I bought the new clock. Piece of crap is what it turned out to be. That's why I didn't get up in time."

"Okay. What kind of sound does the new clock make?"

"A … a not so funny sound."

"Is it loud enough?"

"Yeah. I guess."

"Tooby, if the new alarm is loud enough, how'd you end up sleeping through it?"

Things went quiet at the other end. "That's a great question, Marcus."

"You set it, didn't you? The alarm?"

"Of course, I set it. I set it to 2 a.m., figuring that'd give me enough time to make the 3 a.m. assignment. I set it when I hit the sack at 8 in the evening. That's early, I know, but I wanted to make absolutely sure I got plenty of shut-eye by the time 2 o'clock rolled around. I like to wake up refreshed and raring to go. Trouble is, when the alarm went off, I guess I slept right through it."

"The alarm did go off?"

"I meant when the alarm *should've* gone off."

"So, Tooby, since you hit the hay early, you must've woken up early, even if you slept through the alarm, right?"

"I guess."

"You don't know if you woke up early?"

"Yeah, you're right. I woke up early."

"Why didn't you call me up then, instead of telling me all this now? It still would've been early enough to pay Teleman a little visit."

There was some more quiet. "Oh, yeah. Well, when I said I woke up early, I meant I woke up late. Except I thought I woke up early because the alarm went off."

"I know I asked this already, but I'm afraid I'm going to have to ask it again. So, the alarm went off?"

"Yeah. I guess it did. In fact, now that you mention it, I *know* it did. Except at 2 o'clock in the afternoon."

"Tooby, you mean to tell me you slept for eighteen straight hours?"

"That's a long time, isn't it?"

"Not as long as this phone call."

"Damn clock."

"The clock is fine. You just need to set it to a.m. instead of p.m. I still don't see why you don't just use your old clock. It's already set to a.m., and it works."

"Yeah, except it makes a funny sound."

"Tooby, I have a *serious* sound for you. You want to hear it?"

"Uh, okay."

"You listening?"

"All ears, Marcus."

"Teleman. February twentieth. Three a.m."

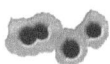

The next day, the twentieth, I said over the phone, "Hey, Tooby. Hear about Teleman?"

"No, what happened?" Tooby said.

"Nothing happened. That's why I'm calling."

"Oh, yeah. Well, Marcus, turns out my nephew came over to visit."

"You never told me you had any brothers or sisters."

"Did I say *nephew*? I meant *cousin*. Second cousin. He's the one who came over."

"Where's he from?"

Tooby seemed confused by the question. "From?"

"Yeah. Where's he live?"

"Uh … Spain."

"Spain?"

"Sure. What's wrong with Spain?"

"Nothing. Nothing at all. Where in Spain?"

"Michigan," Tooby said. "I meant Michigan."

"Oh, okay," I said. "Where in Michigan?"

"Uh, now I can't remember. Name a few cities."

I said, "You're new to this, aren't you, Tooby?"

"New to what?"

"Making excuses. First, with the alarm clock. Now with the second cousin, you don't know where he's from."

"Okay, he lives the next city over."

"What's that mean? There are a lot of next cities over."

I was about to list a few when Tooby said, "He lives a mile down the street. More like a block. Next door, actually."

"You sure he isn't renting your spare bedroom?"

"Yeah, pretty sure."

I took a deep breath. I needed the air. "Your second cousin … he have a name?"

"Uh, Pete."

"Pete an adult?"

"Why wouldn't he be?"

"Because maybe he's a kid."

"No, he's grown up."

"Tooby, why couldn't you have told Pete to hold off on the visit, you have work to do? Most adults can take news like that when it's broken to them gently."

"Oh, yeah. I didn't think of that when he came over."

"Tooby? Can you hear me okay?"

"Yeah. Why?"

"Teleman. February twenty-first. Three a.m."

Tooby and I went back since high school. We hit it off right away and palled around a lot. I taught him the little I knew about business, borrowing things from stores and never returning them. And he taught me about guns and knives, and how to use everyday household items as weapons.

He was smart as a whip, always raising his hand in class and getting the right answers.

What I remembered most was the favor he once did for me. A simple gesture, but it meant a lot.

We were sitting around between classes. We had just got out of U.S. history, and it upset me over flunking the midterm. A few days before, I'd grabbed the answer sheet out of Mr. Patterson's desk and copied it, the way I'd done with all his other exams. This time, though, it must not have been the right one, because I missed every single question.

Tooby never needed answer sheets. He scored As and A plusses without them. Now, as we were sitting there in the cafeteria, he could have been an asshole about it and given me a big lecture along the lines of, "If you studied enough, you wouldn't need to copy the answers," but what he did instead was pat the back of my hand and say, "Not to worry, Marcus. I've got the answer."

Next morning, the entire student body learned that someone had broken into Mr. Patterson's home overnight, put the barrels of a shotgun in his mouth, and squeezed the trigger.

U.S. history class after that was a glum place to be. Lots of my classmates were heartbroken. I missed the guy myself. He was personable and warm. Always said hi to me out in the hallway. But our substitute was nothing to shake a stick at either, considering how, at the end of the year, he ended up giving students whatever grade they asked for.

Sometime between when I flunked the U.S. history final and when I aced the class, Tooby grabbed me by the shoulder, pulled me into a corner, and confided in me. He said the one detail that stood out most about that night was how everything Patterson knew about U.S. history ended up on the living room wall.

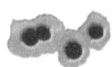

Somebody does something like that for you, blast a hole through an instructor so you can pass a class, you owe him big time. That's why, as soon as I went into business for myself, I hired Tooby right off, before some other company could snatch him up. And that's why I hated to do what I was about to do. See him in my office.

I mean, he'd been up to my office many times, but as a friend. Friends invite friends to their office. But this was different. This involved a dressing down, which I didn't want to do at all. Friends don't dress friends down. But what choice did I have after I'd spotted Teleman myself, earlier in the day but way after 3 a.m., down in the lobby of the very building where I worked, trying to shake a jammed pastry loose in a vending machine.

Maybe Tooby knew what this meeting was about. Maybe not. But, bless his heart, he arrived on time. Darlene, at her desk, was there to greet him. And, like she always did with my visitors, she knocked once on my door, opened it, and showed Tooby right in.

And, like Tooby always did with Darlene, he took a few steps into my office, turned his head, and gave her the once-over. She gave him back a smile and let him look a little longer before closing the door on her way out.

Darlene was something special. A top-notch girl Friday for me and tempting eye candy for any guys who dropped by.

I allowed a few seconds for the effect to wear off, then invited Tooby to sit. There were two empty chairs, and Tooby picked one.

"Do anything memorable early this morning around 3 a.m.?" I asked.

"Aw, geez, Marcus," he said. "Memorable isn't the word for it."

"Then what is?"

"Unforgettable, maybe?"

"Don't they mean the same thing?"

"I don't know," Tooby said. "Do they? I mean *memorable* refers to something you never want to forget, while *unforgettable* might mean something you wish you could forget but can't."

"What was it about this morning at 3 a.m. that you'd rather forget?"

Tooby covered his mouth to cough a couple of times. "Well." He hesitated a little more, then said, "It's like this. There's blood in my urine."

"Oh. That sounds nasty."

"It sure does. I noticed it when I got up to take a leak."

"When was this?"

"Two this morning. I used my old clock just like you suggested. I looked in the bowl and spotted a thin film of red. I just thought it was ketchup from the hamburger I had for dinner."

"What did you do then, being that it was probably getting close to 3 in the morning?"

"I sat around and worried."

"About what?"

"Blood in the urine."

"I thought you said it looked like ketchup."

"At first. But then I got to thinking about what other things are colored red. And that's when blood came to mind."

"How long did you sit there and worry?"

"Until eight, when the clinic opened. I called my doctor, my primary care provider, and he had an immediate availability. I told him I'd take it. So, I drove out there to the clinic and, after searching around for parking, I finally found a slot. The doctor asked me how long I'd been experiencing this, and I told him six hours and asked if that was enough. He said yes and sent me down to the lab where they handed me a cup and pointed me to the john to contribute a sample."

"What's the bottom line?" I asked.

"Blood in the urine," Tooby said.

"I mean, what did the doc tell you?"

"It's some kidney thing," Tooby said. "I forget what it's called. But he said it should clear up in a week or so. But in the meantime, to get some rest. Plenty of rest, he said. And that's what I did after driving back home from the clinic. I crawled into bed to get plenty of rest. And then you called to ask me to come up here to your office."

"So, bottom line …"

"Blood in the urine."

"No, about Teleman. You're able to drive around everywhere, walk into this building, come into my office, give Darlene the wide eye. It shouldn't have taken too much more effort to drop in on Teleman."

"Good point, Marcus. But, you see, my doctor told me that to get plenty of rest, I had to avoid looking at blood."

"He meant *your* blood, Tooby."

"I think he meant anyone's."

"What, he knows what you do for a living?" I asked.

"Well, I put down *butcher* as my occupation. Which is sort of true, I guess. Maybe he meant beef blood. But whatever kind of blood he meant, he told me not to look at it. For peace of mind, he said. He said you can't get plenty of rest without peace of mind. That's why I didn't go knocking on Teleman's door. Because otherwise, he would've ended up in a pool of his own blood, and I would've had to look at it, and then I wouldn't have got the plenty of rest my doctor recommended."

"Hey, I understand," I said, even though I didn't. "The thought of watching Teleman bleed out bothers me, too. We've had a few laughs together, Teleman and me. Jokes flow out of his mouth, nonstop. But, sadly, so do company secrets, if you know what I mean. Maybe you can figure out some way to handle this where you don't have to look at blood. Maybe you can just find a cliff and be done with it."

"A cliff?"

"A very high cliff. Any blood, you won't see, you being at the top and Teleman being at the bottom."

"But, Marcus, I never met the guy. What am I supposed to do? Go up to him and say, 'Hi, Teleman, you don't know me, but I thought we'd take a ride down to the Grand Canyon together, and maybe, while I stand back, you can step out on a ledge to take a selfie.'"

"What's the worst he can do? Say, 'No.'?"

"'No' would probably do it."

"Tooby, listen." I leaned forward, folded my arms on my desk, and looked my old friend in the eye. "You're going to have to work with me on this. I don't want to bring Benny into the picture to finish your job for you."

"Benny? Who the hell is Benny?"

"I don't know how best to put it, but Benny is what you might call a stand-in."

"A stand-in? For me? Marcus, how can you do that to me? How long have we known each other?"

"A long time, Tooby. And up to now, you've never needed a helping hand. But I got to tell you something. You're starting to go weak on me. Why do you think that is? I really want to know."

"Blood in the urine."

You hear that enough, you almost feel like leaping off a cliff yourself. Luckily, out of the blue came a better idea. "What about suffocation?" I said.

"Suffocation?"

"Sure. No blood, and you won't have to ask Teleman anything or drive him anywhere."

Tooby had the look someone gets when he hears a better idea than he could've come up with, but doesn't want to admit it.

I said, "I've always tried to keep the *how* out of it, leave the way of doing things up to you. But this time, Tooby, you need a little boost. You ready?"

"I suppose."

"You got a pencil?"

"I'll remember."

"Teleman. February twenty-second. Three a.m. *Suffocation*."

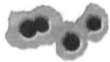

Next day, Darlene showed Tooby in, let him stare at her for a second or two, then backed out of my office and closed the door.

This time, one of the two chairs was occupied. Tooby saw the guy parked there and said "hey" to him, the way some fellows do. The other guy, I guessed, was one of those fellows who don't. He looked over at Tooby but didn't say a thing.

Tooby shrugged it off and took a seat in the empty chair.

I was sitting at my desk, fiddling with an old shoebox until I finally slid it aside to get to the matter at hand. "Tooby," I said, "do you know why I called you in here just a day after I called you in here before?"

Tooby kept glancing to his right at the other guy as if disturbed by his presence. I could see why he would be. The guy was dressed well enough—casual but tasteful threads—but his face brought to mind the recent photos of red rocks and craters that have been coming in from Mars.

"Tooby?" I said again to get his attention.

When he focused on me, I said, "What was the assignment? Do you remember, old friend?"

"Yes, I do. Teleman. February twenty-second. Three a.m."

"What else?"

"Suffocation."

"That's right. And can you tell me what happened at three this morning?"

"The climate," Tooby said. "The damn climate."

That was different. "What about it? I thought the weather this morning was kind of pleasant. Unseasonably warm for a February."

"Marcus, I'm not referring to the weather. It's the climate I'm talking about, which is what the weather does over a long period."

"Okay, what about the climate?"

"You suggested suffocation."

"Simply because the sight of blood was something you wanted to avoid for the time being. For your peace of mind, you said."

"Marcus, the climate isn't helping my peace of mind one bit. It's getting hotter and hotter. And eventually our oceans are going to boil over."

"So?"

"And it's all because the oceans' fishes are eating plastic bags."

"So? What's this have to do with Teleman?"

"Marcus, you can't find any store in the state that sells plastic bags anymore. Any kind, but especially the kind you can slip over someone's head. You can get paper bags, sure. There's a fee, but that's not the problem. I'm willing to shell out the fee because you pay me well enough. But you can't suffocate anyone with a paper bag. You pull tight on it, you'll rip it open, and the guy can start breathing again. You need plastic. But nobody's selling it, because if they did, the continents would catch fire."

What Tooby said almost made sense until I realized it didn't matter. "Tooby, Tooby, Tooby."

"Yeah?"

"Now's as good a time as any to tell you this. Benny took care of Teleman."

"When was this?" Tooby said.

"When else? This morning at 3 a.m. Suffocated him with a doubled-up paper grocery bag secured tightly around his neck with a bungee cord."

Tooby turned his head slowly toward the guy in the other

chair.

"And there's something else, Tooby," I said.

Tooby turned slowly back to me.

"Tooby, it's like this. I bear no ill will against the people I've been forced to retire early. Granger, Ginsburg, and all the rest. They were all fine human beings. But, in the end, they were deeply flawed individuals who turned out to be unreliable. Unreliable is not good for business."

Tooby took a big swallow.

"Your work, of late, has been unreliable, Tooby."

He took a deeper swallow.

I said, "You know I love you like a brother. Like an only brother. Like a long-lost brother who has found his way home and into my heart. A brother I will cherish forever. And that's why I'm willing to give you one more chance."

"Just one?"

"One more, and that's it," I said. "On the other hand, Benny is of the opinion you burned up your last chance with the blood in the urine. But maybe Benny's mind can be changed."

Tooby took an even deeper gulp and turned again to the guy with the Martian landscape for a face. "Benny?" he whispered.

Not getting so much as a glance or a grunt in return, Tooby leaned forward over the right arm of his chair, clasping his hands to stop them from shaking.

"Benny?" he said again, louder this time. Now his voice was quivering right along with his hands. "Benny, please give me the one chance. That's all I ask. I know I screwed up over the past few days. I admit it. And that's because I thought about things I shouldn't have. Like how short life is and how every second matters to everyone. See what I'm saying?"

Tooby paused for a reaction, but there wasn't any. Hands and voice still shaking, he kept on going. "Benny, what I'm saying is, that's why I made up those stories about a new alarm clock and a phony cousin and blood in my pee. I just couldn't do what

I'd been doing anymore. Because if life is short, who am I to make someone's life shorter? Who am I to come up to some slob who might've lived to be eighty and slice open his throat with a samurai sword when he's thirty? See what I'm saying?"

Whatever point he was trying to make, I could see he was desperate to get to it. "But, Benny. What I'm trying to say is this. All the stuff I just talked about is in the past. I don't think that way now. Not one bit. That's because I experienced what you might call an epiphany. I experienced it a few minutes ago when Marcus mentioned my retirement. I got to thinking about the universe and how old it is. It's, what, a zillion quadrillion years old. Now you take a guy when he's thirty and the same guy when he's eighty. That's a difference of fifty years. Fifty years compared to a zillion quadrillion years is nothing. It's zero. Yeah, every second matters, but fifty years amounts to zero seconds. So, if a guy croaks when he's thirty years old, that's the same thing as him croaking when he's eighty. See what I'm saying?"

Benny unraveled his clasped hands and now pressed them together in prayer. "Benny, dearest Benny, what I'm saying, in conclusion, is the following. And please, please listen, I beg you. I swear to you on my mother's grave, even though I put her there, that my reluctance to take a life was just a passing fancy, an anomaly, a blip. My epiphany has taught me that bumping someone off is no different than not bumping someone off. Which means that what I've been doing my entire life is okay and nothing to be ashamed of. I can be myself again. I can go back to being the same reliable Tooby that Marcus has known for these many years. I can proudly declare that my alarm clock works, my second cuz never was, and my piss is yellow."

I waited. And when it looked like Tooby was finished, I said. "I'm sure it would fascinate Benny to hear all that, Tooby. But this isn't Benny."

"Not Benny?"

"Benny's outside the door, waiting."

"Waiting for what?"

"She's waiting to make sure things in here go smoothly."

"*She?*"

"Darlene. Darlene Benny. All these years, you probably never looked down at the nameplate on her desk. She's been working on expanding her résumé. And doing a creditable job of it, too, I might add. She's clever and has spunk. When I asked her about Teleman, she said he won't be telling anyone."

Tooby tilted his head toward the other chair. "Then … who's this guy?"

"I'm glad you asked. His name's Thompson."

Tooby seemed to accept that he'd just wasted half his life confessing to him. "Hey, Thompson," he said.

Thompson turned and nodded, but still didn't say a word.

"He doesn't talk much, does he?" Tooby said.

I said, "He got into a collision with a chemical supply truck. The cargo splashed everywhere. What happened to his face doesn't much matter because he worked the phones. But some of the stuff went down his throat and completely sizzled his vocal cords. A month ago, he was my top phone rep. Deep, resonant voice. Clear diction. A tone that was commanding, yet cordial. He could talk anyone into anything. Not so much anymore."

Tooby kept looking at him with an expression that, from the side, looked like genuine pity. "That's too bad," he said.

"His name's Thompson."

"I know. You told me," Tooby said, still looking at him.

I rolled my chair back and stood up. Tooby turned to face me. I locked eyes with him and said, slowly and carefully, "That's Thompson. Today. Three minutes from now."

I then held out the shoebox.

Tooby sat still for a moment. He slowly got up out of his chair, took the box, and sat back down.

I watched Tooby lift the lid and peek into the box. I watched Thompson as he watched Tooby lift the lid and peek into the box. I spotted the beads of sweat forming on each of their foreheads and found myself hoping with all my heart that this would work out.

Martin Zeigler writes short fiction, primarily mystery, science fiction, and horror. His stories have been published in anthologies and journals, in print and online. Every so often (okay, twice), he has gathered these stories into a self-published collection. In 2015, he released *A Functional Man and Other Stories.* More recently, in 2020, a year we will all remember with fondness, he released *Hypochondria and Other Stories.* Besides writing, Marty enjoys the things most people do. And besides *those*, he likes reading, taking long walks, and playing the piano. Marty makes his home in the Pacific Northwest.

JUST CALL WALLY

BY WIL A. EMERSON

The noise at the front door jarred Walt Mason's head as if thunder had once again shaken the old rafters. He decided the time had come to look for another place to call home. He didn't need to be in the same building where he conducted his business. As he pulled a pillow over his head, the pounding came again, this time with a voice.

"Wally, let me in. Wally."

What the hell. Walt looked at his watch. Three in the morning. He wasn't on night duty. What the hell. As brain fog cleared, he sat up in bed. Damn that Ollie.

Mason pulled the door open, just enough to confirm the excess noise had been caused by the one and only Ollie Hanover.

"It's 3 in the morning. What the hell?"

"I know what time it is. I need some help."

"Go home, come back at noon."

"Can't. Please, let me sit for a while."

"Sit, you can. Don't say a word, don't even breathe." Mason yanked the chain and let Ollie through the narrow space.

As Mason slunk back to his bedroom, Ollie called out, "I need your help now."

"What the hell? Didn't you hear me?"

"I killed Danny Donnelly."

Mason turned around so fast, his neck bones crackled.

"Why in the world did you kill Donnelly?"

"Because Booster paid me."

"That crook paid you to kill Danny Donnelly?"

"Yep, that's what I said. I don't know what to do with his body."

Mason scratched his head as he gazed at Oliver Hanover, the third. The last in a long line of Hanovers, Ollie was somehow missed when intellectual decision-making had developed in the evolutionary human brain. Mason had known Ollie all his life. From kindergarten on, shared the same bus ride back and forth every day, ate the same bologna sandwiches their mothers made the night before. They had parted ways for a while, after graduating from high school, when Walt went to a state college. Ollie stayed behind to do various jobs. Sometimes a job actually included a paycheck from a reputable business. When Walt came back to Marlboro, Virginia, to continue his family's business, he checked in on Ollie frequently.

Then Ollie's parents died ten years ago, in the same month. Of course, their rental of the two-bedroom apartment ceased to be an option for their son. Ollie needed a place to call home. So Walt, like the older brother Ollie never had, rented him a flat in the adjoining building so he wouldn't sleep out in the cold.

Not that Ollie was mentally challenged. He was a math wizard of sorts, good with a paintbrush, but he just couldn't make the neuron-dendrite connections to stick to a reasonable plan of action for survival. Walt loved him and hated him, too. An albatross around his neck for far too many years. He'd lost both wives because of Ollie. Or at least that's what Megan and then

Karla claimed. Didn't question their motives. Walt took care of the payments at settlement time.

So far, Walt had done well with his life. The family business grew, as did the surrounding neighborhood. Always a need for his service to the point he hired three equally capable employees who provided a sense of freedom from the twenty-four/seven requirements of the job at hand. Walt's life wasn't a long list of ongoing complaints. And it wasn't Walt's nature to begrudge his friend a helping hand.

Walt gazed at Ollie. Good-looking, curly red hair always kept neat, blue eyes that begged for attention, a strong jawline. He stayed in the best of shape because Ollie walked or ran twenty miles a week. The women often swooned over Ollie—until they got to know him. It usually took about a week before the shine wore off. If only the motherly type would come along, fold her arms and heart around the guy, and forever protect him from himself. That would be a blessing, Walt thought.

Then Walt might feel like he had a true friend, the brotherly kind, to enjoy as they aged. What wonderful memories they would share as they sat on the park bench in Hoover Square.

With a long sigh, Walt, his gangly legs tired from a long day, sat down in a high-backed chair across from Ollie, who had plopped down like a rag doll in Walt's favorite soft-cushioned recliner.

"Help me get this straight. You killed Danny Donnelly because Booster paid you to do it. Is that right?"

"Yep, that's right. Happened about an hour ago. I hit him hard, out, gone … you know, dead."

"Ollie, if Booster paid you to cut off your hand, would you do it?"

"Hell, no, Wally. What? You think I'm dumb or something?"

"Dumb? What does that mean? Debatable. Your action is a little more complicated than just doing what you're paid to do. If you did this, it is certainly a crime. A serious crime."

"I know." Ollie put his hands over his face. "Now I know."

Walt wasn't sure if Ollie would cry. It wouldn't help either of them.

"I'm inclined to just let you sit there while I finish sleeping. This is your problem, Ollie, not mine." If Walt asked how, when, or where, he'd only be involving himself more in a dire situation, which could lead to being an accomplice or withholding evidence if cops got involved. Walt would have to look up the legal definitions to keep himself distanced from Ollie's criminal act. But curiosity had a firm hold on him, so he asked his own first dumb question.

"How did you do it?"

"Hit him with a bat. You know, Dan's a lot taller than I am. So, it was a stretch. Good thing he wasn't looking at me."

"What? You were behind him, you followed him? He didn't know you were in the room, what?" Walt wanted a cup of strong black coffee. He eyed the kitchen. A two-minute deal. Then he'd have to offer Ollie one, and then neither of them would get any more sleep.

"He came out of Booster's place. Gambling, probably. Not my kind of thing. You know that, Wally. I don't waste my money on cards."

Actually, it's my money, Walt thought. But what the heck, he'd give Ollie credit for staying away from Booster's card games.

"Why were you at Booster's?"

"To kill Danny. Told you, honest. I wasn't gambling."

"I got that part. No concern there. But why kill Danny Donnelly?"

"For Booster. No one liked Dan Donnelly. You know that. A bad reputation. I heard for the last ten years he's a hired gun. A bad person." Ollie shook his head.

"And now *you're* a hired gun, Ollie." Spoken emphatically to make a point.

"How's that? I haven't killed as many people as Donnelly."

The answer took Walt by surprise. "How many people did Donnelly kill, Ollie?"

"Booster said he'd done over a dozen jobs. Can you believe that?"

"It doesn't matter what I believe." Not sure if he should ask or not, Walt forged ahead, his teeth clenched. "I have a delicate question to ask, Ollie. You're not obligated to answer. How many people have you killed?" Walt braced himself, the wooden chair hard on his shoulder bones.

"Like I told you. Dan Donnelly. Tonight. Over and done with."

Was Ollie telling the truth? "Murder is murder, Ollie. Being paid to kill someone would be considered a more serious crime than, say, one committed in a fit of rage."

"Like a husband catching his wife in bed with another dude? No, wasn't like that. Not out to get even or anything. Justified if you ask me." Ollie yawned and looked at his watch. "Time's catching up with us."

This wasn't the first time Walt heard his friend make the "time catching up" comment. He remembered what happened when they were kids and Ollie brought home a bike that didn't belong to him. It wasn't as bad as it first seemed. He hadn't stolen the shiny new bike, Ollie said. He just picked up the one that sorta looked like it might be his. Red, similar shape and design. Two wheels, handlebars, hand brakes. That's what he told the cops when Walt convinced Ollie he had to turn the bike in.

What prompted Ollie to tell Walt had been the wanted poster taped on every storefront on the main drag. A nice color print of the bike that he'd conveniently parked in Walt's backyard. "Time's catching up with us," he said that day to Walt, who had developed a habit of helping Ollie out of his unusual circumstances. Walt dialed the phone, asked an officer to stop by. Walt made sure Ollie explained the situation as he first told it—a detailed story. Out late, dark, cold enough for a jacket in late September, but he'd forgotten to wear something warm. A quick ride was better than a long walk. It wasn't like he'd stolen it, but

Walt had cautioned him to refrain from saying just that. For once, Ollie listened. The cop, not much older than Walt or Ollie, said, "No problem." He patted Walt's shoulder. "Good job, big brother."

Walt stifled a yawn. Before he went back to bed, he needed to conclude this discussion. Of course, it wasn't something to be taken lightly. Not a bike, not the leather jacket from Macy's, not the toolkit from Ace Hardware. Definitely not like the time he rode a stud thoroughbred off Alexander Rodney's farm.

Oh, Rodney was pissed. Big time. Threatened to sue, threatened to take Ollie to court for grand theft, he threatened a lot of things that didn't help the situation at all. He knocked Ollie to the ground and, to everyone's surprise, Ollie suffered a broken arm. Ollie howled like a kid, tears and all. Even when the paramedics arrived, Ollie kept crying. Walt sat with him in the emergency room cubicle, and Ollie finally calmed down. A sedative helped. Necessary, the doctor said, or they wouldn't be able to take proper x-rays to evaluate the extent of the injury. It was broken, no doubt about it. Right arm, too. His working arm. Big, boney lump sticking out mid-way between his elbow and his wrist. Didn't take a genius to figure it out, Ollie howled. Ollie said he knew the minute he hit the ground, it was a nasty fracture.

Under sedation, Ollie said to the doctor and the police officer standing guard at the exam room entrance, "Rodney shouldn't have done that. I didn't hurt his horse." The cop listened. He'd been assigned to the missing horse case. A big, bold move for a guy like Oliver Hanover. Five miles out of town, riding that stallion up and down the back roads, letting it graze and drink from a small creek most folks thought was toxic because it was so close to the rubber plant. It was obvious the officer took a liking to Ollie, defending the rights of a horse.

Ollie knew nothing about breeding horses or even riding them. But, after he saw a television story on the Rodney ranch outside of his city, he decided he had to act and rescue that beautiful specimen of a horse. The story and the success of the local farmer enlightened other "ranchers" after the offspring of his stallion won a state fair championship and went on to a big racetrack payday. Ollie saw it as nothing but a case of injustice.

Who would help the horse if it were not him? Give the magnificent horse a day of pleasure to roam like a normal horse should roam.

"Did the horse give permission?" Ollie said. "I swear, it won't stop with horses. Everybody's rights are disappearing."

As the sedative wore off, Ollie said to Walt, "Time's catching up with us."

Alexander Rodney did press charges. That's when the clock started ticking.

A year in prison? And a five-thousand-dollar fine was nothing to whinny over. But what recourse did Walt have? Ollie jailed because of a joyride? On a big, old horse that pretty much didn't show any dislike with being in a dry barn every day, feeding on a fine mixture of oats, fresh-cut grass, and carrots to produce a strong, sturdy batch of sperm?

When the court date arrived, Ollie dressed in a clean pair of jeans, a blue button-down shirt, and a tan sport jacket. Walt didn't complain, as he understood Ollie thought he'd dressed appropriately to face Judge Henry Adams, who might send him to jail and order him to pay a hefty fine. Walt sat beside Ollie at the defense table in his usual soft black business suit, a gray tie in a Windsor knot over a crisp white shirt.

No one expected Rancher Rodney to show up for the hearing and witness Ollie walk in with his casted arm in a pitiful dark blue sling and his sausage fingers hanging out the end, so big he couldn't bend them. But there he sat, in the first row behind the prosecutor. Big pout on his face, determined.

When the clerk called the court to order, introductions made as to defense and prosecution, statements made as to cause, Ollie was soon asked to swear the truth, the whole truth, and nothing but the truth.

Ollie stood and raised his left arm. "I apologize, Your Honor."

Judge Adams, more salt than pepper left in his hair, leaned forward. "Sir, you were asked to swear to the truth."

"Your Honor, forgive me. I don't mean to be disloyal or disrespectful. I know I should hold my right arm high when I swear to the truth, but I can't do that unless I'm given a lot of heavy drugs and I've never been one to take narcotics. If God gives me pain, I take it like a …"

At that point, the judge said, "You've said enough, Mr. Hanover." He nodded to the clerk. "Mr. Hanover has been sworn in." He dropped his chin and closed his eyes. But neither Ollie nor Walt considered it a prayerful gesture.

"Your Honor, if I may address the court." The lawyer Walt Mason hired for Ollie stood at the end of the defendant's table. "My client is entering a not guilty plea, but he is willing to pay the fine. If the judge will accept this arrangement, then I will ask the court to dismiss the case."

The prosecutor, a wily guy who looked like he lived on noodle soup and string beans, stood up so quickly, it looked as if a hot stick had poked him.

"I object, Your Honor."

His name was Damion Klinger, and it surprised most folks Walt knew that he even practiced law. But Klinger was known, albeit a lightweight street fighter, and the last thing Walt wanted was a fight with the red-faced, bull-headed prosecutor. That's why he had earlier suggested to Ollie's attorney, Jethro Longmire, an old family friend of the Masons, to work a deal with rancher Alexander Rodney. It crossed Walt's mind when Klinger stood that perhaps Jethro forgot to mention the deal to the prosecutor. Walt knew it wasn't his job to communicate between the two lawyers.

Walt closed his eyes. Not concerned about Ollie getting punched by the raging prosecutor. More because the two of them were amid a no-win situation. Ollie would go to jail and Walt would still have to pay the five grand.

Before anyone knew what happened, though, Alexander Rodney stepped forward. "Your Honor, I'd like to talk to you directly. Then maybe we can all go home."

"Order, order," Judge Adams yelled. "Clerk, get that man back behind the rail." He glared at Rodney.

The rancher took two steps back but only because the clerk, six-four and nearly as broad, wore a menacing grin and moved swiftly to do as the judge instructed.

Ollie watched the preceding with his blue eyes wide. As though a riveting movie played in front of him. He jabbed at Walt's arm, but Walt had the good sense not to engage in a conversation right then. Ollie leaned over, an attempt to catch Jethro as he spoke.

Jethro put up a finger—across his lips it went. Whatever Ollie intended to say had to remain unspoken, silence the best defense. Jethro had a nagging suspicion the judge might be in a foul mood and adjourn for the day. That would put a serious dent in Jethro's schedule. Three friends from the VFW Lodge had arranged a marathon of events over the next week. Every other day eighteen holes of golf, poker on the intervening recuperation days. Golf and old buddies held more interest than boring malfeasance or petty theft cases. Even if Ollie admitted to grand larceny, murder in the first degree, or national terrorism, Jethro would still want to be out in the fresh air on a green fairway. Nothing much interested him except hitting a little white ball, slow and easy, all day long. Poker came in second with his friends from the VFW Lodge. To celebrate a good day, a tall glass of Jim Beam would lead to a most satisfactory day.

After the massive, armed clerk backed away, Rodney stayed dutifully behind the rail that separated the public from designated officials. However, Alexander raised his voice again. "Your Honor, I want these charges dropped. This kid, well, he doesn't need any more trouble in his life."

The judge struck his gavel again. "Order. Order," he sputtered. In a louder voice, he said, "Sir, don't you understand you are not part and parcel of this court procedure? We can hold you in contempt of court. Put you in jail. Is that your wish?"

The prosecutor rose. "Your Honor, I concur this is outrageous. No doubt, the defense put him up to this."

The judge growled, "Did I grant you the opportunity to speak?"

That remark led Walt to believe the judge had an ax to grind with Damion Klinger, too.

Alexander Rodney saved the day. Perhaps the week for Jethro.

"Okay, sir." His honor set the gavel down and turned an ear to Rancher Rodney. "Make this the shortest speech in history."

"Won't take twelve minutes, Your Honor." He laughed. "I caused this whole misunderstanding. Sorta took matters into my own hands. This boy didn't mean harm. If I woulda cooled down, none of us would be here and that fine young man wouldn't have his arm all busted up. I'm very sorry, Your Honor." Rodney sat down. Even pulled a handkerchief out of his pocket and wiped his eyes.

Damion Klinger wasn't the least bit satisfied, though. He needed a win to prove his worth. "I object, Your Honor. This is a ruse. No doubt Mr. Rodney is afraid of a lawsuit over the personal injury he caused. That is not the matter of this court. Oliver Hanover broke the law. It is our duty to seek justice today." Klinger leaned on the table, a pitiful posture for a man who had lost his bearing.

Judge Henry Adams, a dedicated, soulful man, court officer for forty-three years, raised his gavel. "Case dismissed. Go in peace." He moved off the bench so fast his long, black robe caused a wave and court documents fluttered to the floor.

Jethro Longmire said as they left the court building, "You owe me a grand lunch at the Wayfair."

"My pleasure," said Walt.

Ollie smiled. "So no jail at all?"

Walt shook his head as the memory faded. That wasn't a particularly terrible memory. But he wasn't so sure the event tonight would have a happy outcome. And Ollie sat across from him in Walt's favorite chair, with his hands on his knees, in anticipation of a "big, fast, fix" from his best friend. The man he thought of as his brother. Walt considered his options.

"Time's catching up with us, Walt."

"Why do you say that, Ollie? Damn, how do you think I can help get you out of a mess like murder? And do you know for sure if Donnelly is dead? You said you hit him once with a bat. So maybe he's knocked unconscious. Takes a while to wake up. Is that possible?" Walt knew he was grabbing at straws. He had to start somewhere.

"Nope, dead. I made sure. Booster said I wouldn't get paid otherwise."

"What makes you one hundred percent sure?"

"Sat there, waited for him to stop breathing. Took about ten, fifteen minutes, it seemed. Pillow over his face."

"A pillow? That's hard to take, Ollie. Willful murder. I can almost understand a whack in the head. Teach the guy a lesson, maybe. But now you're saying you suffocated him. It sounds terrible."

"He's a bad person. He beat up Booster's daughter. They'd been dating, you see. Booster caught him one time, had Danny knocked around by a couple of guys. Didn't do much good. Her face was a mess the last time Booster saw her. Boy, he went ballistic."

"It's murder, Ollie. Doesn't matter why."

"It's justifiable. That's what Booster said. If it's justifiable, then it's a good cause."

"Justifiable? Was he harming you? Did you defend yourself? No, you slugged the guy with a bat, knocked him unconscious, and then suffocated him. You're in big trouble, Ollie. I'm not much good for you now."

"He coulda shot me. Would that make a difference?" Ollie said.

"Did he point a gun at you? Is that what you're telling me now?" Had Ollie made up a lie to gain Walt's sympathy?

"When I slugged him, he turned around and then pulled a big black gun out of his waistband. A Glock or something like that. I think the big ones are Glocks."

"Ollie, you don't know shit about guns. Did he pull a weapon out, aim it at you?"

"Well, he pulled it out, whatever it was, and then suddenly he flopped over. Smack on his back. Head cracked the cement. Gun fell out of his hand. That's when I decided to wait and see what happened. Sat down, there was the dirty old pillow laying by the waste can. Thought about putting it under his head. Make it easy for him. Then he groaned, and I figured the two thousand wouldn't be mine. So I used the pillow to you ... know ... you know what."

"For two thousand dollars. Ollie, that's peanuts. Stupid, stupid decision. Now your life is a total mess. In jail forever."

"Time's catching up with us," Ollie whispered. He looked at his watch. "Sun up soon. People in that alley, deliver stuff to Booster's."

"And what in the hell do you expect me to do?"

"Just thinking out loud. A little help. Over and done with. It's your business."

Walt shook his head and raised his hand to his face. The final straw.

Walt went to his bedroom and put on a pair of black pants he had flung over the side chair. No plans to wear a suit for three more days.

They walked out to the alley, the back entrance used for vehicles to load and unload into the large garage. Walt took out his keys, told Ollie to take the passenger side, and then backed out. Three blocks to Booster's. All of four minutes at the most. No traffic, few lights.

Walt backed the long van into the alley. A simple task, he'd been driving for nearly twenty years and never had a mishap. Bad publicity for his business to be involved in an accident of any kind. He pulled as close to the dead man as possible. Just enough room for them to maneuver Dan's less-than-warm body.

"There are a couple of pads in the back. We'll roll him up nice and tidy. Then you take his feet. I'll do the top end." He could count on Ollie to do exactly as he was told. It was another trait that Walt had always admired about Ollie's flawed mind.

Back in the van, Ollie spoke again. Almost with a reverence. "It's a shame we won't know if he wanted to be cremated or buried."

Walt replied, "I don't think it matters. There is only one option."

Walt backed into the open garage, went to the wall, and pushed another button. A sliding door spread open, and a loading dock moved forward. Ollie helped Walt slide Donnelly's body on the mechanical dock. He closed the garage door, and they went up the stairs to the locked door where the cocooned body lay on the other side.

"There's a gurney at the end of the hall." Walt pointed. Ollie hustled to get it.

"How long does it take, Walt?"

"About two hours. Are you going to wait?"

"Yes, I think I should. Someone needs to give him a send-off. Guy doesn't have anybody. Even a bad guy needs someone in the end."

Walt shook his head. "That's kind of you, Ollie. But you realize this can never happen again. I can't ruin my business. My life." A long sigh followed.

The Mason Funeral and Crematory Service had served Walt Mason and his past family well. Provided a good income, offered personal satisfaction, good standing in the neighborhood. How much more was Walt willing to risk? Two wives, gone. No kids. Little time for good friends. Should this last gesture be the end of Ollie calling Wally for help?

His best friend? It would only take a quick push and shove into the crematorium. He gazed with saddened eyes at Oliver

Hanover, the third. The last of a long line of Hanovers who hadn't been born with the intellectual capacity to make wise decisions. Ollie's skills had taken him on a winding road to nowhere. Walt watched tears run down Ollie's face.

Remorse or intuition?

Wil A. Emerson writes from her home in Raleigh, North Carolina. A transplanted northerner, her stories take a leap of faith for the southern beach reader expecting charm and wit. Wil's been published in women's fiction, a story about a kindly older woman befriending a wishful gal. But most of Wil's stories focus on the dead or deadly. An award winner in the Bould Anthology Award issue 2020, she was also featured in the 2019 and 2021 publications. Her story, "The Works," will appear in an upcoming *Crimeucopia* anthology published by Murderous Ink Press. You can also view her artwork, nature in acrylics, at www.wilemerson.com.

AIDING AND ABETTING

BY ADRIAN LUDENS

Between convulsive sobs, Chesil Ach du Lieber managed to tell her doctor that her husband, Depp, had traveled into the city to attend a business conference. Dr. Obadiah Gee used the distraught woman's cell phone to telephone the man.

The phone rang three times, then: "Hiya, sugar britches, how you doing?"

Dr. Gee cleared his throat. "Excuse me, this is Dr. Gee calling."

"Oh, my mistake! I thought this was my wife. She used to have this number."

"Mr. ..." *Ach du Lieber, or just Lieber?* Gee, didn't know. "Sir, she *still* has this number."

Five seconds of silence passed. "I don't follow."

"I'm calling you from her phone."

"Did she lose it?"

"Good heavens, no. I'm here with her now. I made a house call."

"But you didn't call my house, you called my cell."

"Mr. Ach du Lieber, please stop joking around. Your wife is greatly distressed, and I believe she could benefit from your presence."

"I've been in meetings all day and haven't had time to buy her any presents," the man complained. "What's wrong with her? Spell it out for me, Doc."

"She's suffering a bout of …" He caught himself, unsure of how to best proceed. *Everything is under such scrutiny*, he thought. "Do you remember the title of the rock band Def Leppard's best-selling record? The one that came out in 1987."

"Oh my God! She's burned down a building?"

"No, no. You're thinking of 1983's *Pyromania*. I'm referring to the next record, *Hysteria*."

"What does she think is so damned funny?"

"That would be the word 'hysterical.' I assure you this is far more serious."

"So you're saying she needs a hysterectomy?"

"No," Dr. Gee mentally added, *you harebrained nincompoop*. "She is hysterical and suffering a bout of hysteria. She's convinced your baby is a danger to her. I've tried to get her to take a sedative, but she refuses. I'd advise you to get here as soon as you can."

"Oh God," Chesil Ach du Lieber lamented. "I hear someone coming!"

Dr. Gee listened to the heavy tread of dress shoes bounding up the stairs. "I believe you are right."

"Do you think it's the baby?" Chesil looked fearful.

"No, ma'am." Gee frowned. "I'd say your husband has arrived." At his words, Depp Ach du Lieber entered his wife's bedroom. He crossed the floor to the bed, leaned over, and embraced her. "Darling, are you okay?"

"Yes, I'm fine now. I just get so stressed and fearful." She sighed and dabbed at her eyes with a frilly hanky.

Depp's brow furrowed as he scanned the room. He turned to his wife. "Where's the kid?"

Dr. Gee spoke up, hoping to ease the man's mind. "Your son is resting peacefully in his crib in the next room. I checked on him only minutes before you arrived."

"'Resting peacefully,' he says." Chesil's voice quavered. "Scheming and planning our deaths is what that would-be assassin is really doing in there."

Gee frowned at his patient.

Depp had fixed his attention on the doctor. "I bought my wife an emotional support animal, but it isn't here." He gave his wife a searching look. "Well?"

"I hardly think it fell down the well, darling," Chesil said. "As far as I know, we don't even have one!"

Depp forced an icy smile. "Where is the goat I bought for you?"

"I don't know. And that darned goat is not a good companion at all. Every time something goes wrong, and I feel the need to cry, when I reach for it, the goat just goes all stiff and falls over. He's no comfort to me at all." She dabbed her eyes again with her hanky.

Depp looked at Dr. Gee. "How do you like that? I went to great lengths to have a special myopic goat flown in from Tennessee, and she doesn't appreciate or use it."

Dr. Gee felt rising discomfort. "I believe you mean to say you've purchased a myotonic goat," he said. "Some people call them fainting goats. They have a hereditary condition that causes them to stiffen or fall over when startled. Frankly, I'm hard-pressed to think of an animal less suited for emotional companionship."

Depp lifted his chin. His eyes blazed. "How about a South African scorpion?" he challenged.

"Point taken," Gee said. "Be that as it may, I feel as if I should be on my way. There's not much more I can do here."

Chesil yelped. Depp's face contorted with fear. Dr. Gee turned to see what had disturbed them. Their cherubic tot stood unsteadily, staring wide-eyed at the room's occupants. He took an awkward step, lost his balance, and ended up on his rear end.

Gee clapped his hands together. "Why hello there, little chap! How in the world did you get out of your crib?" He crossed the room and scooped up the youngster in his arms.

Depp stared at the baby with obvious misgivings. "Doctor, meet our son, Lucifer Anton Damien Aleister ach du Lieber. But we call him Chucky, for short."

The doctor gazed into the little boy's innocent blue eyes. He could find nothing at all wrong with the child, nothing that would help explain his parents' unusual paranoia.

He returned the tot to his crib, patted the boy's head, and reentered the bedroom. The fainting goat had wandered into the room while he'd been gone. It bleated once, defecated on the rug, and began nibbling on the end of the bed's comforter.

Chesil started to weep. Depp's haughtiness fell away like a discarded candy bar wrapper. "Doc, please! What can I do for my wife? Better yet, what can *you* do for her?"

"For now, she just needs some rest."

"Just name it and I'll take care of it."

"As I said, she'll benefit just from you spending more time at home."

"Money is no object."

"If you help with the baby—"

"—is there somewhere we can send her? Perhaps a retreat?"

"Pitch in with the cooking and the household chores—"

"—an expensive medication you can prescribe?"

"Most of her problems will be solved if you pay—"

"—my checkbook is ready. Let me find a pen."

"More time with your wife and your son."

"Stop beating around the bush, Doc! Just tell me in plain English!"

"You need to help her—"

"—a medical procedure, perhaps?"

"Feed and change the baby. She's overwhelmed."

"—a frontal lobotomy?"

"What!?"

"What?"

Chesil shrieked so loud it made Dr. Gee's ears ring. The goat stiffened and toppled onto the floor.

"Good heavens!" Gee exclaimed. "What's wrong?"

The woman raised a trembling hand and pointed at the doorway. "He's here," she intoned. "*Spying.*"

In the doorway, Chucky lifted his arms and gazed imploringly at Dr. Gee. He lifted the baby and carried him back to his room. "I am so sorry, my little friend," he whispered. "Between you and me? You seem to have a wig in a hatbox for a mother and a spittoon filled with tobacco juice for a father."

"Uck," the baby replied.

"I concur wholeheartedly." Gee laid the baby in his crib and returned to the next room.

He addressed Depp. "As I was saying. Bed rest for her," he indicated the woman with a nod. "Mr. Ach du Lieber. And for—"

The man raised a hand to stop him. "That," he said, pointing at his wife. "Is *Mrs.* Ach du Lieber. *I,*" he poked his index finger into his chest, "am Mr. Ach du Lieber."

For the first time, it occurred to Dr. Gee that he might be the victim of an elaborate television prank show. "I know that, of course. I only meant—"

"Perhaps it would help if we all introduced ourselves using our first names," the bedridden woman suggested. "For instance, I'm Chesil."

"I'm Depp." The man's finger remained pointing at his chest.

Dr. Gee sighed. "I'm Obadiah, Obie for short."

"Nice to meet you, Obie," Chesil smiled. "I'm Chesil."

Dr. Gee watched her, hoping she'd laugh to show she was kidding. She didn't.

After an awkward silence, Dr. Gee cleared his throat. "I'll just be on my way."

Depp frowned. "Hang on a moment, Doctor."

"What's the matter now?"

"Something's bothering me, something from earlier." The man looked perplexed. Gee imagined a three-legged hamster trying to run on the wheel that powered the man's brain.

"You said goats did not make great—or even good— emotional support animals. Well, why are certain sports stars, like Michael Jordman, Tom Grady, and Waylon Gretzky, referred to as 'the GOAT'? Why do people call them that if goats are not, in fact, the best?"

Dr. Gee wished he'd called in sick this morning and hit the golf course instead. "I believe you mean Michael Jordan, Tom Brady, and Wayne Gretzky."

Depp shrugged. "I don't know who any of *those* guys are, but the question remains."

"In this instance, GOAT is an acronym. It stands for Greatest of All Time."

Chesil frowned. "Where does the goat come in?"

Gee bit down on his lip and counted to five before he responded. "With an acronym, you take the first letter from each word and then pronounce it like a new word. Greatest of All Time becomes GOAT. Acronyms should not be confused with another form of abbreviation called initialism. An example would be vee, eye, pee, which stands for 'very important person.' See the difference? We say, VIP, not vip."

Depp's face turned as red as cherry gelatin and he stared at the carpet.

Dr. Gee pretended not to notice the other man's embarrassment and turned toward the bedridden woman. "Contractions are probably the most common form of abbreviations. I'm Dr. Gee, but of course I don't spell 'doctor' out every time. The acceptable shortened version is simply dee, are, and a period."

"Oh, thank goodness," Chesil murmured, apparently to herself. "I've been spelling the entire word out in my head every time."

Gee scanned the room, looking for an intelligent adult who would commiserate with him. He didn't find one. The closest he came was a glimpse of the baby, who peeked into the room one moment and was gone the next.

"I must express my gratitude to you, Doctor Gee. I have attained a sharper understanding," Depp said. "In this instance, not only is GOAT an abbreviation, but it's also an acronym. One might say 'ad' to refer to an advertisement, for example. Then there are contractions, wherein a portion of the midpoint of the word is eliminated. The letters b, l, v, and d, extracted from the word 'boulevard,' when written on an envelope, are understood phonetically to remain 'boulevard.' Then, of course, there are initialisms, such as BBC—British Broadcasting Company—and DVD, which means 'digital versatile disc.'"

"However, I digress. Our discourse is on the topic of acronyms. GOAT, as you say, Doctor, is 'greatest of all time.' NASA stands for National Aeronautics and Space Administration. SARS is 'severe acute respiratory syndrome'—a severe form of pneumonia. The military is quite keen on acronyms. There is HERCULES, which stands for Heavy Equipment Recovery Combat Utility Lift and Evacuation System. And the oft-overlooked AARDACONUS, which, as I'm sure we all recall, stands for Army Air Reconnaissance for Damage Assessment in the Continental United States. Phonetically, AARDACONUS and the titular character in the cult classic William Castle film *Mr. Sardonicus,* while similar, do not perfectly match. I have thus concluded there was no deliberate intent on the part of the U.S. military when creating that acronym to draw any dualistic parallel."

Gee stared at the other man. Chesil sniffled and wiped her reddened eyes.

Convinced more than ever someone was having an elaborate laugh at his expense, Dr. Gee bounded across the room and threw open the closet door. Finding no hidden camera operator inside, he dropped to his knees and lifted the bed comforter. Only a gleaming pair of eyes belonging to the diminutive goat stared back at him. He stood.

The couple stared at him as if he were mad.

"Oh!" Chesil said, clutching handfuls of bedding. "Don't forget GYAITGDHBIBMFOIYA."

Depp gave his wife a quizzical look. "What is that one, dear? I don't believe I am familiar."

"Get your ass in the goddamned house before I break my foot off in your ass."

The temptation to contribute to the inane conversation became too much. "We could consider my name an acronym," the doctor announced. "My name is Obadiah Gee, shortened to Obie Gee to sound less formal. I am a doctor specializing in obstetrics and gynecology. Thus, Obie Gee—or OBG—is both my name and my job."

The couple gave him blank looks. Depp caught his wife's eye. She frowned. He shrugged.

The doctor decided to leave. Again.

"I'll be on my way," he said.

"Doctor! Wait!" Chesil pleaded.

Gee paused. "Yes?"

"We don't feel safe here," Depp said. He darted his eyes in an exaggerated, sidelong gaze toward their son's room. "Alone. With the baby."

"Why on earth not?"

"He's trying to kill us." Chesil's voice quavered.

"That's absurd."

"Is it?" Depp stepped closer, his voice low. "His face is always red. As if he'd been crying."

"Well, he probably *has* been crying," Gee said. *I would cry too if I were stuck here with you two numbskulls.*

"Ah, but that's just what he wants us to think." Depp both hissed and whispered his words. Gee idly wondered if *hisspered* might be a real but underutilized word as his host went on. "Chesil and I know the truth. Chucky's face is always red, not because he's been crying but because he's been eavesdropping."

"Lurking, creeping around, skulking about, prowling, spying, lying in wait." Gee glanced up and glimpsed Chesil shoving what looked like a well-thumbed thesaurus beneath the comforter.

"I'm not sure I follow," the doctor said.

"Well, *he* certainly does!" Depp grimaced. "Follows us from room to room! That baby isn't natural."

"I recommend an experienced psychiatrist."

"How will that help?" Chesil asked. "He can't even talk yet."

Gee closed his eyes and massaged his temples. He felt a thunderstorm-sized headache coming for him.

"Just suppose," Depp clasped his arms around himself as if terrified. "I get up in the middle of the night and I put on my slippers and robe, intending to go downstairs for some warm milk. At the top of the stairs, suppose my foot slips on something. Suppose I nearly plunge headlong down the stairs, but I catch the railing."

Depp's cheeks had turned a hectic pink. "Now suppose—and this is all purely hypothetical, you understand—but suppose I reach out, intending to identify the object. And suppose I touch it, but in the act of touching it, I inadvertently brush it away. Suppose it tumbles down a couple steps. Suppose I recognize it as a cloth patchwork doll I purchased for the baby. At that moment, I'll *know*. I'll know, and I won't even be surprised! The baby placed it there, deliberately, hoping to kill one of us!"

"Well, now, that's quite a stretch."

"And suppose, the next day, Depp comes home from work to find me dead," Chesil added.

"Dead?" Gee asked.

"Yes. Lying at the foot of the stairs." Chesil's eyes swam with tears. "My neck broken, after slipping on the doll."

"You think you'll slip on the same doll? In broad daylight?" Gee looked first at Mrs. Ach du Lieber, and then at her husband. "Why didn't you pick up the doll on your way back upstairs after getting your warm milk? Why leave it there if you were so concerned and so shaken?—hypothetically, of course."

Depp flushed, and then paled. "The unmitigated gall! You should be helping us, Doctor, not pointing the finger of blame!"

Dr. Gee felt his own cheeks burning. "I'll be on my way," he said again.

"Wait!" Depp grasped Dr. Gee's sleeve. "Suppose after the funeral, I am so distraught I take something to help me sleep. And suppose the baby's bloodlust is not yet satisfied. Suppose you were to stop here only to discover me in my bed—dead!"

I never intend to set foot in this house again, Dr. Gee thought. *The inmates clearly run* this *asylum.*

"He'll have had his revenge on us both!"

"How do you figure?"

"Well, he …" Depp cast his eyes about the room. "He turned on the gas."

"Wouldn't your baby succumb to carbon monoxide poisoning, too?"

Depp frowned. "Well …"

"These scenarios are asinine." Dr. Gee scowled first at Depp and then at his wife. "You two ought to be ashamed. What I see before me are two very spoiled and entitled people who barely have time for each other, much less time for another human being—one who is dependent on them for his own survival."

Mrs. Ach du Lieber paled. Her lower lip trembled. Her husband wrung his hands together and stared at the floor, appearing suitably chastised.

"I ought to call Child Protective Services." Dr. Gee paused for effect. "But I won't. Stop with the insane speculation. Your baby loves you. He needs you. Start loving him, and caring for him, before it's too late."

The couple nodded. Tears streamed down their cheeks. Dr. Gee clapped Depp on the shoulder and bowed in Chesil's direction. Gee picked up his old-fashioned medical bag and strode from the room.

He tramped heavily down the hall.

After ten feet, Dr. Gee glanced back, slipped out of his shoes, and padded in silence back to the baby's room. He slipped inside, hardly daring to breathe. At the far end of the room, something rustled.

Dr. Gee took half a dozen purposeful steps until he stood at the side of the crib. The baby waited, hands on the rail, staring at him with wide, intelligent blue eyes.

Imagine being raised by those two imbeciles. Poor little chap.

As the silence spun out, an understanding passed between them, without either of them speaking a word.

Dr. Gee reached a decision. He put a hand into his medical bag. Mostly an ostentatious affectation, it still contained a few useful items. He found what he wanted and withdrew it. Knowing babies learn by mimicry, he demonstrated the object with a few flicks of his wrist.

"See, baby! Here's something *useful*."

A scalpel.

Adrian Ludens is a program director and afternoon host for a rock radio station, and the public address announcer for a professional minor league hockey team. He lives in the Black Hills of South Dakota with his family. He enjoys reading and writing dark fiction, listening to music, and exploring abandoned buildings and remote locations. Adrian's fiction has been published in several dozen anthologies, including *Insidious Assassins* and *Zippered Flesh 3* (both from Smart Rhino Publications) and most recently in *Violent Vixens* (Dark Peninsula Press) and *Under Twin Suns* (Hippocampus). Find him online at @AdrianLudensAuthor (Facebook), @AdrianLudens (Twitter), and a podcast at homesliceaudio.com/gunners-graveyard/.

LIZARDS AND OTHER VARMINTS

BY SHARI HELD

Monday

Lizard swiveled to stare Okey Lawson straight in the eyes. "You want me to *what?*"

Okey backed away and lowered his eyes. Maybe he'd been too hasty in assuming that Lizard, a down-on-his-luck loner, wouldn't have any scruples about being a gun for hire. "I, uh, want you to take out someone for me. It's a chance to dust off your sniper skills." He paused. Lizard didn't say a thing. Well, hell's bells. He'd stuck his toe in the water. Might as well plunge ahead.

"Won't be hard," Okey said, looking up at Lizard expectantly. "I got it all planned out. The guy visits Ruby Jo every Tuesday, Thursday, and Saturday afternoon at 2 p.m. Like clockwork. She runs the one-woman house of pleasure five miles or so from here. You been there?"

Lizard shook his head. "Go on. I'm listenin'."

"It's a fair piece from town. Won't be anyone around. All you got to do is pop him in the head and hightail it out. You won't even have to dispose of the body. Not good for the entertainment business havin' a dead body in the front yard. Ruby Jo'll take care of that for us. See what I'm sayin'? Piece of cake."

Lizard was the first person Okey thought of when he'd decided Jago Topper had to go. As a former Marine and a crack shot, Lizard was perfect for the job. Best of all, he didn't mosey into town much, and no one knew they'd struck up a kind of friendship during the last couple of years.

But would he do it? What if he'd had a "come to Jesus" moment and didn't do killin' no more? Sweat glistened on Okey's brow. His stomach churned and gurgled so loud he was sure they could hear it clear into the next county.

Lizard rubbed his pointy chin, then pulled his fingers through his piss-poor imitation of a beard. "What's it worth to ya?" He stood up to spit a brown glob into a mountain laurel bush, then settled back down on a stump.

Okey let out his breath, put his thumbs through his belt loops, and rocked back on his heels. Lizard was askin' 'bout money. A good sign. "How 'bout five hundred dollars?" Okey had a thousand hidden in a coffee can in the hayloft. No sense givin' Lizard his entire honeypot if he didn't have to.

Lizard nodded. "Who and why?"

"Name's Jago Topper. He's been bonin' Wylodine. My wife." Okey stopped and looked at the horizon. He was tired of the guys at Junior's garage snickering and elbowing one another when he stopped by to patch a tire or catch up on the local gossip. Okey, along with everyone else in this godforsaken dump of a town in the Appalachians, knew Wylodine had been doin' the dirty with Jago for months now. It hurt Okey's pride to admit that. Even to someone he only saw a few times a year out in the wilderness.

Lizard stared straight at Okey again. "You sure you wanna do this? It's not exactly sumpin' you can undo."

It was Okey's turn to nod.

"Okay, then. Yep. I'll do it. Ain't no skin off my nose."

Okey beamed. "Okay, then. I'll make sure I'm at the garage during the times Jago's visitin' Ruby Jo. You make the hit then. Understand?"

"No problem."

Okey slapped his thigh and laughed out loud. Those same bastards who joked about him behind his back would be his alibi. He wondered who they'd be chewing the fat about next. It didn't matter. It wouldn't be him!

He pulled an envelope out of his back pocket and handed it to Lizard. "Here's half. You'll get the other half when the job's done." Okey reached into his Coleman cooler, pulled out a couple of long necks, and they sealed the deal with some Deadhead Imperial Red.

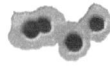

Tuesday

Lizard checked his watch. It was 1:45 p.m. Where the heck was that dang cathouse, anyway? Did Okey say to turn north or south at the old white pine? Lizard couldn't remember. That Imperial Red, and the few that followed, had gone to his head. Besides, keepin' track of time was something he usually had no call for. He assessed the situation. No sun in his eyes if he headed north. And the goin' was easier. He headed north. Half an hour out, he realized his mistake. He headed back. No way he was gonna make it in time. But what the heck. At least old Jago would have some fun before he bit the dust. And it wouldn't be Wylodine he was screwin,' so Okey shouldn't mind.

It was goin' on 3:15 when Lizard set up surveillance on a slope overlooking Ruby Jo's. He hoped Jago would come out soon. He was hungry. In the Marines, they'd nicknamed him Chow Hound because he always got hungrier than an old coon dog before pulling the trigger. He scrounged up half a package of stale Sour Cream Doritos and an old beef jerky stick from his gun bag. He'd barely pulled them out when he heard talkin'. Ruby Jo and a man with a big smile on his face appeared. She gave the lucky cuss a big smackeroo and patted his behind before going back inside.

Lizard looked him over. It was Jago, he reckoned. Tall. Dark hair. Beard. That fit what Okey had told him. Course, that fit about fifty percent of the men around the county, and the other fifty percent were women. This guy walked with a cane. Okey had said nothing about a cane. But, hey, maybe Jago had sprained or twisted something earlier today. He got him in his sight and pulled the trigger.

Yes! He still had it. There was nothin' quite like the feeling a direct hit right between the eyes gave you. Poor sap never even had time to wipe that smile off his face. Lizard packed up his rifle and started to retreat when Ruby Jo threw open the door and ran out, shotgun in hand.

"What the heck? Sam? Sam, honey? You dead?" She took aim with her shotgun and got three shots off. Then she started yellin'. "I know you're out there, you yellow-bellied varmint. Stay away from this place, you hear? You just cost me one of my best tippers!"

Lizard stared at the fiery redhead. God, she was gorgeous. Even if she had her nose in a snit. She was arousing thoughts in him he'd thought were long dead. He watched as she pulled off the dead guy's boots, grabbed one foot in each hand, and proceeded to drag him toward the woods. She was an itty-bitty thing—barely a hundred pounds, he reckoned. Should he offer to help? Naw. That would be a dead giveaway. He chuckled at his own joke. Dead giveaway.

Those boots looked awfully nice, though. He waited until she'd entered the tree line, far enough along that she wouldn't see him—at least not close enough to identify him—then he grabbed the boots and took off for his cabin. The plan was to meet Okey on Wednesday at their rendezvous spot.

Wednesday

Okey didn't even wait for Lizard to sit down before he laid into him. "You haven't got the brains God gave a grasshopper," Okey said. "You shot the wrong man. You killed Sam Nugent."

Lizard frowned. "Sam Nugent. Who's he?"

Okey rolled his eyes. "The poor sod you shot. By mistake."

"Weren't my fault he was in the right place at the wrong time," Lizard said, not quite meeting Okey's eyes.

Okey mentally counted backward from ten. "Sam Nugent was Ruby Jo's client *after* Jago. You were late. And don't you think I'd point out something like Jago walked with a cane?"

Lizard scratched his beard. "I wondered about that. How'd you hear 'bout the mix-up?"

"Funny about that. Imagine my surprise when the man you were supposed to have delivered to the pearly gates tells me Sam Nugent was shot and killed at Ruby Jo's. Jago realized he'd left his sunglasses at Ruby Jo's. When he went back for them, he saw her comin' out of the woods, madder than a mamma bear that finds someone messin' with her cubs. She told Jago. Jago told the sheriff. Now everyone knows." Okey's face felt like it was on fire. It matched the feeling in his oversized belly.

"Sorry about that, Okey. Won't happen again."

Okey didn't say a word. He was good at that. Tampin' down his feelings. Lettin' them gnaw at his gut and fester until he exploded like a dirty car battery. What could he say? He hated conflict. "I think you'd better lie low for now. I'll be in touch." Okey walked away.

"Hey, what about the rest of my money?" Lizard asked.

Okey pivoted faster than a man his size should be able to. "Thanks for remindin' me. I'll take back the advance I gave you seein' as how you shot the wrong guy."

"But I shot someone. That should be worth sumpin'!" Lizard was flappin' his skinny arms so hard it looked like he might be fixin' to fly away.

"You shot the wrong guy!"

"It's called collateral damage," Lizard said.

"Give me a hundred fifty. You can keep the rest."

Lizard grabbed the wad of cash from his back pocket, counted out a hundred fifty dollars, and threw it in the dirt around Okey's feet.

Okey glared at him, retrieved the cash, and started walking away. "Later," he said over his shoulder.

Lizard didn't like the way Okey had left things. The longer he waited to make the kill, the more likely Okey would call the job off. Dang it, Wylodine could be knockin' boots with someone else tomorrow. Double dang it. Maybe she'd have a change of heart and let Okey hit a home run. You never knew with women. He'd never get that money then. No siree, that wouldn't do. Lizard had big plans for that cash. He was gonna buy a fourteen-inch battery-powered LCD HD TV and a shitload of batteries. It would be winter in the mountains before you knew it. He didn't mind being alone. He needed solitude as much as he needed the air he breathed. But come February, when it was practically impossible to get about, the isolation weighed on him. That's when the dark thoughts started taking over his mind, like maybe life wasn't worth livin'. He needed that TV. He was going to move forward with the mission sooner rather than later. He'd bump off Jago. That would force Okey to pay.

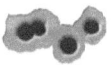

Thursday morning

Okey Lawson woke up that morning at the first cockcrow and stared at Wylodine lying asleep beside him. She was a beauty who hadn't yet hit her stride. She'd been only eighteen two years ago when he'd taken her off her daddy's hands. He didn't know what had possessed him to take a looker thirty years younger than him for his wife. Nothin' good could come of it. And nothin' had. He had to face the facts. There'd always be a Jago. Maybe he should get rid of Wylodine instead.

Okey wasn't a hasty man. He thought about it all afternoon. Back in his daddy's day, if your woman was getting some on the side, you could kill her and say she went to visit relatives. People might raise eyebrows when she never returned. But no one would say a word. After all, it wasn't any of their beeswax. But things were different today. He rolled his options around in his mind and gave each one a good think.

If he wanted to keep it all legal-like, he could divorce Wylodine. But to do that, he'd need to make a trip to the big city. It's not like those lawyer types made house calls. He doubted if the good-for-nothing transmission on his old Ford pickup would make the trip. Naw, he wasn't gonna go that route.

By feeding time, he'd decided against killin' Wylodine. That was, after all, a drastic measure. She cooked, cleaned, did the laundry, and fed the chickens. Who was going to take care of all that if she was six feet under? Besides, she played a mean hand of poker, which came in handy during snow-ins when the ground was covered with a foot of snow. And her smile, when she threw one his way, could melt icicles. She even gave him a little nookie when she was feelin' frisky. At least she used to. Before she took up with Jago.

Naw, he couldn't get rid of Wylodine. He'd reserve his venom for the object of her affection, the man she'd let bone her while he did without. Jago Topper.

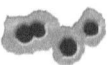

Thursday afternoon

This time, Lizard was prepared. He had a bacon and egg sandwich, a bag of Fritos, and a cola. And he was on time. Early, even. He'd pop Jago. Okey would be pleased and wouldn't yell at him anymore. And he'd get paid. He ate some more of his sandwich and settled down. Soon he was snoring in rhythm with the cicadas.

The sound of voices jerked him awake. Damn! How long had he been asleep? He hadn't brought a watch because he knew he was going to get to his target in plenty of time. He peeked around the enormous boulder he was hiding behind. The man was tall, had dark hair and a beard. And no cane. Must be Jago. He and Ruby Jo were laughin' like he'd just told her the best joke ever. He waited until Ruby Jo went inside. She was wearing a pink dress with big roses on it this time. Dang, she was pretty.

Good thing the men parked a ways down the road. Lizard had plenty of time to pick him off. Then he thought of Ruby Jo and how she'd have to drag his body back to the woods. And in that beautiful dress, too. He stood up, pulled the trigger, and ventilated Jago's head.

He'd barely sat down when Ruby Jo ran out, madder than a she-devil in heat. "I'm warning you, whoever you are. Stay away from my property and stop killin' my clients." She punctuated the last part with another shot of her shotgun. "I just got me a sweet business built up. And you're destroying it. If I ever find out who you are, I'll put a bullet through your head!" She actually stomped her foot.

Lizard got a kick out of that. He liked that little red-haired girl. Maybe he'd invite her over to watch his TV once he got it.

Friday morning

"You shit-for-brains dumbass," Okey said as soon as Lizard opened his door. "What were you thinkin'? I told you to lay low. Only an idiot would think that meant to go and knock off someone else."

Lizard handed him a beer and what remained of his bag of chips. "No need to yell. I got the job done, now, didn't I?"

"Got the job done? I'll tell you what you got done. You plugged a hole in Tadroe Jenkins, one of the nicest guys you'd ever want to share a beer with."

Okey's face was an unhealthy shade of red. "I'm not happy. Hell, the only person happy around here is the undertaker. And Jago. Who's still screwin' Wylodine."

"Man, that guy sure has a strong libido. Wonder what vitamins he takes. I've heard—"

Okey frowned. "Button it, Lizard. The last thang I want to think about is Jago's libido."

Lizard thought a change of topic might be in order. "Didn't Ruby Jo take care of the body?"

"No. This time, she called the sheriff. Said she thought someone was trying to ruin her business."

"What the heck are these doin' here?" Okay stomped over to the corner of the cabin where a pair of shiny black boots stood at attention, picked them up, and waved them in the air at Lizard. "Are these Sam Nugent's boots? Sheriff Buzzie Banks said Sam was missin' his boots. Anything you want to tell me?"

"Well, them're awfully nice boots. He didn't need them anymore. Seemed a shame to let 'em go to waste."

Okey grabbed the boots and headed toward the door. "I'll take these and put them where they won't be found. I don't want to see you again until you can tell me Jago Topper is history."

Friday evening

Lizard's head hurt from all the thinkin' he'd been doing and all the yellin' Okey had done at him. He figured he'd make a trip to town to the Triple B, the only bar for miles around. He had that cash from Okey's down payment. Might as well treat himself. He'd been doin' a lot of killin' lately. It took a lot out of a guy.

Lizard had only set foot in the Triple B once. And that was a few years ago. He stepped inside, got a drink from the bartender, and headed toward a back corner of the room. Jack Daniel's in hand, he settled back in his chair, which he'd placed against the wall, and surveyed the room. Well, dad-burned! Okey was sitting across the room, on the other side of the pool tables. He started to raise his glass to him, but Okey shook his head and looked the other way.

Right. They weren't supposed to know each other. Okey probably wouldn't be very good company, anyway. Lizard polished off his whiskey and held his glass up for a refill. Maybe he'd stop by the liquor store and buy a bottle to go. He shifted his weight from one leg to the other. The bar was getting busier. He'd be leavin' soon.

Lizard didn't see the stranger heading his way until the guy asked to share his table. Lizard automatically started to say no when he saw the Semper Fi pin on the dude's jacket. He nodded toward the empty chair. "Where'd you serve?"

"Iraq. Active service ended in 2009." The stranger sat down and stretched his long legs. "Name's Scott. How about you?"

Lizard nodded. "Camp Baharia. Got out in oh-five. Name's Lizard."

When the waitress delivered Lizard's Jack Daniel's, he held it up. "Oorah!"

"So, you from here?" Scott asked, nursing his beer.

"Nope. Rural Indiana. I went back to help with the farm. Then the family had to sell. I stayed until my dad died. Then there was nuthin' keepin' me there." Lizard emptied his glass and motioned for another. "Got in my vehicle and kept drivin' 'til it broke down a ways from here. Decided to stay."

Scott—Lizard didn't know or care if that was his first or last name—nodded. "I hear you. What did you do over there?"

"Sniper." Lizard grabbed his third Jack Daniel's from the waitress. He was feeling really social. Double dang it, he was even smilin'. He could tell because his facial muscles were complaining.

"Same here. These folks know what you did?"

"Don't know these folks much. That's the way I like it."

Scott held his bottle to the light and took a swig. "You get by okay?"

Lizard nodded. The guy sure was nosy, but it wasn't every day he ran into a former Marine. "Extended my tour to pick up an extra thou' a month and stashed it away. Don't need much."

Scott stared at the whiskey in Lizard's glass. "Well, whatever works for you. I'm headed to Texas to work on an oil rig. I figure a few years of saving my money and I'll be able to retire in style."

Lizard was just drunk enough to take offense at Scott's implied insult. Well, he'd show him a thing or two. Wipe that smug, better-than-you look off his face. Dang, he wished he had a cigarette. Maybe he'd pick up a carton at the liquor store.

"Okay," Lizard said, smacking his empty glass on the table. "You caught me out. I've got a good-payin' gig. Soon I'll be able to ditch this place and live in style, too. And my gig don't involve no manual labor. Yessiree. People around here call me The Exterminator. Man's got a cheatin' wife. One squeeze of a trigger and problem gone. A guy steals a cow. He'd better enjoy it 'cause that's the last dang hamburger he's ever gonna eat."

Lizard noticed Okey glaring at him. Hard. What was his problem? Couldn't a man have a whiskey in the local bar and shoot the shit with a fellow former Marine without Okey's eyes boring a hole into them as big as a pileated woodpecker diggin' for carpenter ants? Out of the corner of his eye, he caught Scott registerin' Okey's interest. Lizard was about to flag down the waitress for another whiskey when Scott suggested they hit the liquor store and finish the evening at Lizard's place.

"A-OK by me," Lizard said as he pulled some cash from his pocket and slapped a couple of bills down on the table.

As Lizard slid into the passenger seat, Okey came out. He climbed into his old Ford pickup and drove by them, glaring at them all the while.

"That guy got a grudge against you or something?" Scott asked.

Lizard shook his head. "It's nothin'," he said as he struggled to fasten his seatbelt. "He's just an ornery old cuss."

"I'm surprised no one's asked you to do him in."

Lizard got a chuckle out of that.

Saturday

Lizard woke up the following morning with a headache the size of nearby Clingmans Dome. He groaned and rolled over, pulling the blanket back over his head to block the sunlight. The next time he woke up, the sun was overhead. It was goin' on 1:30.

"Holy shit! I missed the entire morning." *And, son of a gun, it's too late to whack Jago today.*

"You didn't miss a thing," Scott said.

Lizard about jumped out of his skin. "You still here?"

Scott looked around. "Looks like." He handed Lizard a cup of coffee, then sat down at Lizard's makeshift table—a door over two sawhorses.

With every gulp of coffee, Lizard's memory returned. He remembered telling Scott about the hit and how he'd messed up—not once, but twice. He winced when he realized he'd probably told Scott how badly he needed that money for a TV. God, how pathetic. If his old gunnery sergeant could hear him now, he'd never live down the shame.

"Guess you know I screwed up," Lizard said. "One little hit and I couldn't finish the job."

"Don't worry. I've got your back. I took care of everything for you."

"What?"

"I killed Jago. It was clear you weren't going to be up for the job after all you drank, so I took your rifle, drove into town, and parked close to the garage. I figured he'd show up eventually. I asked some young kid which vehicle was Jago's. No one pays attention to kids. He was glad to point it out. Then I waited until Jago got in and drove off. He stopped to take a piss at the side of the road a few miles out of town, and I plugged him." He smiled. "Now, let's go get your money."

Something tickled the back of Lizard's brain. Not in a good way. Scott hadn't killed Jago in the right place, but that shouldn't be a problem. Then what was botherin' him? Oh, now he remembered.

"What time did you do the job?" Lizard asked.

"About eleven hundred hours, give or take a half-hour. Why?"

"Because I was supposed to knock him off at fourteen hundred hours. So Okey would have an alibi."

Both men looked at each other for a few seconds.

"That could be a problem," Scott said.

"Better go see Okey and get paid now," Lizard said. "Let's go."

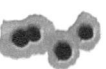

Sheriff Buzzie Banks plunked the red bubble on top of his vehicle and got ready to head out. He didn't need the siren, he just liked to use it occasionally. Make sure it still worked. He'd been the sheriff going on sixteen years now. He hadn't seen this much carnage since the Feds cleaned out the Cassidy brothers'

dope-growing operation. Three people dead in five days. First Sam Nugent, then Tadroe Jenkins, and now Jago Topper. Topper had been found a couple of hours ago. He shook his head, looked around to see no one was watching, and undid his belt a notch. It was a long stretch to Okey Lawson's farm.

He had a hot tip that needed investigating. An hour later, he pulled into Okey's place. Looked like Okey had company. He'd seen the one guy before. Former military. The other guy he couldn't place. Must be a friend of … what was that guy's name? Chameleon? Nah. Lizard. That was it. He got out and stretched his legs.

He nodded at Okey, introduced himself to the other two men.

Wylodine came out with a tray of glasses and a pitcher of water and offered some to everyone. She then sat in the swing, her knitting in her lap, and smiled at the men. To the sheriff's way of thinking, her eyes landed on Scott a little more than was wont. Probably staking out her next partner. They would make a pretty pair. What had Okey been thinking when he married a woman young enough to be his daughter? He didn't see how Okey put up with it. Maybe he hadn't.

"Sheriff, what can I do for you?" Okey asked.

"Got a tip on the killin's we seem to be momentarily infested with. Came out to see if there's any truth to it."

"Sorry, but I don't know anything other than what the guys at Junior's are speculatin'," Okey said. "I'm sure you've heard all the mud-slingin'."

"Hm," the sheriff said. "How 'bout you, Lizard? You heard anything?"

Lizard gulped. "Me? Naw. Haven't heard much about nothin'. Keep my nose clean. Mind my own business—" Scott had a coughing spell and Lizard shut up.

"I arrived only a couple days ago," Scott said. "Been staying with Lizard all that time."

"So, sheriff," Okey said. "You said somethin' about a tip?"

"Yep. Got an anonymous phone message. Said to check out your truck. That I might find something interesting." He nodded toward Okey's mud-splattered pickup. "Mind if I check what's under that tarp?"

"What?" Okey's stomach rumbled. He glanced at Lizard. "Go ahead, there's nothin' there 'ceptin' some tools."

The sheriff walked over to the Ford and drew back the tarp. First, he pulled out a Remington 700 rifle, which he propped up on the side of the truck. He dived in again. This time he held up a pair of practically new boots.

"Okey Lawson, I'm arresting you for the murders of Sam Nugent, Tadroe Jenkins, and Jago Topper. Put your hands out so I can cuff you. Let's make this as easy as possible."

Okey stood open-mouthed and dead still as Lot's wife after she looked back at the burning city of Sodom.

"But, sheriff," Okey finally sputtered. "I didn't kill anyone. I'm innocent."

Sheriff Banks put him in the car and slammed the door. "Time will tell," he said. "Let's get you back to town." He tipped his hat. "Gents, ma'am. Wylodine, you can see Okey tomorrow." They left in a plume of dust, red bubble blaring.

Lizard looked up at Scott. "Well, don't that take all. How'd my rifle get in Okey's truck? And those boots?"

"The rifle would be me," Scott said. "I saw how Okey was glaring at you in the bar the other night. Despite what you said, I reckoned there was bad blood between you. So, after I shot Jago for you, I drove back to town, saw Okey's truck, and dumped the rifle under his tarp. I didn't know he was your client."

Wylodine joined them, smiling up at Scott before responding to Lizard. "You can thank me for the boots," she said. "I saw Okey put something in the barn the other day. When he left for town, I checked it out. Okey wears a size thirteen. These were elevens. I'd heard the gossip. It took little brains to guess whose boots they were. I figured a little tip to the sheriff was in order. Now, can you tell me what's going on?"

"Okey hired me to get rid of Jago," Lizard said. "Permanently. He knew you were …"

"Sleepin' with him," Wylodine said.

"Er, yes," Lizard said. "There were a few, um, mix-ups." Then the implication of Okey's arrest sunk in. "Dang! Okey ain't paid me yet. There goes that TV."

"How much was he going to give you?" Wylodine asked.

"Five hundred bucks," Lizard said. "But he already gave me a hundred."

"I think I can honor that," Wylodine said. "Follow me." She led them to the barn. "In the loft, you'll find an old rusty coffee can," she said to Scott. "Bring it to me."

"Yes, ma'am," Scott said.

He handed the can to Wylodine when he returned. She pulled out a wad of cash, counted out four hundred, and presented it to Lizard. Then she gave Scott two hundred. "I figure you guys did me a good turn. Okey's history. Soon, I'll be free."

She smiled at Scott and ran her hand down the front of his shirt, stopping a few inches south of his belt buckle. "So, what would it take to convince you to stick around these parts for a while, stranger?"

Shari Held is an Indianapolis-based freelance journalist, editor, and author. Her short stories have been published in *Hoosier Noir 3* magazine and many anthologies, including *The Fine Art of Murder*, *Homicide for the Holidays*, *Circle City Crime*, *Murder 20/20*, for which she also served as co-editor, and *The Big Fang* (coming November 2021). When not writing, she cares for feral cats and other wildlife, knits, and thinks up imaginative ways for her characters to get into all manner of trouble!

KILLER FASHION

BY MADDI DAVIDSON

Lying in tall grass while keeping an eye on my target, I itched all over. My skinny camouflage leggings and olive-green tank top perhaps weren't the best outfit for this stakeout, but I was fashionable. I carried a black sling bag with room for binoculars, and in my one concession to practicality, passed on wearing leather flats in favor of a pair of tropical-design Vans slip-ons. I firmly believe that one can be both a killer and utterly stylish.

My assigned victim was hanging out in the pasture, several hundred yards away. Sweet-faced with long lashes and big brown eyes, he was exceedingly well hung and every inch a stud. George was a prize-winning bull owned by a rival to the farmer, Sam Farley, who hired me. Not that Sam and I had traded names, communicating through burner phones and cryptic aliases, but who else other than Sam would be so anxious to keep George out of the Wisconsin State Fair? Gorgeous George had beaten Sam's steer Alfred in every competition over the past two years. I could understand Sam's frustration, but I must say, killing a rival bull lent new meaning to the phrase, "having a beef with someone."

How to dispatch George posed a quandary. While I didn't have a problem hunting and killing deer where there was skill involved, I wasn't keen on shooting farm animals. Nonetheless, I desperately needed the work, and assassin for hire was proving to be the only job, so far, that I could do capably.

Five generations of blond-haired, blue-eyed Thorsens had grown up on the Wisconsin dairy farm, and mine was probably the last. My older siblings—Danny, Sean, and Ben—gave farming a universal thumbs (or hooves) down. Cows held no interest for them, and the feeling was mutual as all three had been mooed at, stepped on, kicked, or otherwise been made to feel most unwelcome by bovine bullies. Considering the tons of dung they had to shovel, I can understand why they passed on becoming yet another generation of cow consorts. As for me, well, I'm lactose intolerant.

I had attended a state college, majoring in feminist theory. Consequently, I found employment difficult, holding a series of low-paying jobs that led nowhere and taught me nothing. Okay, I learned no waitress should expect a tip after tripping over a fluff dog (escaped from a patron's purse) and falling into a table and knocking over an open one-hundred-forty-dollar bottle of Cabernet into the lap of a customer.

My brothers had each majored in business and been fired from several jobs. Yet, they didn't lack for the trappings of success. Glam condos in Chicago, expensive cars, and spending money galore. I was curious how they could afford such lavish lifestyles while I eked out a living.

One evening while sitting in my studio apartment in Madison and drinking his way through a six-pack of Bud, brother Ben listened sympathetically to my tales of workplace woe. The waitressing fiasco had been far from my only screwup. On his fourth beer, Ben recounted his many job failures. By the fifth beer, he confessed he'd found his true calling working with his brothers in the new family business—hitmen for hire. Ben suggested I join them.

He persuaded Danny and Sean that a young, attractive, well-dressed woman would be an asset on certain assignments. It helped that I was a crack shot, having accompanied my brothers on deer hunting trips to the UP—that's the Upper Peninsula of Michigan for you non-Midwesterners. I'd once bagged an eight-pointer. A rack, as they say, definitely bigger than my brothers'.

I shifted my position for the umpteenth time while contemplating what to do about George. Under the hunting ethos that was drilled into me from my very first kill, you didn't shoot an animal unless you were going to use every part—skin, flesh, and organs. I wasn't planning on exercising my butchering skills on George as I didn't want to get blood on my camouflage leggings and Vans. Obviously, garroting was a nonstarter, and I figured it would take a ton of poison to do him in. Blowing up the animal seemed the best alternative. Technically, it wasn't shooting, and what was left of the bull would be charred or loaded with foreign matter and probably wouldn't be worth eating. Maybe the local turkey vultures would disagree. In short, I wouldn't be violating the hunting ethos.

That evening, I snuck onto the farm and set a small explosive device on George's pen. Fortunately, black is an excellent color for secret ops and always in vogue. My ebony, slim-fit, tiered, ruffled pants complemented by a black, long-sleeve crop-top were perfect for planting the bomb and enjoying a drink later at a bar. I was working my way through an Alexander Valley Cab and fending off a pimple-faced college student when the bomb exploded.

In hindsight, the fertilizer I used was probably short on aluminum sulfite since only the fence blew up. However, a large splinter pierced George's forehead, requiring a vet visit and stitches. George's injuries kept him from the state fair. With my fee, I splurged on my first pair of Christian Louboutin pumps, despite the very few places I could wear them in Wisconsin.

Despite the assignment not going quite as planned, my brothers were happy, especially since the jobs I'd done with them as part of my training program had been somewhat less successful.

My first task had been to drive the getaway car for my oldest brother, Danny. We made it two miles down the road before running out of gas. It wasn't my fault that my car's gas gauge was broken, and I didn't have enough money to fix it. As I explained to Danny when he was screaming at me for being a dumb blonde, my lack of financial resources is why I took the job in the first place! Fortunately, we were in Lafayette, Indiana, and close to the Amtrak station. Danny gave me money for gas before hopping on the train to return to Chicago, leaving me to return on my own with the car. I'd emptied the gallon gas container and was about to return it to the service station when Danny called and reminded me to pull the purloined license plates off the vehicle. I never told him that a police car cruised by seconds after the plates had disappeared into the trunk. Phew!

The debacle in Milwaukee was definitely not my fault. Sean, my middle brother, was being paid to blow up a house as a warning to someone. When we arrived at the impressive brick edifice late one night, we noticed lights on and people moving in the home. Sean swore.

"The house was supposed to be empty. We're not being paid enough to kill anyone. We'll have to make do with destroying the garage."

He pulled some explosives out of his knapsack and began placing the charges around the structure. "Here," Sean said, handing me the nearly full bag. "I don't need the rest of this. Take care of it."

So I did. Since it wasn't needed, I dropped it in a trash container. We retreated a short distance behind a grove of small trees, and Sean set off the explosives. The garage blew up, taking out the trash can, which triggered a second, much larger blast. Bricks, stones, metal fragments, and dirt flew in all directions. In the mad scramble to safety, my Versace jacket (purchased used, of course) was torn and I broke several fingernails. I must have strained a few muscles, as I could barely move the next day. Since the family business—inexplicably, I thought—didn't offer workers' comp, I sent Sean the bill for my spa weekend where I had a mani-pedi and a heavenly Shiatsu massage. Wine therapy, too. A lot of wine therapy.

My brothers, less than pleased with my contributions so far, held a family meeting to reassess my employment suitability. I pointed out neither of my assignments had made use of my best assets—marksmanship and design sense. Ben supported me and effectively argued I should have another chance. Consequently, when a vindictive ex-wife contacted us to shoot her former hubby's jewels, my brothers, none of whom were eager to do the deed, gave me the assignment. Ben was volunteered to drive the getaway car.

Our client provided a visitor pass to the tony country club where she and her ex-husband still maintained a family membership. She told us her husband booked a 2:40 p.m. tee time each Wednesday. The club's pool area overlooked the golf course.

Fortunately, clients pay in advance, so I had money to spend on a new outfit and gun. I purchased a major cutout, one-piece, Louisa Ballou knock-off with an ultra-sexy silhouette. For a weapon, I chose the lightweight Walther P22. Yes, I know ".22 pistol" and "accuracy" are rarely found in the same sentence. However, the Walther was easy to conceal in my pre-owned Prada basket bag, whereas a rifle and scope would be a tad conspicuous. Not that anybody noticed, but my black and white suit went smashingly well with the coal-black Walther.

Right on schedule, the target appeared on the twelfth fairway. He was considerate enough to slice his ball, bringing him closer to my position. I've shot a white-tail deer right between the eyes at a hundred yards with a pistol, so how hard could it be to shoot a guy in the whatevers at a mere sixty-five yards? I slipped over to a hedge, which provided cover from both the pool area and my victim. It was just bad luck that when I sighted him in and pulled the trigger, the man dropped his Bulgari sunglasses. (I learned later they cost two thousand a pair.) Like a robin with a worm in its sights, he bent over so quickly that I missed the shot, hitting him in the left … ah … cheek. He fell to the ground clutching his rear end. My second shot found his jewels, despite his rolling around and screaming. Amidst the yelling and general hullabaloo, I slipped out of the pool area and found Ben in the parking lot. Nobody gave me a second look except to admire my figure. Keep the neckline low and your tatas high and no one ever remembers your face.

Having proved with George that I could work solo, my brothers were much relieved. They'd been having issues allocating assignments in places like Bemidji, Minnesota, and Spearfish, South Dakota. Everyone preferred exotic locales, like Texas. Okay, Texas might not sound glamorous to some, but it was heaven to those of us who endure gray, soul-squeezing frigidness for eight months of the year. My brothers now felt I was the perfect one to send on jobs in the boondocks, er, America's heartland. I wasn't thrilled about it, but didn't raise a fuss as the pay was lucrative and I soon could afford a larger apartment and a more extensive wardrobe of fashionable attire.

No official numbers exist for those employed in the killer-for-hire business—the job is not listed in the Standard Occupational Classification System used by the U.S. Census. However, the professional killer profession appeared to be a male-dominated field heavily reliant on ex-military, gang members, and, as with my brothers, dropouts from FFA (Future Farmers of America). For the man who wants to be both well-dressed and an assassin, an underarm holster with a generous-cut blazer looks good and is effective. Also, you can strap a small gun to the ankle, hidden under pant legs.

Neither of these fashions worked for women. Wearing an underarm holster meant walking with shoulders hitched up and arms held out to the side, resulting in a simian-like gait. Bringing the holster further forward pushed one boob up and created a distinctly lopsided look where tight silhouette silk blouses just would not drape properly. Seriously, who wants that? Fashion also required ankles to be kept bare, except for a discreet ankle bracelet or tattoo. Tattoos in my line of work would be dead giveaways, so to speak, so I avoided them like baggy, old-lady capris. Fortunately for me, the killing business is sporadic, and I had oodles of time not only to practice lethal skills but to pursue my love of fashion design. In this instance, killer clothing.

I soon abandoned my brief foray into designing a bra that would hold a weapon. Let's face it, guns are too angular. The development of an interchangeable outfit proved successful. I carried out a hit in St. Paul, Minnesota, wearing a short navy-blue dress, matching loosely constructed jacket with deep side pockets for my Glock and extra clip, and kitten-heel pumps so I looked taller but could still run fast. I appeared to the world as a young woman on her way to a business appointment, which I was—when it comes to offing people, I am *all* business.

I took out my target, then ducked behind a building. When I emerged a few moments later, the businesswoman was gone, replaced by a stylish girl out for fun. I tucked my dress into my jeans, giving a blouson look. The jacket had reversed into gray tweed, and I was wearing street shoes with my hair pulled into a top bun. I hid the gun and pumps in the depths of my bag as I dropped into an Italian restaurant and had a nice dinner with an exquisite Pinot Grigio before heading home.

Not all my ideas worked as well. I'd designed a cute silver necklace with a dolphin pendant to garrote a seventy-five-year-old woman in International Falls, Minnesota. She broke right through the skimpy chain, and her screams left me deaf for days. I had suspected the chain was too weak, but was unwilling to use a less stylish, thicker chain or, heaven forbid, a gemstone/rock necklace. That look was so 1980s.

Fingernails were a challenge. Long ones got in the way when I tried to get off a quick shot, and I was forever breaking them. It was a major problem, especially because I have incriminating tastes in nail polish designs. Since short nails are not congruent with a chic look, I turned to press-on nails, not for use during the kill, but afterward. I could glue on a complete set in five minutes while in the back of a taxi. Or, if I were driving my own car, ten minutes, tops. Naturally, I bought sets in multiple colors and lengths to match my outfits.

My brothers were fully booked up when a request came in to knock off a high-profile businesswoman in New York City. I accepted the assignment with mixed feelings. I'd be able to travel to a place I'd always wanted to see, but I was not happy that I'd be killing Lauren Kane. A British designer and founder of the Contessa clothing line, Lauren was one of my idols. Actors, singers, and supermodels endorsed her designs, and she was a regular judge on a television fashion show. I had picked up an imported Contessa crossbody for a song at the Salvation Army store. Made of beautiful vitello leather, it was the perfect size to hold money, a phone, keys, and a Glock. I could only imagine our client was a frustrated contestant or rival designer jealous of Lauren's success.

Some assassins like to plan everything down to the last brass casing. This meant days or weeks of watching the target and scoping the terrain. My brothers felt the best practice was to get in and out, spending at most one night in the job's vicinity. For the New York assignment, I ignored their advice and flew in a day early to do some shopping. For my wardrobe, I pulled out all the stops. Killer heels, leather pants, and a sleeveless, cream-colored silk blouse. And that was just for the plane. Visiting high-end retail shops required another outfit to give me a subdued wealth vibe. Since I couldn't fly with a weapon, Ben advised me where to pick up a gun once I was in the city, which required yet another change of clothes—I thought I'd go for the scared homemaker look. For the kill, I created a new, trendy assassin ensemble.

New York City! I'll always remember that trip with a warm glow … and a tinge of sadness. On my free day, I spent eight exhilarating hours cruising high-end stores.

The following day didn't go so well.

Lauren was due early afternoon at a filming of the television show "Don't U Dare Wear That," also known as "Dud Wear." I positioned myself near a bus stop down the street from the back entrance to the studio. My heart was fluttering as I smoothed out the front tie of my mustard-colored, palazzo high-waisted pants.

A white limo drew up and Lauren Kane emerged. Long dark hair, flawless skin, three-inch heels, and a clinging scarlet dress that shimmered—she was perfection personified. I just couldn't do the deed. Instead, I rushed toward her, slipped by her bodyguards, grabbed her elbow, and introduced myself as the new junior producer for Dud Wear. As we slipped inside, I whispered to her that I had a gun and if she wanted to live, she was to follow my moves.

"Right this way, Ms. Kane," I said, turning into the first women's restroom I saw. "Please don't let anyone come in," I told her guards as I closed the door. We were alone.

"What's this all about?" Lauren said, shaking.

"They hired me to kill you."

She drew a breath as if to scream, but I covered her mouth, sorry to smear her blood-red lipstick.

"I have an alternative suggestion. Nod your head if you agree to hear me out."

She complied. I removed my hand, adding quickly, "I love your work."

"I need to leave."

"I'm not done. I also design clothes and would like to share my ideas."

Eye roll. "As if I haven't heard that line before."

"I create assassin-wear for women."

She appeared interested, so I pressed on.

"A key feature of my designs is that the outfits transition seamlessly from work to pleasure." I explained the importance of drawing attention away from the face to the bust or butt, using my lacy white bodysuit as an example.

"You see how it reveals just enough of my black push-up bra to encourage the observer to keep his gaze on my chest."

Lauren's excitement grew when I showed her the specially designed pockets in my palazzo pants that allowed me to reach through to the Glock strapped to my thigh. She fingered the pants fabric and examined the seams.

"There is a real market for this if you branch out to include self-defense wear," she said. "I speak from experience."

At my raised eyebrows, she continued. "I've recently received several death threats. When I contacted the authorities, they suggested a bulletproof vest. Really! I refused, of course. No woman looks good in one of those. Instead, I turned to a techie friend who could make a tiny panic alarm for me."

Lauren held out her gold chain necklace with an onyx stone pendant. The onyx was secured in a gold oval, on the back of which she showed me a small, raised button.

"It calls my bodyguards," she said as she pressed it.

The bathroom door flew open and two burly men in black, ill-fitting suits charged into the room. I was down on the cold tile floor before I knew it.

It was Lauren's word against mine that I was hired to kill her. Since the authorities could find no proof that I'd done anything except carry an unregistered weapon and threaten its use to get Lauren alone, they sentenced me to several years in a minimum-security prison.

My brothers, disappointed in my failure, fired me. On top of that, that backstabbing weasel Lauren stole my palazzo pants design, using it as part of her new line of defense-wear clothing for women. I'm currently designing a line of prison-inspired clothing— fashionable jumpsuits with deep pockets for files and lock picks, plus matching accessories such as earrings in the shape of handcuffs. I just know it's going to sell, and I'll make a killing in the fashion world.

Maddi Davidson is the pen name for two sisters living on opposite sides of the country: Mary Ann Davidson in Idaho and Diane Davidson in Virginia. Together they have published several novels, a nonfiction book, and many short stories. Their tales range from the murder of a deranged scientist resurrecting the dodo to a spurned wife hacking the pacemaker of an ex-husband who richly deserved it.

ANGLING

BY BEN GAMBLIN

Marsden Green, built in 1893. One of Seattle's first urban parks. Fifty-two acres, including miles of walking trails, a conservatory, and a playground for the kids. I've been meeting clients here since I rebranded. My preferred spot is this metal bench next to the bocce court. It's tucked off the main path, ensuring adequate privacy, and the nearby shade trees are a blessing in the summer.

Mrs. Franzel arrives at the park around 1:30 on Monday afternoon. I watch from the bench as she parks her town car and proceeds down the trail. Shoulders hunched, hands stuffed in pockets, eyes darting. I scooch over when she draws close and give a friendly wave. She waves back, fingers trembling, and sits beside me.

"Good afternoon, Mrs. Franzel."

"Hello," she squeaks.

"Glad you could make it."

"Mm-hmm."

"Mind if I have a look in your purse?"

"Excuse me?"

"Formality."

"I ... see."

She hands it over. As I'm rifling through the compartments, I nudge her arm and nod at the court.

"Ever play bocce before?" I ask.

She casts me a sideways look. Sure, it's an offhand question, but I've found small talk often calms the client's nerves. Besides, she's half an hour late. A little banter won't kill her.

"I ... can't say I have."

"You should try it sometime. A real hoot."

Satisfied she's not packing any recording devices or other contraband, I give back the purse. She glances around nervously. We're all alone, no one within listening distance, but that doesn't ease the tension in her shoulders.

"Sorry," she mutters, "I'm not sure how this works."

"Don't be sorry, Mrs. Franzel. I—"

"Joan. Call me Joan, if you like."

"I'd rather not. As I was saying, I understand you know Richie."

"We went to high school together." She allows a gentle smile. "Even dated for a short time."

"No kidding? That's wild."

"Years ago, of course."

"Richie also says you'd like to obtain my services."

She nods slowly.

"Did he explain what I do?"

"In a manner of—"

"What did he say?"

"He said you, um … that you …"

"That I shoot people?"

She nods again.

"Good, glad we're on the same page. Who would you like me to shoot?"

"Grayson. My husband." She sighs. Hardest part's over. "He's been unbearable. He comes home late every night, and—"

"Really, ma'am, I'd rather not know your reasons. Personal preference."

"Oh."

"Did Richie tell you my rate?"

"He said to discuss payment with you."

I remove the pen and notepad from my messenger bag and jot down the amount—my standard fee, minus ten percent. Her eyes swell at the figure.

"Richie didn't say it would be *that* much."

"This is actually a discount, seeing as you two are old friends. Will payment be an issue?"

"No, we have the money, but … frankly, I could pay less to have Grayson killed."

"That depends on whom you hire. As for my fee, please understand what I do involves a high level of skill. Not to besmirch my colleagues, but any bum can point a gun at someone and fire a fatal shot. I specialize in *nonlethal* wounds to the lower abdomen. Missing every vital organ on a stationary target requires impeccable marksmanship, let alone a moving one."

She looks away, folding both hands in her lap to keep them from fidgeting. Most clients have second thoughts right about now. The fee, the anatomical descriptions. It's a lot.

"Do I have your guarantee this will work?" she asks. They always do.

"I'm a specialist, ma'am, not a miracle worker. My job is finished when the bullet passes through your husband's body—"

"Oh, Jesus."

"—and with all the variables at stake, it would be downright irresponsible to guarantee any sort of outcome. That said, I've never had a dissatisfied customer."

"Really?"

"Let me put it another way. I've never received a complaint."

I have a strict no-contact policy with clients once assignments are finished, so what I've just said is technically true.

"All right," she says. "Now what?"

"What does Grayson do for a living?"

"He works in commercial real estate. He's an … executive."

Ooh, an *executive*. I'll be sure to use my fancy bullets.

"Let's meet again one week from today," I say, tearing a blank sheet from the pad. "Take this with you. Write down your home address, along with Grayson's office, places he likes to go for lunch, his gym, and so on. I'll also need a recent photo and his car's make, model, and plate number. Please write legibly."

"Couldn't I give you this information now? I have a photo in my purse and—"

"Consider this a mandatory waiting period. If you decide to follow through, we'll meet here in one week to discuss the next steps. Bring that slip of paper, along with half the fee—twenties only. If you change your mind, stay home and forget we had this conversation. No hard feelings, no further contact. Agreed?"

She nods, placing the paper in her purse.

"Is there anything else?" she asks.

"Yeah, one more thing." I lean over, putting us at eye level. "Don't show up late again."

"Of … course. Sorry, I was—"

"See you next Monday. One o'clock."

Mrs. Franzel springs to her feet and speed-walks down the trail without so much as a glance over her shoulder. Moments later, her town car screeches out of the parking lot. Maybe that last bit was harsh, but I have a brand to maintain.

Lou Corbette changed my life. He'll change yours, too, if you let him.

Richie turned me on to Lou—aka the Wizard of Wichita—about two years ago. Up to that point, I had eluded the buzzword bullshit that defines many of today's professions and was leery of Richie's assertions about Mr. Corbette's sage marketing wisdom. To appease him, I agreed to one of Lou's webinars. *Recognition to Recall: Elevating Your Brand to the Next Tier.* Barf, right?

Wrong. From slide 1, I was hooked. Lou's delivery was so engaging and refreshingly rudimentary. No condescension or meaningless jargon, and none of that "sell the product you'd want to buy" crap. Tangible, data-driven methods parsed into digestible concepts that even laymen like me could grasp. Don't meet client expectations—exceed them. Treat every contact as a potential networking asset. Focus on the strengths of your competitors, rather than weaknesses or vulnerabilities. Follow the market like a hawk on a power line (the guy has a knack for similes).

The biggest takeaway came near the end of the course. "Find your angle," Lou said, addressing the camera. Determine how your product specifically and uniquely addresses consumer demands. Integrate these attributes into your image. Stay ahead of the market by redefining the market. "It isn't enough," he concluded, "to be a brand consumers recognize by name. You should be the first brand that comes to mind whenever a consumer needs the type of product you're sellin'. The right angle can bridge that gap quickly and effectively."

I received a cheesy digital certificate for finishing the course. But, more important, I gained a fresh perspective about my job. I'd been contract killing in the Seattle area for the better part of a decade. Steady work, but shooting chumps for money is a competitive field in this country—no shortage of chumps *or* bullets. If I found my angle, as Lou suggested, then I might distinguish myself from competitors. However, nailing down this angle initially proved difficult. Painless deaths only? Two-for-one discounts? Low-interest financing?

Then the fates dropped a breadcrumb in my lap. Maurice Bennett was his name and infidelity was his game, though the way he played it was more like a major league sport. Mistresses, casual squeezes, and one-night stickeroos up and down Puget Sound. Mrs. Bennett told me all about it, even after I asked her not to. The bitterness wafted off her like last night's tequila.

After reaching a threshold with Maurice's hound-dogging, Mrs. Bennett put out her feelers and got ahold of my private line. We convened to discuss the situation at the parking garage where I used to meet clients. She explained Maurice owned Klassy Klean, a chain of carwash and detailing centers scattered throughout lower King County. He'd spend his days driving between the various sites to check equipment and keep his teenage employees in line—maybe hit on a bosomy customer if he had time.

Mrs. Bennett gave me his weekly schedule and I was on my way. After a week of surveilling, I decided to complete my assignment at his Auburn location. It had the poorest exterior lighting and Maurice closed there alone on Tuesday evenings before heading home. Ambush him in the parking lot with a quick double-tap, steal his wallet to stage a mugging, and amscray. With some luck, no one would find him until Wednesday morning. What could go wrong? Funny you should ask.

I parked five blocks away and didn't hear a single passing car during my back-alley jog to the carwash. Maurice was alone when I arrived, as anticipated. His pickup was parked in front of the customer care center, so I crouched down on the passenger side and readied my nine-millimeter. He strolled outside a few minutes after nine, whistling as he locked the door. But before reaching the truck, he stopped short and squared his legs.

"Who's back there?" he shouted.

I glanced around in a panic. A small concave mirror was tucked under the eave—I'd missed it during my surveillance. The murky reflection revealed me as a shadowy figure kneeling next to the wheel well. I leaped to my feet and steadied the nine-millimeter over the truck's hood, only to find Maurice aiming the barrel of a Colt revolver between my eyes. I ducked before he could fire and bear-crawled to the tailgate. For all the details Mrs. Bennett provided, you'd think she would've mentioned his concealed carry.

"Gotcha now, motherfucker," Maurice snarled.

After a deep breath, I dove to the side. Maurice fired first and missed, striking a squeegee bin at the self-wash station. I had better aim. My nine-millimeter round plugged him between the gut and ribcage. He dropped to his knees, spilling his revolver onto the pavement. I could have finished the job right there. He was mumbling, leaking all sorts of fluid, his peacemaker well out of reach. But instead, I picked up my spent casing, swiped his wallet, and bolted down the alley. Sometimes, "screw it" is the best policy.

This is why you collect half upfront. You never know how things will shake out. I figured Maurice Bennett would be an easy assignment. Next thing I knew, I was in the middle of a sloppy carwash gunfight. To make matters worse, the prick survived. My slug had somehow missed all his vitals—so much for "better aim"—and he dialed 911 on his cell before losing consciousness. Maurice underwent three major surgeries and spent a couple weeks in the ICU, but ultimately walked away from the incident with little more than a nasty scar.

In the aftermath of my botched assignment, Mrs. Bennett didn't pay her outstanding balance. No surprise. I didn't deliver as promised. A few weeks later, she rang my private line again and requested another meeting. I agreed, against my better judgment and no-contact policy, though I brought my nine-millimeter to the parking garage in case she was planning something cute.

But Mrs. Bennett surprised me. First, she walked over and hugged me like we were old friends. Then she produced a small satchel containing the other half of my fee.

"I don't understand, ma'am."

"Paying what I owe is the least I can do."

"But your husband is still alive."

"And then some." She smiled, her teeth glowing against the cold concrete. "This entire ordeal has … changed Maurice. He stays home every night, buys me flowers, makes love like he used to. He even took me to Chantal's last Saturday. *Chantal's*. I can't tell you the last time we went out for dinner at a French restaurant."

"To be clear … you aren't angry?"

She giggled. "I haven't been this happy in a long time."

Fireworks exploded in my head. Electric guitar riffs squealed from ear to ear. I'd found my angle. Or rather, it had found me.

I spent the next week conducting market research. None of my local colleagues knew anyone who specialized in serious injuries intended to trigger personal catharses. A few of them even patted me on the back. I must admit, it was ingenious. From a legal standpoint, my assignments would be downgraded to attempted murders in the event I got caught, and landing clients would theoretically be easier if the stakes were less permanent. Theoretically. There was only one way to know for sure. The first few clients I approached with my nonlethal angle were a mixed bag. Some balked.

"No, you don't understand … I want her *dead*."

"*Nonlethal?* I need the insurance money."

"What are you, a fucking Quaker?"

I fine-tuned my elevator pitch, but soon realized it wasn't the delivery that needed retooling. It was my target demographic. At that point, Richie had been recruiting for a few years. He knew plenty of people in the area—the guy's a networking junkie—and he was the one who introduced me to Lou Corbette in the first place. When I enlisted a third-party middleman to handle client engagement, Richie was the ideal candidate. I bought him a beer and gave him my spiel.

"Not bad," he said. "Of course, you'll be committing to matrimonial work. Who else but a spouse would go to this much trouble to change someone?"

"The thought occurred to me."

"Identification is another issue. If they live, they could pick you out of a lineup."

"I'm no rookie."

"Tell that to Maurice Bennett."

"Fuck yourself." I nudged him. "You in?"

"Twenty percent."

"Ten."

"All right, fifteen it is." Richie clinked my bottle. "Was I right about Lou or what?"

Two years later, my brand is stronger than ever. Since the first few jobs proved successful, I've enjoyed steady word-of-mouth among clients without attracting any unwanted attention—compared to murders, my work is low priority for the cops. The transition has also helped me on a deeper level. Years of killing people had taken a toll on my mental health. Since the rebrand, I've felt ten pounds lighter around the shoulders. Food tastes better. Sunshine feels nice.

The results are the actual story, though. Some people change temporarily after catching a slug before reverting to their former selves, but most undergo profound, permanent alterations. One guy took up oil painting and landed a gallery show that paid off his mortgage. Another woman ran for city council on a gun control platform, bolstered by her recent injury—and won, much to her ladder-climbing husband's delight. That doesn't mean the changes are always welcome. Sometimes it's more of a monkey's paw scenario for the client. Take Jeff Keeley, one of my first nonlethal jobs. In the wake of his "senseless attack," he sold his carpet business and moved to St. Lucia, only he brought along his twenty-something girlfriend and not the wife of thirty-two years who'd hired me. Then there's Caroline Jayne. Her estranged husband thought she'd move back home after leaving the hospital, but instead, she phoned to tell him she'd met someone else—a female rehabilitation nurse. They got married last spring. It was in the paper.

That's what people like Mrs. Franzel struggle to understand. I have no control over how someone copes with their trauma, or what form their metamorphosis will take. I aim and squeeze. The rest is up to them. Bottom line, never make assurances you can't guarantee—your customers will never forgive you if you don't deliver. Lou Corbette taught me that, but what else is new?

Mrs. Franzel is ten minutes early for our second Monday afternoon meeting at Marsden Green. Her hands are steadier this time, her shoulders more relaxed. Even her eyes are a calmer shade of blue.

"Good afternoon," she says coolly, flattening her skirt as she settles onto the bench. "Thank you for meeting me again."

"Thank *you*. I trust this means you'd like to move forward?"

"Correct." She holds up her purse. "Do you need to—?"

"Nah, I trust you."

She fishes inside and removes a thick manila envelope, which I immediately slip into my messenger bag.

"Aren't you going to count it?"

"Do I need to?"

"No," she smiles. "I suppose not."

Next, she hands me the paper with a photo clipped to the edge. I glance at the image and skim the information. Every requested detail is there. Her penmanship is outstanding.

"What happens now?" she asks.

"Based on this information, I'll follow your husband for a few days. Get a feel for his routines, his habits. Then, when I'm ready, I'll perform the requested service." I tear another sheet from my notepad and scribble a few digits. "After the job is finished, please wire the remaining balance to this account within thirty days. Anonymous transfer. Burn the paper afterward."

"Of course. Then … that's it?"

"Correct. We'll have no contact once the transaction is complete."

"I understand." She tries to sneak in a deep breath, but her ballooning cheeks give her away. "You've done this many times, haven't you?"

"Yes, ma'am."

"Have you ever killed anyone? Accidentally, I mean, when you meant to wound them."

"No, I have a spotless record. Richie can tell you all—"

"Richie *did* tell me. He has nothing but nice things to say about you. It's just … I couldn't live with myself if anything happened, now that I've thought about it more. Does that make sense?"

I was wondering how long it would take her to break character. Still, she's sturdier than most.

"You have my word, ma'am. Grayson is in skilled, capable hands."

"I just want to help him."

"You *are* helping him. Think of me as a therapist treating your husband. Other therapists prescribe medication, I have different methods. And given the recent opioid epidemic, it's not like pills are any—"

"You don't have to sell me on this. My money is on your bag."

"Fair enough. So we're clear, I only collect full payment if he survives."

"Richie told me that, too. Cold comfort, but I appreciate the gesture." She holds out her hand. "I suppose I won't see you again. Please be careful with my husband."

"Of course." Her grip is tighter than expected. "So long, Mrs. Franzel."

She gets up and strolls back to her town car. Once she's out of sight, I take out her notes and read them more thoroughly. Grayson Kichener Franzel. Jesus, sounds like a vocal warm-up for theater kids. Drives a Beamer 7 Series. Works at the Stowicky Investments Center near Pike Place Market. Packs a sack lunch every day—hasn't trusted Seattle restaurants since a nasty bout of norovirus—but his digestive tract is robust enough for the Godiva Lounge off Third Avenue because he stops there for a drink *every night* after work.

I turn my attention to the photo. Grayson looks how I'd expected. Forty-something, vitamin-deficient, about twenty pounds overweight. Silver-tipped hair retreating at the corners. Bags under his eyes like pillowcases. Here he is on a sunny day, standing next to his wife and two other lovely women. The guy can barely muster a smirk.

I used to feel bad for my marks because I was sending them to the grave. Now I pity them for different reasons. The people I'm hired to shoot are, with rare exception, utterly miserable. They'd have to be to warrant this sort of intervention. Take Grayson here. When did he lose hope? Was it a single catalyst, or more of a cumulative shit-piling? How long has it been since this schmuck genuinely smiled for a camera?

That said, the saddest people make the easiest assignments. A lot of them don't run when they see the nine-millimeter. I'll even catch the occasional smile, like I'm doing them a favor. My first impression: Grayson Kichener Franzel will be a straightforward job. But for Maurice Bennett-related reasons, I don't like getting ahead of myself.

Before leaving the park, I call Richie's cell.

"Yelllllo?" he answers.

"Free tonight?"

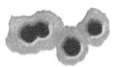

O'Reardon's likes to pretend it's an Irish bar with that shamrock painted over the entrance and soccer jerseys hanging from the rafters. But it's an all-American dive, through and through. The pissy beer and generous pull-tab selection give it away. Branding only gets you so far.

Richie's at our usual table. I find a shot of bourbon and a Rainier tallboy awaiting me.

"Well, well." I take a seat. "Nice to see the three of you again."

"Here's to Monday," Richie says. We clink shooters. "How'd it go today?"

"With your old girlfriend, you mean?"

A rare grin. "I wouldn't call her that. We were sixteen. How'd she look?"

"Pretty, and unhappy. You know her husband?"

"Only by reputation. Joanie and I haven't exactly kept in touch, but I looked up Grayson after she reached out. He's loaded, well regarded in his field. Lousy drunk."

"Are there good drunks?"

"Lousier than most. A DUI and two public tox charges in the last five years alone."

"Cheers to that."

There was a time when Richie and I were competitors—friendly competitors, but hardly friends. Given the constant overlap in our industry, we crossed paths multiple times and formed a partnership of sorts. If he needed to pass on a job because of other commitments, then he'd refer me, and vice versa. This would ensure steady cash flow for both of us, a valuable commodity for any freelancer. Then his left knee blew out a few years ago, and he transitioned to a less demanding role. He's done well for himself. Top recruiter in the Northwest, I hear. Aside from me, he juggles a dozen other guns for hire. He says I'm his favorite client because we go way back, but Richie's a schmoozer. I bet he tells all of us that.

"When do you start?" he asks.

"Tomorrow morning, first thing."

"Should be a gimme."

"Don't jinx it. So what happened with you and Mrs. Franzel? She find some other dude to carry her books?"

"Something like that. Hell if I remember now. Joanie and I had some good times, though. Can't forget those." Richie polishes off his Rainier and squeezes the can. "By the way, I got you something."

"Oh?"

"It was gonna be a surprise, but … I can't wait."

He reaches into his pocket and takes out an envelope. Inside, I find two tickets. "The *Brass Tacks* Tour: An Afternoon with Lou Corbette." A book signing to promote the Wizard's latest opus, four weeks from today. I'm flabbergasted.

"Where did you get these? It sold out in thirty minutes."

"I've got my ways. I'm claiming one of those tickets, of course."

"Of course. What do I owe you?"

"Consider it an early birthday gift."

"My birthday's eight months away."

"So it's belated. You're my favorite client. I couldn't resist."

I could hug the guy but settle for a firm handshake instead. Richie and I are close, but we haven't reached the hugging stage of our relationship.

Grayson Kichener Franzel's jaw creaks open. Both eyes bulge, pupils thick as acorns.

"You've never heard of *equity waterfalls?*"

"Sure haven't," I reply.

"Well, there are two basic, uh, ones." He pauses to hiccup. "European and American. Both have their ... their pros and cons ..."

Christ, not again. This marks the third time in as many evenings that Grayson has given me a rundown on equity waterfalls. Serve this guy a few belts and he won't stop squawking about real estate. He must be a hit at dinner parties.

How did we get here? Funny you should ask.

Surveilling Grayson goes smoothly at first. On Tuesday morning, I park around the corner from the Franzel house, an optic-white modernist monstrosity overlooking Lake Washington. From there I tail his Beamer to the Stowicky Investments Center, then spend the day shuffling between various cafes, bookstores, and souvenir shops within the building's proximity. My usual tactics.

Mrs. Franzel wasn't exaggerating about her husband's drinking habits. Grayson leaves work promptly at 5:30 and strolls three blocks to the Godiva Lounge. I stake out the bar's entrance until he emerges around quarter past nine, red-eyed and off-kilter as he stumbles back to the parking garage. The next night I follow him inside wearing my go-to disguise. Mariners ball cap, tinted eyeglasses, a passable fake mustache I bought at a costume shop—laugh all you want, the getup hasn't failed me yet. I claim a two-top a few seats away from Grayson. Even with bad house music blaring in my ear, I can hear him droning on about new market tax credits to the unimpressed martini sippers sitting next to him.

On Thursday evening, I decide to gamble. I walk into the bar, snag the stool next to him and offer to buy him a round.

"We met?" he slurs, both eyes fixated on the nylon fibers pasted to my philtrum.

"I don't believe so."

He thrusts a clammy hand at me. "Grayson. Pleasure."

I learned a lot that night. For one, Grayson has the bladder of a goldfish. He waddles to the men's room at least seven or eight times in the three hours. No mention of his wife, but he doesn't hide his ring, so he isn't prowling for tail. I learn he has no problem getting behind the wheel with a gut full of whiskey, even after multiple run-ins with the law. I learn American equity waterfalls are more favorable to investors than European ones.

I've noticed something else with each subsequent interaction. Grayson is a consummate blackout artist. Every night I sit down next to him, he sticks that clammy palm in my face like we're perfect strangers and launches into the same conversation topics.

So here we are, quarter to nine on Monday night. One week since I last saw Mrs. Franzel at the park, five business days since I began following her husband. I'd already planned to finish the job tonight—I don't like pushing assignments past the one-week mark—and upon entering the lounge and finding Grayson more pickled than usual, I know my intuition is on point. Let him finish drinking, tail him to the parking garage. Just have to wait him out. Easier said.

"So, both waterfalls have their advantages," he concludes, suppressing a burp, "but ... those Europeans'll screw you every time."

Grayson sucks down the rest of his old fashioned and flags down our server for another. The ice-filled glass rattles like a maraca in his hand, and there's a flicker of desperation in his eyes until she returns with a fresh cocktail.

"Christ," he bellows after a long slurp. "Only Monday, huh?"

"Indeed."

"So what's *your* business?"

"Independent contractor."

"Construction?"

"Lifestyle coaching."

"Interesting."

"Not really. You married, Grayson?"

"Yeah." He fiddles with the diamond setting of his ring. "Unfortunately."

"That bad, huh?"

"How much time do you got?" Grayson takes a healthy guzzle, baring his teeth at the burn. "She's screwin' around on me, for one. Has been for years."

Not a shocker, assuming it's true. After spending a few evenings with her husband, I can hardly blame Mrs. Franzel for sidestepping her marriage vows.

"Then she gets after me for staying out late," he goes on. "Like I'm not doing her a favor."

"Have you tried counseling?"

"Counseling?" He chuckles. "Are *you* married?"

"Nope."

"It shows. Tell the girl to bring my check."

Still mumbling, he slips off his stool and heads for the men's room.

It might sound strange coming from a triggerman, but I do care about my marks. I want them to succeed, to reinvent themselves, to improve on the people they once were. I built my entire business model around that—and my method works, at least most of the time. I'm having doubts with Grayson, though. The guy's so self-absorbed and despondent that he might be impervious to nonlethal therapy. Hell, getting shot might send him screaming over the edge. Not a win for me either. A negative result like that could hurt my word of mouth.

Several minutes pass and Grayson hasn't returned, so I drop a few twenties on the table and head down the restroom corridor. Inside the men's room, I find him passed out on his back, head cocked to the side, tongue within licking distance of the floor tiles. This must be that executive material I keep hearing about. Helping Grayson outside through the lounge without drawing attention is a no-go, and the emergency exit has an alarm.

Thankfully, I have another out. Above the sink is a rectangular window just wide enough for me to fit through, and from my canvassing I know it leads to the alley. I lock the bathroom door and get to work.

Grayson's a heavy fella, but I'm able to prop him up against the stall door. A pool of dribble gathers at the edge of his lower lip. I take out the nine-millimeter, align my sight with the fleshy mound under his ribs, and squeeze the trigger. My silencer handles volume control—the shot is louder than movies lead one to believe, but it's got nothing on the thumping bass behind us—and I snag the casing before it rolls into urinal territory.

Grayson's eyes creak open and his body twitches like he's got the hiccups. He glances up woozily, squinting at the fluorescents.

"The hell was that?"

"I didn't hear anything."

The bloodstain in his oxford shirt spreads to the size of a dime, then a quarter. He doesn't notice.

"Am I all right?" he asks me.

Normally, this is when I get into character. Tell them they're experiencing their final earthly moments, maybe taunt them a little. Nothing inspires personal catharsis like a brush with cruel, impending death. But I can't bring myself to put on that charade with Grayson, looking as pathetic as he does. Besides, it's not like he'll remember later.

"Don't worry." I reach down and yank the wallet from his back pocket. "You'll be fine."

"Good," he says, closing his eyes again. "Thought I was in trouble there."

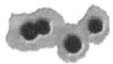

What happens next, I learn from local news coverage.

Moments after I climb out the window, a busboy tries to enter the men's room and finds it locked. No one answers his knocks, so he fetches a key, opens the door, and discovers Grayson on the floor. My shot's on target—clean through without nicking any vitals—but that's the least of his problems. Turns out Grayson is a Type B hemophiliac. In five minutes, he's lost more blood than most people lose in twenty. An ambulance rushes him to the hospital and Grayson undergoes emergency surgery, but by morning he's still unconscious and his prognosis is grave.

Tributes start pouring in from every corner of the Seattle business community. Even the evening anchors on Channel 5 seem somber. "Hang in there, Grayson. Wishing you a speedy and full recovery." I watch the broadcast from the edge of my living room sofa, shaking my head in disbelief. Two years without a single fatality. Now my spotless record is in jeopardy, and all thanks to a stationary target. Christ, they don't get more stationary than that.

Local media covers Grayson all week—rich white guy gets capped and suddenly downtown shootings are newsworthy—but by Saturday they've moved on to other people's misfortunes, leaving me out of the loop and less than optimistic. Richie texts me that afternoon, asking if I can grab a beer at O'Reardon's. I jump at the invitation, hoping he'll bring news of Grayson's condition, but he's only called the meeting to pass along my next referral.

"Some gal out in Kenmore," he says. "Apparently she nags and has a gambling problem. Her husband's hoping to kill two birds."

"I'm on hiatus."

"No worries, it can wait a few days."

"*Indefinite* hiatus."

"C'mon, this was bound to happen. Be proud of your two-year streak." He looks at his watch. "I'm gonna split."

"Already? I thought we could hang out, get drunk."

"I've got dinner plans."

"Who's the lucky gal?"

Richie shifts on his stool. "Just an old friend."

"Wait … don't tell me."

"Don't ask."

"*Joanie?*"

He shrugs. "And?"

"You're going on a date with a woman who hired me to shoot her husband?"

"It's just dinner. Her idea. All this time in the hospital is getting her down. She wants to catch up."

"Catch up with what?"

He narrows his eyes at me. "I wasn't asking your permission, bud."

Richie leaves, but I linger at the table and get perfectly intoxicated—nice and fuzzy, but sober enough to walk home. I fade to sleep that night and wake up in the morning to breaking headlines:

"After undergoing a last-ditch procedure at Seattle General last night, Grayson Franzel has regained consciousness. With another round of transfusions, he's expected to make a full recovery. Speaking of upgrades, Diane, I understand there's warm weather headed our …"

It's funny, watching the entire city celebrate a man who, by all appearances, didn't have a single friend before he caught a bullet. Every local station books an interview with Grayson during the week of doctor-ordered home rest following his discharge. They all ask the same questions. What was going through your mind when you were shot? Has your outlook changed since the attack? How *are* you?

I'll hand it to Grayson. The man knows how to craft an appealing public image. Affable, self-deprecating, and his retelling of the shooting—pure artistry.

"It wasn't fear I felt, so much as … remorse. For my wife, whom I was about to leave behind, and for my family, my close friends. Even the man who shot me, crazy as it sounds. Maybe he steals wallets to feed his children. An unenviable position, no matter his motive. From there I just sort of ... drifted off peacefully, like an afternoon nap."

An *afternoon nap*. His actual words, hand to my heart.

The press tour eventually ends, but Grayson Franzel's spotlight doesn't dim a shade. Once he's fully recovered, he holds a small press conference to announce his immediate retirement from the commercial real estate sector. This shocks his clients and leaves his colleagues dumbfounded, but everyone else applauds the decision when, during the same speech, he unveils plans to establish a charitable foundation for adults and children with hemophilia. "There is no known cure for the condition that affects me and tens of thousands of others in this country," Grayson says somberly, "and treatments are remarkably expensive, financially out of reach for most." Franzel House launches a few days later, largely funded through his personal income.

Meanwhile, I can't stop blinking at my turn of fortune. Days ago, I was ready to take the hit on my record, possibly consider early retirement. Now I'm watching my magnum opus unfold on the nightly news. Grayson Franzel, booze-swilling degenerate one day, selfless philanthrope the next.

So why am I bitter about the whole thing? In a word, Joanie. It's one thing for a client to mix up digits in an address or neglect to mention a weekly card game. But withholding a life-threatening condition that can cause massive blood loss? One hell of an oversight. To make matters more unsettling, she's nowhere to be seen in the shooting's aftermath. Not sitting at Grayson's side during the interviews or standing behind him during his press conference. She hasn't wired the rest of the money either. She still has a week to the deadline, but my patience is waning.

I should be celebrating. In a few short hours, I'll be face-to-face with Lou Corbette, the Wizard of Wichita himself. My nerves have picked an inconvenient time to get prickly. Guess that's why they're called nerves.

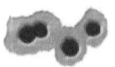

I haven't heard from Richie since our little tiff at O'Reardon's, so I'm half-surprised when I walk into the bookstore with my hardbound copy of *Brass Tacks* and find him lurking by the magazine racks. We awkwardly shake hands. Hug's probably out of the question.

"How've you been?" he asks.

"Living. You?"

"Same."

I nudge him. "Something about Franzel, huh?"

"Yeah, something all right."

"How's his wife?"

"How the hell should I know?" he snaps, then lets out a heavy sigh. "Sorry. That chick is really getting to me."

"Oh?"

"She was all smiles that first night at dinner and, you know, afterward. But ever since Grayson left the hospital, she's gone off the goddamn rails. Constantly crying, drinking all the time. She says she wants to leave him for good. If she thinks she's moving in with me ..."

"Maybe she's just adjusting."

"Maybe." He shakes his head. "Still, not the fun-loving Joanie I remember."

A line forms leading into an anteroom behind the nonfiction shelves. An attendant takes our tickets and we queue up.

"There's something else," Richie says, lowering his voice. "She can't pay the rest yet."

"Come again?"

"They don't have the money. He blew a lot of their savings on that charity."

"Great, so I'm out half a paycheck."

"I'll cover it. Take it out of my commissions."

"Richie, you know that isn't how we work. Sounds like I need to pay her a visit."

"Figured you'd say that." He shrugs. "Do what you have to do."

The line moves quickly. A few shuffles and we're close to the anteroom. Just as we're about to cross the threshold, Richie steps out of line and turns toward the exit.

"What's up?" I call out.

"I gotta go."

"We're almost there."

"I'm a mess. Lou can't see me like this."

Soon he's out of sight. My feet move with the line, but my mind is elsewhere—Richie's given me a lot to contemplate. I enter the room and spot a wisp of gray hair peeking over the shoulders in front of me. Soon, I can hear Lou's voice over the crowd. Next thing I know, the Wizard is a handshake away. Even then, I can barely muster a smirk.

"Howdy," Lou says. His signature drawl is even stronger in person.

"Mr. Corbette. It's … an honor."

"What's your name?"

"Sorry?"

He nods at my copy of *Brass Tacks*. "Who should I make it out to?"

"Right. Actually …" I drop the book to my side. "If you don't mind, I could use some advice."

Lou blinks at me through his bifocals. "What's on your brain?"

"Well, it's my angle. I found one for my brand, like you suggested."

"How's business now?"

"Outstanding, but … the new model's a little riskier. More variables, more room for error, you know how it is."

"Uh-huh."

"Recently, I had a minor crisis. The fire's out now, but for a minute my brand was in trouble. Put me through the wringer."

Lou tugs his bow tie and glances at the line behind me. "Is there a question comin'?"

"Should I take these recent troubles as a sign I need a new angle? At what point do the risks outweigh the gains?"

He scratches his chin. "Have you considered your *angle* might need an angle?"

"Go on …"

"The technical term is microevolution. If your model isn't progressing, your brand isn't innovating. Without innovation, the angle's meaningless. Like putting a custom paint job on a Cadillac that won't start." He leans in. "In your case, I'd say all these variables are the problem. Trim the fat. Take a step back, then you'll know how to move forward."

"And after that?"

Lou grins. "You found the first angle, you'll figure out the next one." He shifts in his seat. "Not to be rude, but—"

"Of course. Thanks so much, Mr. Corbette. You've been a big help. Again."

"Want me to sign that book?"

"Nah, I got what I came for."

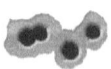

I know Joanie isn't paying up anytime soon, but we agreed on thirty days and I like to honor my arrangements with clients. On the morning of day thirty-one, I arrive at the Franzel residence a little before eight and park around the corner. Grayson leaves in his Beamer a short time later. Then I stroll up to the front door and ring the bell. Mrs. Franzel answers. Her breath catches like she swallowed a fingernail.

"What are you doing here?" she gasps.

"House hunting. Think we're gonna be neighbors."

"Grayson will be back any minute."

"That isn't what his secretary told me. She said he'd be in foundation meetings all morning. Unless *she's* the liar." I gesture toward the living room. "May I?"

She nods and steps aside, taking a seat in a wicker chair near the door. The interior is more luxurious than the house's sterile facade suggests. Polished parquet floors, marble stairs, solid-oak bookshelves. I take a seat on the sofa facing Mrs. Franzel's chair. Her lower lip quivers, tugging both cheekbones.

"I thought you didn't contact people after assignments," she murmurs.

"What I *said* was, no contact once the transaction is complete. You have an outstanding balance, ma'am."

"That? I … I asked Richie to tell you. We don't have the money right now, but soon I—"

"Relax, Richie told me. I don't care about the money. I'm here because you lied to me."

"Sorry?"

"Let me put it another way. You abused my trust."

"I don't understand."

"I've had some time to think this over, so stop me if I say something incorrectly. You hired me to shoot your husband without telling me he had hemophilia. An intentional omission on your part. After our first meeting, you decided you wanted me to kill him. I squeeze the trigger, he croaks, and you're free to do whatever you please. *And* you don't owe me the remaining fee because Grayson's dead and that's my policy. Now he's made a full recovery, and suddenly you're too broke to pay the rest." I run my hand along the sofa. Italian leather, smooth as fresh cream. "Allegedly."

She shakes her head. "I told you, I could have hired someone to kill him for less money. I hired you *not* to. I *care* about my husband."

"Then why do you want to leave him for Richie?"

"Richie told you that?"

"Not many secrets between us."

"I don't know what to say."

"Don't sweat it." I remove the nine-millimeter from my jacket pocket. "Last words aren't everybody's thing."

Her eyes widen. "You're going to *kill* me?"

"Well, yeah ... sorry, I figured you put that together already."

Her body stiffens as she backs into the chair, tucking her knees toward her chest.

"I'll get you the money."

"Again, not my chief concern."

"What about Richie?"

"He and I are in the same trade. I told him I was paying you a visit. He didn't bat an eye."

She drops to a whisper. "You don't have to do this."

"That's funny." I lean forward on the sofa, putting us at eye level. "Back when I killed people for money, they used to say that all the time. I always gave the same reply, too. You don't have to *live* either. The world will go right on spinning, evolving, maybe even improving without you. And soon, anyone with a pleasant thing to say about you will be gone, too. Nobody ever had a comeback for that. In a way, I think they found it comforting."

Mrs. Franzel closes her eyes. I rise to my feet, check the safety, and line up the sights with her sternum. Quick double-tap and I'm gone. But then I notice a slight tremble in my trigger finger. This hasn't happened since my rookie days. Exhaling, I shift my weight to the other knee and try to refocus. No luck. It's still wriggling like a worm. Mrs. Franzel cracks open her left eye.

"Sorry, just a second," I say.

Oh, who am I kidding? I can't kill her. I've spent the last two years training myself *not* to kill people. That chapter ended for me the moment I rebranded. I can't go back to that life, the tension headaches and the night terrors and the stress eating—and if I have to, it won't be on account of fucking Joanie.

Now both of her eyes are open.

"What is it?" she asks.

"Oh … nothing." I re-holster the nine-millimeter and turn toward the door. "It's been a pleasure, Mrs. Franzel."

"You're not going to—?"

"No, I'm not."

"Really?" She sits up in the chair, wiping her eyes. "But … why?"

"Does it matter?"

A shaky half-smile forms. "I suppose not. Listen, I'll pay you as soon—"

"Keep your money. You're debt-free."

"Thank you."

"You caught some good luck today. Use it wisely."

She doesn't stand to show me out.

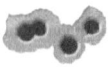

I immediately sever ties with Richie. No parting handshake, no last round at O'Reardon's. I don't return any of his voicemails and eventually he stops calling. Now it's just me, recruiter and shooter rolled into one. I think Lou would approve of my streamlined operation.

Things are smooth and uneventful for a few months into the transition, but then I get the phone call. My pulse jumps when the client reveals his name. I assume it's Richie, playing a sick prank—some nerve after everything we've been through. But the more this guy talks, I realize it's no impersonation.

"Let's meet Monday," I say. "You know Marsden Green?"

The client reaches the park around half past noon. From my bench near the bocce court, I watch him park his car. It's him, all right. I'd know that 7 Series anywhere. He exits, glancing over his shoulder as heads down the trail.

"Good afternoon," he says, sitting beside me. "You're the one I spoke with on the phone?"

"That's me."

He narrows his eyes. "Have we met before?"

"No. But I know who you are, Mr. Franzel."

"You do?"

"Seen you on TV."

He nods. "Then you understand this requires full discretion."

"They all do. But don't worry, I have a spotless record."

"You've been doing this for a while?"

"Long enough."

Grayson sighs. "I was shot a few months ago. You know that if you've heard of me ... it's sort of my claim to fame. A mugging. This punk in a bathroom who wanted to steal my wallet. Christ, I'd have *given* him my wallet."

"Some sick people in this city."

"I'm not angry. Actually, I'm grateful. I was wasting my life. Working a miserable job, unhappy at home. And the drinking, Jesus. Haven't touched a drop since."

"Good for you."

"What I'm getting at is ... this experience changed my life for the better. When I first heard about what you do, the service you provide, it got me thinking. Something like that could be very beneficial to her."

"Her?"

"My wife, Joan." He fiddles with his ring. "Ever since my accident, she's been so … sullen, displeased with everything. Like she resents me for recovering and doing something with my life. I've been tolerating it for a few months now. But frankly, I've reached the end of my—"

"If you don't mind," I interject, "I'd rather not know the reasons."

Ben Gamblin is a crime and mystery writer who currently resides in Tacoma, Washington. His work has appeared in periodicals such as *Déraciné*, *Ink Stains Anthology*, and *The Dark City Mystery Magazine*, as well as story collections from Forty-Two Books, Underland Press, and Writers Co-op. Follow him on Instagram @bengamblinofficial.

SMALL CLAWS, SMALL GUNS

BY JEZZY WOLFE

Those bastard eyes narrowed. They were the color of gasoline, but not the expensive premium-grade gasoline. I'm talking at least twenty percent ethanol-laced, the cheap stuff. The kind that makes your engine sputter. The kind that screams for a quart of fuel additive at the pump. They were eyes you couldn't trust.

I thumbed the hammer of my .45 and tensed my finger around the trigger.

He snarled and stood taller. "I knew you didn't have the balls—"

His chest exploded the instant a deafening crack ripped the air. Red rained on the concrete slab as his body crashed on the garage floor. I was shocked, frozen in place, trying to piece together what happened. Despite the tremble in my hands, I had the good sense not to drop my gun and accidentally discharge my bullet.

I mean, sure. This was what I came for. Argeno was dead. All I had to do was leave the coded message on the voicemail, and my assignment would be complete. I did not need to tell them it wasn't my gun that killed the mark. Probably.

But I needed to make sure I wasn't next.

I lifted my gun and inched to the left. The shot had been fired from somewhere to the right, near a pile of used tires in a corner about twenty feet away. I didn't speak, I could barely breathe. Whoever hid in there could have easily taken me out with Argeno. Maybe they were intentionally avoiding me.

I coughed to clear my nervous throat, and said, "Hello?"

No response.

Even with my gun raised, I was an easy target. Clearly, they were studying me, weighing their options. I wasn't their mark. I lowered my gun but kept my finger on the trigger. "This guy," I said, pointing to Argeno. "What an asshole, am I right?"

I heard scuffling, and brought my pistol back up, ready to fire away, steeled for a fight against my stealthy opposition.

Two round eyes blinked from the shadows of bald Michelins. I could just make out an unusually long mustache. The figure stepped into a shaft of light.

I stood face to face with an otter. Standing on an otter that was standing on yet another otter. Three otters, wearing a beige trench coat. The top otter wore a dark fedora and held a Ruger LCP between its front paws. Otters incognito. The trio eyed me like I was a delicious fish.

"Oh my God," I said, unable to stop myself. "You're adorable!"

Top Otter squealed twice. Maybe it thanked me. Either that or someone stepped on a squeaky dog toy. I never talked to an otter before, so I wasn't familiar with their vocalizations. Top Otter sounded like a cross between a rubber chicken and a Daily Bark toy newspaper.

I took a step toward the otters and extended my hand. Did otters greet strangers by sniffing hands like dogs?

A whistle shrilled from somewhere I couldn't see. The otters dismantled and scampered into the shadows, heading for an exit. Top

Otter still wore the fedora and trench coat, which flapped behind like a bland cape. They were faster than I was. By the time I emerged from the garage, I could see the otters climbing into a van at the curb. There were even more otters in the van with them. A veritable gang of dog-sized assassins packed into an Econoline. I waved at them—not sure why, just couldn't help it—but the door closed. As the van sped away, the ruckus of innumerable squeaky toys being squeezed filled the night air.

I waited until the taillights disappeared, then called my handler.

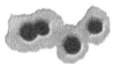

Orman's office sat in a perpetual blanket of sour smoke and wood oil. It felt grimy and pristine at the same time. Orman himself was the same irony personified. His expensive suit was tailored and immaculate, but his hair jutted from his scalp in unruly peppered gray gnarls, and he sported an around-the-clock five o'clock shadow on his jowled chin. I'd been doing contracts for him for a few years, and he never changed … the best-dressed slob I'd ever met. He took a couple puffs off his stubby cigar and studied me.

"So, Argeno is done?" His voice was as smooth as rocks tumbling in two fingers of bourbon.

"Yes."

"And *you* did him?"

"Yeah, I mean, yes." I avoided fidgeting with my sleeves. Orman could sense nervousness a county away.

"Because I have video that says otherwise." *Puff-puff-puff.*

Shit! "What are you talking about?" How did he know? In my head, I could see my paycheck dissolving into nothingness.

Orman picked up his phone and swiped the screen, then turned it toward me. I could see the back of the costumed otter trio, with Argeno's backside in the distance, clearly distracted by me. Top Otter jerked back just a little as they fired off a bullet, which probably hit a few organs on its way through his chest. Whoever held the camera moved farther back as I became visible.

I realized "whoever" was probably the one driving the van. Why did it not occur to me that someone was with those otters? Had I really convinced myself the otters were also responsible for their getaway vehicle?

I guess, after seeing an armed otter execute a perfect hit, I assumed those otters were special enough to also drive themselves home … wherever a gang of assassin otters might live. Full confession, I may or may not have been entertaining myself with visions of how that might've played out.

"Who gave that to you?" I said. I wished for something to soothe my tight throat, like a bottle of water or Maker's Mark.

"That would be the dispatcher who closed the contract." He rubbed the end of his cigar in an ashtray. "Look, Enno, you're a good hire. Someone just beat you to this one."

"I didn't know I was competing with an outside gun for the job," I said, calculating whether I had the funds in the bank to cover my rent without the job. Hint … I didn't.

"You weren't. But I tell you what. We have another contract. This one just came in. Some attorney representing that crazy activist group, PTARG. Worth about 17k if you can pull it off this week. Think you can take it?" He held a manila envelope in his hand and waited for my answer.

"You mean People Treating Animals Real Good?" I'd never tangled with that organization before. They were frequently in the news with their protests and aggressive antics, and even as a hired gun, I found them intimidating. I could appreciate their love for animals, but honestly, I thought they were all just a little more than completely unhinged. That payload was one hell of an incentive, though, and there wasn't much unhinged that a .45 couldn't handle. I almost accepted but paused to ask, "What about that other dispatcher?"

"They were already paid out before this contract came to us. If you act quickly, they won't even know about it." Orman fished a fresh cigar from a drawer and used a palm-sized cutter to trim one end.

It wasn't the answer I hoped for. Still, I took the envelope. I was more intimidated by my landlord than PTARG. No cute and talented otter would steal this job from me.

I squatted behind a bulbous boxwood hedge outside the PTARG headquarters and waited as all but two cars left the parking lot. The attorney, a man named O'Shea, who had the ethics of a dinosaur but the backbone of an eel, was working late with one director, presumably on the upcoming court case. I didn't know why he was being scrubbed, and I didn't need to know. I didn't know who was paying for the hit. I only knew I had two nights left to complete the job. I was ready, in the event he left alone, to fire from the back of the bush, where security cameras couldn't see me hiding in the dark. Unless he was accompanied, or someone else showed up, it would be an easy kill.

The door opened, and my guy came strolling outside, his pace brisk but relaxed. He fumbled for his keys as I raised my gun and aimed. At this angle, I could either go for the heart or head. Either would be effective. Easiest 17k ever.

Squeak squeak.

"Dammit!" I whispered. "No!" I recognized it immediately. Fucking otters, man.

I pushed through the leaves to get a better look, without drawing attention. Four otters approached my mark and were squeaking and squealing at O'Shea's feet. He clearly didn't know how to react, but who would? How often do four chatty river otters approach anyone in a parking lot? Not *nearly* often enough, I say.

Everything happened so fast, I almost couldn't follow it. As he laughed and leaned over to scratch an otter on its head, one other— probably Top Otter—stood on its back feet and pulled a small handgun from a fanny pack strapped around its belly. Two quick shots and O'Shea went down ... just as the door opened and a woman emerged. She screamed and rushed to O'Shea's side, crying frantically, smoothing back his hair, pleading with his lifeless body.

I suddenly realized why someone might have wanted him dead.

The otters retreated quickly, but not quickly enough to escape her notice. She catapulted after them with her jacket, and flung herself into the air, landing on an otter and smothering it in her coat. One otter circled back and picked something up from the grass, and I realized she must have captured Top Otter. Muffled otter cries faded as she struggled to carry the writhing creature inside the building. I slid back, further out of view of the cameras, and hid in shadows as I circled behind the fence surrounding the PTARG building, toward the parking lot.

By the time I got there, the van was already gone ... presuming it was ever there. I needed to get away before the cops arrived. I made it to my car a block over and drove with the lights off for two more blocks, just to make sure they did not see me. I circled around a few blocks and passed by the PTARG building.

I can't say what surprised me more ... that there were no police on the scene, or that O'Shea's body was gone. The sprinkler system sputtered to life as I drove away.

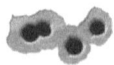

I sat in Orman's office and again watched surveillance of the hit I failed to orchestrate. The video cut off as soon as his body hit the ground, which I found odd and frustrating.

Indeed, the whole situation frustrated me. I lost another contract. The otters beat me to another mark. But there was an added layer now, as the news said nothing about the dead attorney. Nothing about any incidents at the PTARG headquarters, either. The top story during last night's 11 o'clock news had been the fire that broke out at the Bushel's Bacon Beanies plant.

Also, what happened to that poor otter?

Orman said nothing about the otter. In fact, he eyed me strangely when I asked if the otter was safe. I sort of half shrugged and smirked, and then quickly changed the subject. "Isn't it strange they did not call the police after finding his body?"

Puff puff. Orman studied the cigar smoke for what felt like too long and leaned back in his chair. "The dispatcher reported the hit went without incident. That certainly appears to be the case, by the video they provided."

"They mentioned nothing about PTARG taking their otter hostage?"

"How does someone take an otter hostage? It's an animal. Animals aren't hostages, they're just animals."

"That's not what PTARG would say," I muttered.

"What's that?"

"I mean, yeah, it's an otter. But it's an otter that kills."

"It's a carnivore," he said. "Of course it kills."

Orman was not concerned about the otters. Honestly, I shouldn't be, either. Despite their incredibly endearing faces and those huge shiny eyeballs and their long, twitchy whiskers, these otters were trained marksmen.

They were also my biggest competition. And the reason I was short on my rent.

"Got anything else for me?"

Orman handed me another folder and another chance to avoid a pissed-off landlord.

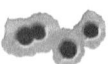

The Manfred hit went without a hitch or interruption. I scored eight grand, which was considerably less than the last two contracts I lost, but more than enough to cover my rent. I figured I could give myself a week before I needed to find more work. Maybe I would switch it up. When I wasn't a hired gun, I alternated between headhunting and landscaping.

Maybe it was time to break out the weed eater.

I was enjoying a burger and catching up on some television when hard knocks shook my front door. I froze and held my breath. Were the police outside? If so, wouldn't they announce it? I checked my doorbell camera on my phone and discovered the lens was covered. Someone didn't want to be seen. I picked up a bat that I kept beside the door and leaned against it.

"Who are you?" I demanded, my mouth an inch away from the deadbolt.

I heard a soft murmur but couldn't pick up anything other than whoever was on my porch was human.

"If you don't at least give me a name, I ain't opening the door."

"Noreen."

I turned the deadbolt and opened the door two inches. A lady in a wide-brimmed hat stood on my porch, her hand pressed over the door-cam lens, her face pinched and impatient.

"Do I know you?" She appeared harmless enough, if somewhat annoyed.

"Can I please come in, Mr. Enno? We have business to discuss." Her voice was clipped. She glanced back over her shoulder, as if she feared being seen. At first, I thought maybe she was the woman at PTARG, O'Shea's mistress. But as she took off her hat, I realized she was someone else.

I opened the door wider and stepped aside. My revolver waited in a secret pocket of my recliner, so I knew if she pulled anything, I could protect myself. She went directly to my couch and sat down.

"Might I trouble you for a drink?" she said.

"Might I trouble you for an explanation?"

"Sure. Once I have that drink." She picked up my remote and began channel surfing.

I might not be the most gracious host, but Noreen was rude for a guest. Even so, I was more curious than annoyed. I rummaged in my fridge and found a half bottle of Grey Goose and a few hard ciders. I opened a cider and offered it to her.

She blinked and stared at the bottle. She probably meant a glass of water. I was bad at socializing.

"Sorry, I assumed you wanted a real drink," I said.

"This is fine. Thank you." She took the bottle and had a long drink, downing almost half the bottle in one pull, and placed it on the coffee table.

So, she really likes cider. I sat back in my recliner, making sure I could access my pocket in case she got any ideas. "Now, what business do I have with you, Noreen?"

"Please, call me Ms. Kittery."

"Oh. Uh … okay?" I frowned. She might be even more socially awkward than I was. "Ms. Kittery."

"I need your help," she said, "to find Shoggoth."

"I beg your pardon?" I could not have heard correctly.

"*Shoggoth*," she said, emphasizing each syllable. "My otter."

At that moment, I knew exactly who sat in my living room.

"You want *me* to help *you?*" I laughed, but not in amusement. "Do you have any idea how much money you've cost me?"

"Do you have any idea how much it costs to shelter and feed a half dozen Asian small-clawed otters?"

"I am gonna guess somewhere in the ballpark of thirty thousand."

"I apologize for moving in on your contracts, Mr. Enno. It was a dirty move …"

"Moves," I said.

"… but it has been hard for me to raise the money to care for them by honest means." She finished the cider, burped, and handed me the empty bottle. "Thanks."

"If you can't afford to take care of them, why do you have them?" I studied her as she crossed her legs and leaned against the sofa arm. She didn't seem like such a threat any longer.

"The otters were part of an aquarium show back in Florida. They were a popular attraction until activists started picketing the aquarium. Made a few bomb threats, even, which scared the public away. They were demanding to take the otters into custody and free them into the wild," she said. Her eyes teared at just the right amount. "Thing is, these otters were rescued as pups. They were never wild. Releasing them would be a death sentence. So one night, I took them with me. I could not leave them like that. I was all they knew. I would never forgive myself if something happened to them."

"When you say activists …"

Noreen nodded. "PTARG. They harassed me for years over the otters."

I chewed over what she revealed. "So that hit on O'Shea was … revenge?"

"Oh no, that was just a wonderfully convenient hit," she said. "Nothing more. My otters are well-trained assassins. Before we started getting contracts from Orman, we worked for a contractor up north. We moved south because there were more prospects, and I figured we could find another aquarium show once I had enough money put away to build a sanctuary for them. Someplace permanent, where I could also be, to protect them." She smiled. "They are my babies."

"You know, some people just get a cat."

She scowled at me.

"Sorry," I said. I offered her another cider, which she accepted, and thought about the missing otter. "So PTARG has Shoggoth now. Do you think they know it's your otter?"

"Yes. I've been receiving threats from the local members. They said they were going to capture all the otters and drive them a few hundred miles off and leave them. Because they don't belong in captivity." We both made a face.

"Do you have a permit for them? They can't just take your pets from you."

"The aquarium held permits. I didn't have permission to take them. But demonstrators shut down the show. And, like I said, I wasn't about to leave them behind." She gripped the cider bottle so tight I worried she might break it.

"Why not just go to the police?"

She shot me a look.

"Oh yeah. Right." I cleared my throat, unsure of what to say. "I am sorry to hear about this. Of course, it would have been nice if you didn't bogart my marks … but I understand why you were so aggressive."

"That is why I am willing to offer you half of the money I made from those hits in exchange for Shoggoth."

"But I don't …"

"That's almost fifteen thousand." She was not going to make this easy.

"Why ask me? I have no skills with animals. The only pets I had growing up were a rock and two goldfish. Animals don't like me."

"Shoggoth likes everyone," she said.

"You probably should have rethought that name."

She clenched the bottle with both hands and, for that moment, she looked worried I was about to turn down the offer. In my head, I heard the frantic cries of the muffled otter being taken away. Even his distress was adorable.

"Dammit," I said.

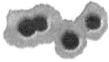

What I didn't know at the time, PTARG was looking for a groundskeeper, for their headquarters and a second location just outside the city. Noreen, of course, knew that. Just as she knew I did landscaping as a side gig. It turned out to be stupid easy gaining access to their buildings.

Noreen suspected if Shoggoth wasn't still in the headquarters, he would be caged somewhere on their second property. What scared Noreen was the possibility they might release Shoggoth before she could locate him. So my plan was, get in, figure out exactly where the otter was held, and then bust him out. I wasn't looking for an elaborate or complicated maneuver. While I didn't want to kill anyone while extracting Shoggoth, I would do whatever I needed to.

The headquarters comprised a nondescript office building, except for an enormous neon sign mounted on the rooftop that read

PEOPLE TREATING ANIMALS REAL GOOD in orange block letters. The grounds were rather small, with just a few strips of grass to mow, and round boxwood hedges that would need regular pruning. I calculated how much time it would take me to finish the job before remembering I was only pretending to be the groundskeeper.

After picking up my badge key from the superintendent, I located the room where my equipment was stored. The door was outside, by the back entrance. I pretended to do my job, but after a few minutes, I returned to the building and searched for Shoggoth. I even searched the basement, which turned out to be nothing more than a makeshift recreational room that hadn't been used in a long time.

Damn. No otter.

I sent Noreen a text to give her the bad news before heading down a hall toward the front. I heard voices coming from a room, and they grew louder as I approached the doorway. I tucked myself around a corner in the hall and listened.

"They are in the silo," the woman said. "Next to security."

"Do I need a team for the extraction?" the man said.

"You can't lift a hundred pounds?" she said. "The barrel is sealed, so you can use the forklift to put it on the truck. Take it to the landfill."

"And the other is a standard release, Liz?"

"God, no," she said. "That beast killed Neil. Put a bullet in it. Dump it by the falls."

I recognized her voice. Liz was O'Shea's mistress. My blood chilled. This was worse than Noreen feared.

"Tonight," she said.

"I can't tonight," he said. "I have tickets to UFC on Ice."

"God, you're an idiot," she said. "Fine. Tomorrow night."

"Yes, ma'am."

I slid back down the hall before they came out and spotted me. Screw the hedges. I was taking the afternoon off.

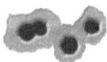

"Thing is, which silo are they referring to?" Noreen and I agreed I needed to find Shoggoth tonight, before Muscles the Ice-Skating Freak got to him. We knew the otter had to be at either the second location or somewhere nearby. But according to the GPS, the area was all farmlands. There were probably a lot of silos out there. And we were almost out of time.

It was growing dark. I'd met Noreen at a public playground, but her white Econoline drew more attention than we intended. We moved to a grocery store parking lot after a group of children pointed their fingers at us and chanted, "Stranger danger!" I suggested she consider painting her van another color.

"Wherever the silo is, it has to be somewhere on their property," I said. "She mentioned security."

"How will you get past them?"

"I will make up something about needing supplies. Grass seed maybe. Tell them I am just there to get an inventory since I couldn't be there earlier." I paused. "We need to dismantle the gate camera. That way, I can make sure you have a way in behind me."

We agreed it would be a wise idea if she parked nearby, in the event I needed help. Also, because an otter probably wouldn't fit in my car.

"Don't worry," she said. "I have it covered."

I decided not to ask what she meant. Noreen proved she possessed incredible cunning every time she upstaged my assassinations. The mission was already more complicated than I expected. Of all the hats I wore, animal rescuer was not one of them.

"In that case, I am headed over. I will see you there. Text me when you arrive." With a brief wave, I left. I could see her in my rearview, going into the grocery store.

PTARG's second property was located just outside the city line, not quite in farm country. I discovered the gate didn't appear to have a barrier preventing access. I spotted a camera on top of the chain-link fencing, but that was about it. The two-story building was lacking a garish sign and instead had PTARG, Inc. printed in simple white letters on the front door. I noticed, once inside, most doors didn't even have locks. I was surprised. Based on their headquarters, I assumed this place would also be locked down.

I found one guy in an open office and knocked on the door jamb. He appeared startled by me, but not especially alarmed.

I introduced myself as the groundskeeper and asked where they kept the supplies. He gave me directions and turned back to his computer.

"So, what is it you do here? If I may ask," I said. I kept my questions casual.

"I'm just an intern. Name's Todd," he said. "This is mostly corporate and accounting over here. Some training. Boring stuff. I don't even think security is on duty tonight."

How could I have lucked out that big? "Is that usual?"

"Normally, we have some security out here. Not a lot, though. Nothing important happens out here. But our regular security guy has been out sick, and they've used temps here and there, but otherwise, it's just us."

"You mean, just the two of us?" Hell, I might not need to shoot anyone!

"There is someone who lives on the property. They are the general supervisor. But they're out for the night. UFC on Ice. I have tickets, myself, and I am about to head out there. I can remote lock up if you need me to."

I thanked the guy and told him I would let him know, leaving him to his computer. Around the corner, I stopped in a doorway and messaged Noreen to let her know about the gate camera and Todd.

She promptly messaged back she was outside the gates and to let her know if I needed her to head inside.

I located the back exit and went outside. I found the closet and checked inside. Among the usual yard equipment, I also found a long-handled saw, an ax, a bolt cutter, and hedge shears. Useful. I shoved a tissue into the doorjamb so the door wouldn't latch and made my way around the grounds.

The property had more gravel than grass and almost no shrubbery. Heavy tree lines surrounded most of the perimeter. I thought about how odd it was that a company with so few actual groundskeeping needs would hire a full-time landscaper.

Even more peculiar was why the property had almost no security.

As I rounded a long building that appeared to include open parking bays, I found three other structures on the property. One was a small house, likely the supervisor's quarters. One was a modest brick structure, which I assumed was a security office.

The third appeared to be a short water tower, no taller than a three-story building, painted bright orange.

I messaged Noreen: I think I found the silo.

The house and security office were both dark. If the supervisor was inside, I preferred not to wake him. I pulled on the door on the silo's far side. It was unlocked.

This was too easy.

Inside, I discovered a hallway circling the building's perimeter. I walked down the hallway once, trying the doors as I passed. Two were empty rooms. The third door was the size of a garage bay, with another bay door the opened to the outside. I pulled the inner door up and flipped a light switch by the door.

The space was larger than I expected. A stairway was sitting on the opposite side of the room. There were shelves on one wall holding various tools and equipment. The room itself looked and smelled like an automotive shop.

In the middle of the floor sat a single white drum.

I didn't get too close to it. Probably because the label clearly warned the contents were acid. Sulfuric acid if I read it correctly. If this was the drum Muscles was supposed to pick up, did it contain O'Shea's body?

Why was PTARG covering up his murder? Maybe his mistress didn't want to be outed, but wouldn't murder override self-preservation?

None of that mattered, ultimately. I was there for Shoggoth. There were no signs of the otter in this room. I made for the stairs.

As I reached the second-floor landing, I heard something downstairs. The screech of metal. Someone closed the bay door.

I unholstered my revolver and slid along the wall, looking for doors. I found a single door and turned the knob slowly, trying to listen for voices or footsteps. Someone had to know I was in there. I needed to find a spot to hide and message Noreen.

Inside the room, I discovered it was likely the only room on the second floor. The large space was a maze of aisles and shelves. This might take a while. I squatted below some shelves and sent Noreen a quick text: Upstairs in silo. Someone downstairs in garage.

Almost immediately, she messaged back: Nyarlathotep killed the gate camera.

What? For a moment there, I worried she had a stroke.

I waited in place. There were no voices. No footsteps. Maybe someone thought the door was left open by mistake. After a few minutes, I stood up. I started searching the shelves.

Halfway into the room, somewhere near the center, I heard it. Faint, but unmistakable.

Squeak?

Yes, it sounded like a question.

I made my way around some other shelves, further into the labyrinth.

In the middle of the room was the cage.

A very defeated Shoggoth lay curled in one corner. A few bowls inside indicated he was fed. If the lady wanted him dead, why were they feeding him, anyway?

"Hi, buddy," I whispered. This otter didn't know me. I had to let him know I was his friend. "Hi, Shog. Shoggy. Shoggs. How you doin', Shoggy?"

The otter just blinked.

"I am here to get you out, Shoggoth. Wanna go? Wanna go bye-bye?" Now I felt really dumb.

But Shoggoth understood. The otter slithered to me and whimpered, almost like he knew he had to keep his squeaks down. I looked at the latch on the cage and realized there was a padlock.

Made sense, I guess. Otherwise, Shoggoth could've let himself out.

I couldn't carry the whole cage, and I wasn't sure what to do. Shooting the lock would be noisy and would risk hurting the otter. But I didn't want to leave him. I remembered the door to the maintenance shed would be unlatched. I turned down the volume on my phone and dialed Noreen.

"I am upstairs in the silo. Shoggoth is here, but this cage is padlocked. I need the bolt cutters from the maintenance closet behind the main building. The door is open. Are you able ...?"

"Sit tight," she said. "I am sending back up."

The call went dead before I could ask how she planned to reach me.

Ten minutes. Give or take. Ten minutes of me sitting on a cold floor staring at a cage holding an otter that's staring back at me. Aside from the occasional whimper, neither of us said anything. Yes, some of those whimpers were mine. Have *you* stared at an otter for ten minutes without whimpering? I bet not.

Squeak squeak.

I expected to see Noreen with the bolt cutters in hand. Instead, two otters wiggled toward me, one with the bolt cutter handle in its mouth. I was equally surprised and impressed. It dropped the tool in my hands and circled my legs. All three otters were excited, clearly eager to be reunited, so I worked quickly. I worried they might get noisy if I took too long.

Fortunately, the padlock snapped beneath the cutter, and the lock fell off the door.

Clattering loudly on the floor.

"Shit!" I ducked down. Whispering to the three otters, I said, "We need to get out of here quickly. No squeaking! You hear me?" I put my finger to my mouth.

One otter … no idea which one since there were three now, and they were all equally cute … put its paw to its mouth and raspberried. They blinked in unison.

Now was not the time to pet them. "Follow me," I whispered.

We wove our way back through the maze and paused by the door. I shot Noreen another text: Have Shog. Is it clear?

To which she immediately answered: Sure

In retrospect, I should've proceeded a little more cautiously. By now, I had messaged her enough to know she rarely used replies like "sure." And she always punctuated. As I headed back down the stairs with three exuberant otters at my heels, all I could think about was getting them far away from PTARG. I wasn't even thinking about the money at that point. I just wanted them free.

I should have known nothing is easy. An organization operating with high security does not leave a place open unless something else much worse is going down. As I crossed the floor, I saw Noreen waiting in front of the bay door.

And then I heard the hammer of a gun being cocked.

I froze.

A woman stepped out from behind a shelf. The woman from PTARG. O'Shea's mistress. She had a gun aimed at Noreen.

"You did me a huge favor," Liz said. "I thought I was going to track them down one by one, but you brought them all to me. Thank you."

"You're not welcome," I said.

Noreen didn't move. Didn't flinch. Not even so much as a blink. I bet she made quite the poker player. If she was scared, I couldn't tell.

"Don't you even think of hurting my otters, you bitch," she said, her voice as even as the night she showed up on my doorstep.

Liz laughed.

"Why would you waste your time on otters," I said. "Shouldn't you be more concerned about your dead lover?" I wanted to rattle her enough to weaken her guard.

"Lover? He wasn't my lover. He was my husband. And a real piece of shit, at that. I was the one who ordered the hit."

Holy. Shit. Confused, I said, "Then why are you trying to take her otters? They were doing what you paid them to do."

"Look, I couldn't care less about Neil. I knew Ms. Kittery here was doing hits for Orman. That's why I went to him. I was trying to lure them to me," she smirked. "Worked like a charm."

"But … why? Why should you care about one lady and six otters?"

"Because otters are wild animals and not pets! She has no business with them. Training them like circus animals to perform tricks for the public. All I wanted was to see them free, back where they belonged. Animals are not pets," she said.

"I still don't get it," I said. "You would murder people over *otters*?"

"An otter killed Mandy."

Noreen blinked. "The Manilow song?"

"My prized koi!" Liz snapped.

"You have pet koi?" I grunted. "Hypocritical much?"

Then a bang ripped the air, stunning everyone.

Well, stunning me, Noreen, and the three otters. Not Liz O'Shea.

She slumped to the floor, blood pooling beneath her.

An otter stood to the far left. It was standing on an otter standing on another otter. They were wearing a wizard's cloak. The Top Otter held a small Ruger LCP in its front paws. The otter squeaked a few times.

"Oh my God," I said without hesitating. "You're adorable." I seemed to say that a lot around these guys.

"Azothoth!" Noreen clapped. "Good boy!"

"You really need to reconsider those names." I shook my head.

The six otters squirmed around Noreen's feet as she pulled a can of sardines from her pocket and opened it, asking them, "Who is a good boy?" A cacophony of squeaky toys echoed in the garage, followed by the sloppy sounds of chewing.

You know, I rather dug those otters.

I refused to accept Noreen's payment after that night. Told her to buy the otters some fish and a river to eat it in.

So she did.

As luck would have it, she needed a landscaper for her property. Maybe I could talk her into naming the next otter something better. Something friendlier.

Mandy, maybe. Or Ruger.

Jezzy Wolfe is a poet and author who has appeared in numerous anthologies and publications, such as Smart Rhino's *Zippered Flesh* trilogy and the *Insidious Assassins* anthology, Crystal Lake's *Shallow Waters* anthology, Western Legends' *Unnatural Tales of the Jackalope*, *Space & Time Magazine*, and *Weird Tales Magazine*. Her debut poetry collection, *Monstrum Poetica*, will soon be available from Raw Dog Screaming Press. When she is not being chased by her ferrets or hiking trails, you can find Jezzy on her blog at jezzywolfe.wordpress.com, on Facebook at www.facebook.com/jezzywolfeauthor, and on Twitter at @JezzyWolfe.

THE BUTCHER

BY ROBERT PETYO

"Get my asshole son-in-law in here right now."

"Daddy, please. I can handle this." Antonia Marino Valdez kept her hands clamped on the chair's edges as she leaned toward the desk where her father again pounded the tiny red box.

"Get him in here now." When his unlit cigar popped from his mouth and landed on the blotter, he stared at it with wide eyes, as if commanding it to return to his lips.

"Daddy, it wasn't his fault," she lied as one hand came up to the bruise on her left cheek. "Let me handle this." She didn't need her father's help to deal with her husband.

When the door behind her swung open, Antonio Marino demanded, "Where is he?"

"I'm sorry, sir." The voice of the thin man in the doorway barely made it across the massive office. "He's not on the grounds right now."

"Where did he go?"

"I'm sorry, sir. I don't know."

"Find him, Gabby, or it'll be your ass on the line." He grabbed his cigar and poked it at his daughter. "He'll pay for this."

"Stop it." She thumped her fists lightly against her thighs. "You're always thinking the worst of David. Always. I know he's not perfect. Nobody's perfect as far as you're concerned. From the moment I met him, you hated his guts."

He stuck the cigar in his mouth and chomped on it for a few seconds before saying, "That's because he's an asshole."

She stood and again stroked her cheek. "I will take care of this."

"Will you?"

"Daddy, have a little faith in me. Do you think I can't handle it? We're working things out. Yes, we've been having a few problems, but I know we can work it out. Don't worry," she said as stepped toward him, lowering her voice, hoping to soothe him. "You'll have your grandson." She knew it disappointed her father that he didn't have any male heirs. It sometimes nagged at her he would have preferred a son. But sometimes it also made her work harder to please him.

"Don't waste your time," Marino said. "He's an asshole."

The attempt to soothe him had failed. She stepped forward and slapped a hand on the edge of his desk. "I refuse to put up with this."

He looked at her hand, still resting on the desk, and for a moment the lines in his face softened. Just for a moment. "Where is he?"

"Let me handle this. I'm going to tell him to stay away from here until you calm down."

He pressed his torso back in the stiff chair. He removed the cigar and held it up like a precious jewel. "I am calm."

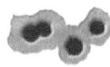

David Valdez read the note again, and when he heard the front door opening, he quickly folded the note and shoved it into his back pocket. "Toni," he called as his wife stepped in. "How did it go?"

"Daddy's really pissed at you. You can forget about that promotion." Exhausted, she moved to him and bent to kiss him on the cheek.

"It doesn't matter." He didn't stand or even look at her. "He won't be mad at me after I take care of the Butcher for him."

Toni carefully sat on the end of the long couch that had been her mother's favorite resting place when she came to visit. Mama had always given her excellent advice on how to handle men, especially her father. "What do you mean?"

"I'm going to kill the Butcher."

"Yeah, right."

"I'm about to find out where he is. Then I'm going to take him out."

"You're crazy." She leaned forward on the couch.

"Then your father will finally give me a little more respect. He'll be kissing my boots."

She munched on her lower lip as she considered that. David was an incompetent who would never be fully accepted into the family business. Her father had given him some simple no-brainer tasks, many of which he fumbled, but that was the only concession he would make to an outsider who married his daughter, a man he only tolerated because he hoped he would give him a male heir. David would never get access to the big money.

David tapped his hip. "I'm tired of him thinking I'm useless. Everybody in your family thinks that."

Useless wasn't the term her father had used. Lately, Toni wondered if maybe her father was a better judge of character than she was. When they first got married five years ago, Toni assumed she would help guide David into the family business. Unfortunately, he showed little interest in working hard. He just wanted to drink, party, and have sex, and not always with Toni.

She clasped her hands between her knees. "You and I have to have a little talk."

"Not now. I'm busy."

"How exactly are you going to bump off a government witness, who is probably hidden deep in some tunnel somewhere with hundreds of agents around him? How are you going to do that and not end up dead?"

David smiled as he stared at her for a long time, his eyes widening with wolflike desire. One hand snaked back to his hip pocket where he tapped his butt like it was a faithful pet. "Don't you worry yourself, my little dear."

She stood. "I am worried. Tell me what is going on. How do you know where he is?"

He thought for a moment, then held his palm out toward her. "It's better if you don't know."

"Stop that condescending crap. You think I'm an innocent little babe? I know a lot more about what's going on in my family's business than you ever will. Now tell me. How are you going to find out where the Butcher is? I want to know what kind of craziness you're planning."

Again, David thought for a few moments before digging his cellphone out of the desk drawer. "I've got to make a few calls, honey. Leave me alone, please."

"Absolutely not, you asshole," she snapped as she took another step toward him, her hands clenching.

The color drained from his face as he reeled back. "Watch your mouth, bitch."

With a growl, she leaped toward him. But he was out of the chair before she crashed into it.

"You looking for another beating?" he taunted as he stepped around her.

She slipped to one knee and twisted her head back toward him. "Fine. Go ahead and cross swords with the Butcher." She carefully got to her feet and adjusted her clothes, making sure everything was in place before she took a few steps toward him and handed him his phone that had fallen on the floor. "But take my word for it. That will be a big, big mistake. You could end up dead." She stiffened with shock as her heart told her David's death might not be such a terrible result.

Were they really drifting that far apart?

He shrugged and turned toward the door. "I need some privacy."

"David, please. I've been trying to help you get into my father's good graces. I've been trying to help you advance in the family. This will be a mistake."

He left the room and slammed the door behind him.

Toni stroked her cheek as she sat at the computer screen in the library. She decided not to do any of this research on one of the family computers because she didn't want her father to get a hint of what was going on. She sipped from her bottle of water and smiled at the head librarian, who busied herself shelving some books.

The Butcher was an accountant who used to work for Marino Investments. His testimony could be damning for the Marino family, though probably not fatal. Her father had survived a lot worse scandals in his twenty years of investing and money laundering.

In fact, Toni and her father were confident his lawyers could crush the Butcher's credibility. Someone bumping off the Butcher to silence him would probably hurt the Marino family's image more than his testimony might. They would come off like a vengeful gang, rather than a respectable business, the image they struggled to project.

But her husband was convinced that by taking the Butcher down he would become an insider with the family and get a big pay raise. He was wrong. Not that she was worried he could ever succeed as an assassin, but she didn't want to take any chances.

She knew the Butcher was being held in protective custody pending his testimony before the grand jury. Her research uncovered a few hints his safe house was somewhere out in the Poconos. One newspaper with Pocono ties hinted that they would have an exclusive interview with the Butcher after his testimony, but they also implied that they were already in touch with him. That told her he might be there, maybe at one of the honeymoon resorts. That would make an ideal haven.

She and David had recently spent a weekend at the Honeymoon Palace, the same resort where they had spent their honeymoon. That had been an enjoyable weekend, a weekend when they were clearly in love, or at least acted like they were in love. But they went quickly back to reality and violent arguments over David's dream that he was entitled to more power in the family.

She squeezed her eyes shut like she was clearing a TV screen. She went back online and confirmed that the number she had gotten from David's phone was to the Honeymoon Palace.

She went out to her car and called Gabby. "There's somebody I want you to follow for a while."

David slumped in the corner of the club at a small, circular table that had only two chairs. He had slept on the couch last night and didn't get any rest. Now, since none of the lamps that hung from the ceiling in the rectangular room were near him, he sat in sleep-inducing twilight, struggling to keep his head up. The guitar player on the low stage across the room was barely audible, doing little to keep him awake. None of the people, heads bowed as they nursed their beers, seemed to care about the music.

"Not too crowded tonight."

David looked up at the skinny, bald man who wore dark glasses and a bulky sweater over tight jeans. After a yawn, he said, "You're late."

"Not too crowded tonight," the man repeated.

David straightened and shook himself awake. "Do you really want to do this secret spy stuff? I know who you are."

The man carefully planted his hands on his hips.

"Fine," David said. He yanked the note from his back pocket. He had to lean to the side and angle the paper to catch some light. "Tuesdays never draw the crowds," he read. "That's why I like it here on Tuesdays."

"Jesus!" The man slapped the paper out of his hand. "What the hell's the matter with you, bringing that here?"

He stroked his palm where the man had made contact. "Cut the crappy games, Blintiff."

"No names," he said as he slid into the seat across from David. "I'm Red Face. Remember?"

"Okay, Red Face. Just tell me where the Butcher is."

"Quiet." He winced as if he'd just been slapped.

"Come on, man. No more games. I'm tired of being a gofer for my father-in-law. I need this. Once I impress the old man and I'm accepted into the family, people will treat me with a little more respect."

"This is about respect, huh? Okay." He rested one wrist on the table while he reached into a pocket of his sweater with the other hand. He withdrew a paper and held it back when David reached for it. "I want a little respect, too. Where's my money?"

David set an envelope on the table and snatched the paper.

On it was an address. He looked up. "Don't play games." He waved the paper. "This ain't where they're keeping him. I know they're keeping him somewhere close to the Honeymoon Palace."

"They are." He pointed at the paper. "That's where you're going to meet Jack Mandorin. He's the reporter who's been in contact with the Butcher. He's meeting him for an interview in two days." He stood and leaned toward David. "You're going with him."

"What? How?"

He stopped him with an outstretched palm. "Money talks, my friend." He turned to leave when someone shoved him down in the chair. His elbow cracked back against the table, and David looked up.

"We have to talk," Toni said.

"What are you doing here?" David asked.

She stood close to the table so that she looked down at them. "I've been following this idiot here." She jerked a thumb toward Blintiff.

He started to stand, but a fiery glare from her was enough to slam him back into the chair. "How much money did you suck out of my husband?"

Blintiff looked at David.

"Cut it out, Toni. And keep your voice down." He looked around the club, but the people hunched over their beers ignored them.

She finally grabbed a chair from another table and sat between them. "We met at the Honeymoon Palace," she told Blintiff. "Remember?"

He nodded but said nothing.

"I knew you were a jerk then, but a harmless one. A poor working shmuck who thought he was going to be a gangster." She felt David's hand on her arm and shrugged it off. "When I saw my husband was in touch with the Honeymoon Palace, I figured it was you. So, I tracked you down and kept an eye on you." She whirled to her husband. "Did he promise you the Butcher?"

His eyes popped like a flashbulb in the darkness, and he again looked around the club. Again, no one was interested. The guitar player had cranked up his volume a bit but was horribly off-key. David stood, shoving Toni away when she tried to stop him. "We can't talk about this here."

Only Blintiff remained seated, pressing the envelope to his chest as he enjoyed the show.

David started toward the exit.

Toni started after him, then turned back and leaned toward Blintiff. "Keep the damn money. I guess you earned it with your scam." She hustled after David, catching him in the parking lot just as he opened his car door. "There is no way in hell you're going to find the Butcher, let alone kill him."

He got behind the wheel but left the door open. "Let me finish this, Toni."

"Do you think Blintiff is some kind of insider? A stoolie who can get you in?"

"I'm meeting a reporter," he said. "The one who's been in touch with the Butcher."

"No, you're not. You'll be meeting another scammer like Blintiff who's going to suck more money out of you."

He jabbed his key into the ignition and turned to her. "Let me see this through. I want to prove to you I'm not useless."

For a moment, her heart pinged like someone was poking her. "I never said you were." David started the engine and tried to pull the door closed, but she kept her forearm against it. "But if you go through with this, then I will realize that you're useless. Don't do it, David."

He knocked her hand away and yanked the door closed.

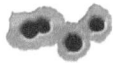

Jack Mandorin had thick glasses with pitch-black frames that matched the thick straight eyebrows that hovered over them. "Here's the way it's going to work, buddy. They won't let me record anything, so you're going to be my assistant who's there to take notes. Once we get inside the room where they keep the Butcher, you take him out, then you knock me out to make it look like you hit me before killing him."

"How will I kill him?"

"Huh?"

"I don't have a gun."

"So what? There's no way you'd ever get a gun in there, anyway."

"What do I do?"

"You got hands, don't you? You're a big guy. The Butcher's a wimp."

David hadn't expected that he'd have to kill the man with his bare hands. "How about you? Why are you in on this?"

"Scoop of the century, buddy." He jabbed a finger across the table between them. "And a nice little payment."

David reached into his inside coat pocket for the envelope. He had little left in his account, but after this, it wouldn't matter.

Ten minutes after Mandorin was gone, David left the bar and scanned the street in both directions before turning down the alley where he had parked. Someone tackled him before he reached his car.

"Hello, asshole."

David had a hard time opening his eyes. He tried to shift his body to the side and realized he was strapped to a chair. "What's going on?"

"You and I are going to have a little talk."

He finally opened his eyes and then squeezed them shut against the sudden wave of light. He slowly opened them again, adjusting to the light, and saw a tall, thin man standing before him. "What are you doing here?"

"Trying to talk some sense into you. That's what I'm doing here."

He looked around the room as best he could and determined there was no one else there, nor was there any furniture other than the chair he sat in. He recognized this place as the cell in the basement of Marino Investments branch office.

"Your wife was trying to talk some sense into you, David, but you just wouldn't listen. I had to take over."

"I don't know what you mean. I'm just trying to help you."

"Shut up. Shut up and listen. I do the talking. We know you have some crazy idea that you can find the Butcher and bump him off."

"I—"

"Shut up. We doubt you could pull it off. Not a schmuck like you. But that's not a problem. If it were up to me, I'd let you go in there and get your ass killed. But we don't want the Butcher hurt."

David flopped in the chair, but he said nothing.

"Someone breaking into the fed's safe house and offing the Butcher would be a disaster for the company. It would make it look like Marino Investments is tied to organized crime and hired a hitman. That's the last thing we want. We want everybody to think we're a respectable business that has a few minor legal problems. That's all. Can't you see that, you idiot?"

"So, why am I here?"

"Are you going to wise up and stop tracking the Butcher?"

Toni answered the phone.

"Do you want to talk to him?"

The voice was so soft, Toni had to ask him to repeat himself. He did.

"Did he ask to talk to me?" When Gabby didn't respond, she knew that answer. "Forget it, then. I'm finished with him. Just do what has to be done."

"Are you sure?"

"He's never going to change." She ran her tongue along the inside of her teeth, top and bottom, as she imagined how Gabby was working over David. Her husband pretended to be a tough guy and was good at knocking around women. But Gabby, who was a lot tougher than he looked, would be too much for him to handle.

"So, what do you want me to do with him?" Gabby asked.

Toni looked across the room at her father, who sat chomping an unlit cigar. She arched her brows and tilted her head at him.

"You're running this show," Marino said. "And doing a damn fine job," he added with a smile. "It's your call."

David would never straighten out, and he had come close to hurting her family. And he had hurt her. Many times. "End it," she said into the phone.

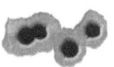

It was four days before they found David Valdez's body in an open dumpster near the Tri-State Electronics factory on Hildebrand Avenue. Tri-State had expanded to that larger property after a low-interest loan financed by Marino Investments. Police determined the victim had been badly beaten and witnesses said he had been boozing it up at a local bar and picking fights with other patrons. That local bar, Fiorello's, had their finances handled by Kellerman Associates, a branch of Marino Investments.

That was the day after Marino's lawyer held a press conference where she announced she was ready and eager to hear testimony from Grayson Bellemy, aka the Butcher. Although she did not explain what her approach would be, she clarified she was going to shred his testimony.

Antonio Marino poked his cigar at the TV screen in the private screening room that could hold twenty people. "She's a good one, that lawyer," he said. "Almost as good as you. Almost."

Toni sat next to her father and was the only other person in the room. "This case is going to fall apart."

He gave a decisive nod and squeezed her shoulder. "Thanks to you. You're certainly moving up."

She smiled at that.

He said, "Too bad things didn't work out with you and David, though, but I knew he was bad news."

"You were right." She stroked her cheek and thought about her mama's advice for handling men. "He was an asshole."

Robert's most recent stories have been published in *EconoClash Review*, *COLP: Big*, *Hardboiled*, *Suspense Unimagined*, *Transcendent*, *Serial Magazine*, *Classics Remixed*, *Thuggish Itch*, *Flash Bang Mysteries*, *The Black Beacon Book of Mystery*, and *COLP: Treasure*.

THE ADVENTURE OF THE ASININE ASSASSIN

BY RICK HUDSON

"Are you alright, Holmes?" I asked. The revolver still smoked in my hand.

"Yes. Yes, thank you, Watson," he replied. "Quite alright."

Moving toward the fireplace to retrieve his tobacco from the pouch on the mantel, Holmes looked down at the peculiar figure that now lay dead on the floor of the study at 221B Baker Street. His shrewd, cold eyes stared upon the masked face. I fancied he was not so much looking at the veiled features, but into the skull itself as if he could peer into its contents.

It had been a singular afternoon. I had been about my practice as a physician between noon and 2:15. On returning to my house, I had found my wife in a particular state of agitation, for a telegram had arrived earlier in the afternoon from my good friend Sherlock Holmes, and she believed it to be most urgent. On reading it, I found that it indeed was. In the message, Holmes hinted at strange and sinister goings-on, and bid me come to

Baker Street immediately. He added I should bring my revolver, and I should bring it loaded. At that time of day, attempting to cross London by Hansom would have been a fool's errand, so I left my house with all swiftness for the nearest station of the Metropolitan Sub-surface Railway. I leaped down the front steps to my home, nearly catching my coat sleeves on the iron railings in my urgency. I attempted to contact Holmes with my pocket telephone but received no response. I dispatched a message of a textual nature, but this, too, remained unanswered.

After a somewhat haphazard and frenzied dash through the streets, in which it seemed that every tradesperson in the city had conspired to congregate on the pavements of the district with the express purpose of impeding my progress, I made it to the MSR station. Fortunately, the rapid acquisition of a ticket was enabled by fortuitously appending an application to my pocket telephone earlier that week, which facilitated such matters. I hurriedly descended into the lower depths of the station, down its steep stairwells and along its interminably long passageways. It is a hellish warren under the streets of London. The walls are all overlaid with cold, pallid tiles on which drip a perpetual condensation that has the semblance of unwholesome perspiration. The very air has a quality and a dankness that one encounters in the last breaths of a fever victim. The other passengers that one encounters here are voiceless specters, but phantoms one pities rather than fears. Terrible, unspoken shames and secrets deeply haunted their eyes. And, like the labyrinth itself, their faces carry the sheen of ague.

Despite my frustrations and heated anxiety, I had not long to wait for a train. I boarded quickly and was soon conveyed from the overbright platform into the lightless tunnels by the pounding and howling locomotive. In that Tartarian world, one sees nothing beyond the windows other than one's own ghost in the glass gazing timidly in return, as if it is you that is the fearful apparition. Occasionally a trackside light will flash by. These luminescences unquestionably serve some mundane and advantageous purpose, but the imagination is impish and bestows on them the character of marsh lights and nightgaunts. One may fancy that the ancients, should they by some miracle be transported to our world, would prescribe some grim and spectacular origin to this vast and lightless maze, perhaps hazarding that it is the burrowing of shambling and crawling primeval gods from some antediluvian mythology that the world has forgotten, and man only remembers in his deepest and darkest nightmares. But, in all truthfulness, the rather Romantic, if rather Gothic, conjurations of fancy are nothing to the real evils that have been committed in that chthonic dreamscape. Holmes, Lestrade, and I have, on far too many occasions than any of us would have liked, found ourselves wandering that Avernal kingdom on the trail of some far too telluric evil. I have yet to transcribe many of these instances, but what unites them is their distance from metaphysical evil and fantasy. They have been all the more horrible for their tawdriness, woeful grubbiness, and deep-set foundations in this very material world.

As the train pulled into Marylebone station, I alighted there rather than continue to Baker Street station itself. My reasoning being that while Baker Street may appear to be the more logical stop, for those more cognizant of London's spiderweb of alleys and backstreets, Marylebone would afford a far more rapid transition between railway and Holmes's address. I shall not detail my hurried and fretful journey, and leave that to your imagination, as I am sure your intellects are more than capable of conceiving of the chaos and activity of London streets and the anxiety of a man desperate to ensure the safety of his friend. Nonetheless, I eventually found myself propelling myself into 221B Baker Street with the fleetness of Mercury, and barely remember mounting those familiar stairs that had witnessed the tread of so many clients, victims, and rogues. Without knocking, I entered, and, in that remarkably familiar room, I was met with the most astonishing sight.

Holmes stood in his dressing gown by his armchair, motionless. He was fixed in the stance and expression of a tiger that faces a hunter's gun—primed and coiled to pounce, but knowing his next movement would bring his end. Indeed, Holmes was facing a hunter's gun, a small pistol held by the most perplexing of figures. The gunman was dressed all in black—shirt, jacket, gloves, trousers, and boots. Further, the assassin had chosen not only to mask himself, but to do so with the grim visage of a skull. Holmes's would-be killer had taken great pains to costume himself as some Gothic angel of doom. Irrespective of the genuine threat this character posed, I could not help but think him to be rather ridiculous, stood as he was in his reaper's garb. From a dramaturgical point of view, the figure lacked the gravitas one expects from Azrael. One always expects such personages to be gaunt and not, well, I wouldn't go so far as to say fat ... but not a little paunchy as our unusual visitor was. Although he wasn't short by any means, he wasn't what I'd call tall either. But it was the assassin's pitiful clothing that undermined the sobriety of the killer most of all. The intended melodramatic effect of the costume was sabotaged by its own cheapness. The mask was of inexpensive material and fastened with an elastic string that threatened to snap at any moment. He had obviously procured it from a fairground novelty stall or similar establishment. The black gloves were of knitted wool. The trousers, jacket, and shirt were ill-fitting and faded in some parts to drab ash, and others bore an oily, gray-blue sheen. The boots were scuffed, the heels downtrodden, and the toes curled upward slightly. It was a most comic and asinine assassin that stood between Holmes and me, rather than a terrifying and deadly vision of execution. However, this clownish figure held a pistol, and that pistol was aimed at Holmes's head. I drew my revolver and aimed it at the masked assailant.

"Stop, damn you!" I shouted. "Drop that weapon now!"

But the assassin paid no heed and continued to menace Holmes silently with the leveled firearm. In retrospect, I feel he may not have been focused on his task, but frozen by bewilderment. Perhaps, now confronted with his prey, the assassin was unsure of what he should do and was hesitating, bemused and perplexed. But at that moment, I did not have the privilege of time in which to ponder such matters. I called for him to desist once more and received no response. I squeezed the trigger of my revolver and it threw the room into a ringing silence that was to last for many minutes.

In fiction, recipients of gunshots hurl themselves somewhat dramatically to the floor as if struck by a mighty blow. But the science of killing has no sense of the theatrical. The bullet struck the ridiculous killer between the shoulders. The body absorbed all the kinetic energy from the shot. There was no excess force to dash the body forward, rather it crumpled to the floor in an inelegant manner, like a sack abandoned by laborers.

And so, I bring us to where I opened this account.

"You knew he was coming?" I said at last. "You sent for me."

Holmes nodded. The silence continued, and I felt no need to break it until a question that had taken some time to solidify in my mind, at last, came to my tongue.

"Why ... why would the man dress as an assassin? And why so obviously? I mean, it's a bit ..."

At that point, Holmes's eyes transfixed mine. A slight smile appeared on his face that I knew to mean, *You've caught up, at last.*

"Because, Watson," he said, "assassins no longer need anonymity. Indeed, they abhor it.

"They have all put themselves upon the aether telegraph where they parade and tout for trade. They promenade and exaggerate their notoriety. There's little call for their trade, you see. And yet so many people dream of becoming assassins. Those who crave dark glamor and adventure. There's a glut, one could say, not only of killers but of those who dream of being killers. They all posture and preen, presenting themselves as assassins to the world. As if wanting it enough will make it so. As if presenting as the thing will *make* them the thing. In reality, most of them work in call centers. There's nothing more dangerous than a dream gone sour, nothing more malignant than a thwarted dreamer. They imagine themselves unjustly chained, like Prometheus, to a rock of mundanity, where they are devoured by their desire for the infamy they are entitled. The wrongness they feel, at an injustice they believe the universe itself is directing at them personally, transmutes them into vindictive, greedy ogres, whose blood runs hot with viscid envy. And their squalid hearts congeal with spiteful dreams of retribution.

"It only takes a human mind to orchestrate the most elaborate symphonies of vengeance. One wronged, ordinary human mind, or more usually a mind that believes that it has been wronged. Our fantasies subpoena monsters from our imagination to enact our evil for us. It does not have to be a visionary or a vivid imagination. The most mundane of minds can do the job quite adequately. The most uninspired of human consciousnesses have universes of resentment and rage from which it can ferment magnificent gargoyles, whole pantheons, and entire mythologies cultivated upon bitterness and disappointment. Stewing in frustration, defiantly raging in the lack of attention they receive, they take it on themselves to be the messiahs of the underdog. But in truth they are the high priests of their own personality cult, mewling for the recognition they believe they are entitled to—some acknowledgment and appreciation. However, the personality is always frail, and the cult equally so. Yet they plot and scheme the most Byzantine campaigns of reckoning.

"But they always make the same mistake, they never realize how pedestrian their concoctions truly are. A third- or fourth-rate intelligence always considers itself to be at the apex of intellectual development, it cannot conceive of the possibility of a mind more agile and adroit than itself. It is this error that brings about their downfall. It is not so much that they are predictable, but that they are calculable."

Holmes paused briefly in his monologue and gestured with his pipestem at the body on the study floor.

"Take our friend here," he continued, somewhat calmer than before. "Martin Griffiths, twenty-six years old. Resident in a rented house in Lewisham, which he shares with three other equally unremarkable individuals. From a relatively young age, he fostered aspirations of becoming a professional writer of penny dreadfuls. He got a job at nineteen in a shop selling such publications and other periodicals of a more onanistic character. He did so, as he believed this would in some way assist him in his ambition. However, he still worked at the establishment, no closer to his goal. He becomes an enthusiastic operator of an aether telegraph machine, on which he soon encounters others of a similar mind. His dream of fame as a penny dreadful writer is evaporating as time passes, and he appoints himself as the deliverer from the injustice of all who perceive themselves to have been swindled by the fate of the destiny they deserve. Night by night, these covens of the deluded stoke each other's fancies of the universe's treachery. Night by night he boasts and postures, announcing what *he* will do to right the wrongs *they* have suffered. He makes an avowal to strike out with a magnificent and symbolic gesture against the tyranny that they all suffer under. He will strike down dead a figure who represents all the success and achievement that they have been denied by heartless reality."

"And that would be you, would it, Holmes?" I asked, taking advantage of a brief pause.

"Obviously."

"And you deduced all that from just looking on this wretched fellow's body? Pieced all that together from telltale tiny details in his apparel and bearing?" Even I, who was well acquainted with Holmes's skills of analysis and deduction, found this difficult to accept. "You foresaw that this very man was not only plotting to kill you, but plotting to do so this afternoon? You were so confident in your prediction that you sent a telegram to my home, trusting that I would arrive in time to intervene in your assassination? I am finding this difficult to believe."

"No. It was far more elementary than that, my dear friend."

He smiled in that particular way of his and, rather flippantly if I may say, regarded his pocket telephone before speaking.

"It was quite simple. Indeed, all too simple, perhaps disappointingly so. There was no need for deduction. The fool announced it to me himself quite clearly and in some great detail. You see, Watson, I had the prudence some time ago of saving to my favorites #Iamgoingtokillsherlockholmes."

Rick Hudson has been writing professionally since leaving school. He writes literary and popular genre fiction (principally horror, fantasy, and SF), and fiction that exits on the fault line between these two forms. His work has been published alongside that of Neil Gaiman, Clive Barker, John Carpenter, Bentley Little, and Storm Constantine. He also contributes articles to consumer magazines available from W.H. Smith's and other major retailers in the UK. Rick is also a university academic lecturing in English literature, specializing in the Gothic and the fantastic.

THE LAST HIT

BY ELDON LITCHFIELD

I'm four minutes to retirement, Sandra thought, checking the wind gauge again.

The night air felt cool on the gritty rooftops. She enjoyed the breeze. The street had its smells and horrid lights, but above the stink lay the comforting quiet of the shadowy roof. She wondered if she would miss the work. She smiled. She was not the aged individual ending a career at the factory or a wizened fool at a firm. She was Sandra Cote, hitwoman supreme and legend of the underworld.

Sandra worked to retire right before hitting thirty-five, a good time to disappear to enjoy the fruits of her labors while at the top of her game. Tonight was to be her last performance, and the highest-paid hit in her career. She planned afterward to fade into mystery, to live the good life in Mexico or on some Greek isle, or maybe Morocco.

So many pleasurable possibilities, she thought. *All I have to do is put a bullet into Kendrick Grimaud, the rapidly rising crime lord gaining influence in Kansas City and who already controlled Topeka. Established crime bosses wanted him gone—three million for the elimination of Mr. Grimaud, aka Uncle Creepy, the Freak Monique.*

Sandra felt the air between the presumed target area and her. She just needed to wait. Adjust, then strike.

Kendrick arrived in a posh car up to the front of Club Necromancer. Sandra had no problem picking him out—tall, sporting long, thin white hair, pale skin, and dressed completely in black, crowned with a top hat. *Like something out of a terrible movie*, she thought.

She adjusted her scope and waited.

Waited ... as Kendrick got out of the car.

Waited ... as he nodded to subordinates.

Waited ... until the back of the head was clear.

Sandra took the shot. Blam.

Kendrick fell. His goons swarmed around him. Job concluded. Three million in the bank.

Kendrick stood up, dancing around and shaking his head while yelling.

She could hear Kendrick from her vantage point. "What the hell? Why weren't you covering me, you imbeciles?" He slapped one of his entourage before bolting into the club.

Sandra slipped off the rooftop to the alley where her motorcycle lay hidden. *No way had I missed*, Sandra thought, but the man was jumping around like he had only stubbed his toe, so that was the only logical conclusion.

Sandra started the motorcycle, revved the motor, and sped off into the night without three million.

That night Sandra contacted her agent, Dan Hood, to report that the first strike had failed, but to tell the contractors not to worry, Grimaud would be dead before the following morning.

Club Necromancer wasn't Kendrick's only haunt. There were Club Titty Kitty and The Foxy Den. Sandra knew Kendrick went out every Wednesday night for business, since associates tended to be agreeable after downing a few drinks while watching naked people twirl around poles, a fact of economics not openly taught in business school.

Kendrick had the honor of being the only one to survive a hit from her, Sandra thought, *but tomorrow night he would die.* Sandra cleaned her rifle and practiced yoga exercises until sunset.

Kendrick arrived at Club Titty Kitty with his bodyguards and a group of sparkle-clad women. Sandra eyed her target from the roof of an abandoned five-and-dime one block away and waited for an opportunity. The women were giggling at something Kendrick said. Sandra aimed at his throat this time. Kendrick stepped to the entrance, obviously leering at the exposed flesh of his companions just as Sandra sent a bullet into his neck.

Kendrick's eyes widened as he fell back onto the entrance carpet. She saw everything through the scope. Clean shot. Job over. Bermuda, here I come.

Except she heard his voice.

"Ah, phuk! Foo keps shutootin' muh?"

She plucked the scope out of her carrying case to focus on an upright Mr. Grimaud. Kendrick pointing to his throat and demanding that his goons run out and find the shooter. The bodyguards fanned out. Clasping his throat, Kendrick hit the wall next to the club entrance. As the hat fell off his head, Sandra noticed the narrow bandage around his head that the long hair had hidden.

Sandra was stunned. There was a dark stain where her previous bullet had hit.

Survival instincts kicked in as Sandra snapped out of her daze and dashed away to her motorcycle. Another night and another failure.

What would she tell Dan?

"He ducked?" Dan repeated.

Sandra took a long drag off a cigarette before answering. "Yeah, bizarre coincidence that he just happened to bend over, which took him out of the line of the bullet. One in a bazillion chance." There was an uncomfortable silence on the other end of the line.

"Listen, Tootsie. The customers said they are losing confidence in your ability to deliver. What the hell is wrong? You never fail, ever."

Sandra wondered about that herself. The bullet struck, but a man does not walk around after bullets have gone into his head and throat.

"Dan, just tell them I will get the job done, plus I'll lower the bill to two-and-a-half million for the inconvenience."

Dan sighed. "Mighty nice of you, considering I get fifteen percent. But hey, I don't need that extra seventy-five thousand dollars."

"Stop whining. Trust me, Dan, this son of a bitch is going down."

The conversation ended.

She reflected on the fiasco. Everything should have come off like clockwork. But next time, Sandra thought, Kendrick was going to die because she was going to use two bullets.

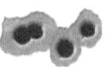

The Foxy Den catered to clients with specialized tastes. Want to see a stripper that was completely covered in bad tattoos, an amputee gyrate onstage to the *Pee-wee's Playhouse* theme, or dancers dressed as cartoon characters engaged in simulated copulation? Sandra knew the owner brought in exotic talent from all over. Kendrick met an associate there named Roscoe Payne, whose vice was watching blind women box in the nude. Roscoe set up transportation of illegal goods ranging from drugs to stolen merchandise. Kendrick met with him in person to establish delivery times, and he never missed a meeting.

Sandra hid in the tall grass one hundred yards from where her target would appear, deciding to use a specialized rifle designed by an expert gunsmith from New York.

She worried Kendrick was not coming for his routine visit. Her worry evaporated as Kendrick's car pulled up to the entrance of The Foxy Den. Bodyguards popped out of the car to survey the surroundings. Another car pulled up with more goons, and these brought out night-vision goggles to scan the area for any attackers. Sandra guessed Kendrick was feeling nervous now, having survived two attempts on his life.

"Don't fret none, Mr. Grimaud, death is on the way," she whispered, waiting for the man to step out. Sandra saw the top of his hat. She wondered if the man was shaking with fear as it wobbled strangely, but as the hat came out further and Sandra noticed it was on a short stick. Sandra felt insulted. Did Kendrick think he was being stalked by Elmer Fudd?

Suddenly Kendrick rose out of the car. He appeared fine. Sandra sighted his head through the scope, then pulled the trigger. Wasting no time, she fired again at the falling figure. Another hit scored under his jaw. Each bullet had struck. Time to slither out of the grass and get away on the motorcycle.

"Motherfuckinggoddamnitshitheadedasswipe! Who keeps doing that? Answer me! When I find you, I will tear you apart with my bare hands! What are you morons standing around for? Find that son of a bitch!"

His hands were on both sides of his face, and Sandra had the insane thought that he was literally holding his head together. He might have a bulletproof vest, but she was going to risk it. No way she could miss the chest. Once sighted, she squeezed the trigger.

Hit.

Kendrick's lanky form spun around, and Sandra saw the large hole in the back of his coat. However, Kendrick did not fall. He wobbled, teetered, and staggered, but did not fall.

"Son of a bitch!" Kendrick and Sandra shouted in unison.

The goons' heads turned in her direction, and Sandra knew her cover was blown. She bolted for her motorcycle hidden down a side road. Sandra started it up and spun out, realizing that her rifle was still back in the tall grass and no doubt would be found, but she couldn't dwell on that now. Sandra got a good look at Kendrick. His bandages had fallen off to reveal a hole in his neck and forehead. His bottom jaw was horribly askew, and another hole was in the side of his head where she had shot him the first time.

It wasn't her aim. The problem was that Kendrick Grimaud just wouldn't die.

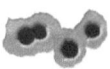

Sandra called Dan after downing four shots of scotch and inhaling fifteen cigarettes.

Dan answered with a charming hello. Shaking, Sandra took another swig of scotch straight from the bottle.

"Yeah, Dan, say, why don't we drop the contract against Cousin Eerie Grimaud there and just move on to something else?" Silence from the other line was like a slap to the face. Sandra reached out for the scotch again but stopped when he answered.

"You messed up again? Baby, this is a third ... I mean two-and-a-half mil ... what is it, is he a little person and hard to hit? Like Kate Moss thin? No, he is a six-and-a-half-foot tall, quasi-albino wearing all black, and he wears a freaking top hat!" Dan went on, Sandra shrank inside.

Dan stopped his tirade.

"Listen Tootsie, this is not protocol, but one party paying for the hit offered to talk with you. Said there was something you should know and would only tell you in person. My MO is to keep the client and agent separated, but hey, maybe he has something you need. It's up to you. I could set—"

"Yes!" Sandra said. "I would like that. Uh, call me back when it is set up."

Dan grunted. "I'm not supposed to let the other members of the paying party know, so this meeting will be super-secret, got that?"

Sandra stated she understood. Dan left a message half an hour later that the meeting was set at 1:30 p.m. tomorrow at The Devil's Alehouse. Sandra wondered why they were meeting at an Irish pub, but the last shot of scotch prevented her from asking much of anything.

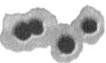

At 1:26 the next day, Sandra entered The Devil's Alehouse, unsure what to expect, only that she would recognize the person by a silver-tipped cane. There was no problem picking out the gentleman from the alehouse's patrons as he was the one swinging a silver-tipped cane above his head shouting, "Oy! Oy!"

Sandra walked to the booth to find a small man in his eighties, dressed in a black and gray suit complete with a bowler hat, like he was on his way to a social function in 1925. She wondered who made such things anymore. The man said hello with an accent Sandra could not place. "So glad you decided to meet, my dear. We have a bit to discuss, but I refuse to have a talk with a dry mouth." He ordered two Offa's Dyke Ales with an order of Glamorgan sausages with crackers.

"Where are you from, England?" Sandra asked.

"Oh, posh on that. I'm originally from Wales, which is occupied by the damn British," he answered. "You see, I'm part of the Welsh Mob," the man stated matter-of-factly.

Sandra scratched her head. "Don't you worry that someone will hear you?"

He laughed. "My dear, who would believe me?"

The ales and sausages were delivered. The old man went straight to business. "I understand you have some difficulties in completing the assignment, and I know why. I needed to meet with you privately because my associates don't believe me. I'm the oldest one in our little circle, you know. All the rest are young punks in their forties, no offense."

"I'm thirty-two," Sandra shot in.

"Of course, my dear. Indeed, huh, must be the light. As I was saying, there are some things in this world that my younger colleagues don't want to consider, even though all the evidence points to it. They are unnerved and refuse to accept the proof. We killed the horrible bastard before. I just think it is terribly indecent of him to be milling around now."

Sandra almost choked on her ale. "Wh … what are you saying?"

The man smiled and nibbled a sausage. "My dear, I was the one that suggested commissioning you. I've been following your career for quite a while. They don't call you the Oklahoma Executioner for nothing." He patted her hand. Sandra couldn't help it and blushed.

"Well, let me start from the beginning. Kendrick Grimaud was a terrible, mean, horrible son of a bitch from Emporia. He started a protection racket in kindergarten. In the fourth grade, he tried to start a prostitution ring, not knowing what a prostitute was, just that people paid money to get one. Neither venture took off, but he found other avenues of mischief. His trouble-making record at school filled an entire drawer. After high school, he worked as muscle to any small-time creep looking for a strong arm. He was unique enough to earn the nickname Creepy Kendrick. Kendrick was looking for the big time. He learned how operations worked, then took over some mob business in Ulysses."

Sandra had held up her hand. "I got one little question here. You're telling me the Welsh Mob runs most illegal operations in Kansas?"

"Yes, of course. Kendrick attempted to hide his extracurricular efforts while still doing work for the mob. They found him out and decided to get rid of him. He was shot thirty-two times, stabbed five times, then shot again, plus kicked in the groin, and afterward an improvised jig was danced around his corpse. They dumped the body in a forgotten well. We all laughed afterward.

"We never should have done it at that hour of the night during the waning and waxing moon," said the old man. "But in our defense, who keeps track of things like that anymore? Kendrick was dead, but that was the puzzle when two months later a man matching Kendrick's description started taking over the criminal element. Within a year he had taken over Topeka and was setting his sights on Kansas City. We sent out enforcers, but they either returned too terrified to be much good for anything or did not return at all. The other mob chiefs refused to admit it was the same person, believing that someone was using the name for its intimidation factor, but I knew different. You see, my dear, Kendrick is one of the … undead."

Sandra leaned back. "You mean he's a vampire?"

The old man laughed, then polished off his drink, motioning for the waitress to bring two more ales. "Oh no, not at all. He is a revenant."

Sandra blinked. "What, he is a priest?"

"Listen, a revenant is an undead creature created from those who were evil during their lifetimes and were murdered. The most wicked of the wicked they are, returning to torment the ones responsible for their death. Kendrick Grimaud is the walking dead."

Her sense of logic should put up more of a fight, she thought, but what the old man said made sense. Kendrick didn't die because he was already dead. A few bullets meant nothing to such a creature, only that Kendrick found it annoying. "Okay, saying you are correct, how do I kill … I mean, get rid of him? Stake through the heart?"

The old man froze, holding his ale in mid-swig. He growled. "When did I say he was a vampire? He is a revenant. R-E-V-E-N-A-N-T. A proper undead of the isles. Not friffin' Count Yorga, and don't say a zombie, dammit."

Sandra made a mental note in the future to keep ales away from Welsh employers when discussing business. "So, what do I do?"

The old man finished the second ale. Without a word, the waitress delivered another ale, absconding with the empty. The old man caught the look in Sandra's eyes. "They know me here." He gulped down half of the pint.

"What you see running around town is a materialization of Kendrick. It has a presence, solid and all, but can't really be harmed. His true body, his anchor in this world, is his corpse. The materialized form gets stronger every time the moon swings from old to new and then new to old. That time between 'not waxing' and 'not waning' is the trick to it. Don't ask me how, it just is. Whatever damage you inflicted on him during your attempts will be gone after the next switchy moon time. What you must do is exhume the corpse, decapitate it, then remove the heart and burn it. Ta-da, no more revenant Kendri ... oh, I get it now ... reverend, revenant. Ha."

She narrowed her eyes at the old man. "If I do all that, are the terms of the hit still valid?"

The old man downed his fourth ale. "Oh friffin' yes, just want the bastard gone."

So I just need to go find and decapitate a corpse and burn its heart, she thought. *Piece of cake.* The old man put down the empty pint and started on the fifth. Sandra assumed the waitress must be in fairly good shape.

"I have to go with you," the old man slurred. "Because I know exactly where the body is buried. If I just explained it, you would just get lost. I gotta see the landmarks. We're a team." He smacked his lips as the waitress swooped in and placed another pint in his reach while snatching away the empty. Sandra now saw the waitress as one of those figurines on German cuckoo clocks that perform a repeated task set by the gears.

"You know, for an older man, no offense, you seem to hold your ale."

He downed the seventh as the waitress delivered the eighth. "Oh, no offense taken," the old man said with a smile. "It's not so much the ale that gets me, mind you, as the OxyContin I take for my back pain."

Sandra left the old man at the Devil's Alehouse after passing a fifty to the waitress to not give him any more drinks. Eleven was enough. She left to pick up an ax, crowbar, twenty feet of rope, and a gallon fuel container from the hardware store. She filled the container with kerosene at the closest convenience store. Sandra arrived back at the pub and ushered the old man out. Guiding him to the motorcycle, she covered a few passenger safety tips with him, such as "don't fall off." She settled in and revved the engine. "Okay, mister, where are we going?"

The old man pointed in no particular direction and shouted, "Wamego, Kansas, my dear." He waved at some passersby. "We're off to decapitate a corpse."

The passersby hurried off. Sandra revved the engine again. "By the way, what's your name?"

The old man burped. "Meredydd Disgleirio Glendower Carwyn Awbry, at your service." *Damn the Welsh*, Sandra thought, speeding off onto U.S. 24 toward Wamego.

Awbry talked constantly during the trip. Sandra couldn't hear any of it. Even if she could, her mind was focused more on the upcoming task. All her past kills were done from a distance. This would be the first time facing her target. A corpse, mind you, but still face to face. Maybe it wouldn't be such a big deal.

Two-and-a-half hours later they were in Wamego. Sandra knew she would've made it in less time if it wasn't for Awbry's traumatic need to stop at every rest area, and wished he hadn't felt the need to announce to everyone they were on a field trip for a cadaver beheading. He never stopped talking. He was still going when they arrived at the dirt road leading up to an abandoned parcel of land used by the locals as a dumping ground. "… and it is a horrible stereotype since we also drink tea. And we make the best sheep. Let me get my bearings now and we will set to our grisly task, eh?"

Awbry scratched his head, then spun around like a dying marionette hanging by one string. "I think they moved some trees," he said. Sandra set her gear on the ground, glad that the area was away from prying eyes. The time was 5 o'clock, and the sun was still two hours from setting. She did not know if such mattered when dealing with revenants. Sandra became aware that Awbry was looking at her. "Are you sure it was Wamego?" he said.

The urge was sudden. Sandra had a Glock concealed under her jacket. One quick shot and …

"You are the one that said Wamego," Sandra said, with her trigger hand shaking.

"Oh, yeah, that's right. Now I recall. Just over here. Right past that rock and a few yards left of that tree." Awbry staggered eastward. Sandra collected her kit and followed.

"This is where we dropped the bastard." Awbry stood shakily over a hole filled with debris. A three-foot-wide sheet of aluminum siding covered the top.

"He's under all this crap." He went over to a large rock to sit down.

She brought an ax and crowbar, but no shovel. She dreaded how long it would take with only two hours of sunlight left. *Oh well*, Sandra thought, *might as well get started.* She then pulled the aluminum sheet to the side and was shocked to see Kendrick Grimaud's decomposed head plainly sticking out of the well. The body loosely buried upright in rocks, dirt, and debris.

She looked at Awbry. "You hid the corpse by putting a piece of aluminum over it? That's it? What were you thinking?" Sandra sat on the ground, rubbing her temples.

Awbry shrugged. "Well, we didn't do a lot of planning, y'see, we improvised a lot. Before we came out here, we stopped at this little place called the Devil's Alehouse and—"

Sandra groaned. "Okay, so I chop the head off, right?" Awbry nodded. Sandra maneuvered onto her knees and braced on the edge of the well, noticing the body was unnaturally well preserved for the time it had been here. It should have been a skeleton and liquefied remains. Reaching in, she grabbed the corpse under the arms and heaved, trying to concentrate on warm beaches, luxurious hotels, and the handsome millionaires she would meet in exotic locations. She pulled Kendrick the Corpse out enough that his head was available for decapitation, looking like the world's most repulsive golf tee. Sandra reached for the ax, hefting it and getting used to the weight. Bracing her feet, Sandra took a few practice swings, then leaned out her foot to jostle Kendrick until his head sloped forward. Sandra thought it looked as if the corpse was considering prayer. Sandra decided on an overhead swing down on the base of the neck and gripped the handle of the ax, raised it.

"One … two … thr—"

"Did you bless the ax?" said Awbry.

Sandra almost flung the ax into the brush but caught it in time, then turned to face Awbry. "You mentioned nothing about having it blessed."

Awbry dismissing Sandra's tone with a wave of his hand. "Don't think you need to. I told you everything I know about how to deal with the thing. Right now, I'm just pulling stuff out of my ass. Go on, I'll hamper you no more." Sandra sighed, affirmed her grip on the ax, and raised it over her head.

"Butter! They don't like butter. Especially if you make a cross out of two sticks. They can't stand it. They go crazy." Sandra turned back around to witness Awbry holding up his fingers, making a cross.

Sandra gripped the ax again, focused, then raised it.

"And kryptonite makes them stronger." Awbry snickered.

Sandra spun around while pulling out her Glock. Faster than the human eye could track, she released the safety just before she pointed the muzzle at Awbry. Six rapid shots produced holes in the drunken man's white shirt. He fell without a sound.

Re-holstering the Glock, Sandra lifted the ax over her head, then hesitated, expecting the old man to gurgle out one last bit of alcohol-inspired nonsense. But Awbry remained silent on the hard ground. Sandra swung the ax, cleaving the head off the corpse. The head bounced around the congested well before settling behind its previous shoulders. Sandra chopped into the chest, surprising herself with her viciousness, and destroyed the ribs. Panting, she stooped down, and then thrust her hand in the chest for the heart, surprised to find the interior of the cavity damp and realizing now that gloves would have been a nice addition to the equipment list. The organ gave a little under her grip, the moist slime of congealed body fluids making it difficult to pull out. She used the ax edge on the body. Sandra finally held the heart of Kendrick Grimaud up to the sky.

Sandra found a circle of rocks that had served as a campfire for transients and set the foul organ in the center, retrieved the kerosene container from the motorcycle, then poured the contents on the heart. She laughed in triumph before realizing that she had no way to light it.

Sandra rushed over to Awbry. She searched his pockets, but only found a pill bottle with two OxyContin in it and a wallet containing a driver's license and twenty-five dollars. Sandra was amazed. According to the license, the old man's name really was Meredydd Disgleirio Glendower Carwyn Awbry. She wondered whatever happened to his silver-tipped cane.

Sandra ran to Kendrick's body, hoping there would be a lighter in the jacket pocket. She smiled, finding a red Zippo with the words Bad Boy on it. She walked to the kerosene-soaked heart and tested the lighter, creating only sparks. Sandra grimaced, wishing the annoying fumes were not giving her a headache so she could …

The lighter lit. Sandra was glad that kerosene did not explode like gasoline as she dropped the lighter onto the heart. A low whoosh of flame covered the circle of stones in a dull blue glow. The heart bubbled and oozed in the flames, causing her to retch.

Afterward, she checked on the heart to find all that remained was a crisp oval that looked like a burnt pancake. Satisfied, Sandra went to Awbry to provide him with a few moments of respectful silence. Awbry had helped her, Sandra thought, and it had been unprofessional to shoot him out of anger, especially six times, but it would not do for the higher-ups of the Welsh Mob of Kansas to know that she offed one of their own. She dragged the body to the well and dumped it in with headless Kendrick, to keep him company, and covered the hole with the same sheet of aluminum that was there before.

Sandra went back to the motorcycle to go home and call Dan.

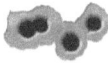

She got her two-and-a-half million.

Dan said the customers were impressed with whatever she had hit Kendrick with. His body had blown into flaming bits and scattered over the parking lot of Club Necromancer. Sandra guessed it happened the same time she had burned the heart. Dan said that some people swore that Kendrick's head screamed a full thirty seconds after he exploded. Her agent asked questions, like why the remains of Kendrick's body had melted into goo. Sandra guessed he wouldn't buy that what had exploded in the parking lot was not one-hundred percent real Kendrick. It didn't matter. She officially retired.

Sandra soaked up the sun on the Italian beach, but it did little to banish her worries. The added payment from the Kendrick job to her own savings amounted to over three-and-a-half million, but nowhere in her assassin career did she bother to take a course in budgeting, and the cost of fancy hotels, lavish dinners, grand shopping sprees, fantastic parties, and exotic spas added up. The idea of having to go back to work was depressing. She had gained weight because of her relaxed lifestyle, and her killer-quick reflexes had suffered from a lack of exercise. She just wanted to soak up the rays to forget the gloomy clouds on her horizon. Someone walked into her sun.

"Excuse me, Perdono, signora che ha guadagnato peso, questo è un messaggio per voi," chirped the waiter. He handed Sandra a small envelope with "S. Cote" scrawled on the outside. Sandra gave him a confused look. Sensing no tip, the waiter left, leaving Sandra wondering if this was some joke on Dan's part. She opened the letter and read the contents.

Dear Reaper Lady,

Hi, I am out of pills but that is OK because I really don't feel much of nothing anymore. No more hangovers, but still get a buzz from the old nip! Did you know what phase the moon was in the last time when we were together? Or maybe there is just something in the ground of Kansas that makes excellent conditions for these things to happen. Imagine my surprise that I was rooming with Kendrick. Anyways, I'm coming to visit you so we can talk about old times. Things have not been the same without you.

Oh, and don't bother looking for the "old me"—guess that phrasing works. I bought the old dumping grounds, had the well blocked off, and had a few tons of concrete poured over the site. Now it's one of the Wamego tourist attractions called the Rootin'-Tootin' Kansas Ghost Town. Family fun for all. What do you think? My only competition is the Oz Museum.

Did you know Wamego has an Oz museum? Neither did I. But there it is.

Be seeing you soon!

Sincerely,

M D G C A

Eldon Litchfield is a writer of the odd and macabre living in Winston-Salem with his spouse and three cats. His influences range from Ray Harryhausen, horrible B monster movies, good monster movies, horror comics, and too many other things to list. He is a patron of a local murder of crows and spends too much time researching obscure lore and should spend more time outside getting some sun. You can find him on Facebook under Eldon Litchfield or read his weirdness at barchiel1.livejournal.com.

KILLINGS 4 SALE

BY BLAIR KEETCH

"How should I explain all the ways I can kill people? Should I list everything in one section? Or highlight each method of murder somehow? What d'ya think?"

A warm summer breeze swirled through the open garage doors and shuffled the papers on my office desk, giving me a chance to collect my thoughts. "Ah, exactly how many services do you offer?" I paused to pick up a stray rose petal from one of the many heirloom rugs lining the floor.

Piper wore black Buddy Holly glasses, which she constantly pushed back on the bridge of her nose in a gesture I found strangely appealing. "Well, it depends on the client, but off the top of my head—strangulation, stabbing, poison, death by revolver, death by rifle, death by auto ..."

"You mean, hit and run?"

"Definitely," she said. "Or it could be sabotage—cut brake lines, but no guarantee that will work. Or a staged car crash."

"That's a lot of ..." I searched for a suitable phrase. "Options, I guess."

Her fedora bobbed up and down in agreement.

"That will be much too crowded if each has its own tab."

"Maybe I should break them into categories? I should mention my specialty is making murder look like an accident."

"I'd suggest a tab that provides an overview, and you click through to another page listing all your talents."

"You mean something like 'About Me' or 'Products and Services'?" Piper shook her head. "Feels too staid. I'm not a corporation."

"You can label it whatever you want, but people still expect a familiar structure. How about *Ways I Kill People*?" I was half-joking, but Piper was not—she broke into a dazzling smile.

"I love it!"

The advantage of having my office inside an unused garage is that it's virtually soundproof and away from the prying eyes of my aunt. Yet, I couldn't help but glance around to make sure we weren't somehow overheard. "You must forgive me, but this is something new to me." While I'd crafted websites for some dubious customers such as a local escort agency (curiously unerotic), this was my first job for a hired killer. "I rarely work on the Dark Web."

Piper looked at me incredulously. "This isn't for the Dark Web. I want as many people to see this as possible. It certainly beats ads on Kijiji."

I blinked away my surprise. "Uh, you advertised in classifieds?"

"Well, it was better than a poster stuck up on the grocery store bulletin board." She pouted, but I couldn't tell if she was serious or not.

"How about I do a rough landing page to see if we're moving in the right direction. Once we've nailed down the ambiance, we can tailor the content accordingly."

Her eyes widened with excitement. "No blood splatters, please. I want something fresh and original."

I nodded and wrote "no blood splatters" in my notebook. I was about to ask about the merits of bullet casings when bright lights shone into the recess of my office like an errant searchlight.

My aunt had returned from grocery shopping, her high beams needlessly turned on as she parked in front of the open garage despite plenty of space on either side.

Piper didn't hide her curiosity and stared at my aunt as she pulled herself stiffly out of the driver's seat. "Peter, put the groceries inside," she demanded.

I tamped down my irritation. "In a few minutes," I said.

"I don't want the milk to get warm. You can talk with your client later." Somehow the word *client* sounded like *hooker*.

Piper smiled sweetly at my aunt. "I'm sorry," she whispered to me. "I didn't realize your mother suffered from dementia."

"I'm his aunt, not his mother. Though that burden was passed to me many years ago." My aunt's voice echoed off the garage walls as she looked icily at Piper.

"It's been a pleasure, my handsome Petey." Air kisses on both sides of my face. "I'll send you some material for consideration."

We watched as Piper straddled her cherry red Vespa and drove off along the sidewalk.

"This soup is cold," my aunt said.

"It's supposed to be cold," I informed her. "It's called vichyssoise, and it's very popular in the Mediterranean on hot summer nights."

"Maybe your harlot will like it, but give me something plain and simple any day." I grimaced. "Plain and simple" meant grilled cheese or shepherd's pie. I had worked as a sous chef at one of the city's most prestigious restaurants. Not trendy, but classic.

Slowly working my way up the ranks until my aunt's constant harping over my late nights and irregular hours became too much. "How can I ever get a good night's sleep with you stumbling home in the middle of the night smelling of wine and garlic?" she often said.

The money was good, but not good enough that I could leave and go out on my own. In a fit of desperation, I quit, hoping to make my aunt happy. But peace and tranquility were as fleeting as complimentary hummus in a vegetarian café.

However, there was a silver lining to my departure. One door closes, another opens—although I was uncertain what the open door would be. For the first few days, my phone rang constantly, the display showing "Côte d'Azur." Probably the head chef, Michel, begging for my return.

Finally, one afternoon, I answered the phone and shouted, "Not coming back. Find yourself another dupe."

"Don't worry, we already hired your replacement." It wasn't Michel, rather the restaurant owner, Jacqueline. She had always treated me with kindness and respect, and I immediately regretted my surly tone. "I'm calling for your other talents."

"Other talents?"

"Well, criticism, for one. You were always commenting on how dull and uninspiring our website is. So, we're doing a complete overhaul and I thought you could help."

"I'm not a web designer," I said.

"You're in luck. I have a great IT person. Technically brilliant, but couldn't design a coloring book for a two-year-old. She wants us to provide creative content. Images, copy, that sort of thing."

And so it began, my yearlong tutorial—some formal courses, others through osmosis as I worked alongside various designers until I struck out on my own—if you could consider setting up my office in my aunt's unused garage following in the steps of Steve Jobs.

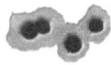

"What's this?" my aunt asked.

"Lamb medallions stuffed with feta cheese." I placed the plate on the table with a flourish.

"Feta? Isn't that Greek?" Then, with a glance of horror at the steamed fiddleheads, she said, "When I was young, only poor people ate these weeds."

I wondered why I tried anymore. Even a lowly omelet pushes her culinary boundaries. Before I could think of how to respond, my phone buzzed with a text.

"It's dinnertime," my aunt said. "Probably some naked selfies from that tramp this afternoon."

I retreated into the kitchen on the pretext of retrieving the saltshaker and surreptitiously checked my phone. Indeed, my aunt's wild accusation wasn't far off the mark.

"Here are a couple of photos for my profile pic," Piper said. "What d'ya think? I'm aiming for sophisticated and sensual. Hope it's not slutty instead."

The attached photos made me swallow nervously. Piper was wearing a black bowler hat. And a dazzling white silk blouse that fitted snugly. Her expression was far from demure. I struggled with what to say, but my aunt saved me with her irritable grumbling. "Come back, your dinner's getting cold."

My sleep was restless. I couldn't shake the image of Piper with her alluring eyes, bright smile, and provocative photos.

I was finally drifting off to sleep when my phone buzzed twice in quick succession. Bleary-eyed, I looked at the screen. Two texts from Piper. Each text consisted solely of a link to a newspaper article. No comments. Not even an emoji—unlike Piper.

I clicked on the first. A headline popped up. *Tragic Accident Kills Local Entrepreneur.* Details were sparse but disturbing.

An up-and-coming businessman—a pool supply store owner—was accidentally poisoned when an ammonia leak occurred in his shop. Police investigated, but they ruled it an accidental death.

The second article had a similar victim, but a different scenario. *Robbery Gone Wrong* read the headline. Another successful retailer, older and more prosperous—this time the owner of a small chain of jewelry stores. Shot point-blank as he left his business to do a bank deposit. Left behind his wife of five years. The photo showed an obviously much younger woman. Enough said.

Before I could read further, another text arrived. "I have plenty more for 'Previous Work' or whatever we should call it." Followed by another image. Piper wearing a half-open men's Oxford shirt. Her blonde hair defiantly poked out from under a beret. She held up a large, phallic gun in a James Bond pose.

Too late for a cold shower, too early to wake up. I turned off my phone and then tossed and turned until dawn.

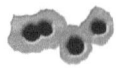

The next few days, my focus was on an entire revamp of a local accountant's website, driven with some urgency because of upcoming tax regulations.

Yet with increasing frequency, I kept returning to the construction of Piper's website. I experimented with the tabs, placement of photos, a scrolling banner. Although a clichéd image, I used a smoking gun as a pop-up image to sign up for her monthly blog.

At first, I had gone with dark colors, but the menacing tone didn't feel right. Instead, pastel colors that admittedly bled into each other. I had photoshopped Piper's image and emphasized her piercing blue eyes. For the links to the news articles, I'd found images of the fatality scenes to give it more impact and immediacy.

I circled back to the link for the second newspaper article and clicked on it again. The jewelry store and the wife's identity were clearly named. I did a quick search and, before I could have second thoughts, I clicked on the 'Contact Us' page and the telephone icon.

"Forster's Fine Jewelry. Virginia speaking."

"Hello," I said, suddenly realizing I was unprepared. "I'm a web designer and I was calling about a shared acquaintance—Piper." I almost sensed a nonchalant shrug at the other end of the line. "I didn't think you would answer the phone yourself."

"I'm full of surprises." She laughed. "Everyone thinks I was just a trophy wife. Did you know that we've added five more stores in the past two years?"

"Sounds like you're building quite the empire."

"Now that all obstacles are out of my way," Virginia said. "My husband reached the limits of his ambitions at three stores."

"About our mutual friend," I said.

"Piper? Delightful girl, killer personality."

"So I gather. I'm constructing her website and she sent me a link to a newspaper article."

"Hopefully not the one in *The Sun*. They made me sound like such a tramp."

"Ah, it was from *The Guardian-Times*, but she wanted to add it on her website."

"Oh that," she said. "We already discussed this. Fine by me."

"You're not worried this might create ... shall we say, unwanted attention?"

"My dear, I've received nothing but unwanted attention for the past five years, ever since I married my husband. I'd call it malicious gossip if there wasn't some truth to the matter." Her voice hardened. "Police consider this a cold case. If anyone asks me, I'll say it's likely a prank."

I nodded to myself. If anyone could pull it off, she could. As I hung up, it occurred to me that Piper and Virginia were cut from the same cloth, though Teflon might be a better description.

"Houston, we have a problem."

"I've heard the line probably a dozen times a month since I was a teenager." I smiled. "I think I prefer Petey."

"Okay, Petey," she said. "There's a major obstacle."

"You've changed your mind?"

"Why would I ever do that?" Her look of surprise was genuine. "I want to advertise my services as professionally and as mainstream as possible." She glanced up at a rustling sound in the garage rafters above.

"Raccoons," I said. "Like you. Cute but ferocious."

She smiled at the compliment. "Do you know how many people need my services? And don't know how to find me?"

"Walking up and down the sidewalk with a sandwich board doesn't cut it?"

She swiveled my laptop back toward her. "This is fantastic. Whimsical, yet ominous. I love it. It's just missing one aspect."

"A link to PayPal?"

Piper shook her head from side to side. Today she was wearing a wheat-colored Panama hat. "Accolades," she said.

"Accolades?" As always, I felt one step behind.

"You know, reviews."

"No problem. I can easily add another tab labeled 'Accolades' if you wish."

"That's not the problem. I'm missing actual content."

"You mean reviews of your killings?"

"Do you ever go out to a restaurant without checking their reviews? Book a hotel? Even order a pizza?"

I hesitated. Earlier that morning, I'd been scanning reviews for roofers. But assassins? It seemed far-fetched.

She saw the skepticism on my face. "Look at me. Do I look like a professional killer? Would you trust me to garrote your girlfriend? Or bludgeon your business partner?"

"Nice alliteration, but isn't word of mouth the best recommendation?"

"My clients aren't the type where their friends are also looking for assassins. And aren't reviews virtual word of mouth? That's why I need a website. It's an extremely competitive field out there. Lots of amateurs, but they have advantages over me—body, brawn, intimidating demeanor." Piper smiled again, and her dimples flashed like lights on a vintage arcade game.

"And reviews offer a level of assurance," I said.

"How's this sound?" Piper made air quotes with her hands. "My life was a dead-end street with an abusive husband, trapped marriage with no opportunities to spread my entrepreneurial wings. Until Piper arranged a fatal accident. Now I have freedom, a new love interest, and a far healthier bank account." She looked at me. "Persuasive, huh?"

"Sounds like Virginia Forster," I said.

"Well, she wrote this before she got cold feet."

"Hence no reviews."

"All my past clients said the same. A few can brush off a newspaper article, but a reference by name is too much."

"What if it was signed anonymously?"

"What's the point of a review if it's anonymous?" she said. "No one will believe it's genuine."

"But the rest of the website is fine?"

"Absolutely" Piper broke off.

A man in a black suit, dark-gray shirt, and wraparound sunglasses stood at the other side of the street staring at us.

"Anyone you know?"

"Never seen him before."

"Not one of your colleagues?" His wardrobe fit the Hollywood version of an assassin. I couldn't shake the feeling I'd seen him before. I rose out of my chair, but a moving truck lumbered down the street, blocking my view. When it finally departed, the sidewalk was empty.

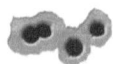

Two days later, I was putting the finishing touches on Piper's website, except for the "Accolades" section, which was still blank. Neither of us could figure out who would provide a review, though I regarded this as a minor inconvenience, while Piper considered it a showstopper.

A light rain fell, but not enough to warrant closing the garage door. My aunt's car pulled sharply into the driveway and stopped abruptly, the car hood almost touching the couch that served as a waiting area.

I shielded my eyes in annoyance from the glare of the headlights. I saw the outline of my aunt behind the wheel. After a moment, the lights extinguished. She clambered out of the car and gave me a smug look. "I just came back from Mr. Jeffries."

"Who?"

"Mr. Jeffries. He lives three blocks over on Huron Street."

My stomach sank. I remembered Jeffries. An auto buff who was usually restoring a couple of vintage cars in his driveway. Worked at a local dealership and always wore black suits.

"He mentioned a couple of months ago he was restoring even more cars and needed some more storage. I told him he could rent the garage anytime he wanted."

I stood up from behind my desk and pushed past my aunt. My head throbbed, and I only caught snatches of words. "Clean up by next Thursday … eight hundred a month." I headed into the darkness of the house, upstairs to my cramped, solitary room, blood rushing in my ears until all I could hear was the roar of an aircraft engine.

"Cheer up. Everything will work out in the end."

I pulled my attention away from the computer screen. "For a cold-blooded killer, that's a Pollyanna statement."

"Look on the bright side of life." She whistled tunelessly.

"Easy for you. I'm the one who's going to be evicted in three days. By a family member, no less."

"There must be alternatives." Piper sipped her takeout coffee. "What about the basement?"

"A hoarder's delight. You can barely walk among the boxes, my uncle's old tools and paint cans, cartons of old records."

"Breaking the fire code, no doubt," she said. "Do you really need an office? Everything's virtual nowadays. You can meet at a coffee shop for clients."

"For clients, yes. But for the design work, I need a fixed server, at least two large-screen monitors, stable Wi-fi …"

"Okay, I get the idea." Her eyes looked around the garage appraisingly. "Speaking of ideas …"

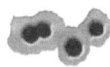

It was the evening of the soft launch. While her website wasn't fully active—the "Accolades" section had a "Coming Soon" graphic floating across the screen—Piper had wanted to go live as soon as possible.

"I guess there's usually a cocktail party with appetizers and glasses of champagne," she said.

"Usually plastic glasses."

Piper paused and took another bite of the pasta I'd prepared. When she'd proposed a low-key celebration of beer and takeout, I'd suggested an alternative—a gourmet, home-cooked meal. However, my aunt's home, with her hovering in the background, would spoil any celebration, so Piper's flat was an obvious choice.

Instead of being too fancy, I'd gone old-school bruschetta made with ripe, locally grown tomatoes. Grilled calamari as an appetizer. Homemade ravioli stuffed with cheese and lobster, with a rich, white sauce. At first, I was disappointed at the table and chairs on her front veranda when I was hoping for a more intimate setting, complete with candlelight.

However, the evening breeze, approaching sunset—even the friendly greetings of neighbors out for a walk—created a wonderful ambiance.

"Give me a moment while I fetch the cheese plate."

"Wait, I have a better idea." Piper took me by the hand and led me inside. She'd placed candles throughout the living room, and their flames flickered from the gentle breeze through the open window. "Let's have each other for dessert," whispered Piper as she gently pushed me back onto the couch.

What followed was a whirlwind of unbridled passion, laughter, and urgent whispers. Somewhere Piper cried out so loudly I swore the neighbors' windows trembled. Afterward, we laid intertwined among the tumble of pillows as I drifted off to a deep, uninterrupted sleep for the first time in years, even with the faint sound of sirens in the distance.

"What did you say?" I asked sleepily as Piper snuggled closer to me.

"Nothing. Just alibi by orgasm."

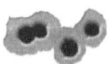

The *Times-Guardian* articles were brief, and coverage faded after a few days. The last article summarized it best.

The tragic fire on Arthur Road that claimed the life of a local seventy-eight-year-old woman was likely "an unfortunate, but preventable, accident," stated Fire Marshall Rick Johnston. "The cause was likely an exploding BBQ propane tank. Many people store them incorrectly and don't even realize they have expiry dates. In this case, arson investigators determined two propane containers in the basement caused the explosion. This also serves as a reminder to keep your basement tidy and not to hoard."

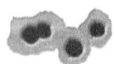

Another spectacular summer afternoon, despite the lingering odor of scorched wood in the air. Wasn't much left of the house.

I sat in contemplation in the dimness of my garage. A pile of moving boxes surrounded me, but only a few. The fire had destroyed just about everything—furniture, all my clothes, even my comic book collection.

As always, Piper was optimistic about our outlook. "It's a chance to rebrand."

Maybe Piper is right. How many people in life can truly start over? I turned back to my laptop and resumed typing.

Out of Death comes Life. My future was bleak, with limited possibilities before me. No opportunities, only obstacles. Then I met Piper, and everything changed. Not only because of her creative ways of killing but her zest for life. A staged tragedy and now my life is full of hope and endless possibilities.

A toot from the Vespa horn as Piper pulled into the driveway.

Highly recommended. I was so impressed with her murderous ways, I proposed marriage.

I returned her cheerful wave and clicked on the rating for Five Stars. I typed Peter H. Reviewer, fiancé, and business manager.

Somewhere in the charred ruins of my aunt's house, I heard a bird chirping. I stood up, smiled, and hit SUBMIT.

Blair Keetch is a mystery writer based in Toronto, Canada. His short story "A Contrapuntal Duet" was part of the 2019 mystery anthology *In the Key of Thirteen*. His story "Deadly Cargo" was included in *Heartbreaks & Half-Truths*, published by Superior Shores Press. "A Crunchy Kind of Death" was featured in the newsletter for It Was a Dark & Stormy book club. "Sleep, Perchance to Die" was part of the mystery anthology *Grave Diagnosis*, published by Carrick Publishing. He is hard at work (when time and toddler permit) on his novel *Flight Risk*. You can find him at BlairKeetch.com or on Twitter at @BlairKeetch.

THE THIRD DATE RULE

BY JEFF MARKOWITZ

Sy looked up from his linguini and white clam sauce and asked, "So, ladies, what do you think?" His aging fingers fumbled at his jacket pocket, revealing a bottle of little blue pills.

Avoiding his lecherous gaze, the twins giggled and continued eating their lobsters.

"But don't you ever think you would want to try something just a little different?"

The twins hid behind their lobster tails, giggling with restraint. Helen, the older of the two—dressed in a conservative wool skirt, cotton blouse, and orthopedic shoes, her silver hair tied up in a bun—was embarrassed by the audacity of her sister's dinner companion. Widowed three years, Helen had been married to the same man for almost five decades. They had made love one way for all those years and never once discussed whether either of them "wanted to try something different." And now, her sister's dinner date seemed to suggest some yet unspecified sexual adventure. And at their age, no less. It was undignified. Ellen, younger by ten minutes, wearing her best lavender polyester pants suit and gold stickpin, melted butter on her chin sparkling in the candlelight, found Sy's suggestion exciting. Ellen had never married. She was seventy-five years old and had never made love, except one time that didn't count, she told herself, one time, lasting nearly twenty years, with her sister's late husband.

She looked Sy over carefully before responding. He was an attractive if somewhat flamboyant man, healthy and robust for a man approaching eighty, still with his own teeth, a full head of hair, and a handlebar mustache. He was wearing green plaid slacks, a green shirt, green blazer, and a bright red bow tie.

"I know what you mean Sy. We're not supposed to feel anything at our age, and most of the time I don't, but now and then I still want to feel …" Ellen's voice trailed off, barely a whisper now, "a man inside me."

Helen was aghast. "Wha … wha …," she tried unsuccessfully to form a coherent thought. Events rolled on without her.

"Oy, well, I hope, if I may be so bold, you might feel that way tonight?" Sy struggled with the pill bottle. "I can still stand erect maybe one time each month, but I think tonight maybe I should take two pills. In case your sister wants to join us."

"No, Sy, my sister won't be joining us. Just talking about it, you're going to give poor Helen a coronary."

Once a month, he would invite a woman from the neighborhood to dinner, and sometimes more than dinner. This was Sy's third date with Ellen. Sy was not so old that he didn't remember the third date rule. Apparently, Ellen also remembered the rule.

Ellen smiled coyly. "Here, let me help you with that." She reached across the table, unloosing the cap.

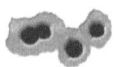

Sy had not been on the job since the end of the second millennium. Retirement had been good to him. After selling the house in Brooklyn, he had moved into a townhouse in New Jersey, a senior community just off exit 8A. After a lifetime of hustling for every dollar, some men find it difficult to adjust to the slow pace of a retirement community, but Sy had made peace with the indignities of aging. He spent his days playing checkers and his evenings watching cable TV. His current favorite was the Crime & Investigation Network. Even in retirement, he liked to keep up with the industry. Only sometimes he missed the excitement of being on a job. Lately, he had felt the loss of purpose most acutely. When the job opportunity came his way, Sy allowed himself to be talked into accepting the offer.

He paid the bill and pocketed the receipt. He would need the receipt later in case he was asked to document his out-of-pocket expenditures. Lord knows he didn't need the money, but there was a principle at stake. They should pay a man in his position the agreed-upon fee plus expenses.

He arranged a rideshare (and another receipt) to take them back to Autumn Acres. Helen and Ellen lived on a cul-de-sac that backed on the eighth fairway. They each owned half a side-by-side duplex. The arrangement gave them the personal space they desired, without ever being more than a few feet apart. They could, and often did, knock on the shared bedroom wall to say goodnight.

Sy had a small home on the other side of the fairway. The rideshare dropped them off in the sisters' cul-de-sac. Sy walked Helen to her side door and waited until she was safely inside. He returned to the car and walked with Ellen to her side entrance.

"Would you like to come in for a nightcap?" Ellen smiled at Sy in a way that made him glad that he had taken the little blue pill.

Inside, Sy built a small fire in the fireplace.

"Please check the damper." Ellen thought a fire would be romantic. A safe, properly managed fire. "We don't want to set off the smoke detector."

Ellen brewed a pot of Darjeeling. While the tea was steeping, she excused herself, returning in a floor-length flannel nightgown and fleece-lined slippers. Sy nodded approvingly. "You look lovely."

"Thank you." Ellen's face reddened. She felt the heat emanating from the fireplace. "Perhaps you'd like to take off your bow tie."

Over the years, his fingers had lost much of their dexterity, but he could still tie a perfect bow tie. He unbuttoned the top button on his shirt and tugged at one end of the bow tie, letting it hang loosely around his neck.

Ellen was suddenly nervous. Other than the affair with her late brother-in-law, Sy was about to be her first. She couldn't rightly claim to be a virgin, not after spending two decades as the other woman, but that was how she felt. She wanted to know more about Sy before inviting him into her bed.

"What exactly are your intentions?"

Under the circumstances, Sy didn't want to talk about his intentions. The little blue pill would do the talking for him. He tried to change the subject, but Ellen was persistent. "Some fancy-dressing, sweet-talking ladies' man won't take me in."

"You're quite right," he said. "I assure you my intentions are honorable."

"Will you respect me in the morning?" Ellen searched his eyes for an answer. "I couldn't stand it if this was, what do the kids call it nowadays, wham-bam-thank-you-ma'am."

Sy didn't want to think about the morning. He didn't want to think about whamming or bamming. "I care for you, Ellen."

"What did you do?" Ellen stammered. "I mean, before you retired?"

"Does that matter? I've been retired for more than twenty years."

"I suppose I'm just nervous." She kissed him on the cheek. "You're sweet."

"I'll be gentle."

And he was.

He took her by the hand and led her to bed.

When they finished, Ellen wanted to talk. "That was ..." but she didn't know how to finish her sentence.

Sy grinned. "Yes, it was."

"When you asked my sister to join us ... did you really mean ..." Ellen lapsed into silence.

What he really meant was unimportant. "I was just being polite." Sy let loose a mighty guffaw. "I didn't want her to feel left out."

"I need to tell you something."

"I know."

But Ellen wasn't listening anymore. She was unburdening her soul.

"When I was a little girl, my parents told me I shouldn't give myself to a man until we were married." Ellen paused, contemplating the lost years. "I never did get married."

Sy didn't know what to say, so he said nothing.

"Helen's husband, David, offered me a solution for my problem."

"A solution?"

"I don't want you to get the wrong idea. David loved Helen. And she, him. But she didn't satisfy him." Ellen took a deep breath before continuing. "That became my job."

"You mean ..."

"Seeing as how I was a single woman living alone, I would need a man to help with small repairs. I'd call Helen and ask her to send David over when he got home from work. Helen must have thought I was a klutz. After all, I broke the knobs on the stove nearly once a week for twenty years. I'd send David back home with a smile on his face, in time for a late dinner with Helen. Sometimes the repair would take until morning." Ellen blushed. "In the beginning, David liked to pretend that I was my twin sister."

"Did she know?"

"I don't think so. They say that twins always know what the other is thinking, and mostly that's true with me and Helen. I don't think Helen cared about sex." Ellen sat up in bed. "I guess we're not identical in every respect."

Sy propped himself up in bed on one elbow and looked into Ellen's hazel eyes. "Maybe not. But she must have cared about the betrayal."

"Why do you say that?"

Sy spoke in a monotone. "Because she hired me."

"She hired you? I don't understand."

"You asked me what I did before I retired." Sy paused, deciding how much he should say. "I was a hitman."

"You were a hitman?" Ellen felt a sudden chill. Followed by a sudden warmth. The warmth demanded more immediate attention. She reached for Sy, grateful to find that the wonderful blue pill was still hard at work.

The hitman was not as gentle this time. But he was careful. And he respected her choices. When they were done, he took a moment to admire her unblemished skin.

Ellen deserved to know the truth. She had a right to know why he planned to take her life before sunrise. In forty years working as a killer for hire, Sy had never once faced a victim who didn't know why. It was an occupational hazard in their line of work. Maybe it wouldn't matter to Ellen, but it mattered to him.

"I met your sister last year, in the card room." Sy paused. "Do you know Helen is a heck of a poker player?"

Ellen shook her head no.

"I think it was poker that got us talking. It was the third, maybe the fourth time we played. She said there was something she wanted to discuss. We took a walk along the golf course. Helen talked. I listened. Before he died, her husband had told her everything. She appreciated his confession and didn't tell her husband that she had always known. She told me that men were weak, and David was no exception. So she had forgiven her husband, but she told me she could never forgive her twin sister."

Sy couldn't maintain eye contact with Ellen. Head down, he pushed forward with the narrative. "I don't know how she learned about my past. I guess these days you can find anything on the Internet if you want it bad enough. Anyway, after some hemming and hawing, she asked me what it would cost. I told her I didn't do that anymore, but she was persistent. And persuasive. She said she would tear up the poker IOUs and give me two large for my trouble." Sy laughed quietly. "Plus expenses, I told her, and she agreed."

The color drained from Ellen's face. "But you didn't … I mean you couldn't … I mean not after …"

"At first, you were a job, no more, no less. I feel very close to you now." It was Sy's turn to blush. "I will miss you. But I can't let my feelings for you stand in the way of my responsibilities." Sy hoped she would understand. "It would be bad for business if people learned I backed out on a contract."

"But you're retired."

Sy shook his head. "My word is my bond."

Sy reached for his pants, lying in a pile beside the bed. He removed a Sig Sauer from a pocket. "I'm sorry, Ellen." Using a pillow to muffle the gunshot and contain the splatter, Sy took aim. He squeezed. It had been two decades, but his muscle memory was intact. A perfect pull.

Sy wondered if Helen could hear the muffled gunshot from the other side of the shared duplex wall.

In the old days, after a hit, Sy would simply drop the gun and walk away. If there was clean up needed, that was a separate contract. But Sy no longer had such business associates, and Helen couldn't ask her maid to handle the cleanup during her next weekly visit. His plan was simple—to carry Ellen's body out onto the golf course and drop her in the water hazard on the eighth hole. He looked out from the back porch. There were still several hours until sunup. The golf course was dark and deserted. The moon was hidden behind storm clouds.

Sy wrapped Ellen's body in a spare blanket and dragged it out the door. He lifted her awkwardly onto his shoulder and made his way slowly in the dark. He had to stop every ten feet or so to put down the body and catch his breath. After several more stops, Sy was gasping. He would have to revise his plan. Even in the dark, he could see far enough to know that at his age, he no longer had the endurance to carry Ellen's dead weight all the way to the pond. He tucked her in carefully under a maple tree and started his way back to the duplex.

He rang Helen's doorbell and waited. The door opened, revealing a nervous Helen chewing on her fingers. "Is it ..."

Sy didn't give her a chance to talk. "Do you have a wheelbarrow? A wagon? Something?"

Helen led Sy to the garage. Inside, she pointed to a golf cart. Not the kind you can ride on, the kind you pull. Helen had not played golf since her husband had died, but she still had the cart, and she still had her bag strapped to the cart. She unhooked the golf bag. "Will this do?"

Sy grabbed the pull cart. "Come with me." Helen put a coat on over her nightgown and followed Sy to the golf course. When they got to the maple tree, Helen helped steady her sister while Sy strapped her onto the cart. They took turns pulling the cart until they arrived, undetected, at the water hazard. He unstrapped the body from the cart and tipped her toward the water.

"Wait," Helen instructed, "I need to say a prayer."

Sy waited while Helen made her peace, the body tipping toward the water until finally it slid into the pond. When the body was fully submerged, they walked as quickly as exhaustion allowed, until they were back at the duplex.

Helen thanked Sy for a job well done. Sy thanked Helen for the use of her golf cart. "But we're not quite done. We need to clean Ellen's condo." Sy paused and stared at Helen. "Actually, you need to clean Ellen's condo."

"Why me?"

Sy grinned. "You're identical twins. Don't you see? It's perfect. You have the same DNA, the same fingerprints. No one will ever know you were in there." Sy knew twins didn't have identical fingerprints. He counted on Helen not knowing. In any event, he assumed she would wear disposable gloves.

Helen wasn't happy with the turn of events. When she entered her agreement with Sy, she understood that her only responsibility would be to pay for the job. That was, after all, the nature of a service contract. She didn't help the landscapers prune her bushes. She didn't help the carpet cleaners steam clean her carpets. But she needed this job to be over with. She would do whatever was required to bring this unfortunate evening to an end. If that meant cleaning Ellen's condo, so be it. She retrieved her bucket of cleaning supplies and made her way to Ellen's side of the duplex. She looked back at Sy, waiting for him to follow.

"I'll just get in the way." He looked at Helen and smiled. His handlebar mustache bounced playfully on his face.

At that moment, Helen understood what her sister had found so attractive. She pushed the thought down, but not before asking, "Will you be here when I finish?"

Sy grinned. "Would you like me to be here?"

"Yes." Helen's face turned bright red. "I'd like to pay you before you go. After all, we probably shouldn't see each other again. Don't you agree?"

"Yes. Of course." Sy knew he needed to stay focused on the task at hand, but his mind had a mind of its own. Long before the notion of a bucket list had become a popular topic of conversation, Sy had always had such a list. He was not the sort of person to focus on the things he didn't have, so his list was short. Just one item. Sisters.

Before he died, Sy wanted to do sisters. At his age, checking that item off his list was improbable. Helen and Ellen were his last, best opportunity.

While Helen cleaned her sister's half of the duplex, Sy poked around in Helen's half. There was a photo album on the kitchen table. Helen and Ellen. Helen and David. David and Ellen. Helen, David, and Ellen. While Sy had been in bed with Ellen, Helen was apparently taking a trip down memory lane. Sy found two large, in cash, in an envelope on her armoire.

Sy located a landline in the bedroom. He didn't want to make the call. He didn't want to do anything except wait for Helen to return. He forced himself to do the right thing. He dialed 911. "I went out to dinner tonight with two sisters. After dinner, I ended up in bed with one of them. That didn't sit well with the other. The sisters argued. Helen shot her sister." Sy hesitated. "I helped her dispose of the body. I didn't want to, but she had a gun."

"Where are you now?"

Sy ignored the question. "Helen is cleaning the crime scene. If you hurry, you can catch her in the act."

Sy wiped his prints off the phone and off the Sig Sauer. He left the gun on Helen's armoire and took the money. He located Helen's purse and extracted additional cash to cover the cost of dinner and the rideshare. It was a matter of principle. The agreement had been two large, plus expenses. The sun was coming up as Sy slipped away. He felt like Sidney Greenstreet, when Greenstreet's character, Kasper Gutman, realizes that the Maltese falcon has eluded him. The search would continue. He would find sisters.

In the distance, Sy could hear police sirens.

Jeff Markowitz is the author of five mysteries, including the award-winning dark comedy *Death and White Diamonds*. His new book, *Hit or Miss*, is part detective story, part historical fiction, part coming of age story, and was an Amazon Hot New Release in Political Fiction. Jeff spent forty years creating community-based services for children and adults with autism, before retiring in 2018 to devote more time to writing. Jeff is the Past President of the New York Chapter of Mystery Writers of America. He lives in Monmouth Junction, New Jersey, with his wife, Carol, and two cats, Virgil and Aeneas.

ONE GOOD THING

BY KEVIN P. THORNTON

When Joe Melancon left Louis Armstrong Airport at eight o'clock that morning, it had been sixty-four Fahrenheit and pleasantly mild. Twelve hours later, he landed in Fort McMurray. It was minus sixty-four and colder than tits on a witch.

He didn't even know why they gave him this job. He had killed nowhere else. He only had a passport because of the timeshare in Mazatlan he bought off the Boss's dumbass son Marco, the one too stupid to run numbers or hookers.

He'd worn his warm Saints jacket and packed a Pelicans ball cap. Still, minus sixty-four, that was damn serious. Walking across the runway nearly killed him, as did the thirty seconds it took to get a cab. Holy crap, he'd never felt cold like that, the kind where it skips the pain and goes straight to freezing your body parts.

He had the driver take him to Walmart and bought winter gear he'd never worn before with names he'd never heard. What the fuck was a tuque? And long johns? He bought them anyway. He didn't buy the boots though—a decision he would come to regret.

He thought about a knife, figured he'd go out for a steak instead, solve the problem that way. He'd killed eighty-seven people, mostly men, in nearly thirty years, but only six with a knife. One by hand, four round the neck, sixteen from buildings, two drownings, and the rest by gun. The drownings were the hardest. It's difficult to escape if you're wet. At least that wouldn't be a problem up here with the ice and all.

He'd started at seventeen when he made his name. He was now forty-four. He scrunched his eyes while thinking. Forty-four minus seventeen left twenty-four. No, twenty-seven. He tried to divide eighty-seven by twenty-seven and came up with a headache, used his phone instead. 3.222222. It seemed not enough, as if he had shirked his work. Less than four a year? Well, he was good at it, so there was that.

Joe had always been loose-reined. He'd never settled into school, never made friends. For as long as he could remember, he'd liked to hurt people.

Joe was the top button man for New Orleans. That is not what he was called. They didn't do that anymore. No made men, no loud ties and double-breasted suits, no button men. Still, he called himself by that title, and so did everyone else to his face.

Behind his back was another thing. The most popular was dumbass psychopath, followed closely by fucking nutjob and other variations on the same theme. Joe Melancon was good at what he did, but he seemed to relish it too much, and he scared the crime community. Especially the women. If you were Joe's current girl, you knew at some point you were going to get hurt. You just hoped he didn't mark you for good.

Joe wasn't bright, but he was efficient, and he was protected. He never did time. The cops left him alone, and he was always elsewhere if there was a Bourbon Street crime sweep, the kind that happened in election years. He was a proficient killer—not liked, not even respected. Just someone who got the job done.

Guns were his favorite—pistols, not revolvers. He could make a suppressor in his workshop, take it apart, and travel with it. That was what was good about being an American specialist. Wherever you worked, there was always a gun to be had.

But this wasn't home, so he'd use a knife.

Canada.

Fuck.

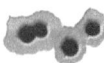

Joe could strangle someone or use a garrote. He'd like to have done that, this being Canada and all. He was fairly sure garrote was a French word, and some Canucks were French, weren't they? Only they didn't look like it. The locals he saw in Walmart looked mostly Pakistani or Chinese, which was the extent of his knowledge of Asia. Some of them were tall and thin like that basketball player, Manute Boll? Ball? Whatever his name was. Anyway, none of them looked French. And he would use a knife because he'd been told to.

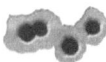

He'd gone to see Levee Levi before he left. Levi looked out for him, gave him advice when he needed it, which wasn't often, but still. And Levi had done the same job, his job, for forty years until he retired to his barbershop and numbers business. Joe didn't know what was more impressive, forty years a button man or being allowed to retire.

"Canada, hey?" said Levi. "That's new. Who wants to kill a Canadian? They're supposed to be nice."

"I know," Joe said. "And this one came from the top. Plus, the special instructions."

Levi didn't ask, he never did. He figured Joe would tell him or not.

"It has to be up close, personal like," Joe said. "No gun."

"A knife, then?"

"Or these." Joe held up his fists. "My first was up close."

"How many since?" Levi said.

"None. It's messy."

"None from eighty-six."

"No," Joe said. "One from eighty-seven."

Levi didn't argue this time. "Get a knife," he said. "Do it smart."

"Why do you think it's different this time?"

"Did you ask?"

"I did," Joe said. "She told me I'd know why when I arrived."

"Maybe it's just Canada. Difficult to get a gun is all," Levi said. "Who was the messenger?"

"Iggy. The lesbian from the strip club. Why does everyone call her Iggy Pop?"

"Has she given you a job before?"

"You know, she hasn't. I was thinking I should be worried, it being different and all. But maybe the Boss heard I've been spending time at the club. Reached out that way."

Levi looked about to say something, didn't. Then, "I thought I told you to stay away from the new girl . . ." He paused as if trying to grab her name.

"Gloria. Her name's Gloria. And I like you, Levi, but you ain't telling me where to not get laid. That's not the advice I need from you."

"You're not going to get laid there. You need to move on."

Joe ignored Levee Levi before he got mad.

Levi changed the topic. "I hear Fabio hasn't got too long." Fabio Loreggian was the Boss, and only a few old-timers got to call him by his first name.

"They're keeping it quiet on the street," Joe said. "Who's gonna take over?"

"Hard to say," Levi said. "The word is he's about skipping a generation. He's been training the grandchildren, the ones who all went off to college." He changed the subject again. "Who's the target?"

"Some local guy, sent up there because he screwed up. All I have is forty, fit, and not expecting a hit. This town, Fort McMurray, it's kind of a punishment. You get sent there if they can't kill you, but they can't trust you."

"I know of it," Levi said. "Mining town with a bit of action. Hell, I probably know some people up there. Italian mamas run the parish and the town will have great pizza and pasta, all the goombahs up there. You watch your back."

"I always do."

Levi muttered a *meh* and, as Joe reached the door, said, "Jimmy Osterberg."

"Who?"

"Rock legend, known as Iggy Pop. That's where Iggy at the club got her nickname. Her actual name is Ignazia, named after Ignatius of Loyola. You should look him up."

And here he was, in minus fuckety-fuck. The breakfast buffet was dry and tasteless, so he walked across to the Tim Hortons, nearly froze his ass off, had coffee and donuts, went back to the room. Somewhere while walking, he stopped feeling his feet. About an hour later, his phone pinged a message. "Job delayed. Hold tight, await further instructions."

Joe waited, watched TV, and was bored. He dressed in all his winter gear and went to the mall, had an early lunch, coffee, snacks, browsed a couple of jewelry stores looking at watches. When he got too hot, he walked to the liquor store, decided he hated Canada. He'd been freezing outside, but as soon as he went into the mall, he started to sweat. Joe took off his coat, tuque, and gloves, but he still had too many clothes on for eighty-degree heating in the shopping center. He figured he'd fix that by going outside again, only to feel the sweat running down his back begin to freeze.

He bought wine, sweated, walked to the supermarket, froze. He bought snacks, sweated, walked to the steakhouse to book a table for dinner, then outside again, then back to the hotel.

"How do you live like this?" Joe said to himself. Anyway, the day wasn't a total disaster. He grabbed a steak knife at the restaurant. Now all he needed was a target, and then he could get out of this place.

Joe didn't want to rent a car because he didn't want to drive. Hell, he didn't even know how to start a car in this weather. He figured there was some secret to it. There were trucks all over the place.

He spent the next two days doing more of the same. The discomfort caused by his continual sweating and freezing irritated him. Half the time, he felt like lying naked on the bed, then he'd get bored, go out, and come back with a bigger rash.

Joe used the lotion in the hotel bathroom. It stung a little, which meant it was doing good, right? He should have gone to the drugstore, but he wasn't that kind of man. He wouldn't even buy condoms, let alone talk to a stranger in a shop about the sweat rash that had now migrated further south.

Then the message came through. "Contact tonight. Be in the foyer at six."

He supposed he should have been surprised when it was Iggy, but nothing about this job seemed odd anymore. She walked in all wind-tousled and sexy, with skin-tight jeans and a coat that reached her knees. The fashion lately was for silver-colored hair. Mostly Joe hated it, but on Iggy it looked like Tom Brady's wife in black and white. She stirred him, and she probably knew it.

"Did you just get in?" he said, all polite.

"Let's go eat."

They were silent on the way. Iggy had a car and took him to the suburbs to a pizza takeout with a sticky countertop across the front, kitchen to the side. The back was a surprise, a small restaurant with four tables, candles in Ruffino bottles, checked tablecloths. It looked like a Scorsese movie or a Billy Joel song.

Joe wasn't Italian. But, in his business, he'd had plenty of meals in places like this. The food was among the best he'd ever eaten. He thought he knew the manager, but Iggy kicked him softly under the table and said cryptically, "Don't recognize anyone, even if you do."

They talked about nothing, like it was a date. Later, the manager put a pot of coffee and a bottle of brandy on their table and left them to themselves.

"They know you in here?" Joe said.

"I grew up in Fort McMurray. Do you remember Carmelina Loreggian?"

"The Boss's daughter? The one who never married?" He noticed the flash of irritation in Iggy's eyes. Carmelina had been short and dumpy, and not even the leading crime boss of New Orleans could marry her off. He remembered. "She disappeared."

"With me," Iggy said. Joe was about to say Iggy couldn't be Carmelina's daughter when she pre-empted him. "My birth mother died," she said. "Carmelina adopted me, and we came here. As far away from my grandfather and New Orleans as possible."

"Smart move. NOLA can be a dangerous town. They tried to whack the old man … what, six times?"

"Eight. Mostly by people who weren't as good at their job as you."

"I do all right," he said, going for nonchalant, but he liked the compliment. She seemed interested in him and knew of things only an insider would know. He talked, mostly tales that made him look good. He was just finishing the story about Fingers Roncalli and his dance in the bath with a live toaster when she stopped him with a hand on his arm and said, "What was your first?" The hand stayed where it was. Despite what he thought of Iggy's lesbian tendencies, Joe felt he was in with a chance. Maybe he could change her persuasion.

"Oak Barclay. He was muscle from Baton Rouge, thought that bought him rights in our town. It didn't. I popped him in the eye with a twenty-two and the slug must have bounced around inside his head some because he was dead before he hit the floor."

"No," Iggy said. "I mean your first. The one that led them to hire you."

Joe was feeling no pain. He'd had most of the bottle of red and was on his third brandy. Plus, Iggy was young and sexy, and Joe believed in himself. He felt like bragging.

"I was still a kid," he said. "Wasn't even old enough to vote. I was living with this woman. Except she didn't tell me she was a working girl. Anyway, her pimp came round, tried to tell me what was what." He paused to make it easy to remember. "We had a disagreement, and I beat him pretty bad. He died on the way to the hospital." He looked at Iggy with his practiced, earnest eyes. "I was about to head out of town when the word came down. I'd actually done your grandfather a favor. This pimp had been holding back and his ticket was about to be punched anyway."

"You must have been scared," Iggy said.

"Concerned?" he said. "I don't get scared."

"Never?"

"Never."

"Wow."

To Joe's ears, she sounded impressed. "Why are you here now? You're not the hit, are you?" Try as he might, he couldn't stop the slur in his words. Iggy seemed not to notice.

"I was here anyway," she said, "seeing friends. I got a call telling me you were stuck. That your job was delayed."

"Any idea why?"

"You'll know more tomorrow."

She got up and put her coat on. Joe did the same, wincing as he did. He had been feeling fine all evening, the red wine and pasta fortifying him. But standing up reminded him of his pain.

Iggy watched him. "First time somewhere this cold?" she said.

"How did you know?"

"You're not wearing your layers properly. Let me guess, you've been freezing and sweating since you got here, and it hurts like hell. What have you used?"

"The hotel stuff."

"Ooh, I'll bet that stings," she said. "Tell you what. My friend has a cabin in the woods with a hot tub. That will soothe you, and we'll put in some bath salts as well."

Joe tried to articulate his thanks for the wonderful idea, but his lips failed him. Still, he felt delightfully content, and he was sure Iggy realized how special all this was. He smiled as she put him in the passenger seat. Then he smiled once more before he fell asleep.

When Joe woke up, he felt as if the world was his to conquer. He was sloshing around in a nice, warm womb, waiting for the glories of birth. Then he opened his eyes and was puzzled. He was in a hot tub, as promised. It was warm but not bubbling, as if it had just been turned off. His feet were getting cold, and he tried to pull them back into the water. But when he looked, they were chained in place. Long, folded towel strips prevented the chains from marking him. He tried his arms. They were bound in the same way. In the background, he could hear Iggy. She was on a phone. She repeatedly said "yes" and "no" for a minute, then said, "GHB. It'll make him happy and sluggish both, the only way I like my men." She laughed a little, said, "I love you, too," and then shut off her phone.

"Hey," Joe said. "Whasshup?"

"You're awake," Iggy said. "Here, drink this." She held a glass to his mouth and Joe slugged it like a camel in the Sahara. Then he peed himself, felt guilty, remembered he was in a hot tub, giggled, thought about telling Iggy he peed, then decided not to because, in peeing his pants, he also realized he wore no pants. He was naked. He tried to think back to how this had all happened. Then he remembered his rash and he giggled again. "My ass feels good," he said.

As if reading his mind, Iggy said to him, "It's an outdoor hot tub. I drove around to here, walked you to the edge, and stripped you before I chucked you in. You were right, by the way. That is a nasty thing you have going on there. And, as for your feet, when did you stop feeling them? You're going to lose some toes to frostbite if you're not careful."

"Sounds painful."

"It is. However, that is not your real problem."

"And what's that?" Joe said, pleased he could talk somewhat. Despite the vague feeling things were not going to plan, he felt like he really needed to justify his existence. "You said GHB. Isn't that like Rohypnol?"

"It's similar, except it makes you more amenable."

"Well," Joe said, rubbing his tongue around his mouth to unstick everything. "It's working."

"What was the name of the woman you lived with, back when you were seventeen?"

"Pearl," Joe said.

"And what happened?"

"We broke up."

"No, Joe, what really happened?" Iggy said.

For a moment, Joe felt something he barely recognized. It was shame.

"She told me she was pregnant, and I was the father. I asked her how she knew. She said I was the only one who did it with her without a condom."

"What did you do next?"

"She left."

"You threw her out," Iggy said.

"I was seventeen," he said.

"So was she. She went to her pimp, Marco Loreggian. He was too scared of you to do anything, despite his dad being the Boss. Uncle Marco knew Pops would make him confront you, and even then you had a bad reputation, some broken bones at school, a boy beaten so bad it looked like he'd been in a car accident."

"Marco the pimp. I bought my timeshare from him."

"So, Pearl went to Carmelina, and she took her in," Iggy said. "Pearl had her baby and was going to go back on the streets. But Carmelina said no. She said you owed her."

"She came to me, told me I had a child, demanded money." Joe remembered everything. It was why he'd tried to lie earlier.

"It wasn't a pimp you beat to death, was it?" Iggy said. "It was Pearl."

"And you're Pearl's daughter," Joe said. "I'm not here to kill anyone. I'm the hit, aren't I?"

"Yes," she said. "You're the hit."

"S'cheating. You tricked me."

"I tricked you? Christ almighty. I reckon if I leave you alone, your cold sores will meet your frostbite and destroy your circulation all by itself. I don't need to trick you. You're too stupid to be up here."

Joe couldn't answer that. It was too confusing.

"So, that's what this is about," he said. "You're going to kill me? But I'm your father."

"You're not my father. You gave up that choice when you killed Pearl—or Xaviera, rather. That was her real name.

"Xaviera? Like the Happy Hooker?" Joe saw Iggy pick up a knife from the edge of the hot tub, the same one he'd taken from the steakhouse. He thought she was going to stab him, but she stopped.

"No, Joe. Xaviera, named after Saint Francis Xavier. Just like she had me christened Ignazia, after Ignatius of Loyola. Do you know why she called me that, Joe? Because Saint Ignatius took a vow of loyalty to the Pope, *his* boss. It was to remind me where my loyalties lie. My mother felt she owed her life to the family, to the Boss, my grandfather. My name was my reminder that I did, too."

Joe had been concentrating so hard, he hadn't realized how cold he was getting, drowsier too. "Why up here?"

"I thought it would be hard to get you somewhere I could kill you back in New Orleans. If I'd known how stupid you were, I wouldn't have gone to all this effort."

"That's no way to talk to your dad." He giggled then, couldn't remember why he was so giggly, then he did. She'd drugged him. Must be why he was so cold.

"Don't say that again, Joe. My dad could have been anyone. You, Pops, some drunk businessman from Atlanta, an Albuquerque second-hand car dealer. And it doesn't matter. I am who I am because of Carmelina Loreggian, not you or any other candidates."

"The Boss screwed Pearl as well? Damn."

"Pops was a horndog."

"Then why did it take so long? You've known for a while."

"Because Pops was protecting you," she said. "Pops was disappointed with his own son, so he fixated on you, convinced himself he could have been your father. You've were safe until he died, which was last week. Did you not get the memo? Oh yeah, that's right. You stopped being important to the family the moment we buried him. Imagine how fucked up all that could have been. You might be his son, and I might be your daughter, or maybe even his."

"Or maybe the Albuquerque second ..." Joe couldn't remember the rest.

"Exactly. Instead, now you're mine."

"But he never showed anything," Joe said. His voice was nothing more than a whisper now.

"How could he? You know what they'd have said if he claimed you as his son, that the Boss was losing it. He adopted you from afar and he tried to protect you. He even set up Levi to be your friend and adviser. You should have listened to him more. Especially about Gloria. Despite all this, I honestly was in two minds, trying to justify keeping a Neanderthal like you around. You might have scraped by but for her."

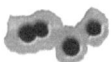

She went inside. Joe could hear her wiping down the furniture, bagging glasses, cleaning up after herself. Cleaning up the crime scene. Joe had done it so often for others, but he never thought he'd be the subject of one himself.

Iggy came back out, carrying a plastic bag.

"Can you feel your feet?"

"No. Nothing."

"Good. You will, soon enough. Everything will freeze. And, as it does, well ... have you ever seen water turn to ice? It expands, taking up more space. That's what's going to happen to the blood in your feet. First, it'll expand, then it will start to explode. After that it will be your legs, then your arms, your torso, and finally your head. It will be painful."

"You're the new Boss, aren't you?" His voice so soft she didn't even bother to acknowledge him. "Why Gloria? Why warn me off her?"

"She's my wife," Iggy said.

Joe laughed. He tried to say what was on his mind, about the world changing too much. But his laughing, pitiful as it was, turned to cold heaves, and then he stopped.

Iggy waited five minutes, then undid the chains. If she were successful, they'd find what was left of the body in the summer, a tourist not used to Canadian winters.

Her car backfired as she left, the sound stirring Joe one last time.

He saw the steak knife on the edge of the tub. It would be enough. They would get her.

He was cold, tired, and lethargic. He would be dead soon. Yet he could do one good thing. From somewhere deep within, he forced all his waning strength to bump the wall of the tub with his knee, just hard enough to knock the knife with his daughter's prints into the water.

Kevin P. Thornton has had about twenty-five short stories published and has been shortlisted seven times for the Crime Writers of Canada annual awards. He served in the South African Air Force and worked for the Canadian military in Afghanistan. He was in a bomb blast in a bar in Johannesburg and under mortar attack in Kabul. If you see him running, go the other way—he's unlucky. He lives in Fort McMurray in Canada, with the kind of life that deserves a picket fence except it's too cold. See his Facebook page at www.facebook.com/KevinP.ThorntonWriter/.

DEERMAN

BY WELDON BURGE

The man wore camouflage attire in the tree stand, a good fifteen feet above the forest floor. The camouflage was ridiculous, better suited for Fallujah than a forest in upstate New York. I could smell the beer on his breath from a mile away. He looked to be nodding off, apparently close to sleep, his rifle resting across his knees. What a doofus. He had no clue I was there, aiming at him with a Glock 43 rigged with a SKYBEN Olight Baldar Mini tactical flashlight—perfect for zeroing in on a cranium.

I trained the small, blue bead of light on his forehead, holding it there in the hope he would open his eyes and realize he was in the crosshairs. I love plugging 'em with their eyes bugged, mouth wide, as they realized a bullet was coming. But he never looked up. In fact, he started snoring. I waited another two minutes, got bored, figured screw it, and plugged him anyway. He toppled from the stand headfirst, slamming into the leaf-blanketed ground at the tree's base.

Another one down.

So many more to go. Seems like more every year.

It was deer season!

I trotted to where the man's body rested, folded like a broken marionette, arms akilter and legs obscenely bent. There wasn't much left of the back of his head. It was a clean kill. Well, not so much clean … but you know what I mean. One and done.

I couldn't linger. It was rutting season as well, and I'd seen a good many does flounce around among the trees. I had a job to do and didn't need the distraction. But you had to attend to natural urges from time to time.

They call us venison. What should I call them, other than idiots? What would they taste like? I heard pork. Of course, I have no idea what pork tastes like either. I'm a vegetarian.

I looked at his rifle, just a few feet away from his corpse. It was a Remington Sendero, a standard deer-hunting rifle. Had a nice scope, too—totally wasted on this buffoon. I debated on taking the rifle but decided not. My two Glocks were all I needed.

I've been on a vigilante campaign ever since Bambi's mom ate a bullet. Enough is enough, ya know? Something had to be done. That's when my crusade began.

As I stood there, admiring my hoofiwork, an arrow whistled just above my shoulder, nicking the hide as it passed. I didn't see the man with the bow, didn't even smell him.

Too risky. I had to move and dashed for the deeper brush.

Bowhunters are the worst! My buddy, Dodger, took an arrow to his flank. Probably would have been better to take him out with a direct hit to the heart. But, no, the killer missed. The bowhunters, two of the bastards, followed Dodger for miles before the pain, loss of blood, and fatigue finally got the best of my friend. The hunters finished him when they found him.

Poor Dodger didn't live up to his name, unfortunately. I'm guessing his head, with his ten-point rack, is mounted on a den wall somewhere, probably over a fireplace, staring into oblivion.

The two hunters? Nah, they weren't so skilled at dodging either. I had some fun with them. Wish I had a wall to mount *their* heads on.

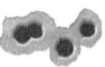

I always thought of myself as a superhero. You know. Deerman. I'd spent years learning my craft, perfecting my firearms and fighting skills. Deerman! Of course, I'm not a man (thank God). And I'd be a superhero with no alter ego, much less a cape. I mean, my alter ego would be a *deer*. How dumb is that?

My father started me on my quest for vengeance. He first taught me how to defend myself. It took years just to master guns. He preferred a Sig Sauer P229. I was more comfortable with a Glock 43. That whole hooves thing. Pretty tricky.

Needless to say, my Pops was the epitome of patience. He made me who I am. I enjoyed all the time my father and I spent in our training sessions. Pops handled taekwondo brilliantly, but I could never get the hang of it. I just didn't have the physique and flexibility for it. Pops was lean and mean.

I never had a chance to learn knifework from him, although he was extraordinarily skilled with blades. A redneck driving a dilapidated Chevy Silverado pickup truck took Pops out. Blinded by the headlights, he never had a chance. I know, the "deer-in-the-headlights" cliché. I was devastated and Mom never got over it. I was even more determined to rid the forest of the scourge.

Damn humans.

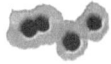

The forest is so tranquil in the early morning as the sun starts to rise. Peaceful. Quiet. Leaves whispering in a gentle breeze. The soft murmur of water flowing over the pebbles of a stream bed. The sweet sound of songbirds, invisible in the thick branches of the trees. This side of heaven.

What a crock!

The forest is filled with horrors, the realm of predators and prey. Potential death waits behind every tree. Every rabbit, every squirrel lives in perpetual terror. The screech of a hawk above could be the last thing they hear.

My home.

Then add humans bearing weapons to the wonderful woods.

Fun, huh?

No wonder I love kicking hunter ass!

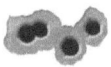

I heard the bowhunter behind me. Sounded like only one of them and, like most humans, he was anything but stealthy. More like bumbling and stumbling—lethal nonetheless. I had to stay on the move. Considering he missed me when I was motionless, he was probably an inept hunter, perhaps one new to the game. I'd likely end up like Dodger with an arrow in my ass if I couldn't evade him.

But I had the element of surprise. The man had probably never faced a stag with dual firearms.

I worked my way through the tightly clustered trees, maneuvers I learned long ago. I knew every turn, every hiding place in the woods. My size made this incredibly difficult. Hiding wasn't the answer to evading the hunters. Best to stay on the move until I could develop a strategy for taking them out.

I then no longer heard the man behind me. I stopped briefly, frozen still and listening. Nothing. And I could no longer smell him. A hunter had placed a scent lure nearby, its odor overpowering any trace of a human. I stood motionless, trying to determine where the man was. If a deer can do anything, standing without flinching a muscle is instinctive. Half the time, a hunter could walk right past you, unaware you stood close by, blending into the background.

Where was this guy? He couldn't have been too far behind me.

The scent lure was horrendously pungent. I mean, I squat and piss on my legs to attract the females. You know, what the humans call rub-urinating. Gets nasty, but the girls seem to dig it. So, I can't complain. The scent lures used by these hunters? I don't know, maybe humans use actual deer urine to make this stuff. Which begs the question: How the hell would humans collect deer piss? What kind of dedication to hunting would be required to squeeze deer bladders? And the scent lures are so *off*. Like the piss was a noxious brew of bear, raccoon, and skunk urine. Never attracted me, but the stench always told me the human idiots were in the area.

The odor was especially potent in this part of the forest. So I knew one of the cretins was nearby.

I saw the hunter too late and had no time to react. This man was a step up from the usual dimwits I encountered. How had he been so quiet? He'd been so loud earlier, making his way through the woods. And the scent lure apparently masked his smell because I hadn't detected that aggressive human odor. Or beer. Or, on occasion, Old Spice.

The arrow speared my left flank, and I suddenly wondered if I'd just been "dodgered." As the hunter approached, I acted surprised, whipping my head as if in fear, and then dropped to my rear haunches. There was surprisingly little pain, but I wanted the hunter to assume it was excruciating.

As the human neared, he lifted his bow and notched another arrow, preparing to deliver the coup de grâce.

That's when I hefted my two Glocks. I smiled at the bewildered expression on his face before I pulled the triggers simultaneously. His head blossomed like a gorgeous crimson peony. A clean kill ... well, again, you know what I mean.

I had to deal with the arrow in my ass. The arrow had passed through fat, not muscle, in my flank. That's why there was minimal pain. I still had to remove the projectile, and the barbed tip would do more damage if I tried to pull it out. The only option was to drive it through.

So I backed up to a tree and started thwacking my butt against its trunk, forcing the arrow deeper and deeper until the barbed tip pierced the skin on the other side of my flank. I snapped off the arrow's tip with my teeth and reversed the shaft back through my flesh. Not fun, but easy enough.

I heard another hunter coming down the path to my right. Probably the dead guy's hunting buddy. They always seem to travel in pairs. Sometimes three or four together. They considered this a "sport." How ridiculous is this, killing my innocent, defenseless brethren? A sport? Well, I made their sport a tad more interesting.

I then saw the man, who also carried a bow. He lifted the bow. He'd seen me. Time to run again. I wove through the tangled brush and stopped near a thick oak to watch. He'd turned to see his fallen comrade, and I heard him gasp. He approached the dead man, turning left and right as if he expected an attack. He had to assume another human had killed the man. He would never suspect an assassin deer.

He suddenly raised his head and somehow saw me through the trees. I always found it difficult to read human faces, but I recognized this—anger. Maybe fear, I couldn't tell. Definitely anger. He raised the bow again. Could he suspect I'd killed the man? Impossible.

I ran.

While dealing with the arrow in my ass, I'd dropped the damn Glocks! I mean, my grip on the guns was tenuous to begin with—you know, the hooves and all. Dropping them was an enormous mistake. I was weaponless and could do nothing now but run. I never saw a third hunter, so I assumed this was the only one who remained. When this was over, I'd backtrack to find the guns. I didn't want to lose those beauties. No hurry, however.

The hunter was distracted, not aware I hid in the thicket outside the clearing in which he stood. He was looking in the opposite direction, his back to me. He reloaded his bow, notching an arrow and pulling back the bowstring.

That's when I noticed the doe thirty yards away, her head bent to the ground, grazing on clover. It was Clarisse, one of my favorites! She didn't see the hunter as he lifted and sighted his bow.

I charged, ripping through the brush. The hunter spun toward me, too late. My rack speared into him. I tossed my head back, sending him flying over my shoulders and into a nearby tree. He'd dropped his crossbow, but he wasn't finished. As he stood, I kicked with my back legs. A hoof to the head is not quite as much fun as pumping a bullet through a human skull. But it was still mighty effective. And certainly more satisfying. His head splattered like a smashed melon, spraying a lovely blood pattern on the tree behind him. It was almost a work of art.

Clarisse approached slowly, smiling the way only a doe can. She nudged my neck and had that certain glow in her eyes. She evidently wanted to show her gratitude. My campaign of hunting the hunters could wait another day. Besides, I needed to take a break from the fun and games.

It was time to do a doe!

Weldon Burge's fiction has appeared in many publications, including many horror and suspense anthologies. Suspense Publishing published his police procedural novel, *Harvester of Sorrow*, the first in the Ezekiel Marrs series. He frequently writes for *Suspense Magazine*, often authoring interviews with fellow writers. Check out his website at www.weldonburge.com.

Thank you for reading
Asinine Assassins

Enjoy this book?
You can make a huge difference!

Reviews are essential when it comes to garnering attention for books. If you liked this book, we would be immensely grateful if you could spend a few minutes leaving a review on the book's Amazon page, Goodreads, or any other review site you prefer. Let other readers know about the stories you most enjoyed reading.

Also, if you liked this anthology, check out *Uncommon Assassins* and *Insidious Assassins* for more wonderful tales.

Thanks so much!

Weldon Burge, Editor

SPECIAL THANKS

Thanks to all the wonderful supporters of Smart Rhino Publications. We especially thank those kind folks who supported us during our Kickstarter campaign for this anthology.

Meghan Arcuri-Moran
Chris Bauer
Robert Brown
Michele Crean
Kevin Davis
Bernie Dlugokeski
Ian Emborg
Wil A. Emerson
Sondra Fielder
Ben Gamblin
Lorraine Hatchwell
Caelin Hill
Julian Himber
Lois Hoffman
Frank Hopkins
Jane Kelly
Dana King

Donald Kudler
Joanne M. Kuhns
Richard Kvale
Dee Lawrence
Derek Lewis
Adrian Ludens
Barbara Mitchell
Robert Petyo
Logan Porter
Lisa Regan
Eric Remington
Lynda Reynolds-Burkins
Rachel Shea
Ricky Sprague
Tony Tremblay
Albert Tucher
Richard A. Williams

UNCOMMON ASSASSINS

Hired killers. Vigilantes. Executioners. Paid killers or assassins working from a moral or political motivation. You'll find them all in this thrilling anthology. But these are not ordinary killers, not your run-of-the-mill hitmen. The emphasis is on the "uncommon" here—unusual characters, unusual situations, and especially unusual means of killing. Here are twenty-three tales by some of the best suspense/thriller writers today.

Stephen England * J. Gregory Smith * Lisa Mannetti
Ken Goldman * Christine Morgan * Matt Hilton
Billie Sue Mosiman * Ken Bruen * Rob M. Miller
Monica J. O'Rourke * F. Paul Wilson * Joseph Badal
Doug Blakeslee * Elliott Capon * Laura DiSilverio
Michael Bailey * James S. Dorr * Jonathan Templar
J. Carson Black * Weldon Burge * Al Boudreau
Charles Coyott * Lynn Mann

INSIDIOUS ASSASSINS

There is a peculiar allure of insidious characters—and especially assassins, hitmen, and their ilk. With this fascination with evil characters in mind, Smart Rhino Publications decided to publish this anthology, *Insidious Assassins*, a sequel to *Uncommon Assassins*.

Jack Ketchum * Joe Lansdale * Lisa Mannetti
Carson Buckingham * Christine Morgan * DB Corey
Billie Sue Mosiman * Meghan Arcuri
Austin S. Camacho * JM Reinbold
Ernestus Jiminy Chald * L.L. Soares * Doug Blakeslee
Shaun Meeks * Martin Zeigler * James S. Dorr
Adrian Ludens * Joseph Badal * J. Gregory Smith
Patrick Derrickson * Jezzy Wolfe * Doug Rinaldi
Martin Rose * Dennis Lawson

SOMEONE WICKED:
A Written Remains Anthology

Avaricious, cruel, depraved, envious, mean-spirited, vengeful—the wicked have been with us since the beginnings of humankind. You might recognize them and you might not. But make no mistake. When the wicked cross your path, your life will never be the same. Do you know someone wicked? You will. The twenty-one stories in the *Someone Wicked* anthology were written by the members of the Written Remains Writers Guild and its friends, and was edited by JM Reinbold and Weldon Burge.

Gail Husch * Billie Sue Mosiman * Mike Dunne
Christine Morgan * Ramona DeFelice Long * Russell Reece
* Carson Buckingham * Chantal Noordeloos
Patrick Derrickson * Barbara Ross * JM Reinbold
Shaun Meeks * Liz DeJesus * Doug Blakeslee
Justynn Tyme * Ernestus Jiminy Chald * Weldon Burge
Joseph Badal * Maria Masington * L.L. Soares
Shannon Connor Winward

www.ingramcontent.com/pod-product-compliance
Lightning Source LLC
Chambersburg PA
CBHW030401180626
46812CB00005B/1875